In the bleak mid-winter –

celebrations of light and joy have brightened lives for thousands

of years.

Solstice, Hannukah, Christmas, New Year's, Twelfth Night

Come join in –

add your own rituals to those of our seventeen talented authors,

and enjoy the holiday spirit that once invaded Regency England,

and still flourishes today!

D1636939

Happy Holidays to All!

The Winter Holiday Sampler

Edited by Kelly Ferjutz

Regency Press
Cleveland Heights, Ohio

THE WINTER HOLIDAY SAMPLER

Copyright © 2000 by Kelly Ferjutz

All rights reserved, including the right to reproduce this book, or portions thereof, in any form.

Regency Press is a division of Crack of Noon Enterprises, Incorporated. The name Regency Press and the Crowned R are registered trademarks of Crack of Noon Enterprises, Incorporated.

ISBN: 1-929085-81-8

First Edition: December, 2000

Printed in the United States of America

0 9 8 7 6 5 4 3 2 1

These stories are all original, and have not appeared elsewhere prior to this publication.

This book is also available in the following electronic versions:
ISBN: 1-929085-52-4   Download
ISBN: 1-929085-53-2   Reader
ISBN: 1-929085-54-0   Diskette
ISBN: 1-929085-55-9   CD-rom
(http://www.regency-press.com)

These stories are all original, and have not appeared elsewhere prior to this publication.

Cover art is based on, and adapted from 'Snowfall Sampler',

designed by **Sharon S. Pope**,

and was charted in the November, 1999 issue of *Stitcher's World*

magazine. Call 1-800-825-8995 for more information.

For our purposes, the design was manipulated slightly by Ty Drago.

Stitcher's World magazine is located in Norcross, Georgia,

and we are both grateful and delighted that

that they have allowed us to use this design.

Gentle Reader --

Thanks to *whoever* invented the Internet, the world of Regency fiction is expanding rapidly, as fans from around the world find each other, and rejoice at having done so. It's a wonderful feeling to know you're not alone -- and even more wonderful if you're a writer. There are an incredible number of very talented authors all over the world, who have never been published, but are patiently honing their craft while waiting for the opportunity to achieve their dream. For readers, this is also a bonanza, for we know that our favorite reading material will never completely disappear, although it may occasionally appear in different formats.

You'll notice in the listings at the rear of this book that several of our titles are available in electronic formats. These include: downloads, 'reader' formats, diskette or CD-rom. The latter two are available by mail, the former are directly to your computer or reader from our computer. More information is available at our web-site: **http://www.regency-press.com**

Following in the footsteps of our first book A REGENCY SAMPLER, we present to you the results of our second contest, based on the winter holidays. The rules were simple: set your story between Advent and Twelfth Night, and indeed, you'll find here stories of Solstice, of Hanukkah, of Christmas, of New Year's Day, and yes--Twelfth Night. Judging was much more difficult this time around, as both the quantity and the *quality* of the entries grew.

Our judges exceeded themselves, I think, in selecting these seventeen heart-warming and cheerful stories. As before our thanks go to: JoAnn Vicarel, Anne Wilson and Becky Katzenmoyer, librarians; and Donalene Poduska, reader, who also found the Winter Sampler that made its way to our cover.

Thanks also must go to Stitcher's World Magazine, whose Sharon S. Pope designed and charted the original *Snowfall Sampler,* which was featured in their November, 1999 issue. They generously allowed us to manipulate their design to better suit our purposes.

This manipulation, along with many, many other computer tasks, was admirably executed by Ty Drago, who also keeps our web-sites functioning and looking so beautiful. Other help, in addition to friendship has been given by Sandra Heath, and is valued most highly.

To those authors whose efforts didn't succeed this time, I wish you well in any future contests, ours or others. It is possible to achieve your goal, but only if you keep writing!

Read and enjoy.

Kelly Ferjutz
Editor-in-chief
Regency Press

The Winter Holiday Sampler

Table of Contents

Tony's been wrongfully branded as a traitor. Surely no respectable woman would wish to become his wife. But that was before he meets Judith, who knows firsthand about being ostracized from society.

The Outcasts

Alexandria Shaw

Chapter One

Tony cursed himself for a fool. The rain poured down, the night was dark and chill, and he was lost. His horse plodded on almost as miserable as his master. Tony peered through the driving rain, hoping to see a welcoming glimmer of light from an inn signifying a warm bed, dry clothes, and food for himself and his horse.

His shoulder throbbed and he felt as queer as Dick's hatband. His great-coat, heavy with rain, afforded him little warmth. It had been deuced foolhardy to start searching so soon after rising from his sick bed, but the longer he waited the less chance he had of proving his innocence.

Six weeks ago he had been a respected officer in Wellington's army in Spain. Now he was a fugitive, branded a traitor to his country and an outcast from his rank. He had his army friends to thank for the fact that he was not lying in prison awaiting trial for treason. They had believed in his innocence and had smuggled him out of Spain and back to England. His sister and cousin had furnished him with a horse, clothes and money, and he had promised to keep in touch but had refused to tell them where he was going. He had no wish to compromise them further.

His only lead was a snatch of conversation which he had heard before he had lost consciousness. He hoped the proof of his innocence lay somewhere in and around Heywood-on-Sea, a small Sussex village, which he fancied was a haven for smugglers, but whether it harboured his traitor, he would have to wait and see. It was difficult to conceive just how some small fishing village in England was linked with a dirty Spanish inn some miles from the sea.

His cousin, John, a government official attached to the war office, had mentioned that his superiors were increasingly concerned about the smuggling activities along the coast and the fact that military information was easily passed to the French by spies who used smuggling to cover their true occupation. In fact, it had been his cousin who had pitchforked him into this havey-cavey business, and John was lambasting himself for having done so.

Tony cursed again. He should have stuck to his military duties and not gone haring off on a wild-goose chase in search of French spies. It had all occurred because he had been getting devilish bored. There had been little military action to keep him occupied. The English had been waiting for the French army to make a move; so he had welcomed the chance to play spy catcher.

It was no use thinking about what he should and should not have done. He was in a devilish pickle now and had little chance of coming about if he failed to find the traitor.

Tony forced himself to take stock of his surroundings. His mind was muddled and he found it hard to concentrate. Exhaustion was taking its toll. Sometime back he was sure he had missed the track through the woods which would have taken him into the village. Should he turn around and try to find it or keep going in the hope that he would come across an inn or even a barn where he could take shelter until the rain ceased? It was to be hoped that he would not take a chill from his drenching. But why worry! If he could not prove his innocence, it mattered not a whit if he died from inflammation of the lungs. Better that, than the gallows.

He was so tired, and no matter how he moved he could not ease the infernal ache in his shoulder. His body sagged in the saddle. His horse, sensing that something was wrong, stopped. Tony jerked awake as his head hit the wet mane of his horse. If he was not careful he would tumble off, and he was sure he would not have the strength to remount. If only he could find somewhere warm and dry to sleep. That was all he could think about for the present.

Was that the rumble of a coach? Who would be out on a night like this and on such a desolate road? He stopped and listened. No! It was just his imagination. Wishful thinking on his part. If, indeed, it had been a coach, he would have been able to ask directions.

The rumble grew louder. It was a coach. He moved to the side of the road and hailed the coach. Too late he realised the coachman would think he was a highwayman. Damnation! What a deuced corkbrained thing to do! He was definitely not thinking straight.

As Tony feared, the driver not trusting a lone horseman in such a secluded area, whipped his horses. The coach lurched past splattering mud. Tony glimpsed a white face peering at him from the window. He urged his tired horse forward. It stumbled and Tony pitched over its head and hit the road, his injured shoulder taking the brunt of the fall. Agonising pain lanced through him and mercifully he lost consciousness.

❉ ❊ ❉

Judith Maybury, the younger of the two occupants of the coach, woke from an uneasy doze as the coach swayed alarmingly with the increased speed. She gazed out the window into the blackness and caught a glimpse of a shadowy horseman by the side of the road. A highwayman!

She saw the rider start toward them and fall as the horse stumbled, and then they were past. Some minutes later the coach slowed, for there was no sign of pursuit. Judith sat back relieved. She replaced the small elegant pistol she had taken from her reticule. No highwayman was going to steal her meager supply of money.

She was puzzled. It seemed an unusual place to encounter a highwayman. As far as she knew, her grandmother's house, Eversleigh, was remote and very few travellers would use the route. No person in his right mind would choose to be out on a night like this and at this time of year. Surely, even on fine nights in summer, the pickings would be slim on such a road.

He must have been a traveller such as herself, she reasoned. But, there was no inn that she knew of on this road or even another dwelling. Judith frowned. Something was wrong, she was sure. Perhaps he had injured himself when he fell? She could not be easy until she was sure that the horseman was unharmed.

Judith knocked loudly on the roof of the coach and called out of the window. "Henry, please stop."

As the coach slowed, the other female occupant, a plump woman of some sixty-odd years, awoke. "My dear, have we arrived? I declare, my whole body is aching. Such an uncomfortable journey! The roads in this area are to be deplored."

"No, Addy. I pray do not be alarmed. We passed a horseman some few minutes back, and I am concerned that he may have been hurt when he fell from his horse. I intend to turn back and discover if my misgivings are correct."

"Yes, Miss Judith," said the coachman opening the door.

"Henry, please turn the coach and retrace our route. I am inclined to think that the horseman my have taken some hurt when he fell."

"Now, Miss Judith, nothing for you to worrit about. We had better keep going in case he had friends waiting to help him with the hold-up. But why he'd be out on a night like this, I dunno," he added thoughtfully.

"Exactly, Henry. I do not believe he was a highwayman. I fancy he was a fellow traveller unlucky enough to lose his way. He may be injured and need our help."

"Miss, is that wise? We have only a few miles to travel to reach Eversleigh House. I can return once I have you safely there."

"No, Henry. If he is indeed hurt, the delay will only serve to worsen his injuries. It will only take a few minutes. We cannot leave him lying without shelter in this cold weather. He will catch his death."

"Now, Miss, I don't know as how you should be doing this."

"Henry." Her tone brooked no further discussion. Even Henry, a loved and trusted retainer, who had known Judith since she was in leading strings, recognised that no further argument, however reasonable, would change her mind.

"Very well, Miss," he grumbled.

They had only been travelling a few minutes when Judith saw a horse nuzzling a motionless figure lying on the road. She jumped down from the coach and hurried to the still form.

"Careful, Miss, there's no saying but what he may be shamming," called Henry.

"That is highly improbable, Henry. Now leave the horses. They are too tired to stray and come and help me at once," she ordered.

Judith knelt beside the man and rolled him over onto his back. He was still breathing, but in the rain and darkness she could not discern if he had sustained any injuries.

"Henry, help me get him into the coach."

Judith and Henry had difficulty lifting Tony into the coach. They were unable to place him on the seat, so made him as comfortable as possible on the floor.

"Judith, my dear, are you sure you are doing the right thing?" said Addy anxiously. "We don't know who he might be or, indeed, what might be wrong with him."

"Addy, he would die if we left him. Would you want that on your conscience?"

"No, you are perfectly right, my dear. Oh, look at your clothes. They are quite ruined," said Addy, "We will never be able to clean them. That was one of your better gowns, too."

"It cannot be helped. It is not as though I will be going into society."

Miss Amelia Addison, Judith's onetime nurse, had agreed to accompany her into her self-imposed exile when London society had ostracised the family because of a scandal.

"Your hair is wet. Just as well you took off your bonnet, my dear. You would have ruined that as well. Oh dear, you will catch your death of a cold."

"Addy, there is nothing that a warm fire and dry clothes will not be able to put right. There is no need to fuss," said Judith firmly. "But, I am afraid that this poor man may contract a chill. He is very cold and his clothes are soaked. Let us hope that a warm bed will put him to rights, for I think it is doubtful that there will be a doctor in Heywood. We will not be able to see if he has any injuries until we reach Eversleigh House. Henry does not think he has any broken bones."

They covered him with a blanket, and Judith gave the order to proceed. Some twenty minutes later they turned in the gates of Eversleigh House. The drive was rutted. Branches of the trees lining the carriage-way hung low over the avenue and brushed against the coach as they rumbled toward the lights of the house visible at intervals through the large overgrown and neglected pleasure garden. The coach drew to a standstill in front of a respectable sized house, but Judith could make out little else of its appearance in the darkness.

Henry rang the big iron bell, and it was many minutes before an elderly man opened the door. Behind him an equally elderly woman, holding a branched candlestick, peered out into the night. "Be that Miss Judith?" the man called.

"Yes. Is that Stanley?"

"Yes, Miss. Come in, Miss. There's a goodly fire in the drawing room and my missus will bring you some tea in no time at all."

"Stanley, we found an injured man on the road. Would you be so good as to help Henry carry him into the drawing room."

Judith walked into the house and was shocked at the state of dilapidation around her. If the rest of the house was like the hall, it would take more money than she had at her disposal to restore it to its former splendor. Cleaning and polishing would not disguise the worn carpet and threadbare curtains, or the ceiling blackened with soot from a fireplace which no doubt gushed smoke whenever it was lit.

The drawing room had a much cheerier aspect and Judith sighed with relief as she stripped off her gloves and coat and warmed herself by the fire. She directed the two men, who were struggling with Tony's unconscious body, to place him on the sofa. With her help they stripped him of his sodden coat and muddied boots. He stirred but did not regain consciousness. A cursory examination failed to disclose any serious injury.

Judith looked with interest at the unconscious man. She judged him to be a little above medium height with a muscular frame. His countenance was pleasing rather than handsome, but there was firmness about his jaw which gave character to his face. She supposed him to be a man of seven- or eight-and- twenty, some few years older than herself. He was undoubtedly a gentleman, or at least a man of substance. His coat and shirt were of the finest quality, and there was a sizeable sum of money in his purse but no card to identify him. His face was pale under a tan, but his breathing was even and his pulse seemed regular and strong.

Addy bustled over and tucked some blankets, which she had obtained from Mrs Stanley, around the stranger. "The poor boy looks sadly pulled. When Henry finishes tending the horses he must strip him of these wet clothes. I'll ask Mrs. Stanley which bedchamber we may use and whether she can put a warming pan between the sheets. I do hope he does not develop a fever. Inflammation of the lungs can be fatal even in young people. Now, my dear, he is as comfortable as we can make him for the moment. Off with you and change from those wet clothes yourself. Stanley has taken up your portmanteau and I have laid out a change for you. Mrs. Stanley assures me that she will have some nourishing soup ready for us as soon as you have changed," ordered Addy.

Judith sighed as she climbed the stairs to her bedchamber. Stanley and his wife had been caretakers at Eversleigh for nigh on ten years, ever since her grandmother had removed to Bath for her health. They had been too old even then to care properly for the house, and no doubt there had been little money to employ other servants to help with the work. Despite the condition of the house, she was thankful that twelve months ago she had inherited it and a small amount of money which, with careful economies, would allow them to live modestly away from the society which shunned her.

Her bedchamber was as threadbare as the hall, but at least it was clean and well scrubbed with a cheerful fire burning in the grate. Thankfully she changed out of her damp garments and rubbed her hair dry. She quickly tied a ribbon around her unruly brown curls and descended to the drawing room, only to find it deserted.

Judith settled herself in a large winged chair by the fire. It was only three weeks until Christmas, and this year's festivities would be vastly different from those of last year. Twelve months ago she was an accepted member of the *haut ton* and one of the guests at the Duke of Howard's country estate. This year there would be but five of them to share the Christmas spirit. In the light of all that had happened Judith was inclined to believe that she was better off with persons who genuinely cared for her.

Mrs. Stanley poked her head into the room. "Are you ready to eat, Miss Judith?"

"Yes, when Miss Addison returns. But where is she and our guest?"

"Henry and my Stanley carried the young gentleman to one of the guest rooms. Your Miss Addison went to help them. The young gentleman was looking poorly. I'm afeared he might come down with a bad fever."

Over their light repast Judith and Addy speculated on their unanticipated guest. "I fancy the young gentleman's a soldier," said Addy. "He has a nasty wound in this shoulder which has only just healed. He is lucky that he did not reopen the wound when he fell, but he does not appear to have taken any further hurt. Perhaps he is home on sick furlough or been invalided out of the Army. And he is as brown as a berry. Surely, he must have been in Spain with Wellington."

"Possibly you are correct, Addy, but I am inclined to think there is a mystery about him. He had no cards on him, and the clothes in his saddlebag did not match the quality of the garments he was wearing. They were more suited to his groom. I find that exceedingly strange."

"Is that so, my dear. No doubt there is a reasonable explanation which he will give us when he wakes. But I am very much afraid that he has taken a chill. He was quite feverish when I left him with Henry. I think I must sit up with him tonight."

"You will do no such thing, Addy. I will take care of him. You are quite knocked up with travelling."

"Miss Judith, it is not proper that a young unmarried lady such as yourself be left alone with a gentleman."

"Addy, who is to know? Besides, what does it matter now. Society has already shunned me, so I really have no reputation left to lose."

"My dear Judith, in time you will be able to return. It will all blow over, mark my words. After all, you are not to blame for your brother's behaviour."

"I am not sure I will wish to return to London. People I counted as close friends gave me the cut direct. It was only Helen who stood by me and then her husband forbade her to be seen with me in public." Her voice was bitter when she remembered the hurt and embarrassment which had followed the flight of her older brother to Ireland, leaving behind massive gambling debts and an estate mortgaged to the hilt.

"Good night, Addy." She kissed her old nurse. "Thank you for sharing my exile. I don't know what I would have done without your help."

"My dear, as if I would have let you come here alone. Your poor mother! I'm just thankful that she is not alive to see what has come to pass."

They climbed the stairs to their respective rooms, Addy to sink her aching bones into a warm bed and Judith to collect a shawl to throw around her shoulders before she went to sit by the bedside of her guest.

Chapter Two

The stranger was still unconscious when Judith relieved Henry of his bedside vigil. "He seems to be sleeping now, Miss Judith, although he is a trifle feverish. Call me, Miss, if you have need of me during the night."

"Thank you, Henry. I will."

Judith crossed to the bed and felt her patient's forehead. Beads of perspiration glistened on his brow and occasionally he turned his head fretfully. She dipped a cloth in lavender water and bathed his face. He sighed but did not wake.

She crossed to a sofa, from which the holland covers had just been removed, and curled up on it with a favourite book of poems, but she found it difficult to concentrate.

Three months ago she had not envisioned that her life would turn topsy-turvy. She had an inkling that all was not well with her brother, but as he was some fifteen years her senior, they had never been close and he had not seen fit to confide in her.

It had come as a great shock to awake one morning and be told that her brother had fled to escape debtor's prison and that she no longer had a home. The following weeks were a nightmare. Their family estate was sold with the entire contents of her home as well as the string of thoroughbred hunters her brother had owned. She had tried to clear some of her brother's debts but there was not enough money after the sale of the estate to pay even one third of them. She had no doubt that her father, an inveterate gambler when he had been alive, had contributed to their ruin. She would have sold Eversleigh House as well, to help pay the debts if her lawyer had not prevented her from doing so. Thanks to his management, she was left with this house and a small income which had come to her directly from her maternal grandmother.

This, no doubt, was to be her home for the rest of her life, so she had better make the best of it. It would be possible, she thought, to employ some girl from the village to help Mrs. Stanley with the everyday household tasks and a boy to help in the garden, but much of the work of putting the house to rights would fall on her shoulders. She was responsible for two elderly retainers and did not have the means to provide them with well-deserved pensions. As well, she had Henry and Addy to support. Christmas was likely to be a lean one this year.

Judith was brought back to the present by a low moan. She crossed quickly to the bed. The stranger was tossing restlessly and muttering incoherently. She bathed his face again and positioned the pillows under his wounded shoulder as best she could. He seemed to calm with her touch, so she stayed by the bedside gently bathing his face.

As the night wore on his fever mounted. She thought at one time she would have to call Henry, for she was hard pressed trying to prevent him from flinging himself out of bed. He seemed to be fighting something, but all she could make out of the words was a vehement, "no." Toward morning, his fever broke and he fell into a deep natural sleep.

It was sometime later that she was aware of someone watching her. She must have dozed off, for the cloth had slipped from her hand and her head was resting on her patient's chest. She sat up abruptly and looked into his brown eyes, still somewhat bright from the last dregs of fever, but alive with amusement.

"Oh dear, I do beg your pardon. I had not meant to..." she stammered, quickly rising and trying to smooth out the creases in her dress and tidy her wayward curls.

"I seem to have caused you no small amount of trouble," Tony said. "The least I could do was allow you to sleep. But where am I? The last I remember I was trying to hail a coach and ask directions, and then my horse stumbled."

"I am very much afraid that my coachman thought you were a highwayman."

"Well, it was a deuced foolish thing for me to do. Forgive me. Let me introduce myself. Tony Ruxford at your service." Tony hesitated briefly before giving his name. Would this lovely creature have heard of his disgrace?

"I am Judith Maybury, sir. I am exceedingly pleased to see that you are feeling better. If you will excuse me, I will send Henry to you now."

"Thank you, I would appreciate that. I feel as weak as a kitten."

"It would seem, sir, that you have only lately recovered from a wound, and after your soaking last night are lucky that you are not still in a high fever."

"I have no doubt, years campaigning in Spain have left me with a strong constitution. I'll be as right as a trivet in no time."

"Then Addy was right, you are a soldier."

Tony hesitated, "Yes, a Captain in the Seventh Hussars."

"I will leave you now. Are you at all hungry?"

He grinned. "Yes. Excessively."

His smile was infectious and Judith felt a strange fluttering in her heart.

Tony watched her leave the room. He recalled with pleasure his waking to a riot of brown curls resting on his chest and the startled look in her hazel eyes when she realised he was awake. He lay for a while enjoying the warmth of the bed and thinking about his hostess. She was attractive, not in a conventional way, for her mouth was probably a little too big and her nose did not have the requisite tilt, but her eyes were large and expressive, and her smile one of great sweetness. Her figure was neat and trim. But, deuce take it! He could not lie here all day. Not if he wanted to clear his name.

Tony flung back the covers, swung his legs over the bedside and tried to stand. His legs refused to hold him and the room spun. He would have fallen if Henry, entering, had not caught him.

"Now, lad, what are you about? Back to bed you go. You've taken a regular rasper and hurt that shoulder of yours again, and Miss Judith told me you were quite feverish last night. A few days more in bed and you'll feel more the thing. Now, don't you fret none."

Tony lay back on the bed, his eyes closed, willing himself to feel stronger. He could not afford the delay but he was realist enough to know that he was in no state to go riding around the countryside, let alone to confront a traitor. Perhaps a day in bed would see him in better frame.

As Henry assisted him to shave and make himself more presentable, he learned a little about Judith Maybury's household. He was relieved to hear that she had no husband. Why that was important he was not sure.

He did not see Judith for the rest of that day, but he met Miss Addison. She changed the bandage on his shoulder and generally treated him like a boy of eight instead of a man of eight-and-twenty. By the time she left he was calling her Addy, and he felt he had known her this age. He was impatient to see Judith again and hoped that she would come to keep him company that evening.

Tony noted the shabbiness of the room and wondered why a young woman would be living in such a place and with so few servants. Both Henry and Addy had told him of last night's events and the fact that they had just arrived at Eversleigh, but very little else. In all probability, here was someone else with troubles.

Tony slept on and off throughout the day and by evening he was feeling a great deal stronger. As he hoped, Judith joined him after an early dinner. She was dressed simply in a yellow gown with the same colour ribbon threaded through her hair and a shawl around her shoulders to ward off the chill of the old house. He looked at her with appreciation and was conscious of a sharp tug of attraction.

"Your fever seems to have left you," she said, suddenly feeling shy, for there was no mistaking his admiring look. "I must apologise for my household. We are still at sixes and sevens, having only arrived last night, and not having been near this place for nigh on ten years."

"Please do not apologise. I am the one to thank you. If you had not come back for me I do not doubt I would have shot my bolt. I am heartily sorry to have put you out, for I have no doubt I have."

She smiled. "Do you play chess, sir? I found this chess set in the library and thought you might like some diversion. I am accounted a fair player. My father taught me."

They played for the better part of two hours, during which time Tony discovered much of her history. "I decided to move to my grandmother's house, away from London and the people who shunned me. I soon found out that I had very few true friends in London society. I was not sorry to leave," she said bitterly, the hurt of her rejection still sharp in her mind.

Tony knew something of that kind of rejection but remained quiet. He was loath to acquaint her with his story in case it would give her a disgust of him, and he did not think he could bear that.

"Checkmate." She laughed delightfully at her win.

"You are indeed a good player. I consider myself a reasonable player but I am outclassed tonight."

"I will wish you goodnight, sir. I think you need your sleep. I will send Henry to you first."

"Goodnight. Perhaps I can have my revenge tomorrow night?"

"Perhaps. We shall see."

❀ ❀ ❀

The next morning he was still feeling the aftereffects of his drenching, but his legs were no longer wobbly and he managed to get out of bed himself. With Henry's help, he dressed, although the bandage around his shoulder prevented him from shrugging into his coat. He was standing by the window looking out onto the wilderness of the garden in front of the house when Judith came in with a breakfast tray.

"Captain Ruxford, is it not too soon to be out of bed?" she asked, concerned.

"I cannot trespass on your hospitality much longer. I …"

The sound of hoof beats and the jangle of harnesses interrupted Tony's reply. He looked out the window and saw several dragoons coming up the carriageway. He had no doubt they were here looking for him. How had they discovered him so quickly?

He turned to Judith. "I must away. I cannot let them capture me," he said urgently.

Judith turned a shocked face to him. "What do you mean?"

"Please, I have no time to explain. I must escape," he pleaded. "Believe me, it is imperative that they do not find me."

Judith made a quick decision. "There is no time for you to escape. Stay here. I will deal with them."

Quickly, she ran down the stairs, intercepting Stanley as he shuffled to the front door. "Stanley, do not tell them about the Captain. We are only the five of us in the house. Take your time answering the door and tell Mrs. Stanley that she is not to mention the Captain."

Stanley may have been slow in movement but there was nothing wrong with his mind, and he grinned at her. "Right you be, Miss Judith."

She left him sitting in the hall chair while the bell clanged impatiently a number of times. Addy was in the drawing room darning some linen. "Addy, there are dragoons at the door. Captain Ruxford believes they are looking for him. We must not tell them he is here, at least not until he has had a chance to explain. Please stall them. I must see Henry and get him to take the Captain's horse from the stable and hide him somewhere.

She dashed outside to the stables and found Henry rubbing down Tony's horse. She quickly explained the situation.

"Don't you worrit, Miss, I know just the place for him."

When Judith entered the drawing room she found a flustered young ensign trying his best to deal with what he perceived to be an agitated old lady who seemed to be incapable of understanding his explanation. He looked to Judith for relief. Perhaps this young woman would understand his request, but he was to be sadly disappointed.

"Oh, my dear," said Addy, "this young man has just told me that there are a company of French spies and traitors lose in the countryside. We are like to be murdered in our beds."

"Spies, traitors! Whatever are we to do?" said Judith, twisting her handkerchief agitatedly and contriving, with good effect, to give the impression of a perfect widgeon. "My dear Sir, we have scarcely been here twenty-four hours and we count only five in number with certainly no men enough to protect us. Murdered in our beds!" Her voice faded, and Judith noted with satisfaction that the ensign was becoming more and more alarmed at the consternation he had caused.

"Miss, please, there is no need to be frightened. There is only one traitor that we know of, and he may already have fled the district."

"Judith, my dear, my vinaigrette," said Addy and fell back on the sofa in an authentic looking collapse. Judith rushed to her side.

Stanley, who had been watching the scene with satisfaction, his facial expression carefully neutral as if the scene before him was nothing out of the way, judged it time to intervene.

"Sir, I think it best if you leave. I will look after them, never you fear. Women! You shouldn't go around telling stories about French spies. Sends them into hysterics."

Returning a few moments later, Stanley grinned. "A masterly performance, if I may say, Miss Judith. Properly routed the young whipper-snapper."

"Oh, dear, I do feel sorry for that poor young man. But it may have been ill judged of us to send him away. Now, I think we all must hear Captain Ruxford's explanation."

❋ ❋ ❋

Tony was in an agony of indecision. Judith seemed to be taking an inordinate time in getting rid of the dragoons. Should he trust her? If he was captured now he would never prove his innocence. Impatiently he paced, until he heard the departing noise of the dragoons. He decided to leave his bedchamber and look for his hostess rather than wait for news of what had taken place.

He walked into the drawing room and pulled up short.

"Captain Ruxford, I believe you owe us all an explanation. Please sit down," ordered Judith, her pistol aimed steadily at his heart. "I am accounted to be a fair shot."

Chapter Three

Tony sat in the chair indicated. "There is no need for your pistol, you know. I am not a traitor." Suddenly, it was very important to him to convince the determined young woman before him that he was innocent. "I am obliged to you all for your help. And yes, I do owe you an explanation."

Judith lowered the pistol, but Tony noticed that she kept it near at hand. The five sat around him and waited expectantly.

"It all happened about six weeks ago. My cousin, John, holds a position in government of a somewhat secret nature, and I received word from him that a suspected traitor was possibly going to make contact with a French agent somewhere near the Spanish village where my company was bivouacked. John furnished me with a description and asked me to be on the lookout, unofficially, of course, for he should not have communicated this information to me and would have been in serious trouble if it became known that he had breached security. I was not to do anything but to alert a Spaniard, Don Diego, who would then take the necessary steps."

Stanley poured him a glass of brandy and he gratefully took a mouthful. "I was never one, I'm afraid, to follow orders well and I was determined to catch this traitor if it was at all possible. I could not believe my luck when he appeared in the village. So, not realising at the time how suspicious this would look, I donned Spanish peasant clothes and followed him to an inn. Imagine my surprise when he met with this same Don Diego who was supposedly my contact. I was just wondering what to do when a third conspirator crept up behind me. In the scuffle I was shot, and so was the person I was following. I lost consciousness, but I did hear Don Diego say something about Heywood-on-

Sea as I blacked out. I have no very clear recollection of much else.

"When I regained my senses, the man I had been following was lying dead by my side and the army had been called. I was found to have a memorandum on me which contained information about our troop movements. Needless to say, the Spaniard and his accomplice were gone and I was unable to corroborate my story. I was arrested for treason, but instead of being thrown into jail, was put under guard while my wound was tended. Fortunately, my army friends believed in my innocence, and when I was well enough smuggled me out of Spain, at great risk to themselves, I might add, and onto a ship sailing for London. I contrived to bring myself home as quickly as possible, although I was laid up with fever for a few days on route. My sister and my cousin John provided me with a horse, clothes and money. The rest you know."

"Surely, your cousin will uphold your story?" asked Judith.

"My cousin has already told his superiors, but because there is no correspondence to substantiate my part in the story there is little he can do. I destroyed his letter after I received it, which, at the time, seemed the most sensible action to take. They think he is only fabricating this story to help me.

"How did the dragoons know to come looking for you in this vicinity?" Judith asked.

"That's a deuced mystery to me. No one knew where I was going."

"Except, perhaps, the traitor," said Judith, thoughtfully.

"Yes, I had not given much thought to that. Perhaps I am not on a wild goose chase after all."

"Now, sir, what do we do? How are we to prove your innocence?" asked Henry.

"We? I take it then, you believe me?" Tony looked at Judith. Her answer was of the utmost importance to him.

"Why, of course, we do," said Addy.

"Judith?" he asked anxiously. Her Christian name came readily to his lips.

"Of course. I am exceedingly sorry about the pistol," she said contritely. "But something bothers me about your story. It's decidedly smoky. Oh, I did not at all mean what you have related," she added hastily, "but, in my opinion there are too many coincidences."

"Bad luck does seem to have plagued me."

"Tell us how we can help?" asked Addy.

"You have done enough already. I'm dashed if I'm going to allow you to put yourself in any more danger. I will depart and cut up your peace no longer."

"No," said Judith. "It is still too dangerous for you to leave here. The dragoons will remain in the district for another day at least. It is better that you stay hidden with us until you are completely well, otherwise you are like to land in an even greater hobble."

"Miss Judith has the right of it, sir," said Henry.

"You will stay here, Captain Ruxford. Tomorrow Addy and I will drive into Heywood, ostensibly to do our shopping, but we will discover whether the soldiers have left the village and where they may have gone."

"But I cannot allow you to do this," protested Tony.

"Now, what danger could we possibly be in? Besides, we are in need of supplies."

Against his better judgement, Tony was cajoled into promising to stay put until Judith and Addy had driven into the village and learned what they could of the soldiers' movements. "I must send word to my family that I am well. I will write a letter and if you could …"

"No," interrupted Judith. "That would not be wise. The address would occasion much comment in the village and the soldiers may hear of it, as, indeed, could the traitor and know of your connections. They would be likely to come back to search more thoroughly. I am of the opinion that it would be better for Henry to go to London with a letter for your sister and cousin. Your cousin may have further news of importance. Henry would not need to take above two days."

"I…" began Tony.

"But you must see that it is the safest way," protested Judith.

"Far be it from me to argue with you. I was just about to say that it was a deuced good notion. I have money, and Henry can take my horse."

"Oh dear, I do sound like a terribly managing female, but I assure you I was only thinking of your welfare."

"My dear Judith," he said, taking her hands, "I will be forever in your debt."

She held his gaze for a moment, her colour high, before lowering her eyes as she read a warmth in his which caused her heart to hammer loudly. Judith, in some confusion of spirits, pulled her hands away and left the room on the pretext of speaking to Mrs. Stanley about dinner. In the hall she put her hands to her burning cheeks and forced herself to confront the truth. She scarcely knew him, yet she was well on the way to falling in love with him.

❄ ❄ ❄

The next day, Judith and Addy returned from their excursion to Heywood to find Stanley and Tony struggling to erect a small evergreen tree in the corner of the drawing room. Heaped on a table were apples, some newly baked biscuits, and numerous strands of coloured ribbon which Mrs. Stanley must have unearthed from one of the trunks in the attic.

"Whatever are you doing?" Judith asked, puzzled.

"I dunno, Miss, I think the Captain's got windmills in his head. He wanted to put this tree up and decorate it with them things there."

"I was sincerely hoping that I would be all finished by the time you returned from Heywood, but it took longer than I anticipated to find a suitable tree. It is a Christmas tree."

"A Christmas tree? I have never heard of it."

"When my father was on the Grand Tour as a young man, he stayed in Germany for a Christmas, and apparently it has been a tradition there for hundreds of years. When my father was alive we always had a Christmas tree in our home, but I have not had one for many years now. I thought it might give the house a festive look. We used to decorate the tree with apples and sweets and coloured paper. Mrs. Stanley could not find any paper so we thought coloured ribbon might suffice.

"What a perfectly charming custom, is it not, Addy?"

"My dear, such a delightful surprise."

"Come, now that you are both home, you must help me decorate this tree while you tell me the news from the village."

Chapter Four

While Tony and Judith had spent a pleasant hour decorating the tree, it had been decided that Tony would act as Judith's groom the following day when they would drive into Heywood. If the soldiers had departed, then Tony would have a drink at the local tavern and see what he could learn, although he was aware that he would have problems understanding the broad Sussex dialect. He had been cudgeling his brains to discover another way which would not involve Judith, but try as he would, he could not think of a better plan for the moment.

When they arrived in the village the next day, the soldiers were still there. Judith felt Tony would be taking unnecessary risks if he carried through his plan, so they returned to Evensleigh House. With Addy's help, Judith spent the rest of the day cleaning and polishing the furniture in the drawing room. It gradually took on a cosier look, especially with the Christmas tree residing in the corner by a cheerful fire. Tony, meantime, banished himself to the stables and with a great deal of advice but little help from Stanley, managed to make three of the stalls more presentable.

"Let us hope the soldiers have departed by now," said Judith tooling the gig towards the village the next day, with Tony sitting beside her, arms folded in the fashion of a groom. "I hope you do not mind being driven by a woman."

"Not when that woman handles the reins as well as you do."

"I was wont to drive my own high-perch phaeton and was accounted a tolerable whip," said Judith, pleased by his approval.

The gig was not the most comfortable conveyance in the weather, but it would have been difficult to drive the coach down the rutted track which lead to the village from Eversleigh House. They were both well rugged up against the bitter wind. Tony had stowed a pistol in the pocket of his greatcoat and unbeknown to the Captain, Judith's little pistol nestled at the bottom of her reticule.

"Judith." Tony's voice held a note of excitement. "There is my cousin. He must have some news. Quickly now, we must catch up with him."

Judith perceived a tall young man, dressed in the height of fashion walking down the main street of the village. "Hurry, take the reins," said Judith.

"Cousin John," she called as she hastily descended from the gig. "Whatever brings you here?" She took the startled young man's hands in her own. "What, don't you even recognise your cousin Judith?" she chided. In a quiet voice she added, "Captain Ruxford is here in the gig."

He glanced over at Tony and then realisation dawned. "Cousin Judith, I did not recognise you. It has been an age since I have seen you. Let us walk a little way. May I offer you my arm? Your groom can follow with your gig."

They walked the length of the street as Judith told John what had transpired. "That is why I posted down as soon as I had your groom's message. I have some news for Tony," said John.

Judith and John stopped at the end of the street, and Tony alighted from the gig and stood at the horse's head. "John, it's good to see you. What has brought you down here?"

"Coz, I have some good news for you. Where can we meet?" asked John.

"You are the best of good fellows, John. I will stay in the village on the pretext of doing some more errands for Judith and we can meet behind that house over there and talk, in say, fifteen minutes."

"How will you return to Eversleigh?" asked Judith.

"No doubt I can hire a hack somewhere. But do not worry about me. John will let you know if I cannot return tonight."

"Take care, Tony," said Judith. They had started using each others' Christian names without really being conscious of having slipped into an easy relationship.

The two men watched as Judith drove back down the street. John looked at Tony's expression. "Do I detect an interest there?" he asked.

"She is pluck to the backbone. But what do I have to offer her? I must clear my name first before I can even think of fixing my interest. Let us not stand here talking. We are causing enough comment by walking in this weather. I will meet you in fifteen minutes."

Tony strode down the street and left John to wander toward the meeting place.

"What news?" Tony asked when he met John a short time later.

"Good news as far as I am concerned. I think I have unearthed the French agent but we need to talk to a fisherman down in one of the huts by the seashore. Come, I'll show you the way."

Meanwhile, Judith drove home thinking over the events of the past few days. How could she have fallen in love so quickly and so deeply? She knew that from first setting eyes on him lying in his sick bed she had been strongly attracted to him, and then somehow she had tumbled into love. The sound of hoof beats behind her made her turn. It was Henry. She waited for him to draw level with the gig. "You have made exceedingly good time, Henry."

"It's a pleasure riding this big'un of the Captain's. A real sweet goer, Miss."

"Did you have any difficulty delivering the Captain's messages?"

"No, Miss Judith. I saw the Captain's sister, Lady Elizabeth Burton, and right glad she was to hear that he was well. But I did not see his cousin. He was out of town on business, I was told, and not expected back for at least a week, but Lady Burton assured me that she would give him the Captain's news."

Judith's heart seemed to skip a beat and her stomach contracted in a knot of fear. "So you never saw the Captain's cousin, and there is no way he could have learned of Tony's whereabouts."

"No, Miss," he replied. "Why, whatever is the matter?" he asked, alarmed at Judith's white face.

"I am very much afraid that Captain Ruxford has walked into a trap. Henry, ride into Heywood. I will follow as quickly as I can. Stop the Captain from going anywhere with his cousin." She prayed she would be in time.

As Judith reached the village and searched frantically for some sign of the two men, Tony and John had reached a ramshackle hut nestled under the over-hang of a cliff. "We need to wait in here for him," said John.

They entered the hut, Tony first. "When did you set up this meeting, John?"

"Coz, what a caper-witted person you are, to be sure," said John, levelling his pistol at Tony. "Haven't you worked out yet that this whole business is all a hum? No, stay where you are," he ordered as Tony, shocked at the unexpected turn of events, moved toward him.

"Whatever do you mean?"

"I mean, my dear Tony, that I am your traitor. I have been selling informa-tion to the French for some two years, but it is becoming more and more dan-gerous and I formed the opinion that it was time I retired. But I need money to allow me to live in the style to which I have become accustomed. With my source of funds about to dry up I had to find another avenue. I haven't a feather to fly with and am heavily in debt. While I remained your heir, I was allowed a certain amount of credit but I knew that I could not count on that for long. And I was right. I had thought that the war would do me the service of disposing of you, but you seem to enjoy a charmed life. My associates, for a considerable amount of money I might add, agreed to help me arrange your death. Needless to say the Spanish business was badly bungled. You were to die there. My ac-complice, as an afterthought, had only enough time to thrust the memorandum into your hand and escape before the army arrived. A masterly stroke, I thought, for surely the courts would take care of you then, but you escaped. You will not escape me this time."

"But why, John? If you had needed money I would gladly have given it to you."

"I had no wish to be your pensioner. Besides, your position in society was also singularly attractive. But enough talking. I have set up a tragic scenario.

My accomplice will attest to the fact that I was unable to save you from the dastardly traitor who killed you and, of course, escaped. I will have my accomplice damage me a little to make my story more authentic. You may be sure, Coz, that the world will see that I am absolutely desolated by your demise. I will be truly sorry, but there is no way out."

Tony stood white faced before him. He could not believe that his cousin, a man whom he regarded as a brother, was about to kill him. It was inconceivable, but everything slotted into place. He had been properly gulled.

John raised his pistol and took aim. Tony decided his only chance was to dive toward him and try to grapple the pistol from his grasp. He would not have time to draw his own pistol. He saw John's finger tighten on the trigger, and he sprang toward John. There was a loud report, followed closely by another. He was somewhat surprised to find that he was still alive and that it was John who was lying on the floor, clutching his chest and looking amazed at the blood that welled between his fingers.

Judith stood by the door, her face pale but determined, the pistol gripped in her hand still pointing at John.

"Judith!" Tony checked that John was not armed with another firearm before gently taking Judith's pistol from her nerveless hand and gathering her in his arms. "My darling girl."

He crushed her in his arms and dropped a kiss lightly upon her windswept curls. She relaxed in his arms, and Tony was content to let her be.

"Captain, I hate to interrupt, but if you don't look to yon cousin you may only have a corpse to take to the authorities," interrupted Henry, dragging John's accomplice, who was decidedly worse for wear, into the hut. "I found him sneaking around the back."

"Damn you, cousin, let be," gasped John as Tony staunched the bleeding. "Think of the scandal to the family name if I am hanged for treason."

"Do you think I care one whit about what society will say? No doubt, you have caused the deaths of many a good soldier, and I intend to see you pay for your treachery."

"Tony, I am persuaded you will need Henry's help to get your prisoners to London. Henry, go with Captain Ruxford. I will drive myself home."

"Judith, I don't like it above half."

"Captain, Miss Judith has the right of it. You cannot handle these two by yourself. Pity the soldiers have left the district," said Henry.

Judith saw Tony and Henry off to London in his cousin's chaise before returning to Eversleigh with the news.

❀ ❀ ❀

It was now five days since the events of that memorable day, and Judith had only a brief word from Tony to say they had arrived safely and that investigations into John's activities were proceeding. Henry was still in London as well, detained as a witness.

There was no word when Tony might return or even if he would return. Her spirits were wholly cast down at the thought that she might only see him a few more times before he vanished from her life. She could not conceive that with his name restored he would want anything more to do with her other than what politeness and gratitude would dictate. Life without him at her side did not bear thinking of.

"Now, my dear, I am persuaded all will be well," said Addy. "This fit of the dismals will never do. It will soon be Christmas, and I fancy we will see him sitting in front of our fire before that."

"One scarcely knows what to think," sighed Judith.

"Judith, my dear, come here. I've never seen the like before," said Addy, staring out the window at two laden coaches which lumbered up the carriage way, preceded by a smart high-perch phaeton pulled by two perfectly matched greys. "I declare, it's Captain Ruxford. I wonder whose crest is on the coach? And, it is Henry driving that very sporting vehicle."

Judith rushed to open the door before Stanley could even get there. Tony jumped out of the chaise and advanced on her in an alarmingly purposeful manner, his arms open, inviting her to walk straight into them. She flew down the stairs and was enfolded in such a close embrace that it seemed likely several of her ribs would not survive. She emerged radiant and breathless from his ardent embrace, and it appeared to her that the winter sun was no longer pale but was shining with particular brilliance.

"Come inside, my love, I have much to tell you," said Tony. He shut the door to the drawing room and drew her down beside him on the sofa. "But first I have an important question to ask."

He took a small jewellery box from his pocket and opened it to reveal a ruby ring of such exquisite work that Judith gasped at its beauty. He knelt before her. "Will you do me the honour of becoming my wife?"

"Oh, Tony, you cannot wish to marry me. You know of my family's scandal."

"And you know of my family's scandal, which is far worse, I might add. Judith, I do love you so, and I cannot bear to think of life without you by my side. Say you will marry me."

"Tony, yes. I would like that above anything else in the world. I love you, too. Much, much more than you could possibly love me. I have been so miserable this past week wondering whether I would ever see you again."

"Now that I have secured your hand in marriage, my love," he said as he slipped the ring on her finger, "I must also tell you that you will not be Mrs Tony Ruxford but the Countess of Warne. I did not use my title in the army."

"Tony, truly you cannot wish to marry me," she said, shocked by his revelation. "Your scandal will be long forgotten by the next Season but I am afraid I will always be society's outcast. You can look a great deal higher for a wife."

"You are the wife I want and I dashed well don't care what society thinks. We will be outcasts together. I have no intention of allowing you to go back on your promise. Come, let me show you your Christmas present. Henry drove it down, a new high-perch phaeton with two prime bits of horse flesh to pull it. We will be busy in the next few days making this house habitable for Christmas. I have brought a number of servants, the estate carpenter, and hampers of food. I intend to make this a memorable Christmas. Then, my darling, we will be married with all the pomp and ceremony I can muster at my country estate in the New Year."

"Tony, I have nothing but a water colour I painted of the Christmas tree to give you."

"My darling, you gave me so much more. You gave me my life and my heart's desire. What more could anyone want?"

He took her ruthlessly in his arms and kissed her soundly. She returned his embrace with fervour, and little in the way of words passed between them for some appreciable time.

Alexandria Shaw lives in Brisbane, Australia and is a speech/language pathologist by profession. She has always been fascinated by the Regency period since first reading Georgette Heyer in high school. Her favourite Regency authors are, naturally, Georgette Heyer as well as Clare Darcy and Shelia Walsh. Alexandria has dabbled in writing since early primary school and has numerous stories in many genres taking up space in her filing cabinet. Her two loves in writing are regency romances and science fantasy for the young adult. Currently, she is working on a Regency novel and a science fantasy for twelve to fourteen year olds. This is her second story set in the Regency period to be published. (First was last year's *An Arranged Marriage* in A REGENCY SAMPLER.)

It's impossible for best friends to be lovers. Or is it? Elizabeth must somehow convince Adam that sometimes best friends do wish to be taken advantage of!

Doing the Pretty

Jane Myers Perrine

"Can you see her, Lizzie?" Adam Bronson, the Baron Fenwick, pointed through the crowd of dancers, his brown eyes sparkling with excitement. "Is she not the most beautiful woman you've ever seen?"

Elizabeth Petersham searched the assembly room but still could not see the paragon Adam had again described to her on their way to Bury St. Edmund. Angela Falconer's beauty and virtue had been a constant part of Adam's conversation since he met her at the assembly a week earlier.

"Over there by the refreshment table. You can see her if you lean this way." And she could.

"She's lovely," Elizabeth agreed. Her rival was tiny, a pocket Venus with enormous blue eyes and silver-blond hair. Elizabeth's heart sank to the toes of her blue satin slippers.

Miss Falconer's light curls made Elizabeth's dark locks seem dull and straight. Elizabeth had always considered herself tall and willowy. Now she just felt skinny.

"Is she rich?" she whispered.

"Lizzie, not now."

"Well, is she? You have to marry an heiress."

"Yes, she is, but that's not the most important point." Adam search the crowd to find Miss Falconer. "Have you ever seen a woman so perfect?"

No, Elizabeth had to admit she never had.

"That's why I need you, Lizzie." He patted her shoulder.

"Me?" She scrutinized his face, looking for a hint of what he was going to say.

"I'll come by tomorrow afternoon. I have a favour to ask."

Before she could ask for more information, a gentleman bowed before Elizabeth, and they joined the set just forming. As she moved to the music, Elizabeth saw Adam standing in the corner, watching Miss Falconer.

The next afternoon brought a repetition of Adam's praises for Miss Falconer. Yes, she was the most beautiful, the most charming, the loveliest woman ever created, Elizabeth agreed.

"But what is she like?" Elizabeth finally asked. "Is she a pleasant young woman? Is she clever?"

"I don't know," Adam answered. "I have never talked to her."

"What?" Elizabeth leaped from the sofa in the parlour where they drank tea. Her sudden movement startled their chaperone, her elderly Aunt Susannah, who awakened with a jerk and looked around before resuming her nap on the comfortable settee in the corner. Not that they needed her. She and Adam had known each other since she was an infant. Her father knew well that Adam would never compromise her.

Confound it, Elizabeth thought. She was almost twenty and had wanted to be compromised by Adam for at least four years, but he thought of her only as his best friend.

Lately, she had thought he might have begun to see her as a woman. There had been lingering glances, sometimes a smile, and once, a touch. Then he'd met the perfect Miss Falconer.

"Why have you never spoken with her?" Elizabeth demanded.

"Lizzie, I wouldn't know how. You and your sister are the only women outside my family I have ever spoken with at length. How could I talk to someone like *her*?" Adam's eyes became slightly unfocused and he grinned.

"Oh, coming it a bit strong, Adam. Sarah and I are hardly beneath your touch."

"Lizzie, I didn't mean that. It's just that, as rough as I am, how could I possibly attract Miss Falconer? My clothes and my hair are not fashionable. I know nothing about London or the *ton*. I have never been to Vauxhall or Almack's. I don't even know how to dance."

Of course not, Elizabeth thought. After his parents had gambled and frolicked away all the estate's money, they'd both died in a carriage wreck and left the shambles to Adam who, at seventeen, had to assume the entire burden.

"Well, you do lack town bronze, but that's because you had other things, important things, to do instead of going to London."

"And I don't regret it. By spending my holidays at Fenwick, I've almost saved the estate, but I still need to marry an heiress to bring it off."

"Why don't you marry me?" Elizabeth asked, then paused for a moment and studied her cup. "I'm an heiress. You and I get along quite well."

Adam choked on his tea. "You aren't serious, Lizzie, are you?"

He was staring at her when Elizabeth lifted her eyes.

"You are serious, Lizzie?" Adam shook his head. "But I couldn't. It would be like marrying my sister. Besides, I won't take advantage of you by marrying you for your money. You deserve to marry a man you love."

With a sigh, Elizabeth put the cup down and, with dread in her heart, asked, "What favour did you come here to ask?"

He leaned forward. "Lizzie, would you teach me to dance? I need you to make me into a beau so I can court Miss Falconer."

Elizabeth looked up at Adam. His dark brown hair was cut raggedly and his clothes reeked of country tailor. She knew every beloved angle of his face by heart. He was handsome but, far more than that, he was kind and loyal and intelligent and industrious.

Did Miss Falconer deserve him? Well, that wasn't Elizabeth's decision. It belonged to Adam and Miss Falconer.

"Let me think." She tapped her fingers on the table as she thought. "First, you must go to London. Visit Weston and get some clothes."

Adam blanched. "Weston? Lizzie, his jackets cost so much. Isn't there a less expensive tailor?"

"Yes, there are cheaper tailors, but if you want to court Miss Falconer, you will need to spend money. Is she worth it?"

"Yes, she is. Isn't she the most beautiful...?"

"And purchase some good boots and get your hair cut," Elizabeth interrupted him. "When you return, we shall begin your lessons in doing the pretty."

❊ ❊ ❊

A few days later, Adam had returned from London and strutted across Elizabeth's parlour. She had not realized what a difference the haircut and clothing would make. The Brutus showed his strong, clean jaw line and emphasized the depths of his dark eyes. A well-cut jacket by Weston displayed his wide shoulders while the tight unmentionables stretched over muscular thighs and calves that had no need of padding.

"Oh, my." Elizabeth continued to study Adam. "Miss Falconer will not be able to refuse you."

"I do look fine, don't I?" A smile lit his features. "Lizzie, I've done my part. Now, you need to teach me to dance and drink tea and chat in polite company."

"You have been drinking tea and chatting with me for years, Adam Fenwick. I consider myself polite company."

"Well, of course you are." He started to rake a hand through his hair.

"Don't do that! You'll ruin the style. Men do not display such behaviour in polite company."

"That is just the kind of advice I need." He patted her on the shoulder. "Thank you, Lizzie. You are the best of friends."

Over the next days, Adam learned to tone down the loud, joyful laugh that so delighted Elizabeth but did not fit in a drawing room. He began to read the *Gazette* and fashionable novels so he could discuss the latest *on-dits* and join in the literary discussions while he drank tea with members of the *ton*.

Then the dancing lessons began in the ballroom. Elizabeth's younger sister Sarah played the piano while Aunt Susannah dozed in a comfortable chair.

In only a week, Adam had mastered the country dances and quadrilles as well as the minuet and cotillion.

"Now the waltz," Adam said as they completed the last step of a minuet.

The idea of waltzing with Adam left Elizabeth breathless. She closed her eyes to calm herself.

"First, let me show you the position and steps to the waltz before we try it with music," Elizabeth said.

"This is how you move your feet." She demonstrated the dance step while he watched, then Adam imitated her movement. Once he seemed at ease, she said, "In the waltz, we face each other. Then you put your hand on my back."

He hesitated for a moment. Something flashed in his eyes, but Elizabeth couldn't read it. Was it longing? Or was it her imagination?

"Adam, it is only a dance. Done often in polite society. I have waltzed several times. Put your hand on my back."

When Adam placed his hand where she suggested, he clenched his jaws and kept his glance fixed above her head. That was fine because Elizabeth wasn't sure she could meet his eyes. Never before had a partner's hand on her back caused her to tingle, actually to tingle.

She swallowed and continued the lesson. "I put my hand here, on your shoulder, then we hold hands like this." She demonstrated before continuing with the instructions. "Now, I am going to count and you are going to move us around the floor. One, two, three; one, two, three.

"Sarah," she called to her sister, "please play for us now."

When their movements fit the rhythm of the music, Elizabeth forced herself to look up, into Adam's face but he continued to study something above and behind her.

"In the waltz, you are supposed to look at your partner. This is a flirtatious dance."

Adam looked down at her. When she met his gaze, she was surprised to see longing there.

"One, two, three," she repeated, keeping her eyes locked on his. A faint spark of hope warmed her heart, and at the same time she felt a delicious shiver down her spine.

Adam stopped moving and studied her face for what seemed like hours while Sarah continued to pound away on the piano, and Aunt Susannah snored. He pulled her closer to him, and his eyes caressed her face. After a moment, he rubbed her cheek with the back of his hand, then he slowly lowered his mouth.

When his lips touched hers, softly, then with more pressure, she threw her arms around his neck and joined in the kiss with great delight.

Then it was over. Adam dropped his arms and stepped back. He swallowed and looked at her.

"I'm sorry, Lizzie. I shouldn't have done that." He shook his head. "But, you see, I didn't know. I didn't know it wouldn't feel at all like kissing my sister."

"Adam..." she began.

"No, I'm sorry, Lizzie. That should never have happened." He turned and strode out the door.

For a moment, Lizzie just watched him leave until she reminded herself that this was Adam, the man she loved and who loved her. He did! He really did! She was allowing him to race out of her life. She picked up her skirt and ran after him.

The cold caught her breath and caused her to shiver when she opened the door, but she hurried outside. When she caught up with him, Adam was pacing back and forth in front of the house as he waited for his horse.

"What just happened?" she asked.

He refused to look at her, refused to acknowledge her presence.

"Adam?"

"Go back inside, Lizzie. It is cold out here." He strode to the other side of the drive.

"Why won't you talk to me?" She followed him. "Are we no longer friends?"

"No, dammit, we are no longer friends." He ran his hand through his hair. "Lizzie, after that kiss we can no longer be friends." He looked down the drive toward the stable.

"Do you want to continue with the lesson, so you can court Miss Falconer?" she asked in an attempt to get him to talk to her.

"No, I do not." He turned to look at her, his eyes filled with pain. "How could I ask her to marry me when I am in love with another woman? With you?"

"Than marry *me*," she shouted up at his impassive face.

"I cannot. You know I must marry an heiress." He clenched his jaw again. "How could you believe that I love you when I must marry an heiress?"

"You were willing to marry Miss Falconer."

"I didn't know what love was then."

"If you do not want to marry me, what you feel isn't love. It is pride."

He looked at her with such yearning that she moved closer to him before he stepped away.

"You are my best friend. I will not take advantage of you," he said quietly, then strode to meet the groom who finally brought his horse.

Elizabeth watched him mount and gallop away. "Stupid, stubborn man." She entered the house in a towering temper, no longer cold. "He will come back," she murmured. "He loves me and he will come back."

※ ❀ ※

But, as the weeks passed, he didn't. Even when Mr. Petersham issued an invitation for dinner, Adam turned it down. Politely, for Adam would not have acted in any other way, but firmly.

Preparations for the holidays began. The house was redolent with secret and the special smells of Christmas. Stir-up Sunday—when the plum pudding full of dates and raisins, was made—came and went with no sign of Adam Even the sight of Sarah dropping the coins into the mixture, her face smeared with dough, could not cheer Lizzie.

Visits to other homes in the neighbourhood to deliver Cook's delicious mincemeat pies were fun, but they had to leave Adam's with the footman.

Mr. Petersham and the groundskeeper discussed the Yule log for days, but even the sight of two men arguing if the log should be oak or fruitwood or as could not pull Lizzie from her doldrums. She was, indeed, blue-deviled.

After she finished tatting a long chain of lace for Sarah, Lizzie searched for yarn to knit a scarf for her father. Instead she found the fabric she had bought to make handkerchiefs for Adam. She pulled the squares from the drawer and sank onto her bed, looking at them.

"Blasted man." She rubbed her hand across the soft surface and realized she might never see him again, would have to face holiday after holiday, Stir up Sunday and St. Thomas' Day and Christmas and Boxing Day and Twelft Night without him.

"Well, I shan't," she said resolutely. Her resourceful brain turned over on idea after another until finally she leaped to her feet to search for her sister.

"I have a plan," Elizabeth told Sarah when she finally found her. "A plan t make Adam talk to me. Will you help?"

Sarah's head bobbed up and down in excitement.

"And you must get Father to help."

"Oh, Lizzie, what are we going to do?"

"Well, I'll do it at the Squire's Christmas party. Here's your part…"

After she shared the sketchy details with her sister, Elizabeth added, "An don't forget, Father must rush in when you hear me laugh."

※ ❀ ※

From the side of the dance floor, Elizabeth studied the room. It was deco rated with ribbons and brilliant bows and furbelows of greenery, but not a sin gle kissing bough, not a bit of mistletoe.

Her glance moved toward where Adam stood with the Squire at the wassa bowl. In the weeks since she'd seen him, Adam's hair had grown, but the bar ber's expert hand was still discernible. He wore a handsome waistcoat with jacket of deep blue. As he laughed at a comment of the squire's, Adam looke around at the guests, his eyes lighting on Elizabeth for just a moment before h jerked his glance away.

When the small orchestra started to play the first country dance, Elizabeth strode across the ballroom to where Adam stood.

"Adam," Elizabeth said, allowing a tear to well up in her eye and slide down her cheek. "Would you please..." She turned toward the Squire. "Please excuse me, but I must talk to Adam."

"Of course." With a nod, the Squire moved away.

"What is it, Lizzie?" Adam's eyes were soft with concern.

"It's nothing." She removed a lacey handkerchief from her reticule and dabbed her eyes. "I just..." She dabbed her eyes again. "I just wanted to be with a friend. Will you please..." she said with a tremor in her voice. "Will you please dance with me?"

Adam took her hand gently and led Elizabeth into the set that was forming. "What is the matter?"

"I cannot talk about it." And well she couldn't, Elizabeth thought, having no idea what was supposed to be bothering her. "Not here."

With only a few minutes of the dance remaining, Elizabeth allowed the tears to flow. "Excuse me," she murmured to Adam. "I have to get away." She turned and ran from the dance floor. As she dashed across the hall and into the small parlour, she glimpsed Sarah and her father by the staircase. Behind her, she heard Adam's footsteps.

Drat, she thought. Not a kissing bough or bunch of mistletoe in here either. She would have to think of something else.

"Lizzie," Adam said from behind her. "Whatever is the problem."

"It's my father," she stammered. None of her plans had included what she should say now, how she would get Adam to compromise her, only that she get him alone. In her thoughts, it had all seemed so easy.

"What's wrong with him?" Adam led her to a chair and settled her in it while he knelt on the floor in front of her. "Is he ill? He looked healthy to-night."

"No, he's not sick. It's...it's..." She sobbed into the tiny shred of handkerchief.

"Not money. He's the warmest man in East Anglia."

"No, it's not money." How could she get him to put his arms around her, to touch her, to do anything which might look compromising? She opened her eyes wide and looked down at Adam, hoping that he would lose himself in their depths.

But he just took her handkerchief and dabbed at her tears. She'd have to throw herself into his arms to compromise herself and hope that he didn't mind the consequences too much. But, before she could move toward Adam, a young woman skipped into the room followed by a young man. Lizzie thought he was a guest of the Squire's oldest son, but she didn't know the young woman.

"Oh, Harold." The young woman giggled. "You mustn't."

Harold, a very handsome young buck, chased her around a table. "Hold still, Becky, so I can kiss you.

"No, Harold!" Becky squealed. Then she saw Adam and Elizabeth, stopped and put her hands over her mouth. "Oh, hello. Who are you? Look, Harold. There are other people here." She gestured toward them. "Two of them. Over there."

"Hello." Harold bowed, then turned to the young woman and pulled her into his arms.

"Oh, no, Harold, not here. We are not alone." Becky giggled and pretended to push him away. "Stop, stop!"

"Come here, sweet." Harold put his hands on Becky's side and began to tickle her.

"Oh, Harold, stop!" Becky shouted, then began to laugh loudly.

Becky had an earsplitting laugh, Elizabeth thought, and realized what would most likely take place when her father heard that sound.

And it did.

Mr. Petersham threw the door open and rushed into the room. Pointing at the couple embracing in the middle of the room, he shouted, "Unhand my daughter, you cad! You have compromised her. You *must* marry her."

Elizabeth groaned and wished she could sneak out of the parlour.

Then her father looked around the room at the four people watching him. Harold held Becky in the circle of his arms and blinked. Becky stared at Mr. Petersham with her eyes wide and mouth open.

Elizabeth attempted to sink into the chair, refusing to look at Adam who stood and watched the scene with great interest. Peeking up, Elizabeth saw him glance from Mr. Petersham to Elizabeth and back, but she could not meet his eyes.

"You're not my father," Becky said. "Why would you say that?"

Befuddled, Mr. Petersham repeated, "Unhand my daughter, you cad," but his voice was much less certain, and he no longer pointed at the couple. Shaking his head, Mr. Petersham turned toward his daughter.

"You're not my father." Becky stamped her foot. "Why do you keep saying that?"

Elizabeth shrugged her shoulders, finally meeting her father's gaze but refusing to look at Adam.

"You are correct." Elizabeth stood. "He's *my* father."

"He's your father?" Becky turned toward Elizabeth with a puzzled frown. "Then why is he calling me his daughter and Harold a cad?"

"I…it's…" Elizabeth gulped. "Well, it's very hard to explain."

Her father turned, his face white and his eyes glassy. He attempted to scurry out of the room.

"Just a minute, Mr. Petersham," Adam said. His words stopped Mr. Petersham in his tracks. "You two." Adam pointed to Becky and Harold. "You two, Becky and Harold, you go back to the party." He nodded toward the door.

"Yes, sir." With giggles and nudges, they stumbled out of the room.

"Now, why don't you tell me what you were doing, Mr. Petersham?" Adam walked toward the older man.

Elizabeth rushed to stand by her father. "Don't blame him. It was my idea." She took her father's arm.

"How interesting. Would you like to explain?" Adam said, his voice level.

"I had a plan." Elizabeth looked up at Adam. "I had to do something."

"Why?" His lips began to twitch a little.

"Well, you were behaving like such a fool. I decided to make it look as if you were compromising me, so Father would force you to marry me." She thrust out her chin. "It was a good plan. Someone had to do something to stop you from making a bumble-broth of our lives."

"Maybe it was a good plan," Adam agreed with a nod. "Until Harold and Becky ruined it." He studied Elizabeth and her father for almost a full minute, then he started laughing. "How in the world did she talk you into this?" Adam asked Mr. Petersham.

"Didn't need to convince me. You're a fine young man. Be delighted if you married my Lizzie."

Adam again studied Mr. Petersham and Elizabeth before he spoke.

"If I *have* to marry Lizzie…"

"If you *have* to marry me?"

"Let me finish, Lizzie." Adam turned back toward Mr. Petersham. "If I have to marry Lizzie, I will try to accept it with the best possible grace."

"Adam!" Elizabeth said.

Adam took Elizabeth into his arms with such enthusiasm and joy that she forgot what she had been about to say, forgave his words and snuggled against him.

He started to kiss her but then looked up at Mr. Petersham. "If I am to be accused of compromising your daughter, I feel it is only fair that I receive some enjoyment from tarnishing both her and my reputations. If you would please leave us alone for a few minutes, we will return to the party an engaged couple."

"Knew I could count on you, my boy." Mr. Petersham hastened from the room.

"Now," he said, smiling down at Elizabeth, "I believe it is time for me to compromise you." He kissed her gently. "Happy Christmas, my love." He smiled down at her.

"The happiest ever." Elizabeth lifted her lips again for his kiss.

Jane Myers Perrine's third-grade teacher told her she would be a writer—and she finally fulfilled that prophecy. In college, she fell in love with Jane Austen so it was natural that, when she finally found time to write, she chose Regencies.

Jane has taught high school Spanish for many years as well as serving as program supervisor in various mental health facilities. Her short pieces have appeared in the Houston Chronicle, Woman's World Magazine, and several on-line magazines. She and her husband George formerly published *The Breathless Moment*, an e-zine of romantic fiction and features for women.

Jane was a Golden Heart finalist with *The Mad Herringtons* and has won awards in short contemporary fiction. She is presently working on a Regency and several short contemporary novels. She recently moved to Buchanan Dam, Texas, with her husband, three cocker spaniels and a very fertile cockatiel.

Sometimes mistletoe can be used for more than just romance. Find out how this symbol of Christmas is utilized in this exciting story of traitors and true love.

Under the Mistletoe

Laurie Alice Eakes

She was not alone in the tree.

Lady Morrigan Wythe froze, knife upraised. Moonlight glinted off the golden blade...and something else.

Another upraised knife.

A shaky but strong hand gripped her wrist, making her knife fall through the branches with a soft rustle. "Lady Morrigan?"

Stunned, she nearly followed the knife's descent. Hoping she sounded firm, not frightened, she forced herself to respond, "Who wants to know?"

"Devenish, a friend...of Lord Fairdown's."

"Lord Fairdown's friends don't—"

"Quiet. Listen." Though low, the man's voice carried the unmistakable ring of authority.

Or did authority lie in his grip on her wrist?

Whatever the source, Morrigan quieted and listened.

"Your father, he always...messages..." Devenish paused and took several wheezing breaths. "I need...your help."

He sounded like he needed an apothecary.

Deciding that the man was probably a vagrant, a soldier whose regiment had disbanded, leaving him destitute and homeless, Morrigan lost her apprehension and annoyance. "Mr. Devenish, if you come to the kitchen door, there is food and warmth aplenty."

"No." Devenish gasped for air. "Dangerous. Need...Fairdown."

"P—his lordship is ill."

Why else would she, a lady of five-and-twenty, be up a tree cutting mistletoe?

The grip on her wrist tightened. "Then you...help?"

"Yes, what is it?" she agreed so he would let her go.

"Thank you." Devenish loosened his hold on her wrist. "A messenger...coming to the Winter Solstice Eve Ball..." His voice trailed off.

Lud, the poor man was mad as well as homeless.

"Mr. Devenish," she said with exaggerated patience, "only neighbors and a few friends from town attend the ball. They're scholars and gentlemen farmers, not men who carry messages of more importance than the latest publications or sheep auctions."

"Not all. Not your fa—"

"My father is the greatest scholar of them all."

And there she'd gone and given herself away.

A sound suspiciously like a chuckle drifted from the other side of the tree. "Knew it had to be you cutting the mistletoe. Don't blame you…not trusting me. But I'm…trusting you. Fairdown said I could if he…failed me."

"Fairdown fails no one." Morrigan barely kept her anger under control as she realized the man wasn't a deranged vagrant, but someone playing a May game at her expense. "Now, your game is up. Let me go."

"No game, my lady." Devenish held her fast. "It's still war…with the Americans, and your father is a link in an espionage chain."

❄ ❄ ❄

Her father an agent of His Majesty's government?

Not possible! Sewald Wythe, Earl of Fairdown, was a peaceable scholar, steeped in his studies of Celtic history and lore. He believed in universal light, the druid philosophy William Blake had rekindled. Fairdown's studies had led to his celebration of the ancient fire festivals.

His celebration of Samhain, the Celtic New Year, had led to his current struggle to recover from a lung fever he contracted while carrying out his ceremony in the rain. His insistence that they go ahead with the annual Winter Solstice Eve Ball led Morrigan up the oldest oak in the garden to cut mistletoe and endure someone's poor jest.

It had to be a jest. Never would her father involve himself in military matters, let alone espionage. Surely Devenish was a friend of her brother, Taliesin, Lord Paxcroft.

Yet what if Devenish played no game?

The slip of paper Devenish had given her clutched in her hand, Morrigan hastened up the back stairs to her father's chamber. She found him dozing before the fire, his evening posset neglected on the table beside him.

He roused at her entrance and offered her his gentle smile. "You got the mistletoe, then?"

"It's in the garden room." She'd wrapped it in a wet cloth to keep the berries white. "I'm far too old to be climbing trees," she added as she sat on the hearthrug at Fairdown's slippered feet.

"Paxcroft wouldn't have done it right. I trust you."

As he had told Devenish he could?

Morrigan gripped her hands together in her lap and looked into her father's lapis blue eyes, the only good feature she'd inherited from her handsome sire. "Papa, is there another reason why you sent me up that tree tonight instead of

Paxcroft?"

"What do you mean?" Fairdown took sudden interest in the posset he detested.

Morrigan removed the tankard from his hand. "Papa, Devenish was in that tree."

Fairdown sighed. "So he came. I hoped we'd have a peaceful Yuletide."

There went the idea of Devenish being a prankster.

More deeply frightened than she had been in the tree, Morrigan asked, "Are you truly an agent for the government?"

"These twenty years, child. But no more questions about that now. Tell me what Devenish said."

Morrigan tensed at the sudden harshness in his tone. "He said you told him he could trust me. He said he was followed and attacked. He got away and hid the dispatches. They're instructions to Admiral Lord Gambier to finalize the peace treaty with the Americans. If they don't reach Ghent by Christmas Eve, or if false dispatches get delivered first, peace negotiations may fail and— Papa, are you all right?"

"Yes, child." With a sigh, he closed his eyes and leaned his head against the winged back of his chair. "I'm a poor parent to involve my daughter in a dangerous business."

Morrigan clasped his hand. "Never you mind that, Papa. The messenger who deciphers the code and collects the dispatches is the one in danger, not I." She grimaced. "Devenish said no one would suspect a mere female."

"No doubt he's right. If the traitor knew he met you in the oak, as he was to meet me, he'd have stopped you on the way back to the house. But Devenish would have had his rifle ready to protect you." Fairdown rubbed his eyes. "What does he wish you to do?"

"Use the mistletoe and some other plants to form the code."

"Ah, the ana—" Fairdown clamped his mouth shut.

Morrigan didn't press. At present, she was more interested in the situation into which she'd been recruited than how to decipher the message. "Papa, why would anyone wish for a war to continue?"

"Profit. Navy men don't want to be put on half pay and lose their chance at prize money. Men who manufacture munitions or supply the military won't have so much business when the conflict with the Americans ends."

"That's monstrous!"

"Yes, child, it is. So I do what little I can to help."

"Then so shall I." She rose. "And at the moment, I can help the best by making sure you get well."

She encouraged him to drink his posset, then rang for his valet to help him to bed. Assured her father would rest, she sought her own bed, though she didn't expect to sleep.

She did rest, however, and woke to a bright gray sky and the smell of her morning chocolate. As usual, she didn't remain in bed; she drank the chocolate while sitting at her dressing table so her maid could brush her hair.

"Simply pin it under a cap for this morning," she directed the girl. "Otherwise it'll be a squirrel's nest by tonight."

"Aye, milady. I'm afraid you're right. The house is at sixes and sevens already. Someone stole a roasted fowl from the larder, and Cook is threatening to take Coachman's whip to all the servants."

"Gracious me!" Morrigan sprang up so swiftly she knocked over her stool. "My gown. The gray merino."

She was off on a flurry of activity that left her little time to think about the strange events of the previous night. A man in the oak and her father an agent for the government shrank to insignificance compared to an outraged cook, anxious servants, and her sister, Isolde, deciding her white woolen gown was too childish for a lady of eighteen and made her look sallow besides.

By the time Morrigan entered the garden room to create the mistletoe message, she was more than ready for a peaceful hour. She had threatened to deliver a severe tongue-lashing to anyone who disturbed her.

The peace, however, brought back the two conversations of the previous night in vivid detail. As she followed Devenish's instructions for placement of white—they had to be white—mistletoe berries, red holly berries, glossy green leaves from both plants, and pine and juniper needles, the significance of her work struck home. A man, one of their guests, would read the message, retrieve the dispatches from their hiding place, and carry them to either the next agent or Gambier himself.

What did the message say?

She understood she was better off not knowing, yet she couldn't stop herself from wondering, studying, experimenting with possibilities. She'd gathered clues from Devenish's insistence that the mistletoe remain white, and her father's half word, "Ana—"

Anabasis? Analecta? anagogy?

Anagram!

The message complete, Morrigan directed a footman to hang the wreath above the archway between the dining room and adjoining drawing room. Then she retreated to her room, fetched pencil and paper, and began creating anagrams out of mistletoe, white, holly, red, and the other color and plant names in the wreath. In an hour, she knew why Devenish insisted the mistletoe remain fresh and white.

She knew the hiding place. It was close—too close for her peace of mind. But a courier attending the ball would need easy access.

Calling herself all kinds of a fool for taking such a risk, she shredded the notes into bits. As an added precaution, she burned the pieces in her bedchamber fireplace. Then, as though this was an ordinary ball, she bathed and dressed in the lapis silk that brought out the blue of her eyes and shine of her auburn hair.

She was ready in time to assure Isolde she looked like an angel in her white gown, which was the truth, and her mother that she didn't look a day over five-and-thirty in her wine satin, which was not quite the truth. Then she descended to the lower floor to make a last-minute inspection of the preparations.

The ballroom was bright and festive with chandeliers blazing and evergreen boughs scenting the air. The supper rooms, composed of dining room and connecting drawing room, shimmered with crystal, silver, and pristine linen.

Satisfied that everything in the public rooms was prepared, she turned toward the kitchen passage—and gasped.

The mistletoe had turned gold.

No, it hadn't turned gold. Mistletoe only turned gold when dried. The berries she had harvested had been white too short a time ago to have dried so completely.

Someone had changed the wreath, changed the message.

She clutched a chair back for support and inhaled several long, deep breaths, forcing herself to think.

Why would someone change the message? Possibly, the courier had made the switch to mislead the traitor. Horribly, the traitor may have captured Devenish again and forced him to reveal the hiding place or code.

Why the traitor would change the message, she didn't know. She didn't know where Devenish was. She didn't know the identity of the Crown's representative.

She knew nothing. She could do nothing. Nothing!

Panic threatened to strangle her. Ruthlessly, she tamped it down. She might do more harm than good if she dashed about like a hair-brained rabbit.

Think, think, think, she commanded herself.

She thought. She stared at the wreath. She realized what she should have done in the first place.

"Parks?" she called for the footman who had hung the message, knowing his duties kept him near the front door. "Parks, where are you?"

"Here, milady." He entered the drawing room and bowed.

"Has anyone been in here since you hung the wreath?"

"Lord Paxcroft and two other gentlemen passed through on their way to the billiards room—"

Morrigan swept up her train and ran down the passageway leading to the billiards room. Tobacco smoke burned her nostrils as she flung open the door and faced the chamber's three occupants.

"Good god, Morrie, what is it?" her brother demanded around his cheroot.

More considerate, Tom Varden, their nearest neighbor, extinguished his cheroot before asking, "What happened, m'dear?"

She tried not to wrinkle her nose at the familiarity of Mr. Varden's address, and eyed the third gentleman, a stranger. Tall and dark with his hair worn in an old-fashioned queue, he was an imposing figure in his blue and white uniform.

His naval uniform.

Uneasy, she said, "An introduction first, if you please?"

"Forgive me." Mr. Varden didn't look repentant. "He's my house guest. Tremain."

The stranger bowed. "Rafe Tremain, my lady," he said in a deep voice with the merest hint of a West Country accent, "Captain of the Red Fleet."

And Lord Gambier was Admiral of the Red Fleet. Did that make Tremain friend or foe?

She inclined her head to acknowledge the introduction. "Pleased to meet you, Captain Tremain. Now, if you will permit, I wish to know if any of you have seen the mistletoe wreath."

Varden and Tremain were too polite to comment on the oddity of her request.

Paxcroft was not. "Did you come charging in here like a runaway nag to ask for a compliment?"

"Pretty design, my dear," Varden said. "All that green, red, and gold."

"Thought the mistletoe was white, m'self," Paxcroft said.

"Gold," Tremain declared. "Definitely gold, like the flecks in your eyes, my lady."

The compliment was too smooth and delivered in too practiced a tone for Morrigan, a lady with six London Seasons behind her. Nonetheless, her cheeks warmed with pleasure.

Paxcroft shrugged. "Thought it was white when I came through the first time. Didn't look the second."

"Were Mr. Varden and the captain with you the second time?" Morrigan asked.

"Course they were. Why—"

"How long in-between times?" Morrigan interrupted.

Paxcroft gaped at her. "Morrie, your wits have gone begging. What difference does it make?"

"How long?" Morrigan persisted.

Paxcroft shrugged. "Quarter hour, no more."

Long enough to substitute dried mistletoe for fresh.

Morrigan bestowed her best smile on all three gentlemen. "Thank you. I will speak to the servants about it. The three of you, please don't remain in here all evening. We need gentlemen to partner the ladies."

"Only if you promise me a waltz," Mr. Varden said.

Morrigan suppressed a sigh. She feared he would ask her first. If she accepted, everyone would presume she favored his suit for her hand. He'd made no secret of his intentions, nor had she made a secret of her indifference. He was striking in looks with his blue eyes and chestnut hair, but she knew his interest lay more in her father being an earl than in her looks, charm, or intelligence, whatever he claimed.

Her smile faltered around the edges. "We are having only one waltz, so I will promise it to no one. Now, if you will excuse me..." She turned toward the door.

Tremain reached it before she did without seeming to hurry, though he had twice the distance to cover. "May I escort you back to the drawing room, my lady?"

With him holding out his arm for her, she could scarcely say no without being rude. Besides, he had a rather fine arm.

Did she like touching the arm of a traitor to England? Papa had said naval men would wish a war to continue.

She stole an oblique glance at Tremain as they traversed the corridor. His stock was silk, his shirt fine cambric, and his gold buttons, braid, and shoe buckles shone without a speck of tarnish. But just because a man didn't look poor didn't mean he was rich or was not greedy.

She mustn't discount Mr. Varden either. He gave the appearance of being wealthy, but his estate was far from large enough to support his lavish lifestyle. He might make money from the war and keep it quiet.

Then, to be fair, as much as it disturbed her to do so, she must consider Paxcroft. He had been in London running up some staggering gaming debts. He could have been bribed.

With a sickening jolt, she realized she was presuming that the traitor had changed the mistletoe.

A pain stabbed through her temple, and she drew a sharp breath through her clenched teeth.

"What's wrong, my lady?" Tremain's voice held concern. So did his eyes. They were the golden-brown of fine sherry and as warm as South Devon sunshine.

"I'm all right, Captain. I still have so much to do, is all. Make certain Cook hasn't frightened the maids into hysterics, see that the butler hasn't drunk the champagne."

Work out the reason for the gold mistletoe.

"I truly must rush off," she added.

"A pity that." Tremain looked up and smiled with a beatific sweetness that had an unholy effect on her senses as she realized they stood directly beneath the mistletoe.

The mistletoe with its false message.

No mistaking the message in Tremain's eyes, when he looked at her again. Less than a quarter hour's acquaintance or not, he intended to carry out tradition and kiss her under the mistletoe.

Morrigan backed away from him. "If you'll excuse me." She didn't wait for him to give her leave; she fled with as much haste as dignity allowed. She needed a quiet corner where she could think what to do.

Halfway across the entrance hall, she caught movement on the stairs and her mother's voice rang out, "There you are, Morrigan. I have looked for you everywhere."

"I'm sorry." Morrigan bade farewell to her quiet moment to think, and climbed the stairs. "I was attending to a minor crisis."

If only the crisis was minor.

"Is something wrong with Isolde's gown again?"

"She has taken down her hair." Lady Fairdown wrung her hands. "I vow I do not know what I shall do with that child. You'd think this is her court presentation and not a simple country ball. Will you help? You always manage to convince her to do what's right."

"Of course, Mama." Morrigan crossed the gallery and made her way to Isolde's room, where she found her younger sister yanking a brush through her hair with so much vigor that the golden strands snapped and crackled as loudly as the fire.

"That maid of mine can do nothing right," Isolde greeted Morrigan. "Just look at the disaster she created."

"Dear me." Morrigan met the beleaguered maid's eyes and smiled. "If that squirrel's nest is what she created, then we must dismiss her at once."

"Then who will do my hair?" Isolde wailed.

"Not I," Morrigan said. "I haven't the time. You'll have to attend the ball with your hair as it is."

"But I cannot!" Tears made Isolde's big, sky-blue eyes even bigger and bluer.

Immune to Isolde's tantrums and sulks, Morrigan shrugged. "You may go sit with Papa or remain in your chamber."

"But I want to go." Isolde flung the brush onto the dressing table. "Oh, very well, Betsy may try again."

"She has a half hour," Morrigan announced, then left the room, knowing Isolde would not be downstairs until the first dance was well underway.

That meant she would have to lead off with Paxcroft in Isolde's place. She must also join Mama and Paxcroft in greeting the guests. Isolde should be there too. So should Papa. Since Isolde turned sixteen, the entire family stood in the entry to receive their guests to the ball.

She wouldn't have a moment to herself for at least an hour. Too much could happen in that hour if the right courier went to the wrong hiding place...

Morrigan halted in the center of the entry hall. The drawing room door stood open and the golden bough of mistletoe shone like a beacon against its nest of green leaves.

A beacon to disaster.

Of course the traitor had learned the code. Of course he was the one who changed the message. He had the greatest reason to do so—lure the Crown courier into a trap and death. That was the most likely way to ensure the dispatches never reached Gambier.

Oh, why hadn't she realized that at once?

"Milady?" Parks approached her from his station by the door. "Is something wrong with the way I hung the wreath?"

"No, not at all." Morrigan pressed a hand to her throat so the footman couldn't see her pulse throbbing there. "But tell me, are you certain no one save Paxcroft, Mr. Varden, and Captain Tremain has been in that room?"

"Several servants have, milady."

"Which ones?"

Parks looked puzzled. "I can't be certain, milady. The door was shut much of the time."

It was a senseless question. The traitor could have paid a servant to change the mistletoe, claiming he wanted it done as a jest.

"Is there ought else you wish to know, milady?" Parks asked.

"Where are Lord Paxcroft and the other gentlemen?"

"Still in the billiards room, milady. Shall I notify him you wish to see him?"

"Thank you, no. I'll go." Knowing she left a gawking footman behind her, she walked into the drawing room and closed the door behind her.

She had less than ten minutes before the first guests were due to arrive. That was less than ten minutes to study the new message and work out the code.

Then what would she do with it?

She would work that out while greeting guests. She needed these last moments of quiet to decipher the code.

Down the far passage, the billiards room door opened. Male voices rose and fell in friendly argument accompanied by varying sets of footfalls. The swift and energetic steps belonged to Paxcroft, and the swift and arrhythmic ones undoubtedly came from Mr. Varden. Of a certainty, the long, lazy stride belonged to Captain Rafe Tremain.

He reached the drawing room first. "My lady, what a pleasure to see you again so soon, and under the mistletoe, too."

"Watch your step, Tremain," Paxcroft said with a note of censure. "She's m'sister, y'know."

Captain Tremain smiled. "I won't hold that against her."

But what can I hold against you? Morrigan wondered.

The answer had nothing to do with traitors and everything to do with the way he looked at her—at her mouth.

He was a cad. She was a fool to react to his flirtation with pleasure.

"Lady Morrigan?" Mr. Varden hastened forward. "Are you certain you won't change your mind about the waltz?"

"No, I'm not certain. I mean—" She caught Tremain's eyes intent upon her, and offered Mr. Varden her hand. "Yes, I have changed my mind. I'd be honored to waltz with you."

Mr. Varden seized her hand. "Thank you. This will be a happy Christmas." Beaming as though she'd just offered him gold, frankincense, and myrrh, he fairly sprinted out of the room.

"Are we to expect a happy announcement by Christmas, my lady?" Captain Tremain asked. It was a polite and not unreasonable question, but his eyes mocked her.

Her face growing warm, she gave him what she hoped was a cool smile. "I hope to announce that my father is truly on the mend by Yuletide, Captain, nothing more."

"And thank God for that," Paxcroft declared. "Nice enough fellow for a neighbor, but don't care to have such a mushroom in the family. And speaking of family, I hear m'mother in the hall. Better go play the dutiful son with Father indisposed." He trotted to the door.

"Don't close—" Morrigan's admonition came too late. The door latched behind her brother, and she stood alone with Tremain between her and the door.

He sauntered toward her.

She took a step back. Too late, she perceived her error. The maneuver had taken her right under the mistletoe.

Tremain stood too close for politeness, too close for comfort. "Forgive my boldness, my lady, but I've faced this same temptation twice tonight, and cannot resist this second time." He curved one hand beneath her chin, tilted her head back, and kissed her full on the mouth. Too soon, he straightened and gazed into her eyes. "Much better than a waltz in my books. But I hope you'll save me at least a set of country dances."

"I won't be dancing." Her voice was steady enough, but her legs felt as useless as wilted carrots.

Tremain's smile told her he knew exactly how his kiss had effected her. "I'll retreat to the billiards room so no one knows you were alone in here with me. Until our dance."

"There won't be—"

The door swung open and Paxcroft stuck his head around the edge. "C'mon, Morrie. We have guests to greet."

And she had more important things to do than feel moon-struck over a West Country sailor, a possible traitor.

❄ ❄ ❄

While she welcomed friends and neighbors to the Winter Solstice Eve Ball, Morrigan made a silent list of possible courses of action. Then she tested each idea for soundness and likelihood of success.

"Lord Riverdon, what a…unique waistcoat!"

She could tell Papa and ask to whom he went for help.

"Good evening, Lady Elizabeth. I'm so pleased to see you were well enough to attend this year."

But Papa would insist on going himself and might suffer a relapse.

"Sir Roger and Lady Bond, how kind of you to come all this way to our little celebration."

Devenish could have gotten away a second time and reached Portsmouth. Help might already be on its way. But if he wasn't able to travel the ten miles, Papa was the only agent she knew.

"Dear me, is it raining, Miss Hammersby? The maids will see your cloak properly dried."

That most definitely left Papa out of it. A wetting could too easily kill him in his precarious health. Devenish had sounded ill, too, and if he'd been injured, he might also die.

Sadly, he might already be dead.

"Isolde? She wishes to make *la grande entrée*, you understand."

By the time the first torrent of guests had passed to the ballroom and she, Mama, and Paxcroft followed, Morrigan knew only one course of action lay open to her. She must go to the false site herself and wait for the courier so she could warn him.

By the time she persuaded Paxcroft to lead Mama in the first dance instead of her, Morrigan had accepted the danger she faced. If it was a trap, it might close on her. She didn't know if they would dare kill her, a daughter of one of the most prominent landowners in Hampshire, but it was a possibility.

What is my one life compared to thousands? she pointed out to herself. *The right messenger—with the right message—must reach Gambier in time.*

How did she get away long enough to work out the new message? How would she get away at all?

A good thing she'd decided not to dance. She wouldn't disappoint any partners when she disappeared from the festivities, except for Tom Varden.

Mr. Varden had the same opportunity to change the berries as had Captain Tremain. He might not have as much reason for wanting the war to continue as would a naval captain, but that didn't disqualify him. If he was the culprit and he disappeared before the waltz, would he suspect what she was about?

A blow on her forearm jarred Morrigan's attention back to the ballroom. "Oh, Your Grace, I am sorry. I must have been wool-gathering."

"Or too interested in that handsome naval officer to listen to an old lady," responded the Dowager Duchess of Ladley as she lowered the fan she'd used on Morrigan's arm.

Morrigan closed her eyes, then opened them again and realized she had indeed been staring at Captain Tremain, who stood directly across the room from her. He, however, seemed interested in Isolde. She had arrived in time for Paxcroft to lead her into the second dance.

They made a striking pair with their mother's golden hair and classical features. Isolde was beautiful, whereas Morrigan knew she was handsome at best.

She stifled a pang that couldn't possibly be envy for the way her sister had attracted Tremain's attention, and addressed the duchess. "I was thinking of all I must do."

The duchess nodded her purple turbaned head. "Yes, perhaps to get him to dance with you. But it won't work, my dear. He's not in your league. Lower gentry at best."

"I don't know what you mean, Your Grace."

The duchess cackled. "Run along, my dear, and enjoy yourself. I'd rather no one thought you were entertaining me and stay away, since you're anything but entertaining this evening."

"I beg your pardon." Morrigan dropped into a curtsy. "I never did make certain everything was all right in the kitchen." With that plausible excuse for her absence, at least for a while, she exited the ballroom and crossed the hall.

She had taken an hour to work out the code from the original design. Surely this second one wouldn't take so long. A pencil and paper would make the work go faster, but if someone came across her, they would think it might strange for her to be scribbling away while a ball was in progress.

Her gaze fixed on the wreath, she ran through possible locations with names that might contain the letters in gold. Nothing came to mind. She scrambled for new possibilities like yellow or butter. But nothing made itself clear to her.

Oh, why had the villain bothered to change the location at all?

At least she guessed the answer to that question—it was too close. Strangers, even guests or their servants, would be noticed skulking around what was strictly the cook's domain.

So where was a prime location for an ambush?

Dairy? That fit if she manipulated the words as she had with the first one, but it was also too close. Lodge? Possible, but the gatekeeper—

"Are you well, my lady?"

Morrigan jumped, then spun to face the speaker. She hadn't heard the door open behind her, but it had. It had closed, too, and Captain Tremain leaned against it.

"Did you follow me?" Alarm made her tone sharp.

"Of course I did." Tremain appeared as insouciant as ever. She could easily imagine him having a picnic during a battle.

"You looked pale," he continued. "Then you made a hasty retreat. Since your siblings and your lady mother were occupied, I decided to make certain you were not about to faint."

"I've never fainted in my life."

So he'd been watching her too?

He smiled. "Good. I'd have been disappointed to find you in a swoon. Instead, I find you staring at that wreath as though your life depends upon it."

"Not my life." She stopped herself before adding, *but mayhap someone else's. Perhaps many someone else's.*

Tremain straightened from his lounging position and held out a hand. "Shall I fight our way to the refreshment table and a glass of punch?"

"Punch? No, thank you. It's too sweet. Perhaps I shouldn't admit this..." She took his hand, which she shouldn't do either. "But I prefer dry sherry."

Sherry like his eyes. Dry like—

Golden mistletoe.

Not gold or any variation of yellow. Dry—no, dried mistletoe. No matter if the arrangement contained no W now. It had to be Dry Down, a mile away on the other side of the park.

It was a misnamed down, for a stream ran through it, a stream large enough to accommodate a rowing boat all the way to the Channel.

Now that she knew where to go, her sense of urgency increased. Somehow, she must find a way to escape.

Captain Tremain seemed determined to keep her close. He tucked her hand into the crook of his elbow and led her back to the ballroom. He insisted she dance with him in a manner that made refusing him impossible without creating a scene.

He danced with easy grace. The figure of the set prevented conversation but lent ample opportunity for flirtation, opportunity he used to such advantage that she blushed like a schoolgirl.

"You're a charming partner, Lady Morrigan," Tremain said as he led her to her mother, who sat with a group of matrons. "A shame you gave away your waltz."

"Yes, it is. I shouldn't be waltzing."

"The supper dance then?" he suggested.

"Thank you, no, I must oversee the laying out of the buffet." She dipped into a curtsy to signal the end of their discourse. "Do enjoy the rest of your evening."

And rot in Perdition if you're a traitor.

If he were a traitor, it would break her heart.

Oh, but she was a foolish old maid to think so about a handsome man. Regardless of the state of his patriotism, he had no real interest in her. Already he was asking lovely Miss Penelope Drummond to dance.

So she'd gotten rid of him. Now she must think of a way to cancel the waltz without either wounding Mr. Varden or rousing his suspicions. A kitchen crisis was always good, but he could send a footman to bring her back.

If only the waltz wasn't so far into the evening.

It didn't have to be. A word to the orchestra leader and an announcement to the guests would move the dance forward.

A quadrille later, Mr. Varden led her onto the floor. He wasn't as graceful as Captain Tremain, but he was a fine dancer just the same. He was polite, too, not attempting to squeeze her waist or draw her closer than the regulation twelve inches. Nor did he flatter or flirt. His conversation was as dull as ditch water. If her mind hadn't been racing ahead, she would have needed to stifle a yawn or two.

Finally, the dance ended. Morrigan was free to go.

She was free, but she couldn't move. The terror she'd held at bay since realizing what she must do, had turned the ballroom floor into a quagmire that held her fast.

Go, now, she commanded herself, *before there's a real crisis to hold you here*. Before it's too late.

Struggling for self-possession, she glanced around the ballroom. Paxcroft leaned against the far wall amid a group of other young men, looking bored. Mr. Varden danced with Isolde and appeared far more animated than he had with Morrigan. Captain Tremain lounged against a pillar talking to the dowager duchess and looking straight at Morrigan.

That sleepy-eyed gaze melted the mire from her slippers. With a murmured excuse to her mother, Morrigan sped from the ballroom. As she hastened to her bedchamber to collect a cloak, she realized she might never see her parents or siblings again.

Don't think of that. Don't think of danger. Hurry. Hurry. Hurry.

She hurried. Holding her skirts as high as her knees, she fled down a side staircase and slipped into the night.

Rain lashed against her face with the stinging bite of a storm straight off the Channel. She drew her hood over her hair and wondered how she would explain her ruined ball gown, if she had the opportunity to explain.

Don't think about that, either.

If only she knew how to use a pistol. To her knowledge, however, the only guns in the house were ancient fowling pieces unused since her grandfather's day. All she had for a weapon was her bodkin tucked into her bodice. The bodkin would do no more than make a man flinch.

Her teeth began to chatter despite her fur-lined cloak. She couldn't have changed her gown without assistance, but she should have put on sturdier shoes. Pebbles from the path cut right through her dancing slippers. Less rain reached her beneath the trees of the park, but the darkness was absolute and she couldn't move as swiftly as she wished to do.

Only a mile to go if she had guessed right.

The missing W plagued her. She occupied her thoughts with more anagrams. Nowhere outside the house even came close to fitting the letters unless she went further afield.

Surely it had to be close.

She should have confided in her father. Too many other lives were at stake for her to concern herself with one man's health, however important he was. He knew the game. She did not.

"Oh, Papa, what have I done?" She leaned against a tree, sobbing for breath, demanding her mind to stop whirling and think.

She pictured the wreath design, a sweep of glossy leaves, a cluster of holly berries, a spray of pine needles...

Her body went limp with relief.

The W lay in the design itself!

Comforted with the knowledge that she had taken the right action, she gathered her cloak more tightly around her, gripped her bodkin in her right hand, and headed across the open down.

She faced no risk of encountering a shepherd and his dog. On such a stormy night, they'd be holed up in the shepherd's cottage. But she couldn't run. She must proceed with caution, approach the alder grove with any acting skills she possessed in full play.

She wished the rain would stop and allow some starlight to guide her. She knew the downs nearly as well as she knew the house, but in the dark and rain, she could still lose her way.

No, she would not. The path led straight across the down to the creek. She would know the instant she stepped into grass.

Her satin slippers caught in the mud. Within moments, her feet were so cold she couldn't feel them. Her silk gloves were no protection for her hands. She no longer knew if she still clutched her bodkin or if she had dropped it along the way. Once, she stumbled on an outcropping of chalk and fell head-long onto the path, knocking a cry from her throat. She rose again and continued. One step. Two...

Was that wind rustling the alder branches? Or was it a person?

She couldn't tell. At least the sound told her she hadn't veered off the path. She was close now, close enough to carry out her feeble plan, the pretense that she intended to meet a lover in the trees.

"Oh, my darling, is that you? What a time I've had—"

A hand clamped across her mouth. An arm encircled her waist, holding her against a solid, male body.

She bit at the hand, but the only result was a mouthful of soft leather. More angry than frightened, she lashed back with her right hand.

She still clutched her bodkin. The thick needle struck home through fabric and flesh. Her captor swore in an undertone that was nonetheless loud enough for her to recognize the voice.

Tremain!

She still didn't know if he was friend or foe. Too much, she wanted him to be friend.

He bent his head so his lips brushed her ear as he murmured, "Take that toothpick out of my side, then don't move and don't make a sound."

Those orders sounded more like they came from a foe.

Unreasonably hurt, she yanked the bodkin free and told herself she was glad to hear his sharp intake of breath.

"Now," Tremain continued, "I'm going to carry you back to the house, where you'll—"

"What're you doing out here with m'sister?" Paxcroft's voice rang across the down like a Christmas church bell.

Tremain muttered something uncomplimentary about the viscount, then swung around with Morrigan still tight against him. "Paxcroft, take your sister and run."

"Don't move." The command resounded from the trees.

"Down!" Tremain shouted.

He dropped to the ground, rolling Morrigan beneath him.

An explosion shattered the night, and Tremain leaped up. Branches crackled. Another shot rang out.

Morrigan scrambled to her feet, trying to see through rain and darkness, trying to work out what was going on. Shadows blacker than the night moved across her vision. Were they fighting men or wind-whipped trees?

She interpreted the sounds more easily than the sights, the thuds of fists on flesh, grunts and curses from pain. Finally, horribly, a banshee wail pierced the air with a power that should have driven back the rain. Then it died in a gasping cough.

"Tremain? Paxcroft?" Morrigan's voice quavered.

"We're here." Tremain sounded a trifle winded.

"Someone's hurt?" Her voice still shook.

"It's Varden." Tremain sounded steady now. "Are you all right, my lady?"

"Perfectly," Morrigan answered.

Then she fainted.

❄ ❄ ❄

"What I don't understand," Morrigan said hours later as she, Paxcroft, and Rafe Tremain sat before the library fire drinking tea with a liberal lacing of brandy, "is why Mr. Varden wanted to lure you into a trap if he already had the dispatches."

Tremain stretched his long legs toward the hearth. He looked none the worse for having had a bodkin stuck in his side, having had to stab a man, and having been closeted with a general and an admiral for two hours. Indeed, he looked rather splendid with his ribband gone and his hair curling around his face.

Morrigan felt hag-ridden with her own hair lying perfectly straight against the shoulders of her warmest and oldest gown.

Yet Tremain smiled at her as if she pleased him, and answered her question as calmly as someone else would discuss the weather. "He never did have them. He intended to replace them with false ones. But the ball made doing so impossible by the time he learned the hiding place. Changing the mistletoe was easy, though."

"So he only changed the message to mislead you?" Morrigan wrinkled her nose. "I feel like a fool thinking he had a trap planned. Did he follow me to the stream then?"

Tremain's mouth twisted into a wry smile. "Don't feel foolish, my...lady. Varden intended to kill me."

Morrigan shook her head, unable to imagine Tremain dead.

"You or just any courier?" Paxcroft asked.

"Me," Tremain replied. "He had an informant in the Admiralty. A double agent, actually." He shot Morrigan a glance that lacked his usual sangfroid. "I've worked for the Admiralty since my ship suffered irreparable damage last January. We knew we had information leaks but couldn't trace the source or the recipient. Eventually, my investigation led to our munitions suppliers, one of whom was Tom Varden."

"So that's where he got his money," Morrigan exclaimed. "I always wondered."

"From there and less pleasant sources." Tremain made a face that fell short of being comical. "I have spent some unpleasant months making myself agreeable to men like Varden. When I traced the purchaser of military secrets to him, I played a double game so I could catch his sources." He turned his face toward the fire. "I wasn't quite successful. That, by the by, is one reason why Devenish and I didn't know one another's names. With those dispatches coming through, we had to take precautions. I finagled an invitation to Varden's house to watch him as closely as possible."

"Mushroom," Paxcroft growled. "He'd do anything to gain advancement."

"Yes," Tremain affirmed, "even entertain me, when he must have known the risk of having me in his house. But my rank gives me connections in high places."

"It'll get him in a high place, all right," Paxcroft pronounced. "A gibbet."

Morrigan shuddered.

Tremain closed his hand over hers. "I know it's not a pleasant end. But Varden was selling information to American privateers and the French before that war ended. Not to mention the fact that he nearly killed Devenish while...extracting information."

"Torture?" Morrigan felt ill. "The poor man."

"Weakling," Paxcroft pronounced. "Shouldn't have given away secrets even under torture."

"He did it," Tremain said with an edge of steel in his voice, "to save your sister."

Paxcroft flushed.

Tears filled Morrigan's eyes. "Varden threatened me? Not to sound vain, but I thought he wished to wed me."

"He did." Tremain's gaze held such tenderness Morrigan's tears doubled and spilled over. "But Devenish didn't know that. So when Varden said he'd hurt you if Devenish didn't talk, Devenish talked. He had no way of knowing Varden would change the message to trap me. He thought Varden would destroy the dispatches and go about his business."

Morrigan wiped her tears away with her sleeve. "No wonder Devenish said I'd be in no danger. He always intended to protect me, and nearly died doing so."

"You could have died protecting me," Tremain pointed out. "And Devenish is quite all right, but if you don't stop weeping over him, I may be sorry he is."

That made Morrigan smile.

Paxcroft looked suspicious. "Where is the fellow? Should go thank him."

"He's in Portsmouth, receiving medical care," Tremain answered. "He managed to reach the Admiralty offices there a few hours ago and warn them. That's why they arrived so soon after we caught Varden with the false papers." He winked at Morrigan. "He told Admiral Dean you're the finest lady he's ever met."

Paxcroft groaned. "Don't puff her up. I want to know more about Varden."

"Don't concern yourself with me being puffed up," Morrigan said. "Swooning will keep me humble for weeks."

"Hmm." Tremain grinned, then turned his attention back to Varden. "His flow of money would have dried up had the war ended. He enjoys luxury, and his estate is small. He needed more money to pay his creditors. The solution was to keep the war going and the money flowing in."

"So he turned traitor." Morrigan felt queasy at the memory of Varden's hands on her in the waltz.

"If he just wanted to do you in," Paxcroft asked, "why wouldn't he let Morrie and me go?"

"I knew too much by then." Though her brother watched her with narrowed eyes, Morrigan turned her hand over so her palm pressed against Tremain's. "To think I suspected you."

"I suspected him too," Paxcroft said, drawing his brows together. "Kept following m'sister around. When you followed her out of the ballroom the second time, I followed you."

"I followed your sister because I kept finding her under the mistletoe."

The only reason why he followed her? Morrigan wanted to, but dared not, ask.

Tremain laced his fingers with Morrigan's, answering her question the way she wanted. "She didn't seem the sort to encourage advances."

"Not Morrigan," Paxcroft agreed. "She's usually the sensible female of the family. But you didn't use much sense tonight, Morrie, going off half-cocked like that. As if a mere girl could stop a traitor."

"She helped," Tremain reminded Paxcroft. "She alerted me to the fact that something was wrong, when she kept asking about the berries being changed to dried ones, changing the meaning of the message."

"The first location was right here," Morrigan said. "It was 'this house larder.' It took me a while to work out that Devenish got the A and other H from branches."

"That you worked it out at all is amazing," Tremain said.

She gave him an arch glance. "For a mere girl?"

"There is nothing 'mere' about you, my dear."

Funny how Mr. Varden's use of that familiar address had set her back up, and Tremain's use of it made her body warm.

"Depends on how you look at it," Paxcroft interjected. "Seems like she's got more hair than wit, haring off to catch a traitor or warn a government agent, however you look at it."

"But I couldn't tell Papa," Morrigan defended herself, having already endured lectures from both parents. "He'd have gone out in the rain and probably suffered a relapse."

Paxcroft looked hurt. "You could have told me."

"No, I—" Morrigan bit her lip.

Paxcroft stared at her. "Good God, did you suspect me?"

"Not very much, but—"

"You're mad!" Paxcroft cried.

Tremain shook his head. "I think she's one of the most logical, courageous females there is, not to mention lovely and warm-hearted."

"Logical? Warm-hearted?" Paxcroft was livid. "I tell you, she needs a keeper."

"She doesn't need a keeper. However, I would like to keep her." Tremain rose and curved his hand under her chin and tilted her face up. "What do you say, Morrigan, my lady, to a Yuletide courtship and a Valentine wedding?"

Morrigan didn't say anything. She rose also and kissed him without being under the mistletoe.

That Yuletide proved the happiest Morrigan had known in her life. Adding to the joy of falling in love, news arrived that Lord Gambier, Admiral of the Red, Henry Goulburn, Member of Parliament and Under Secretary of State, and William Adams, Doctor of Civil Law, along with representatives of the American government, signed the Treaty of Ghent, ending the American conflict on Christmas Eve 1814.

Laurie Alice Eakes barely remembers a time she didn't write—something. During summer vacation from teaching high school English, she wrote her first novel. She enjoyed the experience so much she wrote another one the next summer. After winning or placing in several writing contests, she decided to take writing seriously. Her first sale was a poem published in an international anthology. In 1997, she saw the release of her first book, a nonfiction work entitled *Virginia Wine, A Tasteful Guide.* In May, 1999, her first novel, *The Widow's Secret*, a romantic suspense set in Georgian England, was released by Awe-Struck E-books. *Married By Mistake,* a Regency Romantic suspense, will be released by Starlight Writer Publications in February 2001. Ms. Eakes has two more books scheduled for publication with SWP in 2001 under the Star Service imprint. *Under the Mistletoe* is her first Regency mystery/romance. Besides creative writing, Laurie Alice is a freelance technical writer, takes voice lessons, and hikes, whenever she gets the chance. She lives in the Chicago suburbs, where she is pursuing her teaching certification and discovering that the thrill of romance does not dwell only in the pages of a novel.

Some people need a little extra help in finding their true love. Instead of placing a classified ad, as one might do today, Lord Westerbury decides to take part in a ritual at Stonehenge! Will he be able to conjure up a bride? This enjoyable story will warm your heart.

The Conjured Bride

Kim Damron

Amesbury, Wiltshire
December 21, 1806

"Bella!" The door was thrust open and a young girl burst explosively into the room. "Bella," she called again.

With a sigh, Arabella Wynchcombe dropped the wooden spoon she was holding and, wiping her fingers on her white apron, hurried out of the welcoming warmth of the kitchen and into the salon. "Lydia," she exclaimed in despair as her eyes lit on the damp yellow curls plastered to the red cheeks of her younger sister. "What were you doing out in the snow without a bonnet? Lud, have I taught you nothing?"

Lydia shook her head impatiently. "Bella, listen to me," she said breathlessly, her blue eyes shining like sapphires in the dim sunlight streaming through the windows. "The Druids, they are here. They are marching side by side down to Stonehenge!"

Bella put her hands on her hips and scowled at the younger girl. "For this you take me away from my baking? Of course, the Druids are here. They came for the Summer Solstice as well, you watched them last summer. Now, have you been gathering evergreen boughs for the decorations?"

"Bella!" Lydia stamped one small foot in frustration. "Let me finish! The Earl of Westerbury, he is with them!"

Taking a deep breath, Bella patiently counted to ten. Really, something would have to be done about Lydia's fascination for that man. "Surely that is no surprise, dear," she said gently. "Everyone knows his lordship's uncle was a member of the old order. Since Avery died just two months past it stands to reason his lordship would take his place during the holiday rituals."

"No, no, no!" Lydia shook her head emphatically. "Do you know what Jack told me?"

"Really Lydia, I have told you time and time again not to be exchanging tales with the stable boy."

"The Earl is looking for a wife!" Lydia burst out, unable to contain herself further. "Jack says he has approached the head of the order and that they are to do a conjuring ritual at midnight!"

"Lydia!" Scandalized, Bella crossed the small room and picked up Lydia's bonnet from a chair by the fireplace. "Dearest, you know I want what is best for you, but the Earl is four-and-thirty! You only turned fifteen on your last birthday." Holding up one hand to forestall the argument she saw coming, she crossed to the hall and pulled the front door open, handing Lydia her bonnet and a basket. "Now I want you to put this foolishness out of your head and go trim some holly for me." Seeing Lydia's stubborn pout forming, she pasted a smile to her face and hastened to add; "I am making your favorite crescent cookies for the solstice tonight. If you also gather me some mistletoe, I will let you help decorate them." Placing one hand between her narrow shoulders, Bella gently pushed the younger girl out into the snow.

"But, Bella," she tried one more time.

"The greens, Lydia." With that final admonishment Bella shut the door.

"Lud would you listen to her," Lydia muttered, dropping the basket and bonnet into the snow and sitting on the door stoop. A sleek black cat darted playfully through the snow. "Did you hear that, Maggie?" Lydia called indignantly, holding out one hand. "Most assuredly the Earl is too old for me, but he is the perfect age for Bella. At four-and-twenty, she is very near to being firmly on the shelf, and we do have to save her from becoming an old spinster, don't we?"

Maggie crawled into her lap, purring loudly. Lydia stroked her warm, soft fur. "I can see you agree with me. We'll show Bella. You and I will kick up a lark or two. If the Earl wishes to conjure a bride, I will make sure he finds one." An impish smile lit her features.

Gathering the large cat into her arms, she struggled to her feet, reaching for the basket with one hand. "I suppose for now we shall have to gather Bella's silly evergreens. Then, when the time comes she will not suspect a thing and you and I will do some conjuring of our own!" Satisfied with the plan that half-formed in her mind, Lydia marched happily into the bushes.

❄ ❄ ❄

Robert Ludley, Fifth Earl of Westerbury stamped his feet hard against the ground in a vain attempt to dislodge the coating of snow and mud that appeared to have taken up permanent residence on his once gleaming Hessians. If only he had been paying proper attention to the night Avery made him promise to attend a Solstice with the order. However, the warm fire at White's, combined with a large meal and good brandy, had put him into a mellow mood. By the time Avery had singled him out he had been properly shot in the neck and prepared to grant any request. A frown twisted his features as he recalled what else his expansive mood that night had cost him.

Of course, Avery had been right about one thing. His father's will had specified that he marry and produce an heir before his thirty-seventh birthday, and time was running out. The thought of being leg-shackled to one of those empty-headed ninnies his sister had introduced him to at Almacks was enough to send him into a fit of the blue devils.

Impatiently he swiped at a lock of hair that fell into his eyes. Damn the snow. He did not for a moment believe that the head of the order could conjure him a bride, certainly not the beautiful, proper, compliant wife he imagined for himself, but at least it got him away from Charlotte's damnable matchmaking schemes.

Conjuring a bride at midnight indeed! His lips twisted into a mocking smile as he marched silently beside the Druids. It was much more likely that they would conjure the devil instead. As Charlotte had often admonished him, only a demon would be fit to deal with him.

His smile widened suddenly as he imagined picking and choosing the various traits of his new bride. She would be fair, blond, and beautiful. Guileless, and mercifully lacking a brain-box. Suddenly his mind conjured a face: honey-blond hair fell in ringlets around milky-white skin. Serious gray eyes looked solemnly back at him. Full red lips curved in an inviting smile. So caught up in his daydream was Robert that his step faltered. The white-robed figure next to him gave a sidelong glance. Robert gave him a wide smile. Yes indeed, conjuring a bride of his own making might just be the thing.

❄ ❄ ❄

A smile of delight curving her fine features, Bella stood in the doorway of the salon and surveyed the room with satisfaction, "'Tis beautiful Lydia." Impulsively, she gave her little sister a hug, her serious gray eyes shining with the light of the tapers. "You have truly outdone yourself."

"Lud, Bella, do not get mawkish." Squirming, Lydia wriggled out of the embrace, secretly satisfied with her sister's appreciation.

The large, square salon had been transformed into a winter fairyland, complete with Yule log set in the fireplace. A small tree had been dragged inside and decorated with strands of cranberries and cinnamon sticks tied up with red satin ribbons and a dozen candles. Mistletoe entwined with holly and ivy decorated the carved mantlepiece and hung in bunches from the ceiling. A light dusting of snow floated past the frosty paned windows.

Lydia scampered to one of the lace-covered windows. "Look Bella, it is beginning to get dark already."

"'Tis the Solstice, dearest," she replied distractedly, wandering around the room plumping pillows and adjusting sprigs of holly. "The longest night of the year."

"I wonder if the Druids are cold," Lydia mused, looking out the frosty window.

"The Druids spend much time out of doors," she replied absently. "With their heavy robes, I doubt they feel the cold any longer."

Lydia gave her a sideways glance from her perch on the edge of a velvet-covered chair, "True, Bella. But the Earl is surely not used to such hardships."

Bella whirled to face her. "Not used to hardships, how can you say such a thing? Why, his Lordship fought beside Lord Admiral Nelson at Aboukir Bay." In the dim candlelight an admiring smile curved her lips. Thick strands of honey-blond hair had escaped their confining bun and softly framed her face.

Lydia gave her sister an impish smile. "I had no idea you felt so strongly about the Earl, Bella."

"I have no feelings for the Earl, as well you know," she replied sharply. "My interest stems solely from the fact that he is our nearest neighbor. Now get up from there and help me in the kitchen. Our guests will be here shortly."

Several hours later Lydia crept softly into the hallway. Leaning flat against the wall, she peeked into the well-lit salon. Bella, beautiful in her flowing white velvet trimmed in red, sprigs of fir and holly entwined through her hair, sat with her back to the fireplace. She held a cup of mulled cider in a pewter chalice, and, at her side in a dish, lay a slice of gingerbread and three of the crescent cookies she had made earlier. A smile lit her face as she looked around the beautifully decorated room.

Forming a half-circle around her were their older sisters Sarah and Mary, and Elizabeth, Bella's best friend since childhood. Sarah reached into a large bag and pulled out a shining mirror.

A smile curved Lydia's face. There was no need for scrying to divine the identity of Bella's future husband. Lydia already knew. Well satisfied, she crept back down the hall into the kitchen, and stole out the back door.

Pulling the warm wool of Bella's pelisse close around her, Lydia shut the door softly. Something wet and furry twined around her ankles.

"Lud, Maggie, are you trying to give me a fit of the vapours?" Kneeling, she scooped the soggy black cat into her arms. "It will not bode well for our plans if Bella finds me having an attack just outside the door!"

Maggie meowed her agreement before curling comfortably in Lydia's arms, and purring loudly.

Clutching the heavy black cat close against her chest, Lydia trudged the two miles to Stonehenge in the falling snow. As she neared the ancient monument, she could hear the chanting of voices.

Ducking swiftly behind a snowdrift, she looked on in rapt amazement. The robed figures held their hands aloft beneath the silver moon. In the magical light she could see the loose ropes that bound them together. In the center of the circle, standing directly in front of the holed stone stood a tall man she assumed to be the leader.

Cuddling Maggie's warm body ever closer, Lydia inched slightly forward. The leader's robe was of the purest white. Even in the dim moonlight she could see the glinting gold of the sickle lashed to his side. A long beard, white as the newly fallen snow, fell across his chest. He stood tall and majestic beneath the ripeness of the full moon.

"We come this night to give honor," his deep voice rang through the countryside. He held a staff aloft and Lydia fancied he was the spirit of Merlin himself returned to conjure Arthur and his knights of old. Eyes alight, she watched, breathlessly.

A movement by the leader's side caught her attention. Could it be? she wondered, leaning forward in rapt interest. Yes, it was. Robert Ludley, Earl of Westerbury had stepped from the ranks of the Druids and knelt before the man. Even kneeling, there was no disguising the breadth of his shoulders, the strength of his forearms, and the hooded robe could not disguise the purest gold of his thick, wavy hair. He and Bella would look well together.

"Name yourself," the deep, grave voice of the leader commanded.

"I am Robert, Earl of Westerbury," a strong, husky voice answered him.

"Do you wish to petition the Gods this Solstice eve?"

"I do."

The man looked kindly on the figure kneeling in front of him. "Then have no fears in asking," he said gently.

Lydia scrambled backward in the snow, clutching Maggie close. "Now it is time for fate to intervene, Maggie." The cat regarded her with solemn, unblinking golden eyes. "You do understand, don't you, Maggie?" Those gold eyes regarded her reproachfully. Had Maggie let her down yet?

"We mustn't make a mull of this. We will never have a better chance for Bella to capture his Lordship's fancy. You must go now. Scratch at the door, hiss at the windows, whatever it takes. Get Bella to let you in. She will realize I have gone out. Make sure she follows me."

"Meow!" Springing from her arms, Maggie yawned disdainfully, stretching in the snow before trotting off into the darkness.

"And hurry," Lydia's soft voice called after her.

❄ ❄ ❄

Alone in the large salon Bella stretched languidly in front of the warm, crackling fire. Closing her eyes lazily, she inhaled deeply of the cinnamon and nutmeg that permeated the winter air. An amused smile tilted her lips as she thought back to the divination Sarah had done earlier.

"Peel this apple, Bella," she had entreated, holding the fruit aloft.

Bella had taken it, feeling rather silly. "Really Sarah, isn't this what maidens are supposed to do on All Hallows?" she had asked as she skillfully peeled the apple.

"I think Sarah is right," Elizabeth had agreed. "'Tis a Yule tradition. Now throw the peel over your shoulder."

Thoughts of a certain tall gentleman invaded her mind, causing warmth to flood her cheeks as she took the apple peel and threw it over her shoulder. "Look!" Sarah exclaimed.

Opening her eyes, Bella turned to see the peel lying on the carpet. It had landed on its side. "What does it look like to you?" she asked tentatively.

"Don't be a ninny," Sarah said teasingly. "It is obviously an 'L'."

"L?" Bella's breath caught in her throat as colour stole into her cheeks. "Well then, I shall marry a man named Lawrence."

"Silly," Sarah teased. "It is the surname the apple peel reveals."

"What is the Earl's surname, Bella?" Mary chimed in with an impish smile.

They had teased her unmercifully for a few moments longer before turning their attention back to the mirror to divine the gender of the child Elizabeth carried.

Curling her fingers around the warm pewter of the cup, Bella took a long sip of the spicy cider, allowing its warmth to steal through her body as her thoughts went perversely to Robert Ludley. She had encountered him, quite by accident, at Amesbury market just two weeks before. She had reached for the red ribbons displayed by Mrs. Barnes at the exact moment he had reached for a length of cord. His strong hand had touched hers briefly, his sherry-coloured eyes widening slightly as they looked into hers for what seemed like an eternity.

He had opened his mouth as if to say something, and then a grating female voice had sounded from the closed carriage close by. He turned, distracted, and, foolishly, Bella seized the opportunity to slip into the crowd.

A faint scratching at the door roused her from her memories. Setting the pewter chalice aside she crossed to the window and peered out into the moonlight. Before her the snow stretched out into infinity.

The scratching came again.

Curious now, she moved to the door and turned the latch. A sheet of icy air and snowflakes blew into the house as she pulled the door open.

"Meow."

She looked down to see Maggie on the stoop. Leaning over, she pulled the wet cat into her arms.

"Are you looking to come inside for the night, Maggie?" she asked softly. "I suppose you will want to sleep with Lydia."

Stroking the damp fur, Bella moved quickly up the stairs. "Lydia," she called as she reached the landing. "Lydia," she said again, moving quickly down the hall. That was odd, she thought quite suddenly. Lydia's door was open. Maggie began writhing in her arms.

"Calm down, Maggie," she whispered as she stooped and placed the cat on the floor before crossing to the open doorway. Apprehension weighted her chest as she glanced into the empty room. Maggie's soft fur brushed against her ankles. Kneeling, Bella regarded the cat seriously. "Why do I get the feeling the two of you are in on this together?"

Wide yellow eyes regarded her solemnly. "I suppose you are to lead me to her." Crossing her arms over her chest, she frowned slightly. "Well, I do not need you. I know well enough where she has gone."

Bella hurried down the stairs, Maggie close on her heels, stopping long enough to note that her good heavy pelisse was missing from the kitchen. "I suppose I should be grateful she has some protection from the weather," she murmured, snatching up a warm cloak and flinging it over her narrow shoulders before pulling the door open and marching resolutely into the snow. "Thought you would kick up a lark, did you?" She eyed Maggie sternly. "Well, Lydia will find herself in a hobble when I get finished with her," she warned as she trudged out into the snow.

❄ ❄ ❄

Kneeling in the snow beneath the full moon, Robert waited, unsure of what to do next. The Druids had formed a close circle around him, solemnly chanting. As the cold, wet snow seeped through the cloth of his breeches, he looked around him with newfound respect at these men who followed their beliefs so passionately.

A hand touched his shoulder. He looked up to see the Master of the Order smiling down on him. "Come, Robert," he said, holding out one hand.

He stood and followed the man through the shadowy stones.

"Look." Robert looked to where he was pointing. Between two of the megaliths he could see out into the snow. "Free your mind. Only then will you find your destiny."

Wise blue eyes looked appraisingly into his; a cold, thin hand grasped his shoulder. "I think if you look inside you, you will find you already know the answer to your questions." He turned and quietly departed, leaving Robert alone in the shadow of the ancient monument.

Taking a deep breath of the frosty air, he focused his attention on the snowy landscape in front of him.

The sound was so faint he almost did not hear it. He took a step forward, glancing around the moonlit country.

There she was, her Nordic beauty ethereal in the glowing silver light. The heavy woolen cloak she pulled close around her did not hide the ample curves of her figure. She turned, straight nose etched against the silver night. Honey-blond hair had been caught up into a twist and fastened with sprigs of holly and ivy.

As Robert watched, fascinated, the wind blew her cloak open, revealing the prim style of her white velvet gown trimmed with ribbons of green and red. When he had lost her in the marketplace he had been frantic. Knowing instantly that she could mean something incredible in his life, he had been determined to find her.

"Lydia!" The whistling wind snatched the word from her mouth. She looked around franticly, lines of worry etched across her forehead.

Robert looked behind him. The Druids were continuing their solemn meditation, seemingly oblivious to the lady's distress. Quickly he ducked through the stones and ran to her side.

"You," she exclaimed, the surprise in her voice echoed in her eyes.

"What are you doing out here?" he asked.

Bella's eyes darted around nervously. "My youngest sister, Lydia—" her voice was breathless. "She has long been fascinated with the Druids. When I went to her bedroom earlier, she was gone."

"You believe she came here?"

She nodded, shielding her eyes from the blowing snow with one hand. "I am certain of it. I must take her back inside quickly. She will be freezing in this weather." She added absently, "Pray forgive me for disturbing your rites this evening."

Robert glanced back at the circle of Druids, sitting expectantly in their circle. "I feel certain they will understand."

"Meow!"

Bella looked up to see Maggie bounding through the snow. Dropping to her knees, she held her hand outstretched. "Have you found her?"

Maggie sniffed at her hand for a moment and bit her thumb lightly before meowing again and bounding back across the snow. Bella jumped to her feet, pulling the cloak tight around her shoulders. "Maggie knows where to find her."

"Come then," he replied briefly, taking her elbow and guiding her through the snow.

Silently the Druids rose and followed. Just ahead of them, Maggie's black figure could be seen bounding through the snow. Unconsciously, Bella quickened her steps. In the distance beneath the full, silver moon, a still figure could be glimpsed lying motionless in the snow. Pulling her skirts close around her Bella started to run, Robert close behind her.

"Lydia!" Sucking in a deep breath of the frosty air, Bella fell to her knees beside the motionless figure. "Lydia," Bella whispered again through the tears that welled in her throat threatening to choke her.

"Allow me." Leaning over, Robert gently gathered Lydia into his arms. "Where is your house?"

Bella pointed. "Wynchcombe cottage."

"Wynchcombe?" Straightening, Robert started across the snowy plain, Bella at his side. "Then you are Major Wynchcombe's daughter?"

Absently brushing at the light dusting of snow that fell across her mantle, Bella nodded.

"I should have known why you looked so familiar." He glanced sideways at her.

A flush crept across her skin at his admiring look. "I must apologize again for disturbing your rites."

Robert glanced over his shoulder. The Druids had formed a half-circle, and were following several steps behind them. "The rites had concluded; they were meditating."

"What were you doing?"

A self-deprecating smile tugged at the corners of his lips. "I was waiting for you."

His eyes sought and found hers, and for a moment they were both very still. "Lydia," Bella said softly.

Robert nodded, cradling the still figure close against his chest. "She will be fine. I promise you."

Content with the feel of his solid presence beside her, Bella led the way through the snow to the cottage. Welcoming yellow light streamed through the salon windows, leaving patterns on the snow. Running ahead, she pulled the heavy oak door wide, savouring the warmth of the fire on the spice-scented air that rushed out at her.

Robert swept through the door, looking around briefly before gently laying his burden on the heavy carpet in front of the fire. Dropping to her knees, Bella tenderly pushed at the heavy yellow curls plastered to Lydia's forehead. Her skin was cold as ice. "I keep telling her to wear a bonnet," she whispered as tears blurred her vision.

"Allow me," a deep voice intruded on her sorrow. Looking up, Bella noted that the leader of the Druids had knelt at her side. Swiping quickly at the tears that glistened on her cheeks, she nodded briefly.

"Were we too late?" Robert asked, slipping a comforting arm around Bella's shoulders. She smiled at him gratefully.

"She is deathly cold," the Druid replied as he retrieved a clear bottle of amber-coloured liquid from the leather pouch hanging from his corded belt. "But she is also young and strong."

Bella looked on in amazement as he pulled the cork from the bottle and carefully poured a small amount between Lydia's slightly parted lips.

A deep sigh sounded through the room and Lydia's eyes flickered slightly. The icy white of her skin warmed to a glowing ivory as a warm flush traveled across her skin. Her chest rose and fell as she began breathing rhythmically. Her eyes opened slightly. "Bella?"

"I am here, love." Swiping quickly at the tears that ran down her face, she caught one of Lydia's small hands between both of hers and squeezed tightly. "I am here."

"Thought I would kick up a lark," she said softly. "I did not think it would be so cold."

Swallowing over the lump in her throat, Bella smiled. "No matter, love. You are here now."

After squeezing Bella's shoulder lightly, Robert stood, hands thrust deep in his trouser pockets as he took a step backward toward the door.

A light touch on his shoulder halted his movement. Wise blue eyes looked unblinkingly at him.

"One can, perhaps, conjure a bride. To conjure love, however is not so easy." The Druid nodded toward Bella, holding Lydia in a close embrace by the firelight. "Do not let fear make you walk away. Good bye my friend." Stopping long enough to touch both Bella and Lydia lightly on the forehead, he stole quietly through the door, the rest of the order close behind him.

Robert looked over to the fire and found Bella's gray eyes regarding him seriously. "Thank you."

"Really, Bella!" Disengaging herself from her sister's clinging arms, Lydia rose slowly to her feet. "Surely you can think of a more appropriate way to thank his lordship." Darting across the room she pulled Maggie into her arms. "In the meantime I will go get some cider." Ignoring Bella's shocked expression, she skipped happily from the room.

Cheeks burning, Bella stood slowly, dropping the soggy cloak from her shoulders. "Lydia is right, I'm sure. You must think me terribly ungrateful."

Robert looked at her silhouetted against the firelight. "Well, there is a way that you could make me forget your ungratefulness."

Bella saw a mischievous smile curving his full lips. "How is that?" she asked warily.

"The Druids agreed to conjure a bride for me by the light of the full moon. Since your unexpected appearance broke up our meeting, there is only one thing you can do..." His voice trailed off as a wicked smile lit his features.

Bella stood motionless as he took a step closer to her. "Do you know what that is, Bella?"

Heart in her throat she shook her head slightly.

"You must be the replacement for my conjured bride."

"Oh," was all she could think to say as he reached out and gently cupped her chin in his hand.

"I have not been able to get you out of my mind since that day at the market."

The intensity of his words warmed her heart. "I, too, have thought of you."

"Then say you will marry me, and we will look after Lydia together."

"I will," she replied softly.

Pressed close against the wall in the hall, Lydia looked on happily as the Earl kissed Bella soundly. Hugging Maggie's warm, furry body close up against her, she smiled merrily. "Well Maggie, now that the Earl has found his bride, what shall you and I conjure next?"

Kim Damron is a native Texan, currently living in Dallas with her new husband and inspiration for all things romantic, Richard. She credits her life-long love of Regency romance to her grandmother, Phyllis Haupt (to whose memory this story is lovingly dedicated) who introduced her to the world of Regency England by giving Kim a stack of novels by Barbara Cartland. This is Kim's first published Regency story and she hopes that many more will follow.

Hannukah is a time of celebration and remembrance. David, however, has forgotten his roots and traditions. Should he play it safe and marry someone he doesn't love or risk losing his heart to a very special young woman?

The Hannukah Invitation

Debra Vega

David took the letter from the silver tray his groom, Hall, held out to him. He tried not to snatch it, for he did not want to reveal his anxiousness. He dismissed Hall, then opened it. His face fell in disappointment. He had expected an invitation from his friend and business associate, Sir Robert Westbrooke; was counting on it, in fact. He held instead an invitation from an old friend. One he had not seen in over three years, since he was newly widowed.

He looked it over. A simple request to join the family for the beginning of the holiday festivities. How strange. Since his wife's death, he had scarcely noticed the holidays coming and going. His move from Finsbury Square to Mayfair had separated him socially from many of his erstwhile neighbors. A few had come to the more fashionable side of London in the interim, but they were as lackadaisical about observing the holidays as he.

The first night of Hannukah. How Hannah had loved to prepare for the holidays! Hannukah had been one of her favorites.

He tried to ignore the pang he felt from the memory and sat at his desk. He reached for a sheet of paper, took up his pen and began to scratch out a polite refusal. Then he stopped and put it aside. What was the harm? He missed Emanuel Belisario, a contemporary of his father's, but a good and learned man. He was a bit of a puzzlement, however. He was as successful a diamond merchant as David was a stockbroker. Yet Belisario remained in Finsbury Square, when he could easily afford to move to a more fashionable neighborhood.

David decided he would not like to give the impression that he now thought himself too good for his friend. Swiftly, he wrote an acceptance, then rang for Hall.

"Sir Robert has called, sir," said Hall, taking the note. *So it is to be personal*, thought David, pleased at the distinction. He rose to his feet and hurried to meet his guest.

"Ah, Mr. Parnas! How good it is to see you," said Sir Robert as David entered the room. He stood by the fireplace, a short man, handsome once, now rotund and red faced in middle age.

David bowed. "Welcome, Sir Robert. It is always a pleasure to have you call."

His guest eagerly accepted an offer of refreshment. They sat by the cheerful fire and exchanged pleasantries while sipping some of David's fine Madeira, then discussed one or two business matters. Sir Robert soon came to the point of his visit.

"We shall want you to come to dinner tomorrow evening. 'Tis short notice, to be sure, but my daughter has just announced her intentions to visit a friend in the country for the Christmas holidays. I did point out she will miss our ball next week...but you know, flighty females...she did, however, tell me particularly that she wishes to meet you before she leaves."

David thought of the message already on its way to Finsbury Square. How stupid of him! He could not have known the dinner would be so soon. He quickly did some calculations in his head. Could he keep both engagements? Sundown, the time for the candle lighting, was early at this time of year. The Westbrookes usually dined at nine.

"I have an engagement earlier in the day, but shall be delighted to join you for dinner."

"Capital!" Sir Robert's eyes danced. "My daughter will be so very pleased."

"I look forward to meeting Mrs. Kingsbury, and to seeing Lady Westbrooke again."

Sir Robert left soon after. David went back to his desk to write more letters, but was soon distracted. He began ruminating over how grateful he was to Sir Robert. Many of the *ton* were tolerant of receiving wealthy Jews into their precious inner circle, but none he knew were as open and warm.

David knew that, if he were Gentile, fashionable society would be happy, even eager, to receive him fully into its embrace. Mothers would push their daughters at him, a rich widower with a house in town and one in the country, still quite young and with no children. But such was not the case.

The meeting with Sophia Kingsbury could change that somewhat. She was also widowed, reputed a beauty and not more than five-and-twenty. But she had a flaw, an unforgivable one as far as the *ton* was concerned. There was a breath of scandal in her past.

Oh, just a mere breath, but enough to stain her reputation. They said her husband had discovered she had a lover. The lady had great good luck, however. Before he could denounce or divorce her, he died in a hunting accident.

David could not help smiling at the irony. This flaw made her perfect for him. It was far from unheard of for younger sons of distinguished families to marry Jewish heiresses, but most Gentile ladies of good birth would not care to make an alliance with a Jew, no matter how rich. Mrs. Kingsbury was still received in the houses of her family and a few others, but there were those who snubbed her, and he knew from Sir Robert that these snubs hurt her. It did not help that her husband had left massive debts and she had only a small marriage settlement left. She probably would never fully regain her social standing, but marrying into a fortune would help considerably—even marriage to a Jew.

He shook his head and wondered when he had become so cynical about marriage. His and Hannah's had been a love match. He supposed that was the reason. He did not care to have love again. It hurt too much to lose it. A well-born wife who would help him travel the inner circles of society, who was attractive and grateful to him for at least a partial restoration of her former life, would do very well for him.

❈ ❈ ❈

"Oh, Mama! It is dreadful!"

Rachel looked at herself in the mirror. She pulled at the edges of one of the sleeves of the offending gown, then clawed at the neckline. "Simply no one wears such a high neck and long sleeves in the evening! I look like a country bumpkin!" She had not the least idea of what a country bumpkin looked like, for she had never been in the country, but she was sure it was something very bad indeed.

"My love, I beg you to respect your uncle's wishes as long as we live in his house," said her mother.

A thin woman with a scrawny bosom and arms, a gown with a high neck and long sleeves suited her mother very well. But Rachel felt her dress of that same style, though made of a very fine muslin, decreased her charms.

She turned from the mirror. "Why must we live with Uncle, Mama? Papa left us well-provided for."

Her mother looked shocked. "What can you be thinking? It is far more proper that we live with your uncle. You must stay until you are married, or at least of age."

Rachel tossed her head. "Then I hope I shall marry very soon."

At this her mother smiled. "From your mouth to God's ears."

Rachel looked in the mirror again. She found her reflection on most occasions pleasing. She had fine dark eyes, lustrous brown tresses, and while her complexion had more of an olive cast than was à la mode, it was clear and bright all the same. Now she felt she looked perfectly wretched. Her father had never objected to her dressing in the finest fashions. Why did her uncle have to be so beastly about it?

She immediately felt guilty, thinking thus about her uncle. He was so obliging in other ways and had been such a comforting presence when her father died. And to be fair, he did not give blistering lectures about fashionable dress, as she had heard from the rabbi. But even many of the most pious members of the synagogue did not disdain the latest fashions, no matter what the rabbi said.

"Come, my dear, and smile," said her mother. "I promise you, if you keep that frown, you never will get a husband."

She sighed. "Yes, Mama." She tried to smile at her reflection. It was a minuscule improvement.

"And remember that today is the beginning of one of the most joyous times of the year. We must welcome it in the proper spirit."

"Yes, Mama."

They came down the stairs a short while later, Rachel convinced that lingering at her *toilette* would not improve anything that could overcome the gaucheness of her dress. Her uncle nodded approvingly as they came into the drawing room.

"My dear child, you are perfectly lovely."

She tried not to wince. "Thank you, Uncle."

For all his prejudices against the latest fashions, her uncle still managed to look quite the part of an English gentleman himself. Though she thought him ancient, she had to allow he was still vigorous and, while not handsome, had a dignified bearing.

"I have invited a friend to share the lighting of the candles with us," he announced.

"Yes?" Her mother sat on a settee. "A gentleman, I presume? Unmarried?"

Rachel felt her face flush as she sat next to her mother. While she was as anxious to be free of her uncle as her mother was to see her a bride, she did not like to give that impression to him.

"Yes. He is a widower...."

"A widower?" Rachel could not help gasping out the question. Was this man as ancient as her uncle?

He smiled at her. Evidently, he divined her concerns, for he said, "He is not yet thirty years. His wife...I believe you may remember her, Miriam...died of a putrid fever about two, no, I think it is three years now."

"Then it is someone I know?" asked her mother.

"Yes, indeed. It is David Parnas."

Her mother immediately became excited. "Ah, yes!" She turned to Rachel. "It would be a very fine match for you, my love. He is a stockbroker and has a house in Mayfair, is that not right, Emanuel?"

"Mayfair!" she cried. So much more fashionable than Finsbury!

But her uncle looked serious. "Yes, it is one thing that grieves me, that he will not live closer to his own people, or not participate regularly in the services. And it happens all too often nowadays..."

She stopped listening. Everything her mother and uncle had said made David Parnas sound most appealing. Would he be handsome, she wondered? And kind and thoughtful like Papa and Uncle? She hoped so. Her dress started to vex her again. A man who lived in Mayfair, and who must regularly mix with the *beau monde*, was sure to find her a dowdy upon first impression.

Her heart skipped a beat when she heard someone at the door. Soon after, David Parnas entered the room. Her uncle made the introductions, and she studied him through her eyelashes as she lowered her head slightly and curtsied in response to his bow.

Oh, he was quite marvelous! So handsome, so imposing! She had never seen a man so tall. Nor, she thought, with a sinking feeling in her stomach, so fastidiously dressed. The cut of his black coat, the snow-white waistcoat and skillfully tied cravat were perfection. He was sure to despise her as someone lacking taste and elegance.

He also had a deep, rich voice, but what it said was alarming. "I regret I must make apologies the moment I arrive, but my visit will have to be quite short. I am engaged elsewhere this evening for dinner...an obligation I could not get out of."

She could see both her mother and uncle were as disappointed as she, but her uncle said, "Of course, we are sorry to hear that, but are pleased you could join us this evening at all."

"No more pleased than I am to be here." He sat on a chair next to the settee. He turned to her mother and said, "My wife...she loved the holidays, you know. It is not the same when one is alone."

Oh, no! If only he had not given her mother such an opening. She could guess the next words out of her mother's mouth, and turned out to be frighteningly accurate.

"It is not right to be alone, for so long. You must marry again, Mr. Parnas."

"I intend to, Mrs. de Costa. You are quite right...it is wrong to be alone."

These words caused a noticeable ripple of excitement in the room. Rachel even imagined he was looking at her as he said this, but she couldn't be sure, since she couldn't stop looking at her hands in her lap. Could she have made a favorable impression so quickly?

"It is time to light the candles," her uncle said.

They gathered at the table that held the menorah, which was set by a front window so people passing by could see the light. Her uncle, as was traditional for the head of the houshold, lit the candles. He lit the *shamash*, the candle used to light the other candles, and while reciting the three prayers in Hebrew, lit the first one for the first night.

Afterwards they repaired to a table in another room where cheese, fruit, and glasses of wine had already been set out, since no one was permitted to do any work the first half-hour after the candles were lit, not even the servants.

As they went back to the drawing room, her mother gave her a gentle poke in the ribs. Rachel knew that meant she should sit next to Mr. Parnas and speak to him. She smiled at him. He bowed slightly and waited for her to sit on the settee, then joined her.

"Mama says you live in Mayfair," she said after taking a small sip of wine.

"Yes, that's true."

An awkward silence followed. Would he not even attempt to make conversation with her? She tried again.

"Do you like it there?"

"Yes, very much."

"Do you ever miss living here?"

"I miss seeing my friends socially. It was why I wanted to come here tonight. I miss your uncle's company very much."

Her uncle saved her from having to think of something else to say. "I miss yours as well, my friend."

As they chatted about mutual friends and business, she wondered what was wrong with her. Some instinct told her that he was not a shy man. She knew she was a pretty girl. She'd had her share of admirers. Obviously, his intention to marry did not come from any great revelation he'd had when first meeting her.

What a foolish creature I am, she thought. To be almost the age of twenty and still so girlish!

Then she wondered if he had already fixed his sights on someone particular. Of course, she thought. That was what he'd meant.

In spite of her disappointment, she felt like laughing. Poor Uncle, his plans were for naught.

The clock chimed, and Mr. Parnas soon rose to his feet. "Again, I apologize for the brevity of this visit, but I must leave now that the half-hour has passed."

They rose as well, and bowed and curtsied.

When he was gone, her mother said, "Well! That was very quick indeed!"

Her uncle shook his head. "He has been gone too long from his friends. His new ones are more to his liking, I daresay."

"Still," her mother said, walking over to Rachel and cupping her chin with her hand. "He did seem impressed with our girl."

She wrenched her face away. "Oh, Mama! How ridiculous!"

"Why do you say that, my dear?" asked her uncle. "He did say…"

"Yes, yes, that he intends to marry…does it not occur to either of you that he has already chosen his intended?"

In the silence that followed, Rachel knew that she had hit her mark. Her uncle looked especially troubled.

"I hope that doesn't mean he is looking to…that is…"

"What, Emanuel?"

"That he has found a Gentile bride."

"Oh! No, no," said her mother. "I'm sure not."

"He is wealthy, Miriam. A good match for penniless ladies who offer rank and good breeding. Opportunities may open up for him after such a marriage that don't exist now."

"Emanuel! How can you say such things? Why, his was always a disinterested heart, as I remember. He and his wife were a true love match."

"Perhaps." Her uncle smiled ruefully. "But things change. People change."

Rachel had to see it her uncle's way. As she drained the last bit of wine from her glass, she decided to put David Parnas out of her mind forever.

❄ ❄ ❄

David found it difficult not to laugh almost the whole journey back to Mayfair. How blind could he be? His old friend Belisario had set a marriage trap for him!

It had never crossed his mind. All of Belisario's children were long married. He had not counted on an unwed niece. Not the most elegant creature he'd ever seen, but a pretty thing who could not be wanting for suitors, especially with the substantial dowry such an uncle could give her.

He supposed he should feel flattered, really. Belisario must have chosen him out of personal regard.

How fortunate he'd had an excuse to leave early. He hoped he had not hurt the girl's feelings by being so curt, but why give her a false impression? His future was in Mayfair, not Finsbury.

He soon arrived at the Westbrooke's. He took a deep breath as he alighted from the carriage. This evening would be a very important one in his life, he knew.

He soon found himself mingling with Sir Robert's other guests in the drawing room. Many he knew already, either through other social engagements or business. He met with the usual polite but slightly cool reception. Sir Robert soon appeared, with his wife and a young woman who surely had to be his daughter.

They went around the room, greeting their various guests. They were leaving him for last, he assumed.

Finally, they stood in front of him.

"Mr. Parnas," said Sir Robert. "You remember my wife, of course?"

"Of course." He took Lady Westbrooke's chubby, pink, ring-encrusted hand in his and brought it briefly to his lips. She simpered at him.

"And may I present my daughter, Mrs. Kingsbury?"

She curtsied and held out her hand. As he took it he noted it was much whiter and slimmer than her mother's and exuded the soft scent of lavender.

The four exchanged pleasantries for a while, then the two younger people broke away from the father and mother.

"My father tells me, sir, that you have given him much valuable business advice."

"I hope that he has found it so."

"Oh, he has. He is most grateful to you. Father had suffered many setbacks...I wish my husband could have had the benefit of such advice."

They conversed thus for a few moments. He was a trifle surprised at her knowledge of financial matters, but that did not impress him most. He could not help but think that her beauty had been much underrated. She had soft auburn tresses and eyes so dark a blue they almost seemed black. She wore a gown of silver and white in the latest style. She no longer had a girlish bloom, but her skin was a flawless creamy white.

"Mr. Parnas, may I present my cousin, Mr. Crowley?"

A handsome dandy of about thirty stood in front of them.

Mr. Crowley put a jeweled quizzing glass up to his eye and studied David for a moment. As he lowered it he turned to Mrs. Kingsbury and said, "I say, Sophia, is this the Jew you were talking about meeting tonight?"

David tried not to let any of the muscles in his face move. He had never been spoken to thus in any home of his Mayfair friends.

Mrs. Kingsbury acted as though she had not heard him. "How is your law practice, Harry?"

"Tedious, absolutely tedious. I would give it up if I could." He turned to David. "'Tis the fate of younger brothers, Parnas. Not all of us have the talent to make our own fortune."

"Of course, you could marry it," said Mrs. Kingsbury.

"True, very true. If I could find a rich widow...but you will not have me, Sophia. But then, you are not very rich, are you? Perhaps I could find a Jewess with a large fortune...you must know a few, Parnas, could you not help me?"

"I..."

Mrs. Kingsbury looked genuinely angry now. "Harry, you are being unaccountably rude."

"Am I? I do apologize."

David said coldly, "There is nothing to apologize for."

She slipped her arm in his and said, "Pray excuse us, I must introduce Mr. Parnas to my friend, Mrs. Lewis." She steered him to another part of the room.

"I hope you were not offended by my thoughtless cousin," she said.

He had been deeply offended, but he knew he walked on eggshells and so dismissed it with a slight incline of the head.

"Of course he was merely joking about wanting to marry me," she said.

"I assumed it was all a joke."

A gong sounded. The people in the room stopped conversing and began heading to the dining hall.

"May I escort you into dinner, Mrs. Kingsbury?"

She gave him a smile full of promise. "It would be an honor."

By the time tea came out, David was sure that, on balance, the evening had been a great success. Mrs. Kingsbury seemed everything a well-bred woman should be, and he wondered if the gossip about her had even the slightest bit of truth to it.

He could not help but notice that some of the other guests, while polite, did not give her much attention. She was a member, but not quite part of the world they traveled. It was the same with him. He decided such a thing could only bond two people closer together.

Just before he was ready to leave she said to him, "I shall be leaving tomorrow for the country and return very soon after the New Year."

"May I call on you when you return to town?"

Her eyes seemed to sparkle at the request. "I would be delighted."

He gave his thanks and farewells to the Westbrookes. Yes, indeed, the evening had been a great success.

※ ※ ※

The next morning while breakfasting, however, he began to regret the way he had behaved at the Belisario house. He had been rude to a perfectly nice young woman and her mother, relatives of a man who had his highest respect. He might not have been as crass as Harry Crowley, but still it had been very ill bred of him.

He wanted to mend the situation. Since he could not make any engagements with Mrs. Kingsbury at the moment, he decided to invite the Belisario family to his house.

He called for his housekeeper, Mrs. Salomon. She disapproved of his laxness in following their religion, he knew, and probably stayed only for the same reason that he kept her—respect for Hannah's memory.

"Yes, sir?"

"Mrs. Salomon, I wonder...do you remember where we put my wife's Hannukah menorah?"

She looked a trifle surprised, but also pleased. "Why, of course I do, sir. I have kept it polished, as well. Will you be wanting to light the candles tonight?"

"Yes...yes. I will also have guests. Will you please arrange for wine and food for after the candle-lighting?"

"Yes, sir."

After breakfast he sat at his desk and wrote out the invitation. He sent it off, hoping that he had not offended them so that they would not come.

※ ※ ※

"Oh, my love, what wonderful news!"

Rachel, who had been sitting in her uncle's massive library, looked up from her book. "Mama! What could it be? You look quite beside yourself!"

"I am, my dear, I am!" Waving a paper she sat next to Rachel. "I knew you were wrong about Mr. Parnas."

"Whatever do you mean?" She took the note from her mother and read it. When she finished, she clucked and gave it back with a dismissive gesture. "Oh. Is that all."

"Is that all? My child, this means..."

"Absolutely nothing, Mama, except that Mr. Parnas is a well-bred gentleman who returns his social engagements."

Her mother's shocked look in response to this was almost comical. "How can you say such a thing? He would not return it so quickly if he were not eager to see you again, my dear."

"Ha."

"I do not understand you. Since when have you become so contrary?"

Rachel could not help smiling at that. "Mama, I am just being realistic."

"Well, I say it is a hopeful sign."

"Hopeful! You were ready to take me out to buy wedding clothes."

"Rachel!"

She suppressed another smile. "I am sorry, Mama." She picked up the paper once more. "Well, it is kind of him to think of us. And…I would so like to see his house in Mayfair. It must be very grand."

Her mother became excited again. "Yes, yes. It must be."

Rachel suddenly thought of something. "Oh, dear me."

"What is the matter, love?"

She shook her head decisively. "You must make my apologies, Mama. I simply cannot go."

"What?"

"I cannot go to an evening engagement in Mayfair in one of the dreadful gowns Uncle forces me to wear."

Her mother's face deflated. She evidently considered it a distressing problem, too. Then she smiled again and said, "But that does not matter, my love. Your uncle has to decline the invitation. He has another engagement."

"What difference does that make?"

"Well…I do not like to defy my brother, but we could dress you as we please since he won't be here to see…"

"Fool Uncle? Oh, Mama." She folded her arms together and frowned.

Her mother bit her lip. "Do you think it very wrong, Rachel?"

She burst out laughing. "I am only joking with you. How clever you can be!" She threw her arms around her mother and hugged her.

The two giggling conspirators watched out the window until her uncle had left for his engagement, then dressed Rachel with the utmost care. They were afraid for even one of the maids to see her, so they did not send for one to help. Luckily, her mother was very adept at dressing hair.

Rachel waited upstairs as her mother asked the groom to call for a carriage, then tiptoed down the stairs when she heard it arrive, sliding past the servants and hoping none noticed that her gown would have shocked her uncle into an apoplexy.

They laughed and laughed as they drove away. Oh! Would Uncle be angry if he found out, she wondered? Well, Mama was her mother, and had some authority over her mode of dress, did she not?

❊ ❊ ❊

David greeted his guests in a much warmer manner than he had left them the previous evening. He expressed regret that Belisario was not with them, and would be alone for his own candle-lighting ceremony.

"My brother was quite affable about it, Mr. Parnas, I assure you," said Mrs. de Costa.

I'm sure he was, thought David. He would want to give his niece every chance.

But that was an uncharitable thought, and he decided to banish any others from his mind. Tonight he would repair any damage to their friendship, and that would be that.

He had to admit the girl improved a great deal on second viewing. Her red velvet gown complemented her coloring delightfully, and, he could not help noting, she had an equally delightful figure. He thought he detected a slight coolness in her manner at first, when the night before she had seemed dazzled by his presence. He could have been imagining that, however.

She was certainly, however, dazzled by his house. Both women took a turn about the room and exclaimed over this bit of furniture and that, asked several questions about particular pieces, and approved of the Grecian Revival decor.

"Did you choose it yourself?" Miss de Costa asked.

"I must admit that I did, most of it."

"I congratulate you on your excellent taste," she said.

"I thank you."

"Is this not a lovely menorah, Mama?" said the girl, pausing at the small table in front of the window, where Mrs. Salomon had placed it along with the candles.

"Oh my, yes."

"It belonged to my wife." He turned away suddenly and pretended he had an overpowering desire to warm himself by the fire, memories of past holidays crowding in his mind.

An awkward moment passed before Miss de Costa said, "I do so like a room that has many books. Do not you, Mama?"

"Yes, and it is a good thing, your uncle has more than anyone I know."

The pain from his reminiscing faded. David turned from the fire and asked, "Do you like to read, Miss de Costa?"

Her mother answered for her, "Oh my, yes! My brother finds it quite amazing in a girl."

He smiled at that. She did not strike him as a bluestocking, but the girl had an undeniable intelligence to her dark eyes, and he found that he liked it. "What do you read, may I ask? Novels? Poetry?"

She inclined her head in answer. "I see that you think young ladies do nothing but stuff their heads with silly novels and love poetry all day long."

He laughed out loud. "Not at all, Miss de Costa. You wrong me very much. My wife..." Why did he keep bringing Hannah into the conversation? He forced himself to continue. "She enjoyed novels and poetry, that is all."

The girl's face softened as she said, "It must have been so difficult to lose her."

He noted that her mother gave her a gentle poke in disapproval of the comment, but he thought it very kind of her. He sighed before he said, "Life goes on, does it not?"

"Of course it does," said her mother.

"Yes, Mama, but I think the people who part from us also stay with us a little, and that is something to cherish. Is that not the case for you with Papa?"

Her mother nodded in agreement, a sad smile on her face. The girl turned to him again. "Do you not think so, sir?"

"I think…I think you are a very wise young woman."

She smiled her first genuine smile at him, and he could not but notice what lovely full lips she had. The thought disturbed him so much that he tore his gaze away from hers and asked if they were ready for the candle lighting.

They were just about to proceed with the brief ceremony when Hall announced the arrival of some unexpected guests.

David's jaw dropped in surprise and vexation as Sir Robert, Mrs. Kingsbury, and Mr. Crowley entered the room.

Sir Robert said, "Oh, but you have guests. Perhaps…"

"Nonsense, Sir Robert," David said, trying to recover and sound as ebullient as possible. "This is a most welcome surprise."

He turned to Mrs. Kingsbury and saw her studying Mrs. and Miss de Costa intently.

"Forgive me," he said. He proceeded to make the introductions, and prayed that Crowley would not say anything that would upset his guests.

Crowley merely bowed and made pleasant remarks, though he studied Miss de Costa for a second or two longer than was necessary through his quizzing glass.

The de Costas looked at David expectantly, and he knew they were waiting for him to start the candle-lighting ceremony. He turned to the Westbrooke party.

"I hope you will excuse us, but we are celebrating one of our festivals tonight, the holiday of Hannukah. I was about to light the candles."

"How charming!" said Mrs. Kingsbury. "May we join? Or is it not allowed?"

David smiled, relieved at her enthusiasm. "Of course, all are welcome."

When the candle lighting was over, Sir Robert asked, "What is it precisely that you are celebrating, may I ask?"

"The overthrow of the Greeks by the Jews, Sir Robert. The candles commemorate a miracle, for there was only oil enough to light the temple one day, yet it burned for eight days."

"How extraordinary, celebrating a revolution. Something similar to what the Americans do, is it not?"

"I have never thought of it that way before, but must own that it is similar. But we only light candles, we do not set off fireworks."

Everyone seemed to find that quite clever and laughed.

He ushered them into the other room for the cheese and wine. Mr. Crowley stood behind Miss de Costa as she picked up a plate and leaned close to her ear. "My heavens, what a lot of cheese."

She smiled and blushed. "There is a reason we eat it tonight, sir. "

"And will you not tell me what it is?"

She moved away from him and said, "It is rather a gruesome story."

"Is it? Now I am intrigued."

"The leader of the Greeks, he…" she lowered her voice a bit. "He desired a Jewish widow named Judith."

David felt his fingers tighten around his wineglass, but he said nothing, and hoped Crowley would continue controlling himself.

"Pray go on, Miss de Costa," said Mrs. Kingsbury. "Now I am intrigued as well."

"She was virtuous but also wanted to help her people. So she visited him in his tent…"

Sir Robert, having already downed one glass of wine and about to pick up another, laughed. "Is this a story for mixed company, my dear?"

"Oh, I assure you, Sir Robert, it is perfectly all right," said Mrs. de Costa. "We tell the story every year, to remember."

Miss de Costa continued. "She brought him a basket of cheese and fed him so much he fell asleep. Then…"

"Yes?" said Crowley.

In a dramatic voice she said, "She took his sword and cut off his head."

"Did she now!" Crowley seemed utterly delighted.

"Well!" exclaimed Mrs. Kingsbury in mock horror. "You kept your promise, Miss de Costa. It is thoroughly gruesome."

"I think it a marvelous story," said Crowley.

"Yes, you would."

The story had the odd effect of breaking the ice. Crowley remained respectful and sociable. David wondered if Mrs. Kingsbury had criticized his behavior of the previous evening and he was trying to prove to his uncle and cousin that he could be civil to Sir Robert's Jewish friends.

Crowley also seemed enchanted with Miss de Costa. And, David was appalled to discover, she seemed to like him, too. She listened to him attentively, and he could see her blush once or twice in response to something he said. He wondered what her uncle would think of that.

Mrs. Kingsbury noticed him observing them. "Is she a relation?"

"No. The niece of a friend." He wanted to explain to her that he had merely invited them to return a social engagement, but thought that would not help matters. Inviting an attractive single woman to his house the day after he began paying court to a young widow probably seemed very strange, he knew. He counter-attacked instead. "Mrs. Kingsbury, you quite surprised me tonight. I believed you were leaving for the country today."

"I changed my mind this morning as we breakfasted. So much more going on in town, and my friend has a full house of guests. She will not miss me. I also thought I'd rather not miss my parents' ball next week."

"Well, I am very glad that is so."

"Are you?" She looked him in the eye.

He matched her gaze. "Yes. I hope you will allow me to engage you for the first two dances at the ball."

She smiled. "I would be delighted, of course." Looking at her cousin again, she said, "Harry seems quite taken with your friend's niece."

"Hmm. I suppose he is the sort who flirts everywhere."

"Oh, yes, you could say that about him. But I don't think I've seen such a handsome, pleasant girl in an age." She turned to her father. "Do you not agree, sir?"

Sir Robert, who had been paying more attention to his wine glass than the conversation, started and said, "Very handsome, very handsome, my dear."

She fixed her dark blue eyes on David again. "Has she a fortune?"

He hesitated, then said, "I assume she does. Her late father was a diamond merchant, as is her uncle."

"How fortunate she is. Beauty and a fortune, she may marry as she pleases."

"As long as her choice pleases her uncle and mother."

"Do you not think they would approve of Harry?"

"No, I do not," he said, much more vehemently than he intended.

"Why so?"

Sir Robert heard this part of the conversation and joined in. "Would be foolish of them, in my view. My nephew may not be rich, but his rank, his connexions, make him an excellent match for a girl in her situation."

David realized he might have offended them. He tried to amend it.

"Her uncle is very pious, much more so than many of his station. He would show great disapprobation for any match of this sort. I was not speaking of Mr. Crowley specifically."

Mrs. Kingsbury gave him another one of her piercing looks. "And you, sir? Do you share his views on these sorts of marriages?"

"I must allow that I do not. But I am not the one who would make such a decision in Miss de Costa's case."

He could not tell if this pronouncement pleased her. She suddenly said, "I would like to get to know Miss de Costa better. I shall sit with her awhile and speak to her."

As she crossed the room to join her, it dawned on him that perhaps she did see the girl as a potential rival. He was impatient to have an opportunity to speak to her alone and clarify the situation, then thought perhaps that he should not make an issue of it.

She waved Crowley to the other side of the room, and the rest of the visit had the men divided from the women. There was nothing in the conversation of the women that was worrisome, only a discussion of laces and shoe styles and other usual feminine prattle. Soon, the de Costas were ready to leave.

As they were about to part, Mrs. Kingsbury said, "Father, would it not be enchanting if we invited Miss de Costa and her charming mother to our ball?"

His face lit up. "An excellent notion! You must come, dear ladies, we would most enjoy your presence."

Miss de Costa looked quite flustered. "I am honored, Sir Robert, but..." She looked at her mother for help.

Mrs. de Costa said, "We would be delighted, but of course we must consult with my brother first to see if we are already engaged for that evening."

"I hope you shall both be there," said Crowley. "I would be honored if you would reserve the first two dances for me, Miss de Costa."

"There!" said Mrs. Kingsbury with a wave of her hand. "Now you must come, or Harry will be disconsolate."

David could not imagine why this scene perturbed him so, but he hoped heartily that they would *not* come to Sir Robert's ball.

❋ ❋ ❋

In spite of every effort to enter the house quietly, her uncle saw them as he came out of his library carrying a book. He naturally voiced strong disapproval over Rachel's choice of gown and requested they talk of it in his library. She thought he would not mind so much when he found out that she had been invited to the home of Sir Robert Westbrooke, but he did.

He put his book down on a table with a decisive thump. "I should not like for you to go. Certainly not if you mean to dress like that."

She drew her wrap around her more tightly.

"But Emanuel," her mother pleaded. "It is a very singular honor. And she will see Mr. Parnas."

"Yes, I must speak to both of you about that. I feel Rachel should not see him again."

Both women looked at him, surprised. "Why, Uncle? I thought you liked him."

"He is a fine man, and I would not have thought of him for you otherwise. But I have heard from one of his colleagues that he intends to court Sir Robert Westbrooke's daughter."

"Oh, dear, I see," said Miriam.

Rachel tried to be indifferent to this revelation. She picked at the edge of the lace on her wrap and said, "I cannot say I am very surprised. She is an uncommonly elegant woman and the daughter of a baronet."

"Nor am I, but this only means there is no cause for you to go to this ball. Better to stay here and keep social engagements that will be more advantageous to you."

"I cannot say that I see any harm in her going," said her mother. "And the Westbrookes would be very insulted, I think, if we turned them down."

He looked at them for a moment, then turned his head away. "Of course, Miriam, if that is your decision, you must abide by it. I do not like for you to think that I command you to do or not do anything. Rachel is your daughter, after all."

Rachel said quickly, "Oh, Uncle, we do value your judgment and are most grateful for all your kindness to us."

"Of course we are! But as we were invited personally...I cannot see the harm, I really cannot."

"Very well," he said. He turned to Rachel. "I suppose I cannot persuade you to dress in a more modest fashion?"

"I...my gloves will cover most of my arms, you know. And I will add some lace to the neck of my ball gown, if it would please you better, sir."

He sighed. "I suppose it will have to."

"Thank you, dear Uncle!"

As Rachel prepared for bed, she thought over the events of the evening. She had to admit that for all her attempts to remain indifferent to David Parnas, she could not be. How attentive he had been before his other guests had arrived. And how astonishing to see him still mourn his wife after so many years! He was a man of deep, genuine feelings, just the sort she'd hoped for herself someday. It had been so difficult to be indifferent to him, in fact, that she had permitted that odious Mr. Crowley to pay attention to her in a vain attempt to make him jealous. It had not worked at all. As soon as Mrs. Kingsbury had entered the room, it was as if she no longer existed.

Even so, she did not think he loved the other woman. Respect, perhaps a bit of awe, that was all she could detect, no genuine attachment. How distressing that he would take that in place of the happiness he must have shared with his first wife.

He had seemed unhappy when her mother had tentatively accepted Mrs. Kingsbury's invitation. Was he ashamed of his heritage? Rachel was not sure, but decided to give him the benefit of the doubt, for she hated to think he was not as agreeable as he appeared.

Not that it mattered much. After the Westbrooke ball, it was improbable that she would see him again, and the next time she heard anything of him, it likely would be to read his wedding announcement in *The Times*.

❊ ❊ ❊

Accompanied by Mrs. Salomon, David lit the eight candles and said the prayers for the last night of Hannukah.

It was also the night of the Westbrooke ball.

During the mandated rest period, he thought over the past few days and his meetings with Mrs. Kingsbury. He had to admit they had little in common, sharing few tastes and pursuits. He strongly suspected that when she visited his house she was already plannning changes to the decor.

Even so, he liked her well enough and was sure she liked him. And was that not all they could ask of each other? It would be a marriage of convenience, but that did not necessarily have to result in an unhappy one.

He felt matters were going so well, in fact, that as he dressed for the ball he decided to make his offer that very evening.

When he entered the ballroom at the Westbrookes, he found the de Costas had already arrived. He was a trifle surprised that Belisario had not persuaded them to decline, but pleased to see Mrs. Kingsbury introducing them to some of her other guests. How kind she is, he thought. So like her father.

Miss de Costa looked ravishing in her ball gown, and he noticed that Crowley stayed close to her side.

"Look at how besotted Harry is!" exclaimed Mrs. Kingsbury after she greeted him. "I hope he does not get too far gone, or the girl will have the whip-hand of him."

Besotted! Over the girl's money, no doubt. Had he not come right out and asked to be introduced to a wealthy Jewess? David regretted deeply that he had been the cause of such a meeting, however indirectly.

While Mrs. Kingsbury spoke to some of her friends he engaged Miss de Costa for the second set of dances. She readily accepted.

Perhaps I should warn her about Crowley, he thought. But no, the girl seemed sensible, and if she was not, her uncle and mother would protect her from such an unadvised alliance.

The music began. As he led Mrs. Kingsbury to the dance floor, he could not help but watch Crowley and Miss de Costa. Crowley turned out to be an excellent dancer, and the girl quite a vision of gracefulness. He heard one or two people in the line ask who she was.

Mrs. Kingsbury's sharp eyes caught him watching them. "You seem to have appointed yourself some sort of guardian of that girl, Mr. Parnas."

He tried to treat that as a joke and smiled. "No, indeed I have not, madam."

"Then I hope, if Harry does pay his addresses to her, you will perhaps put in a word for him with her uncle."

That surprised him so much he almost fell out of step with the dance. "I doubt anything I would say could make a difference. Are you saying…"

"I cannot read my cousin's mind, but it would be an excellent match for him, in my view. She is a lovely, unspoilt girl. "

"And rich."

"Yes, and what of it?"

He could not answer that. Was she telling him, in her way, that money was his sole attraction to her? But to be fair, he could not say that deep feelings were his motivation in pursuing his own suit.

They switched partners for the next set—Mrs. Kingsbury danced with her cousin and he fulfilled his engagement with Miss de Costa.

"Are you enjoying the ball?" he asked her, noting how the lights in the room picked up red and gold colors in her dark hair.

"Oh! It is quite lovely, do not you think so?"

"Yes, Sir Robert is a marvelous host."

They danced for a while longer in silence, he not able to stop watching her move to the music. He almost missed what she said to him.

"I beg your pardon?"

"I said, my uncle has told me we will soon be wishing you joy."

"I…I do not know where he could have gotten such an idea."

"Are you not paying court to Mrs. Kingsbury?"

He felt heat rise to his face.

She blushed, too. "I do apologize. I would not have said anything, but was under the impression everything was quite settled. People were talking of it before you arrived."

"What people?" he demanded.

"Why...Mr. Crowley, mostly."

He did not know why he felt so angry. "Mr. Crowley is quite mistaken. There is nothing settled between myself and Mrs. Kingsbury."

"Oh, dear me, I hope I have not offended you, sir."

"Not at all. It is all Mr. Crowley's fault. He should not have misled you."

The dance ended. He led her back to her mother, then thought it would be a good idea if he asked the older woman to dance.

"How kind! But I do not dance. Much better if you ask Rachel again."

The girl looked appalled at her mother's forthrightness. "Oh, Mama..."

"I would be delighted, Miss de Costa, to be your partner again." They settled on which dance, then he went off to find Crowley.

He could not see him in the crush of people. He soon found himself caught up in conversation with Lady Westbrooke, who stopped him to introduce him to some people whose names he did not bother to catch. When, finally, he managed to break away, he caught sight of Crowley slipping out of the ballroom. So much the better. They could talk in private.

David lost the other man in the hallway, but after wandering a few moments heard Crowley's voice coming out of a small sitting room. As he approached the door, David opened his mouth to announce his presence, but before he could, he was shocked to recognize the voice of the other person in the room. It was Mrs. Kingsbury.

"Harry, you are a fool."

"I will not do it. I will not marry that girl."

"I thought you liked her."

"You know there is only one woman I see. I had hoped to make you jealous."

David peeked around the open door until he had a view of the pair. Crowley stood over her as she sat in a chair, fanning herself with her fan. She turned away from him abruptly. David jumped back so she would not see him.

"You must marry *somebody*. I cannot have you mooning after me and making me the subject of gossip again. You almost ruined me forever with your silly calf love."

Crowley straightened up, his face red with anger. "You cannot be serious about marrying a Jew. That will ruin you socially for certain!"

She turned and faced him again. "It does not signify. He will no longer be a Jew after we marry. Then all anyone will care about is that he is landed and rich."

David had to bite his lip to keep from gasping out loud.

"Are you sure he will agree, Sophia? He was celebrating that festival of theirs the other night."

"For the benefit of some friends, that is all. He must know that is part of it, and I doubt he cares one way or the other."

David stepped away from the door. He entered the ballroom in a daze. Fortunately, no one tried to speak to him. He made his way to the terraces surrounding the room and stepped out into the sharp December night. He barely noticed the cold.

'He must know that is part of it.' Deep down, he had suspected it all along, but hearing it aloud suddenly made it real. He had believed he would not care one way or the other, just as she said. Suddenly, he found that he *did* care. In a way, it was like burying Hannah all over again. He could see her face before him, the disappointment she would surely have felt if he had considered such a step while they were married. He could not blame Mrs. Kingsbury for expecting such a thing, but he should not have expected it of himself.

"Mr. Parnas?"

He turned to see Miss de Costa shivering in the night air. "You should not be out here."

"Nor should you. Are you well?"

"Yes." Her look of concern was so genuine, he suddenly blurted out, "You must think me a fool, Miss de Costa."

She looked taken aback. "Why do you say such a thing? Of course I do not."

"You are kind. Your uncle would think differently."

"How so?"

Before he could stop himself, he poured out the whole story about Mrs. Kingsbury. He almost instantly regretted it, but to his relief she did not look at him with either pity or contempt.

Instead, she turned and looked into the ballroom and said, "This world—it is beautiful, there are so many things that are wonderful about it."

"And some not so wonderful."

"True. But one does like to be a part of it, just the same."

He noticed again that she was shivering. He offered his arm to her. "What could I have been thinking, keeping you out here in the cold? Pray, let's go back inside."

She took his arm and they stepped back into the ballroom. They found chairs in a relatively quiet corner and sat down together. Ignoring most of the people and activity around them, they spent the next hour talking.

❊ ❊ ❊

He dreaded no task more than having to go back to the Westbrookes the next day to break off with Mrs. Kingsbury. He knew that it would harm his friendship with Sir Robert, perhaps irreparably, and for that he was exceedingly sorry. But it had to be done.

He had not stayed for supper the previous evening, using the excuse of

having to escort the de Costas home because Mrs. de Costa had a sick headache. He had not seen Mrs. Kingsbury again, and was glad of it. He did not
want to see her until they were in private.

When he arrived, he was told she was not in. Instead of leaving his card, he
inquired for Sir Robert. He thought it prudent to apologize again for his hasty
retreat from the ball.

When he entered the drawing room, he was amazed to see the normally ju-
bilant man looking pinch-faced and drained. Sir Robert even dispensed with
the usual pleasantries.

"Forgive me, my friend, I do not know what to say to you."

Puzzled, he said, "Is something amiss, Sir Robert?"

"Aye, grievously amiss. I shall come right out and tell you. My daughter
and nephew Crowley are, as we speak, on their way to Gretna Green. She left a
letter last night, and we found it this morning."

For almost a full moment, David found he could not speak.

"Such a foolish match, on both sides! My wife is abed, and I doubt she will
rise from it anytime soon. I do not know what could have come over them.
And," Sir Robert said, turning to David, "I cannot imagine the disappointment
you must feel. My daughter abused you, sir. There is nothing I can do but offer
my humblest, profoundest apologies."

If Sir Robert had not been such a good friend, David would have laughed.
He reminded himself that this was a crushing blow to a man he respected, and
immediately assured him that he understood.

"No promise existed between us, Sir Robert. If she had an attachment to
her cousin, better she knew her own mind before…"

Sir Robert looked grateful and murmured, "Most kind of you, Parnas, most
kind."

He left the Westbrooke house with an amazing jumble of feelings—relief,
amusement, and, yes, a bit of injury to his male vanity, he had to allow.

Fortunately, that latter feeling had receded by the time he received a short,
hastily scrawled letter from Mrs. Kingsbury.

Dear Mr. Parnas,

*I have left London, perhaps permanently. I wish you to know how much
I appreciate your attentions of these past days. In my opinion, my father could
not wish for a better friend than yourself.*

*You will no doubt have heard by the time you receive this letter that I
have married my cousin Crowley. Our attachment has been one of long dura-
tion. I hope I had not given you any false impressions during our brief asso-
ciation. If I did, I apologize from the bottom of my heart.*

Yours,

Sophia Crowley

He showed the letter to Rachel on his next visit to Finsbury Square. He knew there would be many more such visits, had known it since the moment she had taken his arm and they had come in from the terrace at the ball.

She read it and exclaimed, "Selfish woman! She most certainly did give you a false impression—she did to everybody."

He looked at her fondly, grateful for the ferocity of her feelings. "Do not be so hard on her, my dear. The heart and head are not always in agreement."

"But her poor father and mother!"

"Aye, it is a very sad time for them. I must admit, however," he said, taking her sweet hand in his, "that it is a most fortunate occurrence. She, perhaps, would not have been as forgiving if I had been the one to break it off."

"I suppose you must feel grateful to the odious and persistent Mr. Crowley," Rachel said, folding her other hand shyly over his.

"You mean to say," he teased, "that you did not really like him? Not even a little bit?"

She was still young and guileless enough to take him seriously. "Oh, sir, how can you..."

They broke apart quickly as her mother came into the room. David regretted the intrusion exceedingly; he had thought to steal a kiss from those lovely lips. Plenty of time for that, he thought. Mrs. de Costa must have noticed they had been holding hands, because she smiled a knowing, pleased smile.

"Mr. Parnas, my brother would like to know if you would come to dinner tomorrow."

"I would be delighted, Mrs. de Costa."

He was delighted by any invitation from his friend Belisario. He would remember all his days how his life had been altered forever by the Hannukah invitation.

Debra Vega was born and spent part of her early childhood in Seville, Spain while her father was stationed overseas in the Air Force. When he retired from the military, the family settled in New York City. Debra earned a degree in film studies at Queens College and has worked for various entertainment-related companies, including as a reader for a film company. After moving to Miami, Florida, she recently started a small business selling collectibles over the Internet. Debra has been writing fiction for about 10 years. *The Hannukah Invitation* is her first published work.

Fans of O. Henry's tales will love this short story by the inimitable Nina Coombs Pykare. If only all cases of writer's block could be solved this way!

The Promise

Nina Coombs Pykare

I stood inside the door of Lackington Allen, Booksellers, shaking snow off my half-boots and the hem of my pelisse. Water dropped from the brim of my bonnet, and I removed it long enough to shake it, too, then put it back on. Our house was within walking distance and so I hadn't had to hire a carriage; most fortunate, given our reduced circumstances. Of course, I would not ordinarily have ventured out in such snow, but today my need had been great.

However, now that I had arrived at my destination, I feared I had acted precipitously. I was there, but I didn't know where to look for what I needed. I did know to stay away from the shelf that held the work of Lady Incognita. No one must know that I, Louisa Penhope, was Lady Incognita. Not even my two elderly aunts and my younger brother and sister back in the house knew anything of that.

I swallowed a sigh worthy of one of my heroines. My newest romance of terror, *Escape from Evil*, had ground to a dreadful standstill, and nothing I did seemed to get my pen moving again. There would be little celebration of Christmas for me unless I could once more be writing.

I had, of course, made the necessary arrangements for our household—the holly branches, the Yule log, the ingredients for plum pudding and other delicacies, the little gifts for everyone. And if I had to, I would put a good face on it and be jolly with the rest of them. But since I was the sole support of said household, I had to get this story finished or the weeks *after* Christmas would not be jolly at all.

I pushed that from my mind and considered my characters. I had a heroine, Melisandra Melitone, a young woman in straitened circumstances very like my own. She was easy to write about—I knew quite well the dread that filled her heart, the fear of not being able to care for those who depended on her. I had my villain, Count Salmont, a man of smoldering passions and dark deceits. I had never known anyone nearly so evil, but I had no problem showing his evil ways. And I had a hero, Anthony, Viscount Pemberton, a man of honor, upright and courageous. Handsome, too, of course.

It was the viscount who had brought my story to its present imbroglio. He simply refused to come to life for me. My first hero had been a more simple man, molded after my deceased Papa, though without his unfortunate propensity for gaming. But the hero of *Escape from Evil* was a real lord, not a lowly baron who had had little to do with society. And I had, after all, no real conception of such a man.

I had missed my comeout because of Papa's death, and since then I'd been completely occupied at making enough income to support our large household. But if I did not soon finish this book... Hence my trip to Lackington Allen's in the forlorn hope that I might find there some volume that would tell me how a gentleman thought, that would help bring my hero to life. But I couldn't simply ask a bookseller for such a book, not without the possibility of giving myself away. And among all these books, how could I find the right one?

I moved past the circular desk and on into the shelves, gazing at the titles as I passed. What was I to do? Where was I to look? A wave of weakness swept over me and I dabbed at my brow with my handkerchief. I could not afford to give way to the vapors. Too many people depended on me. But the thought of them all going hungry made the handkerchief slip from my trembling fingers to the floor where it settled by my wet half-boots.

I bent to retrieve it. Handkerchiefs cost money, after all, and it was money, or the lack thereof, that haunted my every moment. And then a pair of Wellingtons appeared beside me. Shining glossy Wellingtons that looked as if they'd never seen snow.

I looked up—and up. Past tan pantaloons and a coat of green Bedford cord and a brilliant white cravat—to a face that made my heart flutter in my bosom. The stranger was over six foot tall, with dark hair and dark eyes, handsome in a dangerous way. The way of a hero.

He stuck out a gloved hand. "May I assist you to rise?"

I took his hand. It wasn't proper, but I took it anyway. There was strength in it—and heat I could feel through both our gloves as he helped me to my feet.

"Do I know you?" I asked, though I knew I didn't. I had never had occasion to know a man like this. If I had, I would not have forgotten it. Not ever.

He shook his head, and his unruly dark hair brushed his cravat. "I'm afraid I haven't had the pleasure of meeting you," he drawled. "But I should very much like to."

He smiled. Strong white teeth, a kissable mouth. Color flooded my cheeks. What was I thinking? I knew nothing of kissable mouths. Nothing but what I wrote.

"You—you look like the hero of a romance," I stammered.

Now why had I said that? I shouldn't even be speaking to this man. He was a complete stranger, and yet I felt that somehow I knew him.

"I'm honored you should think so," he said with a little bow. "And since I *am* a hero, let me say that I see that something is amiss with you." He looked around and gave me the smile of a conspirator. "Perhaps you will let me ride to the rescue. If there is something I can do to help you, please, do tell me."

I hesitated. I am, after all, a well brought up young woman, not accustomed to speaking to strange men. I knew I should turn my back on him and proceed about my business. But this *was* my business, supporting my family, and here was the chance to learn what I needed. This man didn't know me. I didn't have to tell him why I wanted to know certain things, or about Lady Incognita. I didn't even have to tell him my name.

I looked down. He was still holding my hand! Regretfully, I withdrew my fingers from his. "Could you—that is, would you—" My tongue didn't want to work properly, but I forced myself to go on. It wasn't likely I'd ever have such an opportunity again. "Could you tell me what it's like to be a lord?"

His dark eyes sparkled. "You want to know what it's like to be me?"

My heart palpitated in my bosom. "Yes," I whispered. "Please."

He considered for a moment, his eyes focused on the distance. Then he smiled at me. "I'm not due at Brooks for some time yet." He looked around, but no one was paying us any mind. "Perhaps you'll allow me to walk you home. And on the way I can answer your questions."

I hesitated for only a moment. The man was a stranger, true, and if he walked me home, he would know where I lived, to say nothing of the impropriety of such a thing, letting a stranger escort me anywhere! I might not have a maid or any of the other accoutrements of a lady, but I knew what was proper. Still, I could dismiss him before we reached the house. And besides, I trusted him. I could not say why, but I trusted him completely. And so I put my gloved hand on the arm he offered me and let him lead me out.

❄ ❄ ❄

Some time later, we arrived at the corner of my street. He did not pause but turned at the proper place and moved toward my house. I did not ask how he knew which house to go to. And I did not feel threatened by his knowledge. By that time I felt that we'd known each other for a long time. And with what he'd told me about himself I was sure I could make my viscount come alive. *Escape from Evil* would be finished on time now. Our Christmas could be a truly merry one.

He escorted me up the walk to the door. "Thank you," I said. "You have been so kind. You've no idea how much this means to me."

A strange look crossed his face. "Perhaps I do."

There was that smile again. The rakish smile of a hero, yet somehow sad.

He took my hand in his again. "I ask only one thing of you."

"What is it?" My voice trembled, my heart palpitated as bad as any heroines.

"That you finish the book you are writing. Finish it before Christmas comes."

I swallowed my gasp, but a little squeak escaped me.

He smiled at me. "Yes, I know that you are Lady Incognita. I know that you are writing a romance of terror. I ask only that you finish it—before Christmas comes."

There was something in his eyes, something strange, almost desperate. What had this lord to be desperate about?

"Promise me," he repeated urgently, looking deep into my eyes. "It is of the utmost importance to me."

"I promise," I said, meaning it with all my heart. "I shall finish the book before Christmas. I promise."

The lines in his face relaxed. "Very good." Slowly he bent toward me. My eyes closed as his lips just brushed mine.

"Thank you," he said. "When your promise to me is kept, so shall mine to be kept to Melisandra."

My eyes flew open. "Melisandra? I didn't tell you—"

But he was gone. And in the fresh snow along our walk and outside our front door there was only one set of tracks—mine.

I went directly to my room and wrote until the evening meal. I would finish the book before Christmas if I had to write all night, every night. My promise would be kept. And so would my hero's.

Nina Coombs Pykare is a multi-published author of novels, novellas, short stories, articles, and puzzles and poems for children. She has also taught the novel writing workshop for Writer's Digest since the workshop's inception in 1988.

For almost three years she lived on a mountain in Tennessee with the love of her life. When he died, she returned to Ohio to be near her family, now numbering four sons and daughter, plus four grandsons and five granddaughters. Nina likes dogs, all kinds, and she's crazy about horses and the West, expecially Montana. She believes that love is the most important thing in the world.

The Legend of The Lost Bride comes to life in this tale of mystery and forgiveness. Ned must conquer his propensity for playing hide and seek from the parson's mousetrap in order to find true love and happiness.

Hide and Seek

Cathy Peper

Hiding

A blast of wind struck Worthing Abbey with enough force to shake the ancient panes of glass. Edward Worthing, Lord Peyton, glanced out the window. The clouds hung low in the sky, dark and brooding with the threat of snow. He shivered as another gust caused the house's massive oak-hewn timbers to groan in protest. Two nights before Christmas wasn't the best time for outdoor activities, but he had to get away from Lady Mary and Miss Coleman. He supposed he could go up in the attic, but he'd had a horror of the place since he was ten years old. Seeing only one other avenue of escape, Lord Peyton, better known as Ned to his friends, ducked into the library and stood with his ear to the door. He barely dared to breathe until the pair of young women passed by. Only when Lady Mary's strident tones had faded into the distance did he exhale with a whoosh and allow his tall frame to sag against the stalwart walnut paneling. He was deuced weary of being pursued.

"Hiding from someone?" a voice piped up, shattering the comfortable illusion that he was alone. His little sister, Lady Rachel, or Rae, for short, sat curled in an oversized leather chair, a book clutched in her hand.

"Brat," he said, sauntering into the room. Envious of her peace and quiet, he sprawled into the chair next to hers. "Lady Mary is on the prowl again. I cannot imagine why Mother invited her here."

"She wants you to marry her."

"No." Ned shook his head. "Mary may be the well-dowered daughter of a duke, but not even that can compensate for her haughty personality. Mama has her faults, but she wants the best for me."

Rae continued to regard him dubiously. "Then why does she hold a Christmas house party every year where the only guests are eligible young women?"

"Indeed. Answer that, by all means." Another voice, thick with amusement, spoke from above their heads.

"Clay." Ned arched his neck until he could see his friend, Barclay Biddle-combe, where he stood in the gallery that overlooked the library. "Have you been here all the while?"

"Long enough to see you looking as beleaguered as a fox on hunting day. Why do you let her do it?"

"Do what?" asked Ned.   ·

"Host these infamous gatherings," said Clay. "One of these days you are certain to be caught in the parson's mousetrap."

Ned shrugged. "I have to marry sometime. Why not let Mama put the girls through their paces first? Besides, I'm in little danger of actually getting leg-shackled. Mama is too particular."

"Are you certain?" Rae asked. "She seems delighted to have Lady Mary here. So much so, she barely kicked up a dust when Lady Catherine accepted a proposal the week before we left London."

"Leaving the field to Lady Mary and Miss Eliza Coleman," Ned mused, lungs constricting. Rae had a valid point. "Well, Lady Mary will never be my bride," he insisted. He thought it no more likely that he would wed Miss Cole-man either, but since she was a pleasant, soft-spoken girl, he kept this thought to himself. Admirable as she might be, he'd felt no special spark in her pres-ence and did not intend to marry for any reason other than love. He'd seen enough of his parents' fighting to be disillusioned about marriages of conven-ience.

Suddenly a loud banging sounded down the hall, followed by pounding footsteps. Ned's anxiety returned. Had Lady Mary tracked him to the library after all?

"Lord Holbrook! Lady Holbrook!" an excited voice called from just out-side the room. "He's coming! He's coming! We will all be murdered in our beds!"

Rae rolled her eyes. "Percy. He wants Mama and Papa."

Ned muttered an expletive under his breath, then shot a glance of apology up at Clay. "Every family has eccentrics," he said by way of explanation. Knowing how angry his father would be if he were disturbed, Ned stepped out of his sanctuary and intercepted his distant cousin, Percy Worthing, the local vicar. A hand on the smaller man's shoulder brought him to an abrupt halt. "Put a damper on it, Percy."

"But Napoleon is here! The invasion army has landed." Percy tried to shake free of Ned's hold. "I warned your father, but he wouldn't listen."

Ned frowned. Percy had long been obsessed with the fear of a French inva-sion, though the likelihood of such an event had faded years earlier. Neverthe-less, as long as the two countries were still at war, Ned supposed anything was possible. "I seriously doubt this is an invasion, Percy," he said. "What did you see?"

Percy swallowed, the fear in his eyes as patent as it was unwarranted. "A boat, directly off the coast."

Ned relaxed. "Smugglers."

"No!" Percy shook his head. "The free traders are not out tonight. Don't ask me how I know that," he added, apparently anticipating Ned's next question. "Something is amiss. I feel it in my bones."

Ned frowned, recalling how inhospitable the weather had appeared when he'd considered stepping outside to escape Lady Mary. Could Percy really have seen a ship down in the bay?

Rae touched his arm. "Whoever is out there may be in trouble."

"Agreed," Ned replied, though he hated to fall in with the delusion of his harebrained cousin. "I should investigate. Rae, start the servants heating water and tell Mama to prepare some rooms, just in case. We may be bringing in wounded."

"I'm with you," Clay said, hurrying down the library stairs to join them.

Ned nodded and turned to Percy. "Show me this ship."

"But Lord Holbrook—"

"My mother will tell my father," Ned said, though he doubted it. His parents rarely exchanged more than a few words. The earl was probably three sheets to the wind by now anyway and in no condition to provide much help.

"I spotted the ship from the vicarage, but you should be able to see it from the cliff tower." Percy unwrapped the muffler from around his neck and handed it to his cousin. "I'm not going back out there."

Ned draped the damp wool around his throat as he strode into the hall. "Potts!" he shouted for the butler. "We may have a ship wrecked down in the cove." Ignoring Percy, who still clung to his heels, he continued his instructions to the servant. "Have Jim and Tom meet us on the beach. Bring blankets!"

Moments after plunging into the brewing storm, Ned regretted his impetuousness. Everyone knew Percy was a loose screw. He'd probably imagined the whole thing, and Ned had fallen for it like a nodcock. Tucking his hands under his arms, Ned lowered his head into the razor-sharp wind and hurried to the tower. His grandfather had built the folly right on the edge of the cliff, providing a spectacular view of the shore below.

"There she is!" Clay pointed toward a smudge of pale gray marring the slate blue of the angry sea. "She's down."

"It's a difficult climb from here," Ned told his friend.

"*I'll* follow *your* lead," Clay said with a wink.

Though his teeth chattered from cold, Ned grinned as he acknowledged Clay's hit. When they were at school together, Clay had usually been the leader. Ned had been a relative latecomer to Eton, forced into the harsh reality of the public school system only after the death of his older brother. Lady Holbrook had wanted Ned educated at home, but Lord Holbrook had insisted that his heir attend Eton and Oxford, as all the earls had before him. Ned had been something of an outcast when he'd arrived at Eton as a strapping twelve-year-old, but fortunately for him, because of his size, not even the resident bullies had wanted to take him on. After he'd helped Clay out of a tight spot, the two boys had become fast friends.

"Come on then," Ned said, taking off at a lope. Sleet obscured his vision and the steep incline was treacherous in the icy conditions, but Ned never slackened his pace. Clay slid once, nearly sending both men over the edge, but they made it down without further mishap. As soon as they reached the rocky level ground of the beach, Ned sprinted across it. Icy cold waves lapped at his feet. He could see the ship clearly now, outlined against the gray of the sky. Her mast had broken and the sail hung at a drunken angle. A few sailors struggled in the surf, their cries for help nearly lost in the howling wind.

"Wait here for the footmen to arrive," Ned yelled to Clay.

"What are you going to do?"

"Get these men to shore and search for other survivors."

Clay glanced across the roiling sea, his face set in grim lines. "I'll help you."

"No. I've been swimming these waters all my life, Clay. I know what I'm doing."

"I'll assist the sailors," Clay insisted. "You swim out to the boat."

Realizing his friend wouldn't be swayed, Ned nodded and headed for the ship, charging knee deep into the foam. The water was choppy and icy cold, but it wasn't the discomfort or the danger that made him pull up short. To his right, he glimpsed a shadowy figure, almost indistinct in the darkness. His heart, which had been racing since his near plummet from the cliff, stalled, then began to beat erratically. Could it be? A cloaked silhouette stood at the edge of the water, her white face ringed by a spectral hood. Ice pellets stung Ned's eyes, but his focus never faltered. The Lost Bride! It had been years since he'd seen her, years during which he'd almost convinced himself he had imagined the whole incident, but the sight of her now brought it all back to him in chilling detail. He had seen her on the cliff then, in the half-light of dawn, pacing back and forth with her gown swirling around her ankles. The image had haunted him. Almost forgetting the peril of the shipwrecked passengers, he started for the specter.

"Lady," he called, reaching an arm out toward her. "You've come back."

She turned at the sound of his voice and stumbled in his direction. "Thank God you found us! Please help me."

Wondering if it were he, and not Percy, who was around the bend, Ned braced himself for the heart-stopping chill of a ghost's insubstantial hand. When the very solid weight of a waterlogged female plowed into him, he staggered, though he topped the young woman by nearly a foot. She was certainly no ghost!

"My father is still on the boat, as are a few of the sailors, but I pulled my mother to safety." She tilted her head toward the beach, drawing Ned's attention to another dark-clad figure kneeling on the rock.

He gripped the young woman's shoulders. "I'll find your father," he promised.

"No," she said firmly. "I'm coming with you."

"It's too dangerous."

"That's why I'm coming. I will not allow my father to die out there."

"I told you I would—" She brushed past him, before he could finish, and plunged into the water.

"Let her go," the girl's mother said, pulling herself to her feet. "Isabel has always gone her own way. But help her. Please help her to find him."

"I will," he said. "Will you be all right here?"

"Yes," she said impatiently. "Please go!"

Again he charged into the sea. The fierce cold numbed his body, and he figured he would only be able to make it out to the ship once. Had Isabel made it? She had already fought her way to shore once, surely she must have faltered by now. He fought against an unusual wave of grief, akin to what he had felt toward the Lost Bride. If only Isabel had listened to him.

By the time Ned reached the wreck, he was shaking uncontrollably. When he tried to pull himself up onto the boat, his fingers could not maintain their grip, and he fell back into the churning sea. As he surfaced, he heard a cry for help. He recognized Isabel's voice, though it sounded rough with strain.

"Where are you?" he called, frantic.

"Here!" she called.

The sound came from his left, and as Ned turned, he saw her clinging to a piece of planking. A man lay across the board, his dark hair pasted to his skull.

"There's no one on the ship," she gasped. "I already checked. My father must have hit his head. I got him this far, but I haven't the strength to bring him to shore."

"I'll take him," Ned said. "But you must come, too. Do not even think of slipping away again. I'll not have your death on my conscience."

She nodded, her gray eyes wide in a small, pointed face. They were beautiful eyes, Ned thought, but not having time to dwell on them, he pulled for the beach. The weight of the unconscious man and the young woman dragged at him, but the groaning of the ship's timbers as it continued its inevitable descent into the sea spurred him to greater effort. Waves crashed over their heads. The shore seemed to grow farther and farther away with every stroke.

"Hang on Isabel," he yelled back to the girl, unsure if he was talking to her or himself.

When he heard his name being called, he realized he must be close to the shore. That knowledge, as well as his desire to know more about the girl, compelled him to push his exhausted body forward. Just when he thought he would have to send Isabel on alone, he felt the rasp of the shingle against his frigid skin. Seconds later, arms pulled him from the water and wrapped warm blankets around his drenched clothing. He shook so hard he could scarcely stand, but he saw that the others were being cared for too.

"That was a brave thing you did, old man." Clay spoke softly in his ear.

"Foolish, perhaps," Ned replied, still choking up water.

"Never that," Isabel said. She turned from her mother's side to stare up at him, her luminous eyes shining.

Ned returned her gaze. Even shivering and drenched with sea water, she was pretty, with a dainty build and elfin features. He felt inexplicably drawn to her, more so than to anyone else in his life. However, that was only because of what they had been through together, he assured himself.

She smiled tremulously. "How can I ever thank you? You saved not only my life, but my father's as well."

Embarrassed by all the fuss, Ned shrugged. Turning from the girl to her father, he bent over the elderly man. Blood flowed sluggishly from an ugly cut on the man's forehead, but there were no other obvious injuries. He called for his footmen. "Tom, Jim, come give me a hand. We need to get these people up to the house before we all catch our deaths."

❄ ❋ ❄

An hour later, after a steaming bath, hot mulled wine, and a change of clothes, Ned could still feel the intensity of the life-and-death struggle surging through his veins. But he wasn't bored. Isabel, the water waif, piqued his interest as no woman had in years. She certainly put the matrimonial candidates his mother handpicked for him to shame. Her presence even made facing his parents' inevitable disapproval worthwhile. Grimacing at that thought, he left his chamber and headed downstairs.

He found everyone except his father assembled in the drawing room. His mother and Rae drew him aside the moment he appeared, but a quick glance at Isabel assured him that she had been given dry clothes. She wore one of Rae's gowns, a simple, long-sleeved frock of pale gray, pinned at the waist to keep her from tripping over the hem. Damp, ash-brown hair tumbled to her shoulders and her gray eyes gleamed nearly silver in the candlelight.

"They cannot stay here," his mother whispered in his ear. "Do you know who they are?"

"No," Ned replied, surprised by her words. "Have the sailors been seen to?"

"They were taken below stairs," Rae said, then turned to her mother. "Mama, it *is* Christmas."

"We can scarcely throw an injured man into the street in any event," Ned added.

"He can go to the village inn," Lady Holbrook insisted. "That man lying upstairs in *my* house is none other than Lord Stephen Tremayne!"

Involuntarily, Ned glanced over at the Tremayne women. He had heard the baron's name bandied about when he was a boy, though he couldn't recall the exact details. Lady Tremayne clutched at her daughter's sleeve, her face pinched and anxious. Isabel, however, remained unbowed, her bearing regal despite her lack of inches.

"I tell you," Lady Holbrook said. "I will not stand for it!"

"What the devil is going on here?" A new voice, slurred with drink, but nonetheless authoritative, cut through the commotion. "Can a man not find a measure of peace during the holidays?"

"Father." Ned swallowed. His throat felt raw from saltwater exposure. "A ship foundered in the bay. We have taken in the survivors. All is under control."

"Well then..." Lord Holbrook began to drift away, but his wife forestalled him.

"Lawrence, they must go." She grabbed her husband's arm. "They are *Tremaynes*."

"Tremaynes? Lord Stephen Tremayne is here at the Abbey?" Lord Holbrook's voice rose with astonishment and a hint of something else that Ned could not identify. "I must see him!"

"Impossible," Lady Holbrook snapped. "He suffered a head injury in the accident and has yet to awaken."

"Then what choice do we have but to let him stay?" Lord Holbrook drawled. "Where is your Christian charity? Does it not extend to rakes?"

"Rakes? Byron is a rake. Tremayne is a byword for every indecency— gaming, dueling, birds of paradise." Lady Holbrook made the last accusation with a sideways glance at Rae. "We are responsible not only for Rachel's safety, but for our other young guests as well."

"The man is unconscious, my dear. I think the girls' reputations are safe for the nonce."

"If Lady Mary or Miss Coleman object, they can leave." Ned didn't care if he sounded rude.

"But—" Lady Holbrook stammered.

"He stays, Freddie," Lord Holbrook told his wife in a tone of finality.

Ned glanced at him in astonishment. His father rarely used that tone, but when he did, no one overruled him. "Shall we get something to eat then?" Ned suggested, hoping to divert his mother's attention. "Near drowning makes a man mighty sharp set."

At that moment, Clay appeared in the doorway to announce that the servants had set up a cold collation in the dining room. The others filed out of the room at once, leaving only Isabel, Clay, and Ned.

"I must go to my father," Isabel said with a wan smile. "*If* we are to stay, that is."

"Of course, you are to stay." Ned pressed her hand in reassurance. "I will have a tray sent up for you."

"Thank you. I am a trifle peckish. Actually, I could eat a horse," she murmured before sweeping from the room.

Clay chuckled behind his hand. "What a night," he said, clapping Ned on the back. "But look at the bright side."

"The bright side?" Ned asked, dragging his eyes reluctantly away from the departing Isabel. "And what might that be?"

"Lady Mary is sure to set her cap for you now." Clay chuckled again. "Not even the daughter of a duke can resist a hero."

The Kiss

Isabel blinked back tears as she gazed down at her father. The doctor had been summoned, but she doubted he would arrive until after the storm broke. It scared her to see her father so pale, his only movement the gentle rise and fall of his chest. The cut over his eye had been bandaged, but he still looked very different from the vital man she knew so well. He looked...old. He was old, of course. But Isabel had never thought of him that way until now.

Nor did she think of him as a rake, though she had heard the tales, some of them from her father's own lips. Apparently, his reputation remained strong, even after twenty years of marriage and relative seclusion in the wilds of Cornwall. She stabbed at a chunk of chicken with her fork, glad that Lady Rachel, rather than Lady Holbrook, had brought up a tray. The Countess was just the sort of high-stickler she deplored, the type that placed a higher value on propriety than human kindness. Isabel swallowed. The food was good and she was hungry, but the emotional upheaval of the last few hours made it difficult to eat. Her temples throbbed, and she was grateful that Lady Rachel, despite her obvious curiosity about the notorious visitor, had not lingered. The younger girl had stayed only long enough to inform Isabel that a servant would be sent to relieve her in a few hours.

Isabel sighed. She did need rest. But she also needed some time alone with her father, time to assure herself he would be all right. Time to acknowledge the guilt she felt over his injury. She had been at the helm when the mast broke. In addition, had it not been for her, they wouldn't have even been near the treacherous Sussex coast when the storm erupted. Of course, had her parents not been too busy brangling to notice the danger, her father, a more experienced sailor, would have taken the wheel from her, perhaps preventing the accident altogether. As it was, she could only be grateful that no one had perished in the wreck. No one, other than her father, had even been seriously hurt.

Two hours later, the promised servant knocked on the door. "Miss? I can take over now."

A quick glance at her father showed Isabel that his condition had not changed. She vacated her place beside him, thanked the maid, and headed toward the comfortable room Lady Rachel had shown her earlier. The bed was hung with rose damask and looked inviting, but tired as she was, Isabel knew she would be unable to sleep. Her body ached with the effects of unaccustomed exertion and an assortment of scrapes and bruises. Worry for her father, as well as a lingering feeling of remorse and resentment, clouded her mind. Worst of all, however, was the continued fascination she felt for Lord Peyton, the man who had saved her life, but also the man who had brought her to this pass. Had it not been for her own lovelorn curiosity, she would not have taken the ship in so close to shore. But she had wanted to catch a glimpse of the fabled Worthing Abbey, acknowledged for both its architectural beauty and the cachet of being the home of London's premier catch.

Well, she had seen it all right. She was even a guest in its time-honored chambers. However, now she owed Lord Peyton her life, in addition to having given him her heart several months ago. She felt almost as though a trap were closing around her. Trying to convince herself she felt nothing but a *tendre* toward him did little to soothe her. She needed fresh air, but considering the weather, decided to settle for a walk in the conservatory. Lady Rachel had pointed out the glass enclosure at the end of the west wing when she'd shown Isabel and her mother to their rooms.

After strolling around the conservatory's perimeter, Isabel sat upon a stone bench near the fountain and closed her eyes. She took a deep breath of humid air. In a few minutes she would return to her room and get some sleep.

The next thing she knew, she felt a hand upon her shoulder and heard the sound of a faintly amused masculine voice. Lord Peyton's voice. She opened her eyes to see him standing in front of her. "My lord!"

A hint of shadow touched his dark blue eyes, though his lips curled in a smile as he gestured toward the bench. "May I?" Without waiting for her reply, he sat and brushed a flower petal from his dressing gown. "Difficulty sleeping?" he asked.

She nodded, unwilling to admit that she hadn't even turned back the covers on her bed.

He propped his shoulder against the fountain. "You need not be ashamed to be afraid. I, too, can still feel the sea's icy grasp."

"I'm not afraid."

"Why come here, then? Why not stay in your room?"

"This is the next best thing to being outside." To her annoyance, he kept silent, his dark eyes seeming to bore into her very soul. "I need fresh air when I'm troubled."

"Ah, then you do admit to being troubled, though not afraid."

"Of course I'm troubled," she snapped. "My father is no longer young. He may fall ill from exposure even if the blow to his head leaves no adverse effects."

"By going back for him you probably saved his life, though at great risk to your own. You have done everything you can, Miss Tremayne."

"I know." She bowed her head, studying the scarlet embroidery on his slippers. The fancy footwear looked rather incongruous on his large feet. Of course, she was not accustomed to seeing men in their nightclothes. The impropriety of their situation struck her suddenly, making her mouth go dry.

"What were you doing out on such a night anyway?" Lord Peyton asked.

She swallowed. She couldn't bear it if he guessed she'd been spying on him. "The storm was unexpected," she began, trying to think of a plausible explanation for their presence in his cove.

"But why were you at sea?" he persisted. "Were you travelling somewhere for Christmas?"

"Yes, of course." She jumped on the idea. "We usually spend Christmas at Tremayne House, but this year we decided to do something different. Father and I love to sail."

Curling his legs beneath him, Ned swiveled to face her. "Have we met previously?" he asked. "You seem familiar."

His silk banyon gaped at the throat, exposing an inch of hair-sprinkled chest. Fascinated by this rare glimpse of masculinity, Isabel fought to concentrate on what he was saying. She was disappointed but not surprised to realize he did not remember her. "We met at Lady Finchley's alfresco breakfast," she said. "You told a tale about smugglers."

"Of course, Mad Jack." He smacked his knee. "I had just uncovered that little gem of a tale. Can you believe that the particulars of his exploits were recorded by one of my ancestors? I found the book here at the Abbey." He gave her a sheepish grin. "Too late, then, to try to conceal my shocking bluestocking tendencies from you."

She returned his smile. "I thought only women were reviled for scholarly pursuits."

"Untrue. Men can suffer just as much abuse. I'm no scholar, though. Just ask my father. He's been working on a serious study of the Worthing family these past ten years. I dabble."

Though the tone was light, Isabel thought she caught a hint of pain underneath. "I enjoyed your story," she said. "You told it well."

The smile flashed again. "You flatter me."

Isabel could tell by the light in his eyes, however, that he agreed with her assessment. "Not at all," she replied demurely. Thinking back to that sunny afternoon, she recalled how smitten she had been with him. Entranced by his way with words, as well as his undeniably handsome exterior, she had watched him carefully the rest of the season. Women flocked to him in droves, and even men seemed to seek him out. He might be lacking in the eyes of his father, but the rest of the world disagreed. The last thing he needed was more adulation adding to his conceit. Still, he had a way about him...

In a distant part of the house, a clock chimed midnight. Isabel started, as if a spell had been broken. She stood, nearly tripping over her skirt in her haste. "It's late," she said.

"It's Christmas Eve," Peyton said, slowly rising to his feet. "I must claim a forfeit."

"A forfeit? What do you mean?"

He pointed toward the fountain. Sprigs of greenery, including the distinc-tive white-berried mistletoe, were wrapped around the pinnacle. "Don't tell me you sat here unaware of the lure that hung over your head?"

Her eyes widened as he stepped closer. *He was going to kiss her.* As his chest filled her field of vision, the scent of sandalwood mingled with the earthy smell of growing things. She stood on tiptoe and braced herself against his solid frame.

"Isabel," he muttered as he dipped his head.

"Edward," she gasped as his mouth brushed feather-light against hers. His name sounded foreign on her lips, as shocking, almost, as the weakness that filled her limbs. When he finally drew away, plucking a berry off the vine, she nearly cried out in protest.

"One less for the others," he murmured.

Isabel took a steadying breath and felt the ground solidify beneath her feet once more. "You really believe the mistletoe loses its powers once all the ber-ries are gone?"

"Absolutely."

She tilted her head back to see his face. "You speak with such passion" she whispered. "One might be tempted to think you believe the things you say."

He looked faintly uneasy, as if he were a small boy caught in a misdeed. "And if I do believe them? What then?"

"Then I pronounce you a dreamer," she teased.

"Is that so wrong?" He laughed, pressing the berry into her palm just before he took his leave.

"I suppose not," Isabel murmured as he disappeared from view. She opened her hand and studied the berry, knowing she would keep it forever. It might be all she would ever have of him.

The Lost Bride

The next morning Ned led a party into the woods to bring in the Yule log. To his delight, Isabel accompanied them, but he was too involved with his du-ties as host to speak to her privately. He hoped to do so when they returned to the house, but his mother caught him as the log was carried inside and wedged into the huge fireplace at the end of the hall.

"Ned, I need to speak with you," she said.

Ned winced and excused himself from the company.

"Yes?" he asked, hoping the edge to his voice wasn't as apparent to his mother as it was to him. Out of the corner of his eye, he watched Isabel drift away from the crowd and head back upstairs, probably to check on her father.

"Not here," Lady Holbrook said. "Somewhere private." She led him to the Egyptian saloon and directed him to sit upon a Turkish ottoman while she re-clined upon a couch. "It has come to my attention that you have been showing an inordinate interest in the Tremayne chit. You must understand that an alliance there will not be tolerated."

"Why not, Mother?" he asked, feeling ill at ease in the ornately decorated room. "She is perfectly eligible."

"Eligible! The Tremaynes have been under the hatches for decades. They gained their wealth through piracy, but have never been able to hold on to their money. The current Lord Tremayne came into the title at the age of two-and-twenty and immediately proceeded to squander what little was left of the family fortune."

"I understand there is a family estate," Ned said, remembering that Isabel had told him that they usually spent Christmas at Tremayne House.

"Yes," his mother grudgingly admitted. "In the wilds of Cornwall. It must be entailed or it would be gone, too, by now. It will do the daughter no good. And the mother is a provincial Nobody."

"Sounds as though you have worn out another copy of Debrett's peerage," Ned murmured. "And all because I paid some attention to Isabel?"

Lady Holbrook folded her arms across her chest. "I'm always looking out for your well-being."

"Doing it a bit too brown, Mama. Besides, I have no need to hang out for a rich wife."

"Perhaps not, but why marry a poor girl? If Lady Mary is not to your taste, and indeed, she may be too high in the instep, I will endeavor to do better next year."

Ned pushed up from the ottoman with a sigh. "You do that, Mama."

"Where are you going?" Lady Holbrook demanded.

"Back to my guests. Father is about to light the Yule log."

"Then I suppose we had best go." Lady Holbrook rose and twitched her skirt into place. "Have I made myself clear, Ned?"

"Excessively." He turned to leave, but she caught his arm and stared at him through narrowed eyes.

"Was it all a hum, then?" she asked. "A gentle warning to Lady Mary that she should not expect an offer?"

"We must hurry or risk missing the festivities," he said, ignoring her probing.

With a sniff, Lady Holbrook preceded him out the door. "I hope you know what is due your name," she said over her shoulder.

Ned's hand tightened slightly around her elbow, though he kept his voice low. "How could I forget?" He made his way through the crowd, never a difficult feat for a man of his size, not stopping until he reached his sister's side. "Is Father here yet? He usually lights the Yule."

"I believe he has gone upstairs," Rae replied, her eyes wide with curiosity. "Lord Tremayne has regained consciousness."

❄ ❄ ❄

Isabel had not planned to go downstairs for Christmas Eve dinner, but to her astonished delight, when she had returned to her father's bedside after bringing in the Yule Log, she had found him awake and alert. A weight of guilt slid off her shoulders as she saw him sitting up in bed, his gray eyes, so like her own, as bright as ever.

"Father!" she cried, crossing the room and taking his hand in hers. She bowed her head, falling silent as relief clogged her throat.

Her father patted her back for a moment before easing her up. "Don't make a fuss, Kitten," he said. "I'm fine as fivepence."

His apparent good health notwithstanding, Isabel had wanted to remain by his side, but her father insisted she go down to dinner. Her mother, who had recovered her equanimity with her husband's return to health, urged her to go as well.

"We have much to be thankful for," Lady Tremayne had added, with a loving look toward her spouse.

So Isabel had borrowed a willow-green gown from Rae, stuck a sprig of holly in her upswept curls, and gathered in the salon, with the rest of the guests, before dinner. Now, as she sipped her sherry, she wondered how her parents could be arguing one moment and smelling of April and May the next.

Dinner was an elaborate and traditional affair with a roasted boar's head and a peacock set out in all its glory. Numerous side dishes included plum pudding, eel, a bisque of pigeons, and after all the other courses were removed, cups of steaming punch.

After eating, the guests retired to the hall to sit in front of the roaring fire and swap stories. The enormous Yule log crackled cheerfully in the hearth where it would burn until Twelfth Night, the close of the holiday season, highlighted at Worthing Abbey with a fancy dress ball. Finally, a sliver would be taken from the log to use to light the next year's Yule. As everyone settled into chairs, all eyes turned to Lord Peyton, for although ostensibly the floor was open to anyone with a story to tell, the viscount was well known for his dramatic flair.

Isabel chose a wing-backed chair on the outskirts of the room. The other women sat near the fire, with the exception of Miss Coleman, who found a place beside Mr. Biddlecombe. Lord Holbrook and the vicar also kept in the background, but Lord Peyton took center stage. He wore a close-fitting double-breasted coat of Sardinian blue and matching pantaloons. His waistcoat was deep red, providing a sharp contrast to his snowy white cravat. He looked complete to a shade, reminding Isabel why he was considered such a prize catch on the Marriage Mart by mothers and daughters alike. His mother's holiday house parties were legendary in London, but even with the *crème de la crème* assembled every year for his inspection, Lord Peyton remained a bachelor. With a pang, Isabel acknowledged that he was unlikely to break tradition and ally himself with the modestly dowered daughter of a minor noble

nan, particularly when that nobleman had carved a swath of scandal in his
/outh. No, if she allowed herself to place any significance on his kiss, she
vould end up with a broken heart, instead of one that was merely bruised.

"I thought I would begin tonight with a sad story," Lord Peyton began, in-
errupting Isabel's thoughts. "I first heard the tale of the Lost Bride as a boy,
ut it remains a favorite to this day. "

Rae made a slight sound of protest. "Really, Ned, after what happened I
on't think—"

Peyton silenced her with a quick shake of his head, then swept the audience
vith his gaze before trying again. "Long ago a young man fell in love with a
eautiful woman. When she accepted his proposal, the fellow was ecstatic. On
heir wedding day, the bride dressed herself in silk and lace in honor of being
oined forever to the man she loved."

Clay mumbled something to Miss Coleman, and she giggled.

"The man and woman celebrated their nuptials with friends and family,"
he viscount went on. "People said they had never seen such a lovely bride.
Afterward, they hosted an enormous wedding breakfast. At the breakfast,
omeone suggested a game of hide-and-seek. The groom consented and sent
is bride off to hide, not knowing he would never see her again."

Isabel gave a soft gasp. At the sound, Peyton's eyes met hers. He held her
;aze, frowning, and Isabel felt singed by his stare.

"The wedding party searched high and low for the bride, but never found
er," Lord Peyton continued after a moment. "Eventually, they gave up. As the
/ears passed, rumors arose that she hadn't been human at all. That she had
een one of the Fairy Folk, and they had come to take her home."

Isabel suppressed her gasp this time. In Cornwall the fairies were known as
ixies, and although she had never seen one, on several occasions she thought
he had felt their presence when she was alone. "How is that possible?" she
lurted out, seeking reassurance from Lord Peyton that such a thing could not
appen.

"She may have been a changeling," he replied. "A fairy child given to hu-
nans to raise. Whatever she was, the groom did not remarry. How could he?
Ie could never find another to match her. So he grew old, and rather vague, as
f part of him had already gone to join her." A twig snapped in the grate, send-
ng a shower of sparks on the hearth. It was the only sound in the room as eve-
yone, even Clay, focused their attention on Lord Peyton. "Many years later
nother generation set upon a game of exploration. They found an old trunk in
 little used room of the great old house and opened it to see what was inside.
magine their horror when they found the bones of the Lost Bride, still draped
n her lace and silk. It seems she had hidden herself in the trunk and the lid had
ome down on her, knocking her unconscious. By the time she came to, the
thers had stopped looking for her. Her cries for help went unheard."

For a moment, no one spoke. Then Mr. Worthing, the vicar, cleared his throat. "Well, dear me, cousin…" His voice trailed off, then he tried again "Perhaps we should have another tale. Of the Christ child, this time."

"As you wish." Lord Peyton eased his long length back in his chair.

"But what happened to the groom?" Isabel asked. "How horrible it must have been for him!"

"Undoubtedly so," Lord Peyton agreed. "But he had his answer. He no longer had to wonder what had become of his bride."

"But did he really know?" asked Clay. "Perhaps someone killed her and stuffed her in that trunk."

Miss Coleman giggled again.

Rae tugged her shawl closer. "That story gives me a fit of the dismals. And when I recall--"

"I think anyone would be blue-deviled after such a tale," Mr. Worthing said repressively, cutting Rae short. Heading off anyone else, he began: "Once upon a time, in the city of David…"

Although Isabel remained focused on Lord Peyton's tale, she closed her eyes and tried to listen to the vicar. His pleasant voice lacked the power of the viscount's, still, the familiar story of the miracle birth soothed her, eventually erasing the tension evoked earlier by Lord Peyton. The telling of ghost stories was a popular Christmas pastime, she knew, but they had always frightened her. She hoped there was no truth to this particularly sad one. Lord Peyton had told the tale with conviction, however, his blue gaze resting on her several times as he spoke. She shivered as she recalled the unfathomable look in his eyes. Had he been trying to warn her off? Feeling cold so far from the fire, she stood and wandered closer to the flames. She empathized with the bridegroom in the story. She, too, had given her heart to a lost cause. Feeling the weight of Lord Peyton's stare on her once more, she turned to find him watching her, a brooding look on his handsome face. He looked so distraught that her first thought was to go to him, but as she took a step in his direction, his expression hardened. The vulnerable curve of his mouth curled into a sneer as he turned his back on her and offered his arm to Lady Mary. Chilled, in spite of the fire Isabel froze, watching them walk out of the room. She felt more alone than ever before in her life.

Christmas Day

Christmas day dawned bright and sunny, but after morning services in the village church, flurries dusted a dry powder over the ice-laden snow from the storm. The Worthings and their guests spent the day quietly. After the fanfare of Christmas Eve, Lady Holbrook liked to keep things simple. No activities were ever scheduled. Food from the night before was left out in the dining room and everyone was instructed to help himself. Ned usually gave each of his would-be wives a small gift—his way of letting them know not to expect anything else of him.

This year he had bought fans, three in all, each painted with a different flower. He had already given Lady Mary the one with a rose, and Miss Coleman the one sporting a daisy. He sat now in the library with the bluebell fan spread across his lap, tapping idly at the delicately carved ivory sticks. He'd originally intended it for Lady Catherine, but since she'd become engaged three weeks earlier and had not even attended his mother's party, she had no need of it now. Should he give the extra fan to Isabel?

Irritated, Ned snapped the fan closed and tossed it on the desk, heedless that such cavalier treatment might well shatter it. He crossed his legs in front of him and stared down at the toes of his well-shined boots. Last night, as he was telling the tale of the Lost Bride, the memory of when he had first met Isabel had struck him with a powerful force. It was at Lady Finchley's picnic, as Isabel had claimed. He had told a story then, too, and she had gazed at him with the same admiration she had shown last night. He was unsure why he had forgotten her. The breakfast had been in early summer—June, he thought. Since then, he must have seen her at other ton functions. Perhaps the innocent longing in her gaze had sent him scurrying away posthaste. Whatever the reason, the fact remained that her presence here was too coincidental to be an accident. She had followed him, sure as the sun followed the stars.

Reaching a decision, Ned rose, slid the fan into his breast pocket and went in search of his most bothersome guest. He spotted her cloaked figure strolling down by the shore, along the shingle.

"Nice morning for a walk," he commented as he drew alongside her.

She smiled as she looked up at him. "I like being outside."

They strolled for a few moments in silence, but finally Ned could no longer postpone what he had come to see as a rather unpleasant duty. He drew to an abrupt halt, causing Isabel to pause as well and glance at him with curiosity. "Here." He handed her the fan. "I brought you something. Happy Christmas."

"How lovely." She traced the bluebell design with her finger. "I have nothing for you, I fear."

"Don't you?" he asked, a bit more harshly than he intended. "Did you not expect to see me when you came sailing into my cove?"

Her cheeks were already red with cold, but they turned a shade pinker at his accusation. "I…" She hesitated. "I never thought to actually meet you."

"But you did sail here deliberately?" he persisted.

Isabel ducked her head. "I wanted to see where you lived," she admitted in a small voice.

Ned closed his eyes as she confirmed his suspicions. "And you crashed your boat to have an excuse to come ashore and join my mother's yearly gathering of potential wives for me."

Her head came up at that, her gray eyes as frigid as the waves lapping the shore. "If you believe I risked my own life, not to mention that of my parents, to join your stupid party, then you are more of a coxcomb than even I thought."

"It wouldn't be the first time a girl has tossed her handkerchief at my feet," he said, feeling rather foolish. How had she turned the tables on him? She made it seem as though *he* were in the wrong.

"Well, don't bother picking up my handkerchief," she snapped. "My parents and I will remove to the village inn tomorrow. We can stay there until my father is well enough to travel."

When she held out the fan to him, Ned glanced at it, then raised his gaze to her stormy eyes. "Keep it," he snarled.

Isabel raised a brow. "In remembrance of this visit? No, I think not."

"Then throw it into the sea for all I care," Ned responded. A silence fell between them again, but this time it was hostile rather than amicable. "See here." He cleared his throat. "There is no need for you to stay in the village. We have plenty of room at the Abbey."

"Really? I'd rather find shelter in the stable. Besides," she added sarcastically, "think of your sister. My father is awake now and a threat to her innocence."

"You think to mock me, but he does have a reputation."

"Aye, and blood will tell. That *is* what you are thinking, is it not? That I'm just like my father?"

The hood of her cloak blew back, exposing her ash brown hair. She had styled it simply, pulling it into a coil at the nape of her neck. The look accentuated her widow's peak and the brilliance of her eyes. Though not a classic beauty, she had a vitality that transfixed him. Nevertheless, she had chased him, just like the others. If only she could have been different!

"I thought you cared for me," she said when he didn't speak. "That night when you kissed me under the mistletoe—did it mean nothing to you?"

"I've kissed dozens of girls under the mistletoe," he said wearily, thinking of the scores of simpering young women who had tried to entice him, each hoping she would become his wife. Then he thought about the night when he'd kissed Isabel. She had looked so forlorn, exhaustion and concern for her father etched on her brow. "Isabel—"

But she wasn't listening. She'd turned and was scrambling up the cliff, taking the slick slope far too quickly. Ned held his breath until she reached the safety of the tower. He remained on the beach long after she was out of sight. By the time he returned to the house, not only had his hands gone numb, so had his heart. He would probably kiss a dozen more girls under the mistletoe, but he doubted he would be picking any more berries off the vine. No, perhaps Isabel had cured him of that. Perhaps he was no longer a dreamer.

Seeking

Nearly two weeks after Isabel had fled Worthing Abbey in tears, she returned, this time with an invitation in hand for the annual Twelfth Night masquerade ball. Glancing down at Lady Holbrook's precise handwriting, she hoped she wasn't making a mistake. Rae had added her own plea to the formal missive. Her words were seared in Isabel's mind: *Please come, he misses you.* But just as clearly, she recalled the contempt in Lord Peyton's eyes when he accused her of following him to Sussex.

She had conspired with Rae, through a series of letters, to arrive unannounced on the afternoon of the ball. No one else knew she was there. Rae had organized a game of charades to keep everyone busy, managing to slip away long enough to whisk Isabel out of her hired conveyance and into the same room she had occupied before. Her choice of costume, however, had been Isabel's own idea, an idea that seemed increasingly presumptuous as the moment neared for her to walk downstairs.

As she adjusted the lacy veil over her curls, Isabel wondered what Lord Peyton would think when he saw her. Would he be surprised, or even flattered, when he saw how she was dressed? The elegant silk gown draped over the wide hoops of a previous century flattered her slight figure, but her resolution faltered nonetheless. More likely, the viscount would think this another ploy to foist herself upon him. Taking a deep breath, she left the room.

The party had already begun. Music filtered up the stairs as she descended them. Half of the hall had been cleared for dancing while the other half held tables covered with food, including the remains of the Twelfth Night cake. Judging from Mr. Biddlecombe's antics at the far end of the room, he must have found the bean, which was hidden in the dessert and conferred upon him the honor of being chosen Lord of Misrule. In keeping with ancient tradition, he would reign for a night. Wearing a "crown" of brightly colored paper and carrying a staff of knobby wood, he was busy assembling his "court". Lord Peyton stood off to the side, easily identified by his height, despite his hooded robe costume. He gazed into the hearth where a fragment of the Yule log still burned. Isabel took her position near the door and waited for him to notice her.

She didn't have long to wait. She knew the moment he spotted her by the way his body tensed. Had he recognized her, or was it only the costume that held him immobile? Isabel's heart fluttered in her chest, but she persevered. Knowing he couldn't see through her veil, she opened the fan he had given her and waved it in front of her face. He would recognize her now, she knew. The bluebell pattern was unmistakable. She watched carefully over the top of the fan as he drew to his full height. The hood threw his face into shadows, but the set of his mouth looked grim. It was time to make her move.

Turning, she slipped through the doors, scurried outside, and found her way to the tower. Snow spilled over her high-heeled shoes as she raced up the stairs to the balustraded walkway and ducked into the aperture of the doorway. To her relief, the latch turned beneath her hand. Rae had unlocked the door as promised, and Isabel stepped within. Shaking with nerves and cold, she fumbled with the tinderbox but managed to light a brace of candles and position herself by the seaward window by the time the latch turned again.

"Why are you doing this?" Lord Peyton's voice rasped just above a whisper as he crossed the threshold.

Isabel slowly turned to face him. He had thrown back the hood of his costume, and even in the dim, flickering light, she could see the shock on his face. "Why am I doing what?" she asked. Though she'd been certain he would follow her from the party, he was not reacting as she had expected. Hoping for joy, she'd been prepared for anger, but never this. He was looking at her so strangely, almost as if he feared her. She lifted the veil over her head as he came near.

"Why are you dressed like the Lost Bride?" he asked. "When I first saw you...I thought you were really her."

"You thought I was a ghost?" she asked incredulously.

"I thought I saw her once before. When I was a boy." A dimple appeared briefly in his cheek. "A dream, no doubt, brought on by the horror of the tale and too much rich food."

"A logical explanation," Isabel agreed as she drank in the sight of him. She had almost forgotten how handsome he was. None of the men who had courted her during her season could compare with him. To her surprise, he reached for her, his fingers resting on her bare shoulders before trailing down the silk of her sleeve. He drew her close, close enough for her to see that his smile, charming though it was, did not reach his eyes. "Edward," she whispered, forcing herself to step away from him. "What is it?" In choosing her costume, she'd thought only to show him how much the tale of the Lost Bride, and her visit to the Abbey, had meant to her, but there was more here than he was telling her.

He let her go, though regret touched his face.

"Tell me why you are so haunted," Isabel prodded.

"I identify with the bride," he said at last. "I first heard the story sixteen years ago, on Christmas Eve, when I was a boy of ten. Fascinated, I went up in the attic after everyone was in bed and began searching through centuries worth of accumulated miscellanea. I found no dead bodies, of course, but I did find a trunk. Unable to pass up the opportunity, I climbed inside."

Isabel closed her eyes against a shaft of pain. "What happened?"

"It was just like in the story. The lid came down on me and I couldn't get out."

"What did you do?" She stepped beyond his reach, wandering over to the far window, where she stood, gazing unseeing at the house. No wonder her foolish choice of costume had unnerved him so deeply.

"I yelled, but no one heard me. The next morning my parents directed the servants in an all-out search. Eventually, they found me, shaken, but unharmed."

Unharmed? Isabel wondered. "And the ghost?" she asked, turning toward him.

"A year later, early on Christmas morning, I thought I saw her walking along the cliff. As I said before, it was probably no more than a boy's fancy."

"Yet still she influences you." Isabel pinned him with a sad stare.

"How so?"

"You have no intention of marrying any of the young women assembled here each year," she explained. "You find fault with all of them. Like the Lost Bride, you are caught in a perpetual game of hide-and-seek—with you doing the hiding, of course."

"I scarcely think that is your concern," he said stiffly.

"But I am concerned," Isabel retorted. "No. Let me finish," she said as he started toward her. "By the time the Lost Bride awoke to her danger, it was too late. Everyone had stopped looking for her. I wonder whether that will happen to you, too. When you finally decide you no longer want to be alone, the hordes of women may be gone."

"As long as I still have my title, income, and the Abbey, I'll still be a 'catch' on the marriage mart," he said sardonically.

"Is that what you want? To be married for your money?"

"No!" He grabbed her and gave her a slight shake. "I *do not* want to live my parents' lives—their isolation, the contempt they show one another."

"And you thought you would get that from me?" she asked in disbelief. "Find someone you truly love, Edward."

"I love *you*," he said, his face set and still, as if he were pronouncing sentence upon her rather than declaring his devotion.

"Do you?" she asked wistfully. "I thought you did, but when you realized I had followed you from London, that I was no different than all the others drawn to you—well, you hurt me deeply."

"I should never have said that. You are nothing like Lady Mary or Miss Coleman. They may admire the Abbey, or desire my money and social standing, but they feel nothing for me. You gaze at me with your heart in your eyes, Isabel, and that scares me even more than a marriage license."

"Right now my heart is beating so fast I can barely breathe," she admitted. "Why are you afraid to be loved?"

His hand cupped her left elbow and lingered. Their breaths hung in the air like smoke. "Fear can be overcome. I sought you out, ghost or not, January cold and all." A pulse throbbed in his neck, but this time when he smiled, the blue of his eyes lightened to sapphire. "I kissed you once under the mistletoe. Would you kiss me again without it?"

Instead of answering, Isabel placed her right hand around his neck and drew his head down. At the touch of his lips, warmth kindled inside her to rival that thrown by the Yule log itself. This was the man she had loved since the moment she'd first heard him speak, the man with whom she wanted to share her life.

"Shall we tell the rest?" he asked eagerly.

"Tell them what?"

"That you agreed to marry me."

"I have not! I'm scarcely eligible, you know. Besides, you have yet to ask."

"But I will," he said, unabashed, but tender. "And you will accept."

"Coxcomb." She slapped him playfully on the arm with her fan. "Let's go tell them."

Cathy Lynn Peper lives with her husband, young daughter, and a lab/husky mixed-breed dog in the St. Louis area. She has been a lover of romances, particularly those set in Regency England, for many years, and was lucky enough to find her own hero in her husband of eleven years.

Hide and Seek was inspired by the ballad, *The Mistletoe Bough* by Thomas Haynes Bayly, which was in turn inspired by an ancient folk tale known as *The Lost Bride*. "As I was researching British Christmas traditions in preparation for this story, I fell in love with the eerie poem and couldn't resist basing a story on it. I wish you all the happiest of holidays which will, hopefully, include some time curled up with a good book in front of a roaring fire."

There's mischief and robbery afoot at the White Lion Hotel. More is afoot as well. Be prepared to be surprised in this delightful tale by Regency favorite Sandra Heath.

$\mathcal{A}$ Winter's Tail

Sandra Heath

Before I commence this strange Christmas anecdote, let me assure you that every word of it is true. I had always been a skeptic when it came to the supernatural, finding it impossible to believe in such things as ghosts and fairies because I had never seen one. That was before I stayed at the White Lion Hotel in Bath. I only spent one night there, but come the next morning this old lad believed in everything supernatural!

My narrative commences in London—Berkeley Square, to be precise, and the fine town house of Lord William Acland, youngest son of the Duke of Glastonbury. I had been in his lordship's household for a considerable time, and felt greatly honored when he said he regarded me as part of the family. It is not often that one who has served so long and so loyally is shown such very particular appreciation; and certainly not often that one's old age is rewarded as handsomely as mine has been.

Never in my fondest dreams did I expect to end my days in the lap of country luxury, for I am an ordinary Londoner, not quite born within the sound of Bow bells, but close enough. Hard work and devotion to duty had always been my motto, so the thought of retirement did not at first appeal, but when I became less active, and getting up of a winter morning made my poor old bones creak, I knew I could not go on much longer. It saddened me that soon I would not be able to perch up behind his lordship when he drove around Mayfair in his bright yellow cabriolet. By the way, that is why I am called Tiger, on account of that being the name given to the diminutive grooms who ride behind those particular vehicles. Oh, Lord William and I cut a very handsome dash, he in his Bond Street finery, I with my side-whiskers and striped coat. It used to amuse me no end to see heads turn as we skimmed by.

However, I am in danger of wandering from my story. As I was saying, old age had crept up on me, but then two years ago his lordship—who is the very personification of grace and kindness—informed me that he and his dear sister,

Lady Julia, believed the grime and smoke of London were proving detrimental to my health and welfare, and they wished me to go live with Lady Julia at beautiful Durleigh Park in Somerset. This was in mid-December 1819, and his lordship was going to spend Christmas there, so it was decided that he would take me with him. I confess I shed a tear or two; in private, of course, for it is not meet that a fellow should blub.

And so it was that, the day before Christmas Eve, I said farewell to my good friends in the capital, and took my place next to Lord William in his traveling chariot. Yes, that is right, I actually sat inside with him! Can you believe it? I felt like a king and was so overwhelmed by my unexpected promotion that the winter chill did not touch me. Mind you, the fine warm blanket his lordship tucked around me did help a little.

Off we set in the morning sunshine, just the two of us in a chariot that was laden high for Christmas, with hampers, gifts, and various other items her ladyship had requested from the fine emporiums of Pall Mall and Piccadilly. Yuletide's imminence was very evident in the streets of the capital, with cartloads of holly and mistletoe rattling in from the country, and noisy flocks of geese and turkeys cluttering the roads. Ribboned wreaths were attached to doors, windows were festooned with garlands of greenery, and there was even an occasional glimpse of a drawing room adorned by one of those newfangled German Christmas trees brought here by our dear late Queen Charlotte. The season's greetings were on everyone's lips, and there was that exciting atmosphere such as only Christmas can bring.

At this point perhaps I should describe Lord William. He is a debonair young gentleman, with fair hair, bright blue eyes, and the wickedest smile you ever did see. No one is more attractive or charming, and few can be more certain of vouchers for Almack's, there not being a lady patroness of that exclusive temple to high fashion who doesn't wish to seduce him. Some very superior claws have been unsheathed on his account, I can tell you! And some very fancy fur has flown.

Oh, lord, I'm wandering from my story again. We left the capital in bright winter sunshine, and the chariot kept up such a good pace that for a while it even seemed we might reach Durleigh Park before midnight, but as we came into Bath the weather began to close in most disagreeably, with a freezing fog that reduced us to walking pace. Lord William decided we would halt overnight at the White Lion Hotel, which stands in the shadow of the abbey and Pump Rooms, and has one elevation that faces over the paved precinct in front of these two famous attractions. The White Lion is a plain four-story building built of the fine golden stone that has made Bath what it is. There is a roofed wrought-iron balcony running around the second floor, and at the time of which I speak it had been lavishly draped with seasonal greenery. Darkness had long since descended when we arrived, and lighted candles stood in all the ground-floor windows, where the curtains had been left undrawn to show off the wonderfully decorated rooms inside.

I followed Lord William as he entered the vestibule to secure suitable accommodation, although I waited respectfully at a distance in the shadows by the main staircase. The owner of the hotel, a Mr. Standish, came in person to welcome such a notable guest, and it wasn't long before Lord William had been offered the finest rooms, a suite overlooking the precinct.

Mr. Standish was a bowing, scraping, ingratiating man who was odd to look at in that he had a long pointed nose, big round ears, and very small hands and feet. His gray hair was short and exceedingly neat, he had a decided liking for gray clothes, and when he walked he almost seemed to flow. That is the best description I can manage, but trust you can picture him well enough. I did not like him at all, and even though he did not even see me there in the shadows, let alone speak to me, he made me feel very uncomfortable.

Anyway, I watched from my shadowy vantage point as Lord William was invited to enter his name in the register. Mr. Standish hovered beside him, as if something of great import were on his mind, and at last he came out with it. There had, he said, been a number of very mysterious burglaries in the area around the abbey, including the hotel, and he felt obliged to mention this unwelcome fact. His lordship straightened curiously. Mysterious burglaries? In what way? Mr. Standish looked a little embarrassed, then confessed that each one had been from a locked room with the occupant asleep inside at the time. The authorities did not even know how these crimes had been committed, let alone where the stolen goods might now be, and it was being whispered that magic had to be involved.

As you can imagine, Lord William took this with a pinch of salt, for he was certain there would be a far more rational explanation for the thefts than magic! However, he did not wish to insult Mr. Standish by saying as much, so he merely thanked him for the warning and assured him he would take every precaution, even to wedging a chair against the door handle. At this Mr. Standish gave a rueful smile and replied that it would do no good because even rooms that were firmly bolted on the inside had been quietly pilfered while the victim slept innocently on. Lord William did not believe this either, but politely refrained from comment. He was still smiling to himself as we went up to the suite a few minutes later.

Now, I haven't told you quite all that occurred while we were in the vestibule, but I will come to the rest of it in a moment or so. First of all let me explain what happened when we retired that night. I could have had the suite's smaller bedroom, but with his lordship's permission chose instead the fireside chair in the drawing room. Beds are all very well, but one cannot do better than a warm, comfortable chair. Lord William had a few second thoughts about Mr. Standish's burglaries, and so jammed a chair under the handle of the door, making it impossible for it to be opened unless the chair was taken away. And so we both went to sleep; at least, he did, I just could not nod off because I had Mr. Standish looming large in my mind all the time. I may be getting on, and failing in many ways, but my sense of smell has not dulled at all, and if ever I smelled a rat, it was Mr. Standish. He was up to no good, as they say, and I made up my mind to keep a sharp eye on him.

With all this suspicion running through my mind, my restlessness became so bad that sleep seemed to get further away rather than closer, so I decided some fresh air might prove beneficial. The balcony I mentioned earlier ran past the suite, and was reached by double French doors from the drawing room. The catch of these doors wasn't quite closed. Now, I don't want you to think that this had any bearing on the burglaries, because it didn't. The simple fact was that the servants who had decorated the balcony with festive greenery had not been all that careful about closing the doors when they finished. Anyway, the long and short of it was that I only had to give a small push, and the doors swung obligingly open.

On going outside, I found myself looking at the abbey and the precinct. The fog had thinned a little, perhaps on account of the lighted flambeaux outside the adjacent Pump Rooms, where a Christmas function of some sort was in progress. Sedan chairs waited outside, and I could see carriages drawn up beyond the colonnade that stood between the precinct and Stall Street. In the abbey the organist was practicing very late. He was playing—Good King Wenceslaus followed by The Holly and the Ivy, I recall—and I found the seasonal melodies truly pleasing. So there I stood, sampling the night air and trying not to shiver in the cold, when suddenly the abbey bell chimed the hour. This old boy nearly jumped out of his skin, I can tell you, and decided pronto that the fireside chair had its attractions after all.

But as I was about to slip back into the suite, a shadow moved across the faint light shining from the next room along. Now, I happened to know that room was unoccupied, and that the light was therefore from the lamplit passage because the door stood open. Who would be walking around at this late hour? Nosy being my middle name, I went to spy through the window. I saw Mr. Standish standing in the passage. He was still fully dressed, and seemed very furtive as he glanced back toward the staircase as if he heard something. Then he walked on out of my sight. Now, the lamplight fell in such a way that I could still see his shadow after he'd gone. That is, I could see it, then I couldn't. He was walking slowly, and naturally enough his shadow was moving at the same pace, but suddenly it disappeared completely. It was as if *he* disappeared! Oh, I know you think I'm exaggerating, but it's true. My hair fair stood on end, and I felt quite unnerved. I wondered where he'd gone, of course, and so I slipped along to the next room after that. It was occupied, as again I knew full well, because Lord William and I had seen a certain young lady en-

tering it as we came upstairs. Except that she wasn't just any young lady, but
Mr. Standish's niece, Miss Perdita Standish.

Now I definitely do have to digress a little here, in order to tell you what
else happened down in the vestibule while his lordship was engaging the suite.
Miss Standish had been out on some important business or other and returned
to the hotel just after we arrived. It was immediately clear that she and her uncle were not all that well acquainted, indeed there seemed the awkwardness of
virtual strangers between them. For instance, she nearly called him Mr. Standish, and only just corrected herself in time to call him Uncle Standish. Their
acquaintance did not seem set to get any better either, for she asked him to be
sure to awaken her in time to take the London mailcoach the next day.

Lord William gave Miss Standish a very comprehensive appraisal the moment she entered, for she had a pretty turn of ankle, and an even prettier face,
with wonderful auburn hair and the biggest green eyes you ever saw. His lordship has always had a taste for redheads, and she was a particularly attractive
example of her kind. We learned later that she had been left an orphan some six
months earlier, and had been obliged to leave her home in Cornwall in order to
go to Chelsea, where she would reside with her other uncle, Mr. Standish's elder brother. She was only staying overnight at the White Lion, having been
obliged to break her journey in Bath in order to conduct the little matter of
business from which she had just returned. This business concerned the collection of a small jewelry casket that years before had apparently been left for repair at a Milsom Street goldsmith. It was a family heirloom that had been presumed lost, until she happened to find the receipt while collating her late father's papers.

It was clear from Mr. Standish's reaction that this was the first he had heard
about the casket's rediscovery. His eyes sharpened, and he stiffened like an
animal that scents danger. Oh, yes, I know you snigger to hear me describing
him thus, but that is exactly how he seemed. In fact, he was so alarmed to see
the casket again, that I almost thought he would snatch it from her. But he
contained himself, so much so that after a moment or so he was all amiability
again. Oh, the smell of rat was strong in my nostrils, I can tell you!

Anyway, that is what happened in the vestibule, and now I must return to
my exploits on the balcony. After seeing Mr. Standish's shadow disappear so
oddly, I hastened to peer in through the next window along, that of Miss Standish's room, where I could see a sliver of light through a crack in the curtains.
Please bear in mind that I had the tale of mysterious burglaries ringing loudly
in my ears, and that only a second or so had passed since Mr. Standish's
shadow vanished. The room was quiet, and Miss Standish—Perdita I shall call
her from now on—was sleeping like a babe, her hair spilling over the pillow
like molten copper. Nothing happened. I could hear my heart pounding as I
waited. Then, just as I was about to give up and return to my fireside chair, lo

and behold, Mr. Standish was in the room! How he came there I did not know, just that one second there was no sign of him, the next he was there!

My eyes widened with shock, and the hairs on my neck stood up all over again. It just wasn't natural the way he came out of nowhere like that! As I watched, he began to go through his niece's belongings! Yes, the scoundrel was actually robbing his own kith and kin! I saw him eagerly seize and go through the jewelry casket she had earlier collected in the town. When I say go through, perhaps that isn't strictly true, for it was empty. Yet he examined it in such minute detail that I knew he was seeking a hidden compartment!

For a few moments I remained so thunderstruck that I couldn't do anything, but then I raised the alarm. Oh, did I set up a racket. I made such a noise at that window that I fancy I could have awoken the dead in the abbey! Mr. Standish gave a start, dropped the casket, and disappeared. Yes, disappeared. Into thin air. I had been looking right at him, for heaven's sake! It took my breath away, and I fell silent and just stared.

Perdita had awoken the moment my din commenced. She sat up in bed, holding the sheet to her chin, looking very frightened. Then she saw her jewelry casket on the floor, and with a cry rushed from the bed to pick it up. She did not look for the secret compartment, so I knew that she had no idea of its existence. I couldn't help wondering what could be in it that was of such interest to her uncle. Anyway, because the casket lay on the floor like that, Perdita knew that her room had been entered, and she was clearly very frightened. After hastily putting on her primrose merino wrap, she pushed the casket and the few bits of jewelry she had brought with her from Cornwall into her reticule, looped it safely over her wrist, then rushed out into the passage to raise the alarm. In order to do that she had to unlock the door first, and I noticed particularly that the key was on the inside! So how on earth had Mr. Standish come and gone? By the chimney? I think not, especially with a good coal fire burning in the hearth. Mysterious he had called the burglaries; mysterious they certainly were.

Well, I had to find out what happened next, so I ran back along that balcony as fast as my old legs could carry me, then in through the French doors, and out into the passage at Lord William's heels as he dashed from his bed in response to Perdita's cries. The whole hotel had been aroused, and other guests thronged the passage, some of them in quite a state because they realized that they too had been robbed. Into this uproar stepped Mr. Standish, now in a nightgown and tasseled night cap, as if he too had been aroused from his slumbers! The villain aped dismay about what had clearly happened, and made haste to send someone for the watch and other relevant authorities. In next to no time everyone had been persuaded to go downstairs to the dining room, where Mr. Standish, the very personification of solicitous regret and concern, ordered mulled wine and hot mince pies to be served. I did not know quite what to do. After all, what I had seen defied reason. Mr. Standish had used the word magic to describe the burglaries; did that mean he was a wizard who could appear and disappear at will? Who would believe that? So, for the time being at least, I decided to await developments; after all, he had not been able to find whatever it was he sought, so he would have to try again. And he only had tonight in which to do it, because Perdita was leaving on the morning mail for London.

While statements were being taken from everyone in the dining room, Lord William fussed around Perdita, making all the romantic headway he could! He was very smitten indeed, and I could tell by the shy but warm smile she gave him that Miss Perdita Standish was the future Lady William Acland. It was love at first sight, and the force of it seemed to send them both into a daze. Such is the power of the heart. Perhaps it was the fact of their departures in opposite directions the next morning, for time was definitely not on their side. So they did not make many nods in the direction of etiquette, and before long were secretly holding hands.

I was very pleased for them both, because in spite of her close blood ties with the execrable Mr. Standish, I knew her to be all that was good and gentle. This I had discovered as everyone herded down to the dining room, for I found myself being trampled by an angry squire who was anxious to be the first to register his list of stolen property. In spite of her own distress, Perdita had drawn me safely aside to comfort me because my foot had been stepped on very heavily indeed. Once in the dining room, she procured me a warm drink and quiet corner, and did not leave me until she was assured I was all right. Such kindness made a friend of me for life, and my regard for her has not faltered from that day to this.

Eventually it became clear to everyone that there was nothing more that could be done regarding these latest burglaries, for they were just like all the others. Mr. Standish made it seem he was all of a pother about the whole business. He kept wringing his hands and declaring that it would do his hotel's reputation irreparable harm if these crimes persisted. Oh, I had to give it to him, he was a splendid actor! The authorities departed from the hotel feeling baffled and helpless. Secured doors had again been no obstacle and items had been stolen. No evidence could be found, no explanation presented itself, and there seemed no hope for the return of the purloined articles. I could have told them they were wasting their time trying to solve the mystery, for this was certainly no ordinary pilferer!

It was three o'clock on the morning of Christmas Eve when everyone at last returned to their rooms. They were all disgruntled and uneasy and did not expect to sleep again that night, but they reckoned without Mr. Standish's generously offered mulled wine! It wasn't long before I heard snoring from behind doors that had again been secured to no avail. Lord William had escorted Perdita to her room, but she was understandably nervous about remaining in a chamber that had definitely been entered by the enigmatic intruder. Lord William insisted that she slept in his suite, and before you leap to a shocking conclusion, let me assure you that he kept guard on a chair in the passage, his pistol at the ready! However, he was not at the ready, for the mulled wine soon overcame him, and he nodded off.

Naturally, I stayed in the passage as well, although as soon as his lordship fell asleep, I made certain to keep well out of sight, for I was sure that Mr Standish did not yet know I existed. He had not seen me when we arrived, and I was certain he had not noticed me since then. There was a floor-length curtain by a window at the top of the stairs, and I hid behind it, waiting for him to make his next move. An icy draft came off the window, and I was soon stiff and cold, but I remained at my self-appointed post. All of an hour must have ticked slowly by, and just as I was beginning to truly yearn for my warm fireside chair, I heard Mr. Standish's stealthy tread at last.

He came up the staircase, and paused in surprise when he saw Lord William asleep on the chair. After a moment he went on past me and, after making sure Lord William was soundly enough asleep, continued to what he still believed to be Perdita's door. I held my breath, waiting to see what happened next. But then Lord William stirred slightly. My attention darted to him, then immediately back to Mr. Standish—who in that split second had disappeared. My jaw fair dropped, for he had done it again! Lord William slept on as I slipped from my hiding place and went to the door of Perdita's empty room. It was empty no more, for as I put my ear to the wood, I heard Mr. Standish moving around inside as he searched for the casket.

I guessed it would not take him long to realize why Lord William was keeping guard outside the suite, so I scuttled back to my hiding place behind the curtain. Well, all that came out of Perdita's room was a mouse, a small gray house mouse such as are found in every building. It poked its nose beneath the door, and sniffed very cautiously. Perhaps I had left a faint trace of scent. After a moment it ventured a little further, then glanced up and down the passage. When it was satisfied there was no danger, it dashed along by the skirting board, right past dozing Lord William, and into the suite where Perdita slept soundly in his lordship's capacious bed.

I couldn't believe what seemed to be the case, so I hastened to her old room and listened again at the door. There was utter silence, and I knew Mr. Standish was no longer there. Yet only a mouse had left. The inescapable conclusion was surely too incredible to possibly be true! I slipped along to his lordship's door, and listened there. Sure enough, I could hear Mr. Standish searching inside. I knew then that he and the mouse were one and the same!

Oh, don't laugh, for it is the truth! He could change his form in the blinking of an eye, from man to mouse, then back again! My eyes lit up with grim determination, for I knew I had him! At least, I hoped I did. I was getting on, and speed was one thing I didn't have too much of any more, but I had to try. So I gave a loud screech that had Lord William on his feet before he was properly awake. The mouse shot out beneath the door so fast it was upon me before it realized. I pounced, and that was the end of it. No more Mr. Standish.

His disappearance was a cause célèbre for a while, because I certainly could not admit that I had killed him! Mouse or not, it was a crime, so I wisely kept quiet. The White Lion was searched from top to bottom, for fear he had been murdered by the mysterious burglar, but all that was found was the great store of valuables he had purloined from his guests and the good citizens of Bath. He had done it all by entering rooms as a mouse, becoming a man to effect the theft, concealing the stolen property up the chimneys, then slipping out again as a mouse. Later, when the coast was clear, he would return to gather his little treasure troves. I knew this was how he had done it, but to everyone else his modus operandi remained a puzzle. To this day there are many who believe he was a magician.

I discovered the secret compartment in Perdita's casket and was able to draw attention to it in a seemingly innocent way. It proved to contain a letter that showed that Perdita's late father, not Mr. Standish, was the legitimate owner of the White Lion. The letter was apparently the only evidence of this, and Mr. Standish knew it had been hidden in the casket, the subsequent loss of which—to say nothing of the untimely demise of Perdita's father—had left him safe in his deception.

Perdita became Lady William Acland early in 1820, and she sold the hotel in 1821, when all the legal problems of the Standish family had been resolved. It was recently renamed the King George, in honor of the new king, and is doing very well. There are no strange burglaries there now, of course. I'm thoroughly enjoying life here at Durleigh Park with his lordship's sister, Lady Julia, and I have nothing to do all day long, except sit out in the sun in the summer, and by the fire in the winter.

Anyway, that astonishing night in Bath was two long years ago now. I think of it every Christmas, and have a little chuckle. Well, if there is one thing I used to be good at, it was catching mice. How else do you imagine a cat could give good and faithful service? By the way, there's something I haven't told you. Lady William shares her uncle's strange power. She is expecting her first child and has such a craving for stale cheese that Lord William has become quite alarmed. He has forbidden her to eat it, which does not suit her at all. So she slips down to the kitchens as her other self, and sets about the cheese in the pantry. I let her do it, of course, for she is my friend, and one does not eat one's friends.

Sandra Heath was born in Cilfynydd, Pontypridd, South Wales. Her late father was an officer in the Royal Air Force, and at the age of eighteen, while living in Germany, she met her husband Rob, whosefather was also in the RAF. They have been together for thirty-some years (married for thirty-three) and live near the cathedral city of Gloucester, England. Their only daughter, Sarah-Jane, is now married and living in Lancashire. Sandra began writing in 1971, when two-and-a-half year old Sarah was dangerously ill in hospital with sus-pected meningitis. Having always avidly read historical novels, especially those dealing with the controversy over Richard III, writing such a novel her-self offered a form of escape from the stress and anxiety caused by Sarah's ill-ness. Sarah recovered, and the completed novel, called *Less Fortunate Than Fair,* the story of Richard's niece, Cicely Plantagenet, was accepted for publi-cation. Sandra has been writing ever since, and loves every minute of it. She is often assisted by her two Siamese cats, who think a keyboard is for walking over/sitting on/knocking to the floor/depositing food on/you name it... How-ever, they're a little short on helpful advice regarding plot, character develop-ment, and continuity! Still, one can't have everything.

Lord Lawton is too toplofty for his own good. Not every eligible maiden wishes to marry him. Especially not his new neighbor, Holly. Or, at least, that's what she says.

The Magic of Christmas

Donna Smith

"But we can't have a kissing ball without mistletoe!" This complaint was issued by a very pretty young lady, who was looking critically at an ornate construction, which had aspirations of becoming a kissing ball. The morning room at Havenhill House was littered with greenery and red ribbons, with wreaths and swags in various stages of completion.

"Well, we don't have any and we can't seem to find any, so we will just have to do without." The answer came from another pretty young lady similarly engaged.

The laughing brown eyes of the first young lady looked into the serene blue eyes of the second and their owner said, "I know where some is growing."

"Where? Oh, but Holly, you know we can't go there!"

"Why not?"

"You know how strict Lord Lawton is reputed to be about his property. It could cause a horrid fuss to be found trespassing there. He might set his dogs on us."

"He wouldn't dare."

"Well, he might not, but I have no wish to find out. He is not the most charitable of neighbors, you know."

"Even an old ogre should have a little of the spirit of Christmas."

"We don't know him well enough to know if he is an ogre. We don't even know if he is old. No one in the neighborhood has met him or even seen him. He brought all his servants with him, so there's no one local to tell anyone anything. Even Father knows nothing."

Ivy twirled the ball about to view it from all sides, and continued, "Why are you so set on having mistletoe anyway? It's not as though anyone would be allowed to kiss us." Ivy's countenance softened as she thought of the squire's son, who had been most attentive lately.

"What if the occasion should present itself when no one else is around?" At Ivy's glance of protest, Holly conceded, "Yes, I know. There aren't that many interesting young gentlemen around here." She sighed. "Oh, let's go, Ivy. He shall never know that we have even been there. It's not so very far into his property. I'm sure we shan't be caught."

"But, Holly, you know what father has said. If you get in any more scrapes he is going to send you to London to Aunt Agatha to learn proper manners."

Holly was quiet for a moment. She had been found out when she made a wager on the steeplechase with two of the footmen. She had been caught in clothing borrowed from a stable boy, as she galloped her horse across the fields. And yes, her mother had seen her kissing the vicar's son one Sunday after services. That had created quite a stir, which didn't seem quite fair as the kiss had been rather wet and totally unsatisfactory. But she had been on her best behavior for some time now. Perhaps Father had forgotten.

"But this is important. You know we have always found Christmas to be magic. Well, it can't be magic if we don't have everything just right. We need mistletoe."

Ivy reluctantly agreed. She always found it hard to resist her sister, even when she sensed they were overstepping their bounds.

They went to fetch their cloaks and put on stout boots. The motif of their names even carried through to their apparel. Holly wore a cloak of red with a hood. Ivy chose a soft green wrap with a little green hat. Taking a basket and sharp scissors, they set off. The weather was clear but cold, so a little walk would be just the thing.

Sir Edmund Tolliver was normally a gentleman of good common sense and judgment, not given to flights of fancy, but when his wife was delivered of twin girls on Christmas Day his exuberance was such he could not be constrained from naming them Holly and Ivy. His good wife was not in complete accord, but recognized that in this instance her views could not prevail. So Holly and Ivy they were.

The girls did not look alike, although both were beautiful. Holly grew taller than her sister and had black hair and brown eyes, like her father's. Ivy was slight, with soft brown hair and blue eyes, much like their mother. As they grew, the girls became more and more like their namesakes. Holly was sturdy and a bit willful. She was most interested in outdoor pursuits, and was a bruising rider. She was her father's helpmeet and his confidante on matters involving his estate.

Ivy was soft and rather clinging. She was becoming as much a mistress of the household as her mother was. Her watercolors were much admired.

Holly and Ivy had always felt that the Christmas season belonged to them, which, of course, it did. They always participated in all aspects of the celebration, from decking the halls to preparing the feasts, to singing the carols, particularly the one for which they were named.

When they were tiny girls, first brought down to see the house bedecked with greens and the candles burning and the Yule log blazing, Holly had said to Ivy, "Look, Ivy, magic." And ever since, that had been their signal for the happiness of the season.

They grew up most contented. When they were seventeen, their mother broached the question of a London season, but their father was not agreeable and the girls not interested. Their father argued that a London season would likely mean marriage to someone from afar and living wherever a husband took them, He did not take kindly to losing his girls entirely.

The twins had visited London once and were not impressed. They found it dirty and smelly and full of proud people whom they did not wish to know.

"And besides, they don't even celebrate Christmas! Not properly, at any rate," Holly had announced. They wanted to live in the country and were perfectly happy with country pursuits. Yes, finding acceptable husbands in their near neighborhood would be a problem, as suitable gentlemen were rare, but they left this problem in their father's capable hands.

Ivy had recently begun to notice the squire's son, and her mother was hopeful of an announcement forthcoming soon. But Holly was unattached, and her mother sometimes despaired at the lack of possibilities in the area. Something had to be arranged before Holly's behavior put her outside the bounds of polite society.

While Holly was much sought after, she was not that eager to marry. Her life suited her, and she could not look forward to becoming a dutiful wife.

The girls walked down the gravel road, just a short way past the edge of their father's property. There was a dense hedgerow on their neighbor's boundary, but Holly knew of a slight gap just past the holly tree which grew so tall. She found it easily and held back the branches so her sister could enter.

Although they had glimpses of a meadow in the distance, they had entered into a gloomy world, one with little sunshine and one where the growth was dense before them and under their feet. Ivy shuddered a little, but Holly soldiered on.

"It's not far."

"Thank goodness," said Ivy. "I feel as though I have stepped into the evil forest of some old fairy tale." She winced as a briar caught her cloak, and yanked it free. Thank goodness it wasn't her best.

Holly felt a moment of trepidation. They were trespassing. But it was in a good cause.

It was only a few yards further to the huge tree where the mistletoe was growing. They could see the leaves and berries, but they were high in the tree, perhaps out of reach.

Holly began to lift her skirts and tie them about her waist.

"What are you doing?" cried Ivy.

"I shall try to get some. We've come too far to go home empty-handed."

"But even if you climb, I don't see any that will be within reach."

"It may look better from further up." So saying, Holly grasped one of the lower branches and began to climb.

"Careful," pleaded Ivy. She was trying to be brave and resisted the urge to cover her eyes and not look.

"Actually," said Holly, panting a little, "the view is much better from up here. Makes the place look almost as though it belongs to a human." She pulled herself higher, and paused. "Do you see any mistletoe near me?"

"Oh, no, Holly. It grows too far out and the branches are too thin. Let's go home."

Just as Holly considered this proposition, they were both alarmed by the sound of dogs—large dogs—baying. Even as they both listened, the sound grew closer.

"Come, Ivy, up the tree. Hurry. I'll come down and give you a hand."

Thankful that she was country raised, Ivy managed to clamber up the tree. It was not a moment too soon, for just as she achieved one of the lower branches, two hounds broke out of the underbrush. They paced about the tree trunk, announcing their find.

"Ivy, if you faint I will never forgive you. Just take deep breaths and hold on tight."

Following in the footsteps of the dogs was a most impressive stallion bearing a rider of imperious demeanor. His dark hair was disheveled and his dark eyes seemed to snap. Most would account him handsome, although some might be put off by the harshness of his features.

"What have we here? A couple of pigeons in the tree?"

"Please call off your dogs. We mean no harm." Holly hoped her voice did not shake.

"Harm enough to trespass, I think."

"If you will call them off so we may come down, we would be most obliged." Holly struggled to keep her voice calm.

"Aye, come down. Stay, boys." The dogs sat near their owner, alert to his every whim.

Abandoning all pretense of dignity, Holly clambered down, affording the gentleman a brief view of tidy ankles and most of her lower limbs. As soon as her feet touched the ground, she hastily undid her skirts and pulled them down about her. She was short of breath but she turned to face her captor.

"Good morning. Do I have the honor of addressing Lord Lawton?"

"You do indeed. Have you been sent here or did you decide to invade my grounds on your own accord? Does your mistress require something of mine?"

"Our mistress?" Holly was taken aback. "I believe you mistake us. I am Holly Tolliver and this is my sister, Ivy. Oh, come down, Ivy." Ivy complied, her face red from blushing.

"The Misses Tolliver. What an unexpected pleasure. Have we been introduced?" Now his tone was stern.

"You know we have not. We live just a short distance from here and have come to find some mistletoe. I do suppose we are trespassing, but not many in this area are so strict with their borders."

"Oh, really? So you are allowed to run loose throughout the neighborhood? Are there others like you?"

"Others?"

"I was wondering about *Mistletoe,* or possibly *Noel.* Would they also think the season gives them full rein to go where they wish?"

Holly was truly taken aback. She had never before encountered such disdain. Did he think them hurly-burly misses with no regard for propriety? They were, after all, the Misses Tolliver, not quite without standing. Well, not in such good standing at this particular moment, perhaps, but not to be despised and laughed at.

Drawing herself to her full height, and throwing one edge of her cloak over her shoulder, she replied in as haughty a voice as she could muster, "I do not know why you should be so suspicious of us. We weren't meaning to really steal anything…" Her voice faltered as she realized their actions could be construed in that way.

"You intended to bring my mistletoe back after the season? Hmm, could that be another excuse to seek my acquaintance?"

Holly turned white with anger as she took his meaning. "How unhandsome of you. Of course, we should have known what to expect from a man of your reputation."

"I am shocked that such knowledge did not deter you."

"I am not so lily-livered." Ivy tugged at Holly's cloak, but was ignored. "You seem to be lacking in any sort of Christian charity, to say nothing of the spirit of the season. You hide here like an ogre in his castle, and you are certainly off the mark if you think we have any interest in your person. Who would wish to know such as you?"

Lord Lawton felt a twinge of suspicion that he had misread the situation, but he could not falter now.

"Well, you are a cheeky little miss. I am attempting to gain some control over my field and forests, so I must request that you desist from trespassing at least until I have done so."

"As though a little mistletoe would be missed."

"Of course it would not. But it is my mistletoe and I shall have the disposing of it."

Holly thrust her chin into the air. "How very obliging of you." Pushing Ivy before her, she fled the field of battle. "And a very Merry Christmas to you!"

He paused for a moment, watching their progress and then rode off, his hounds trailing behind.

When they had reached the road and were trudging home, Ivy ventured: "You were not very civil to him. We were in the wrong."

"Of course, but he didn't need to be so toplofty and high-handed. He acted as though we were the lowliest of country misses and as though we had some kind of designs on him."

Walking rapidly to keep up, Ivy said, "But we are country misses."

"Yes, but that is no reason to treat us that way." They walked on.

"Do you think he will tell father?" Although Holly asked the question with a casual air, Ivy could tell she was concerned. Ivy was worried too, but there was little use in repining over something they could not undo.

"Let's hope not," Ivy said.

❄ ❄ ❄

Their antagonist rode slowly home. He had been surprised by the girls and suspected he had acted like a coxcomb. That saucy little miss had goaded him into it.

Lord Lawton usually was thought to have the best of manners. He was considered a leader of the *ton* and had the breeding and wealth necessary to maintain such a position. He had, however, grown tired of overheated rooms too full of perfumed and pomaded people. He was weary of gossip and backbiting. He was sick of gambling and silly wagers which cost some their very lives. And so he had purchased this estate and had come to renew and rusticate, to fill his lungs with fresh air, to engage in a little usefulness by restoring his holding. He had not been sociable, preferring for the time some quiet and solitude.

He was also running away from the hordes of mamas and misses who dogged his steps. He did not mean to marry, at least not yet, and he was not going to be baited and trapped. There had been many attempts to corner him in compromising situations. Young misses had faltered and fallen just outside his town house so that they might be invited in to recover and thus perhaps meet him. Others had complained of overheating at balls, attempting to lure him out onto the balcony alone. So far he had managed to escape.

But he did not mean to be in bad standing with his neighbors. The chit up the tree had implied that he was seen as a sort of nasty recluse. That was not the image he wished for himself. He might be able to acquit them of planning a ruse to come to his notice. And just because he was rusticating did not mean he did not appreciate a winsome face and a well-turned ankle. He must gather his wits and reconsider.

❄ ❄ ❄

"I am beginning to feel the coming of Christmas," Ivy said as the twins walked to the village for a few last-minute things.

Holly did not reply. She was, in fact, not focusing on Christmas. As yet, her father had not said a word about her transgression, but it might be that he did not want to spoil the season. She was going through the familiar rituals, but the spirit was missing. She kicked at a small stone in her path, then winced at the effect on her cold toes.

The village showed signs of the holiday to come, with greens and wreaths on shop fronts and in windows. Cook needed more raisins and a bit more cinnamon. Ivy wanted to see if any interesting green ribbons could be found.

They sauntered along, greeting friends and neighbors. They complimented Sarah Lovedale on her new bonnet. They gave their parents' greetings to Farmer Jones.

Suddenly, Holly stopped, stiffened, and clutched Ivy's arm.

"We have to cross the street. Here he comes!"

Ivy, smiling at a young man approaching, was puzzled. "Who? It is only Stuart…"

"Lord Lawton! We can't meet him. Not now." Holly felt almost in a panic. "Come on."

So saying, she pulled Ivy by the sleeve and out into the street, directly in the path of a curricle and pair. The driver did his best to control his beasts, Holly did her best to pull Ivy out of the way, but Ivy turned her foot and fell.

She lay, crumpled in the center of the road, like a fallen leaf in the prime of summer. Holly knelt by her, engulfed in tears and guilt. "Oh, Ivy," she cried, "what have I done?" She felt rather than saw Lord Lawton approach.

"Go away," she said.

"Hush," he said, "we must not brangle in the streets. Your sister needs assistance."

Ivy was swooped up in the capable arms of Lord Lawton and carried to the dry goods shop, where the proprietor quickly found a chair for her.

"Oh, Ivy, I am so sorry." Holly was chafing Ivy's wrists. Lord Lawton gestured to the shopkeeper who produced a somewhat dusty vinaigrette.

"I believe she just fainted," Lord Lawton said. "This will bring her around." Ivy was soon coughing and shaking her head, pale but protesting that she did not want a fuss.

"You must excuse me, but we must make sure that you have no other injuries." Lord Lawton began to run his hands along her arms, then her fingers. Satisfied, he turned his attention to her lower limbs.

"Is that absolutely necessary?" Holly asked.

"I do not believe she has broken any bones, although she may have twisted her foot. Are you able to stand?"

Ivy, though white faced and shaking, murmured that she was fine and would be up and about in just a few minutes.

Walking a few steps away, Holly turned and motioned to Lord Lawton, who approached. "I must thank you for rescuing my sister. It was all my fault that she had this accident, and I cannot thank you enough. If I had not drawn her out into the street, this would never have happened. I am sorry."

"Hush," he said in a low tone. "Too much humble pie is not your style."

She stared at him. "Do you think I take this lightly? She could have been killed."

"She wasn't."

"I shouldn't wonder if you think I put my sister in danger as a ruse to gain your attention."

"No, I do acquit you of that."

"How kind of you. I am quite overwhelmed by your regard."

"It is your sister who is in need at this time." Lord Lawton looked over at Ivy for a moment then turned back and murmured to Holly. "She is doing a little better, but she needs to be taken home. I shall take her in my curricle." He approached the storekeeper, with whom he had a brief conversation.

"How kind he is," Ivy whispered.

"Kind? He has totally taken over. He is the most toplofty man ever. And it is plain that he has the worst opinion of me. It is probably just another way of making maygames of us."

"Oh, Holly, stop. Once you get a thought in your head…"

Lord Lawton returned, shopkeeper in tow. "I am sorry that I only have room for one of you, but Miss Ivy needs to be taken home as quickly as possible. Under the circumstances propriety is not a question, but just in case, the shopkeeper's helper will ride up behind." Drawing on his gloves, he turned to Holly. "Mr. Jones is arranging for you to be taken home, Miss Tolliver, as I feel it would not be wise for you to attempt to walk after such a happening."

"Of course I can walk," Holly said. "Do you think me some kind of die-away maiden?"

"Not at all," replied Lord Lawton. "But sometimes one has unusual reactions after such an event."

Already beset by quivering knees, Holly could still not give up. "Nonsense, I have always…"

"But today you will make an exception. Ah, here is my curricule. Shall I carry you, Miss Ivy, or will you walk?"

Holly watched as Ivy was handed up into the elegant equipage, and a warm robe arranged for her benefit. Ivy was smiling up into the eyes of her rescuer. Holly determined to put a proper face on the episode. But now she was sure that she would be bundled off to London first thing in the New Year.

The shopkeeper said, "Here we are, Miss. Farmer Harris is driving by your place, and he will give you a ride." Holly looked at the wagon, bearing a full load of mangel-wurzels, and had to suppress a shudder. But she would not hurt the feelings of Farmer Harris and she *was* a little shaky, so she climbed into the wagon and tried to be cheery about it. Yet she could not forget the elegant curricle.

❋ ❋ ❋

The next days were filled with preparations for the holiday. The Yule log was brought into the house with much groaning from the men who carried it. They were rewarded with a tot of whiskey and a bit of Christmas cake. The smells of holiday baking permeated the house. Cook cried and threw her apron over her head, wailing that her fruitcakes had been eaten by mice and was little consoled to find that the stable boy was the actual culprit who had been picking off morsels. She vowed that to get her own back she would make the best Christmas pudding ever.

It was late afternoon of Christmas Eve, and the early midwinter dark had descended. The candles, clustered in every conceivable corner, were all lit and cast a soothing glow about the room. Holly felt a *frisson* of excitement. The best time of the year was almost here.

The twins were sitting in the parlor. Both were dressed in their holiday best—Holly in a gown of red velvet, and Ivy in green. Their mother said that if they were in London, such bold colors would not be acceptable, but since they were among family and close friends it would pass.

Ivy had made a rapid recovery from her mishap. Her ankle had not even been sprained, although she did favor her foot a little. There had not been time to talk about her ride home with Lord Lawton, what with all of the hustle and bustle of making Ivy comfortable, and the rest of the preparations. Indeed, Holly wished to avoid any possible painful confidences. She sighed, then jumped up from her chair.

"I think a little music is called for." She seated herself at the pianoforte and began to play. Ivy did not join her but remained seated on the divan. Holly played on, some of her zest beginning to fade.

Just then Rose, the housemaid, entered the room, bearing a box. She handed it to Ivy, who looked at it curiously. It was hat box size, nicely wrapped, and a card was addressed "To the Misses Tolliver." Holly left the pianoforte and came to join her sister. "Open it, Ivy." Nestled in a bed of tissue were three large clusters of mistletoe. There was no indication of the sender, but both sisters knew the source.

"How lovely," said Ivy, as she picked up one of the clusters. "Now our kissing ball will be complete. Isn't he thoughtful?"

Holly did not answer. She looked at the gift with questioning eyes. Was it thoughtfulness or a subtle threat? Or was it just the kindness of a neighbor? Taking down the kissing ball which hung from the chandelier in the center of the room, she attached one of the clusters of mistletoe to it, before rehanging it. At least that part of the holiday would be perfect.

❄ ❄ ❄

The Christmas Assembly was much anticipated by the twins, for all of the two years they had been allowed to attend. It seemed to them that it was largely in their honour. They fairly sparkled with joy. Both wore white, with crimson ribbons for Holly and green ones for Ivy.

Even though the crowd was almost exclusively their neighbors and friends, somehow they appeared different, dressed to the nines and on their best behavior. It was a friendly gathering, rather less decorous than those held in the cities. Everyone was enjoying themselves, if not behaving to tonnish standards, when the happy crowd noticed Lord Lawton standing tall at the room's entrance.

He was dressed all in black, with impeccable white linen. He held a quizzing glass in his hand, and gazed over the crowd. The buzzing which arose from the assemblage could not have escaped his notice, but it did not change his posture. He was greeted by the Squire, who often served as an informal master of ceremonies, and soon was taken on a round of the room, introduced to each man and matron, as well as to many of their offspring.

As Lord Lawton and the entourage he had collected approached the divan upon which Holly and Ivy were seated, Holly rose and implored her sister to do likewise.

"Why?" asked Ivy, who was sure her young gentleman had spotted them and would soon come to engage her for a dance.

"Do you want him trumpeting all over that he found us up a tree, to say nothing of trying to steal his mistletoe?"

"Oh," said Ivy, rising to join her sister. "Do you really think he would do so?"

"I have no wish to find out."

But their escape was blocked by the arrival of a solid young man who asked Ivy to dance. As they moved away, they left Holly exposed to the Squire and Lord Lawton. The Squire made them known to each other. Lord Lawton bowed, and Holly curtsied. To her surprise he made no mention of their earlier meetings but simply smiled and passed on.

Well, she thought, at least he is not going to make my conduct public, at least not yet. She could not avoid visions of London and Aunt Agatha, but since the hammer of fate had not yet fallen, she decided to put them out of her mind.

The crowd buzzed as Lord Lawton progressed about the room; the general consensus being that it was most condescending of him to come to the assembly, that he was a most handsome fellow with most handsome manners, and that probably he would take his place as a leader of country society. This prospect hardly filled Holly with glee. She doubted that she could ever enjoy any occasion of which he was part.

As usual, Holly was a favorite partner and was not required to sit out any dance unless she chose to do so. Yet, somehow, even as she danced and laughed, she always knew just where Lord Lawton could be found in the room. At a break in the music, as she watched out of the corner of her eye, Lord Lawton began a leisurely progress in her direction. Was there a chance he meant to approach her? She did not wish to find out. She clasped the arm of Stuart Darrowby, chum of her childhood, and whispered into his ear. "Dance with me."

"Oh, Holly, you know I hate to dance." She pinched his arm—only slightly—and he said, "Well, if you really have to," and led her onto the floor.

"Try to look besotted with me!"

"What? What hoax are you planning now? Are you going to get me into some kind of trouble?"

"You are such a nodcock, Stuart. Can't you just once do a favor for a friend without going into all sorts of questions? At least smile at me."

So smile he did, and as it was a rollicking country dance, there was not much need for more. Holly would have preferred to seem cool and collected, not bouncing about, but it was not to be.

She saw Lord Lawton being introduced to her father, and engaging in conversation for a moment. Then their eyes scanned the room until they lit upon her. Were her deficiencies being discussed at this very moment?

Holly fled to the entry hall and then up the staircase to the upper rooms which were not being used. There she sat, on the stair next the top, rubbing her upper arms as it was a little chilly, and ruminating on her sins.

The door to the assembly room opened, and Lord Lawton emerged. He paused and took a smoking case from his pocket. Probably going out to blow a cloud after a nice piece of work on my indiscretion, she thought. As he turned in her direction, she jerked farther into the gloom, and her fan fell and clattered down the stairs.

He looked up. "Miss Tolliver? Allow me to return your fan." He ascended the stairs and did so. Then, without a by your leave, he sat on the stair just below hers.

"Not dancing, Miss Tolliver?"

"Oh, no, no, not just now. I am just a little warm, yes, a little warm and in need of a bit of solitude."

He did not take the hint, but surveyed her with his grey eyes. "Solitude? At the most festive time of the year?"

"Just a tiny respite, and I think I am almost ready to return..."

Just then, softly but clearly, they could hear the orchestra striking up a waltz. It sounded almost like a tune from a toy music box.

"Dance with me, Miss Tolliver," he said suddenly.

"Dance?" she echoed, as though he had suggested something so out of the ordinary that she could hardly comprehend it. But she said "Yes," and arose, and collected herself to return to the assembly room.

But he said, "Just here. Just now." And he put his arm around her, and they moved to the large landing at the top of the stairs and began to waltz.

As they moved together gracefully to the distant music, she felt magic. Not the well known magic of Christmas, but a new sort of magic, one she had not known before. She could feel his regard, but she could not lift her eyes to his face. The feeling might disappear.

"You dance divinely, Miss Tolliver." His voice was low and compelling.

She whispered, "Magic!" And she lifted her head and smiled at him. His arms could not help drawing her closer. Around and around they spun, until she could not be sure if she was dizzy from the dancing or, indeed, in a completely new and magical world.

The door to the outside slammed below them, and Holly stiffened. Dancing, alone, here in the dark! If it did not give Lord Lawton a very strange opinion of her, it would certainly not suit her father. She backed away, gave her partner an uncertain smile, then dashed down the staircase.

Lord Lawton watched her descent. Perhaps there were more benefits to rustication than fresh air. Perhaps there was a kind of magic in a country Christmas.

❄ ❄ ❄

Christmas had come and gone, and Boxing Day was soon history. The end of the twelve days was in sight. The holly and the ivy and the mistletoe were all gathered up and consigned to the fire. Holly had saved a bit of the mistletoe, secretly hung well back in her clothes press. She hoped it did not bring any bad luck to the household, as keeping the holiday greens was said to do. That would be another thing to add to her list of transgressions.

For the first time she could recall, she was restless and anxious. Her father had not called her to task. How long would he keep her in suspense? Perhaps it would be a good thing if Father did send her off to London. Perhaps then she could shake this feeling of listlessness and longing. Aunt Agatha would not stand for such.

Ivy was nursing a little headache, and suddenly the heat of the small parlor was just too oppressive. Holly decided a walk might help her feel more the thing. She took up her cloak and went out.

Walking did help. The clear, cool air helped. But Holly had not paid much attention to the weather signs, and she was quite a distance from home when it began to rain. Actually, it began to pour.

At first Holly did her best to bear up under another burden. Then, feeling the cold rain trickle down her neck and the muddy slush conquer her boots, she began to laugh. A good drenching would be just the thing to improve her mood.

Just then she was overtaken in the road by a smart curricle driven, of course, by her nemesis. All that was wanting was this.

Lord Lawton stopped his horses, stepped down, and then approached, removing his hat and bowing.

"Miss Tolliver, may I be of assistance?"

Holly struggled to contain her laughter. She knew she looked a sight, and the rain was beginning to thoroughly dampen Lord Lawton also.

"Let me drive you home, Miss Tolliver. You may not stay much drier, but you will be home faster." At her nod of acquiescence, he took her arm and helped her into his carriage.

He must think I am a Bedlamite, in addition to my other shortcomings. Holly labored to seem composed.

"How is your sister?" Lord Lawton appeared to be intent on his driving.

"She is well recovered from her mishap but has a bit of a headache. I must thank you for the mistletoe."

"Ah, yes, the mistletoe." Lord Lawton did not look at her, but she could see the corners of his mouth begin to turn up. "The author of our difficulties."

"Difficulties? Oh, yes, I was very rude, was I not? I was in the wrong. So, of course, I had trouble admitting it."

"Do you always have such trouble?"

"All too often. That is why I have to be sent away to London to learn some manners, or so my father says. Did he not mention it when you spoke to him?"

"I? I have only exchanged the most common of pleasantries with your father and only for a short time at the assembly."

Holly felt the beginning of a sense of relief. "Oh, I cannot wish for you to be duplicitous but if you could feel that ..."

"You don't want me to mention your attack on my mistletoe? Why should I? It was nothing but an exchange between...shall we say neighbors? Nothing of consequence, I assure you." He turned to her and smiled, and all of a sudden Holly began to hear the faint strains of a waltz.

All of the pent up anxiety she had been hoarding began to dissipate, like bubbles bursting on the surface of a pond. "Oh, thank you, thank you. I was so afraid I would have to go to London and be nice and totally grown up and perfectly behaved all the time. I could probably do it, but I shouldn't like it at all."

"I would not like your father to send you away just at this time." He did not look at her, but the waltz music grew slightly louder.

Holly smiled. "I did not plan to call myself to your attention. I didn't even know you existed."

"No, you only knew about an ogre and a recluse. I am not always so puffed up with my own consequence. Please forgive my presumption."

Holly's eyes danced. "Hush, my Lord," she said. "Such humble pie is not your style."

Lord Lawton laughed, and put the reins in one of his hands so he might avail himself of one of hers with the other. It seemed a good fit.

At last Holly felt the full force of the magic. It had come after all—even if it was late.

"I thought you had taken me in disgust. You would have been quite right to do so."

"My dear girl, even now when you are sodden with rain you are not disgusting. From the beginning I admired your spirit. I am also not immune to a pretty face."

"Do you think I am pretty? How nice. And charming?"

"No, you are a brat. I fully expect you will lead me a merry chase."

"I?"

"Yes, and we shall have to have the most extravagant celebrations o Christmas."

"So there will be magic." She sighed happily.

"There already is."

In perfect charity with each other they rode on in the rain.

Donna Smith would, of course, write about twins; she has two sets—on of girls and one of a boy and a girl—all grown now. They are all techies of on sort or another and are a great support to their mother as she labors to becom computer literate.

A social worker by profession, Donna began to enjoy Regencies as an anti dote when the world would become too much for her. She envied the *ton* fo being able to shut out every unpleasant thing and focus on their own sybariti pursuits. She wished she could do the same and has often wondered how sh would look in a turban.

For parts of three summers, she and her husband participated in archeologi cal digs in Yorkshire. They have many fond memories of Scarborough and th Vale of Pickering.

The Smiths live in Milwaukee, Wisconsin.

*Mam'selle needed a lesson of her own! Anne certainly isn't in need of a hus-
band to tame her bullying tendencies, as her governess had decreed. But perhaps Mam'selle is right, for suddenly Anne's former beau appears, and Anne is
wishing very much to marry.*

A Gift For Mam'selle

Eileen Ramsay

Anne looked in wonder at the glorious vision in the Drawing Room. That
morning it had been no more than a splendid pine tree brought down from
Papa's Scottish estates, and now, here it stood, transformed into a thing of
splendour and delight.

"Well, Anne. Has your old Papa surprised you?"

Anne turned to her father and hugged him. "It is delightful, Papa, and the
children—and your guests—of course, will be enchanted. Who did all the
work?" she asked shrewdly for she could scarcely imagine her dear Papa
climbing ladders, as someone must have done, to tie all those little candles to
the branches or to twine those silver garlands about the tree.

"Why, Mam'selle of course," answered Lord Inchmarnock, as he had answered so many of Anne's questions for the past twenty years.

Anne frowned. She and Mam'selle, who had presided over the schoolroom
for longer than Anne cared to remember and who was now becoming quite a
thorn in the flesh, deciding that even at the advanced age of four-and-twenty,
her oldest charge required guidance, were at outs with one another.

In fact, The Honorable Miss Anne Louise Fotheringham was so out of reason at odds with her Mam'selle that she had taken the fine Paisley shawl she
had ordered for her former governess's Christmas gift and had given it to her
youngest brother, Tom, to bestow on their grandmother. Tom never had the
readies for gifts, and, since Grandmama was spending the holiday season with
them, it was imperative that he have a decent gift for her.

"And pray, who has been presiding over the schoolroom while Mam'selle
was amusing herself?" asked Anne and immediately hated herself for being so
out of reason cross.

Amusing herself was hardly an adequate description for the labor of love
that stood before her.

"La, love," said her papa, "if that's your mood this afternoon I shall see
safety in my library."

"Will you please hold the ladder while I blow out all these candles, else we
may have the house burned down around us?"

"No, indeed I won't. Ain't that why I pay exorbitant wages to several
footmen? Call one of them."

"This is a surprise for the children," said Anne crossly, "and you know per
fectly well that they will wheedle it out of any of the servants. Hold the ladder
Papa."

His Lordship smiled meekly and did as he was bid, and just as well his old
est daughter did not know his thoughts which were as like Mam'selle's as two
peas in the same pod. Miss Fotheringham would be the better for a husband to
counteract her bullying tendencies and to keep her in order.

He watched Anne climb the ladder and blow out the candles, and although
he did not dwell on the fine turn of her ankles, he did think that his daughter
was a remarkably well-looking young woman. From the tip of her sadly un
fashionable red head to her exquisite, and no doubt extremely expensive, little
green pumps, she was—pardon the natural bias of a besotted parent—perfec
tion. And why she had refused several offers from bachelors of the first stare
he could not understand.

Goodness knows, both Lord Fitzcanon and Sir Hugo Smythe-Barrows had
haunted the house from the first moment of her first season, but each had
eventually retired from the lists and married elsewhere. Then, last year Brom
field had returned from one of his missions of diplomacy and tried to fix he
interest. That had seemed to be going along nicely and la, just when the poo
man had summoned enough courage to ask his permission to speak to his
daughter, Anne had told her papa roundly that she had no desire to marry.

Did she love where it was not reciprocated, he had asked her? Surely she
did not feel he needed a housekeeper, or her young brothers and sisters he
constant care. Goodness knows 'twas impossible to move in any of his homes
without falling over some servant as devoted to his progeny as he was himself.

No understanding the heart of a woman, thought his lordship and returned
to steadying the ladder.

Anne climbed down and insisted that he remove the ladder from the room
"Or call Pisham, Papa, if to carry the ladder is an affront to your dignity. He is
the only one who will resist the children."

"Oh, I'm not so top-lofty, miss, that I can't carry a ladder." His Lordship
chuckled and proceeded to demonstrate the same. "And you'll pocket the key
until the magic hour, I take it."

"Yes indeed," said Anne as she locked the doors of the yellow drawing
room behind them.

She left her father in his library and went above stairs to her bedchamber to
think. It was a lovely room on the front side of the house, and so she was able

to look out at the small park in the center of Belgrave Square, and should she wish to, she could look up the street a little to the town house of the Earl of Crawford and his family. But why, pray, should she have the smallest desire to do so?

She looked. The lights were on, but then, so too, were theirs. It was four o'clock on a December afternoon and lights were on all over London.

She turned from the window as two tall forms in long white drab driving coats with far too many shoulder capes sauntered out of the darkness and ran lightly up the steps to Lord Crawford's house. "Crawford and his brother," said Anne as she played with the boxes on her dressing table. "Would-be Corinthians and, fie, is not Thomas setting up his nursery? They should, the two of them, be better employed." And, not that it mattered in the slightest, but how unimportant they must deem their dinner engagement if they could allow so little time for changing their dress. Oh, what did Lord Crawford or his brother mean to her? They could arrive for dinner in top boots for all she cared.

She opened a small blue box that had stood first on her mama's dressing table and then on Anne's for as many years as she could remember and listened to the tinkling sounds of an old French carol; *Il est ne, le Divin Enfant.*

Memories of her beloved mother came flooding back. Anne closed the lid and the music stopped, but still she held the box, and in her heart she heard the music. Mama had bought it in Paris during her wedding trip, just the year before that dreadful Revolution, and she had given it to Anne the Christmas before Tom was born, their last Christmas as a complete family.

Anne looked at the golden angels on the lid. The blue and gold box had been fashioned in some little town in the south of France and was supposed to represent some old French folk tale. To Anne, it spoke only of her mother.

Miss Fotheringham sighed as the tap on the door announced her maid.

"Lay out my amber silk, Cissy, if you please. I must just run up to the school room to see the children."

They were waiting for her.

"Anne, tell us. Make Mam'selle tell us," three voices demanded at once.

The three youngest of the large family clustered around their sister, demanding to be told of the surprise that was being prepared.

Anne resisted all their importuning.

"Perhaps the treat is for Grandmama," she teased.

"Grandmama," said Tom in astonishment, "but she's too old for treats, Anne."

"Oh, indeed," said Anne, who saw a good way of having her young brother spend more time with his grandmother. Poor little Tom, for no reason at all, seemed to fear his grandmother, who still wore the rather stately costumes of her own generation, finding the delightful fashions of the Regent's court "*too revealing by half.*"

"You may pester Grandmama, Tom, and I will give you and Sophia," she added, turning to Miss Sophia Fotheringham, "a hint. Our grandmother is a very close friend of our dear Queen Charlotte, and it was Her Majesty who is to be thanked for your treat."

As she had hoped, that started the children begging Mam'selle if they might visit their Grandmama in her bedchamber. "For she'll be dressed for dinner, Mam'selle," explained Sophia. "She dresses early and then rests."

"Miss Anne?" began Mam'selle, a hint of sadness in her voice, but Anne was severe. She was not yet ready to forgive the governess for hinting that she needed a husband and children of her own to manage.

Manage, indeed. If to know what was best to be done was managing, then let me manage.

"I have no desire to *manage* your schoolroom, Mam'selle. I do know that their grandmama has expressed a desire to see more of the little ones, but you must be the judge."

Well pleased, Anne returned to her room. Her grandmother would enjoy a visit from the children, and she could be trusted not to spoil the surprise. Mind you, there had been the brightness of an unshed tear in Mam'selle's eyes and that was unforgivable. She would go and chat after dinner, as she was used to do, telling Mam'selle all the droll things said during dinner, and that would show the governess that she had quite forgiven her.

Anne's maid, Cissy, was waiting to help her into her dress and to arrange her hair.

"When is the Christmas tree to be revealed, Miss Anne?" Cissy asked as she deftly separated Anne's lovely curls and piled them up on her neat little head.

"To the babes on Christmas Eve, Cissy, and then, of course, it will be a focus for the rest of the holiday festivities."

"I should not wonder that Lord Crawford will adopt it for next year," said Cissy artlessly but Anne refused to rise to the bait.

"I am sure Lady Inchmarnock is not the only person who has been honored by the sight of our dear Queen's Christmas festivities," said Anne, deftly ignoring the reference to her neighbor, Lord Crawford. "From what her ladyship tells me, it is an old custom in Germany, and her Majesty has had decorated trees at Windsor any time these past forty years. No doubt many members of the peerage have decorated trees as part of the holiday festivities."

"Can't say I've ever heard of it, Miss Anne, her Majesty always living so quiet. Mam'selle says as she never heard of it in France."

"Since Mam'selle left France when she was a child, I can well believe it," said Anne crossly. "And I do hope you have not been gossiping in front of the children. I do not want their pleasure diminished in any way."

"Lord, Miss Anne, I have to say, having looked after you for eight years, that Mam'selle is right, and who would ever think to hear me speak well of the French, cutting off heads as they do all the time, but you are beginning to sound like their mama instead of their sister."

Anne realised that Cissy did not mean that her mistress was beginning to sound like the mama of all the head-cutting-off French, but she stood up angrily.

"Enough, Cissy, when I need advice from you or Mam'selle, I will ask for it. I have no intention of abandoning my poor father and I will thank you to remember that."

Cissy wondered if sometimes his Lordship might prefer to be abandoned, if a man who had six children, a doting mother, a large circle of like-minded friends, and several over-anxious servants rushing to his aid at all hours, could be said to be abandoned. Still she said no more, and beyond fastening the necklet of delicate diamond stars around her mistress's neck, had no more to do.

When Anne went downstairs, Grandmama was in the red drawing room with Lord Inchmarnock and she was laughingly telling her son of the artless wiles used by his youngest children to discover the secret of the locked room. "Tom even told me he had the most splendid gift for me; I do believe that was in way of a bribe."

Lord Inchmarnock laughed. His youngest son found difficulty in keeping a halfpenny in his pocket. He could not imagine a *splendid gift* from that source.

Immediately Anne felt guilty. She had quite forgotten to replace the gift for Mam'selle and now, with Christmas Eve tomorrow, there was no time. No time now to think, for the guests were being announced.

"Sir John and Lady Cazin" and a few minutes later, "The Earl of Crawford, The Honorable Thomas Crawford and Mrs Crawford."

Thankfully, since the Dowager Lady Inchmarnock was present and therefore had the honor of sitting by the senior male guest, it was Thomas Crawford and not his magnificent older brother who sat beside Anne at dinner. He chatted to her artlessly of his family's plans for the holidays, of the *splendid fun* he had engaged in that afternoon at Jackson"s.

"For we had spent the entire morning, Anne, going over Estate papers, and so, while Milissa was wrapping gifts for the servants, Giles bore me off for some sparring practice."

Anne, who could think of no good reason for grown men to take part in— what she termed—degrading and dangerous sports, managed to mumble something satisfactory.

Just at that particular moment she happened to glance across the table and saw that Lord Crawford was looking at her, a faint smile in his eyes. She knew she should have all her attention on his brother, but something held her there. She did not know that she smiled back, as sweetly, as subtly, until she remembered her position and turned again to Thomas who surely had not been saying something about *stripping to advantage*. What could he mean? She set herself to keep her full attention on both Thomas on her right and Sir John on her left until her grandmama rose to lead the ladies from the table.

She forced herself not to look at Giles as she left the room and sat down on the delicate settee beside her grandmother when they returned to the drawing room.

"No indeed, miss," teased her ladyship. "I am quite thrown into the shade by your loveliness, and besides, Lady Cazin and I have months of gossip to catch up on. Do you go and sit at the pianoforte. Gentlemen find an accomplished and attractive woman impossible to resist."

"Grandmama, there is no gentleman in the party I would wish to attach."

"Then you are no granddaughter of mine. Were I four-and-twenty and unattached, I would set traps for Crawford. I saw him look at you when he hoped you were looking elsewhere."

Anne smiled sadly. "Grandmama, I made a perfect cake of myself over Giles when I first came out and he...he sent me away."

"Good gracious, child. He had just inherited and had debts to his ears and several younger brothers and sisters to rear. There was no help from his mama, too glad to rid herself of her responsibilities. What would you have had him do? Offer for you and bury you in a ruin in the country while he rebuilt the estate and educated his brothers and sisters, not to mention managing affairs so that young Thomas might wed that silly chit? Go and play... something by Mr. Handel would be nice. Her Majesty is uncommon fond of his music."

Since Her Majesty was no doubt sound asleep at Windsor, Anne wondered what good her appalling interpretation of Mr. Handel's music might do, but she obediently sat down and improvised until she was calm. Surely Grandmama did not mean her regard for Giles had been reciprocated? Of course it was not. He had sent her away quite rudely. Lowering to reflect that even so, no other man had ever taken his place in her misguided and inappropriate affections.

She obliged her grandmother by finding a book of Mr. Handel's music and soon lost herself in trying to acquit herself adequately.

"Permit me to turn for you," a voice said at her shoulder. She turned to see Lord Crawford standing beside her.

How appalling: she could feel a telltale blush flooding up from the very neckline of her dress. She must look a positive fright.

"I am persuaded Grandmama will wish me to dispense the tea, my Lord," she said, standing up and trying to look straight at him.

"Nonsense. I'm persuaded her ladyship has never addled her insides with that devil's brew. Should she want anyone to pour, she'll ask my Aunt Flaminia."

Anne looked across at Lady Cazin. "I had forgot she was your aunt," she said as she returned to her seat.

He sat beside her, and the seat was not wide. Despite her best intentions she was aware of his firmly muscled thigh through the thin stuff of her dress and tried to edge away.

"You were not used to be so missish, Anne." His lordship smiled. "But that was in the days when I was your old friend, Giles, and not this *My Lord.*"

Anne felt ready to sink. She had not been missish when she had blurted out her love for him, and here he was laughing at her over a childhood folly.

"My old friend Giles, My Lord," she said sadly, "would not continue to taunt me for a moment's indiscretion."

She made as if to move away, but he grasped her hand, and she could do nothing without drawing unwelcome attention to her plight.

"I remember me no indiscretion, Anne. I remember only a lovely girl who offered me what I wanted more than life itself and which, at the time, honor forbade me to accept, and which—forgive me—I have dared to hope might still be mine. You have not married, and better men than I have courted you. My situation is…"

But what his situation was, Anne was not destined to learn that evening.

"The tea tray is here, Anne my dear." Her father had come up behind them. "She will be furious, of course, but I think your grandmother is tired and should seek her bed. We don't need ceremony with you, Giles, my boy. You won't mind being thrown out early."

"Papa," said Anne, quite astonished.

"Good gracious, Miss, what have I said. Crawford knows he can find you here any day until we remove to the country. Now, Giles, I'll show you…indeed, I can't. Anne, m'dear, since you have the key will you show his lordship that Christmas tree. Hasn't he a notion to treat Thomas's babes?"

"They're too young, Papa," said Anne, who was ready to die of embarrassment.

"That's for their parents to decide, my love," said her father calmly. "Go you with his lordship and light some of the candles for the effect. Deuce take it, we will all come. I can't wait to show it off."

Anne could do nothing but run up to her bedchamber to fetch the key of the yellow drawing room. When she came down, Lord Crawford was waiting by the door.

"I am charged with the duty of lighting candles, Anne. No doubt you will explain this mystery."

In some embarrassment Anne opened the door, and the Earl saw the tall fir tree by the window.

He looked at it in consternation and then said, "Very nice," in a flat voice.

Anne smiled at his puzzlement. She could hardly wait to show him. "There are candles on every branch," she said. "Do you light the highest ones and I will take care of the lower limbs." She blushed as she said that word but luckily he could not see her face.

They worked quietly with only the light of a five-branched candelabrum to guide them until, at last, his lordship stepped back from his labours.

"I never saw anything prettier in my life," he said, but he was not looking at the tree. "Anne, my very dear, may I speak?"

She looked at him, so tall, so splendid, and knew that her heart was in her eyes. She moved toward him. She looked into his eyes, eyes that told her that he had loved her forever as she had loved him, and only duty and responsibility had kept them apart. Time enough to tell him that she would have welcomed poverty if he had been there to share it. He held out his hands and she moved breathlessly forward, ready to take them.

"Pretty indeed," came the chorus from the door, and whatever he might have wished to say would have been drowned in the exclamations from the doorway where the Dowager Lady Inchmarnock, leaning on her son's arm, and accompanied by all their dinner guests, stood looking at the vision of magic and delight.

"That Mam'selle of yours has outdone herself again, Inchmarnock," congratulated his mother. "I hope you value her as you ought."

Anne dropped her gaze from her grandmother's piercing eyes. It was she who, hovering on the brink of happiness, did not value her governess.

Later, after the last guest had set off and Anne had accompanied her grandmother to the door of her bedchamber, she hurried on up the stairs to the Nursery floor.

She was distressed to hear Mam'selle's soft voice answering Tom's more plaintive tones.

"There, *mon brave*, I will tell you a story. You will fall asleep, and when you wake it will be Christmas Eve."

Anne stood quietly, wondering perhaps if she should go in. It was not part of Mam'selle's duty to comfort her brother.

"It was Christmas Eve many years ago in France, and the little church where we worshipped was cold and dark with no candles or singing to welcome *Le Divin Enfant*, the Holy child. Those were terrible days in France, and it seemed as if the whole world was afraid. A few of us from my village had dared to go to the church and, yes, the Abbé was there. Poor old man, his heart was broken but not his spirit. He was determined to celebrate the birth of the Prince of Peace. We were too afraid to sing, too afraid that soldiers of the Revolution would hear us, but not the old priest. I can still hear his frail old voice, but I could not join in. I was too afraid. I kneeled down and hid my face in my hands and prayed. And then, Tom, I was aware that even through my closed fingers I could see a great light, and my ears, Tom, how they were filled with the most glorious music.

"I raised my head, opened my eyes, and closed them again, because the light was so strong. I blinked and opened them again and for a few blessed moments I saw great choirs of golden angels. They were crowded around the old priest and the humble little manger, and they were singing such songs of joy.

"The Abbé went on with the Mass and then all was dark and we stumbled out into the woods. No one seemed to have noticed and I thought it was an hallucination but Monsieur L'Abbé smiled at me. He said, 'Did you think, my dear, that *Le Bon Dieu* would allow no welcome for His son? Every Christmas Eve, the angels come to sing for joy at the birth of the Prince of Peace, and those who have eyes to see, *ma petite*, will always see them.'"

"Even at our house?" Anne heard her little brother whisper.

"Whereever love is, Tom," said Mam'selle, "there too, is *Le Bon Dieu*."

Anne turned and hurried to the stairs so that Mam'selle would not see her. She reached her bedroom and found poor Cissy dozing in a chair, waiting for her.

"Go to bed, Cissy dear," she told her. "I can manage by myself and, Cissy," she added with a smile as her maid reached the door, "Lord Crawford will call tomorrow morning."

When the maid had gone off, happily planning her mistress's appearance for the morrow, Anne sat down at her dressing table. She picked up the blue and gold box with its representations of the Christmas angels. Touching the angels gently, she smiled. After all there, would be a beautiful gift for Mam'selle.

(Well, of course—everyone wonders about those Christmas trees. Including the author, who sent us the following author note:)

"About Christmas trees. When my younger son was a baby I began re-searching Christmas customs and was fascinated to read in a book (while somewhere in Southern California) that, contrary to the accepted belief, Prince Albert did NOT introduce the Christmas tree to the United Kingdom. Could I find that book years later when I was asked to verify this fascinating little nug-get? No. Eventually I wrote to the Royal Archivist at Windsor Castle and got a lovely reply. The book was correct. 'We know from her diaries that Princess Victoria had Christmas trees as a child but the Hon. Miss Georgina Townshend, who was at the Royal family's celebrations, Christmas 1800, reported that the Queen–that's Charlotte–entertained the children in the German manner.' She then describes the tree.

The archivist also points out that George I and George II and their wives were all German and probably brought their customs with them. Looks like Prince Albert is the first 'spin doctor' because he certainly popularised Christmas trees in Merrie England.

Laurence Whistler's *English Festivals*, published in 1947, mentions that Caroline, wife of George IV had Christmas trees. Caroline married George in 1795 and died in 1821, when Victoria was but four years old!"

Eileen Ramsay lives in Angus, Scotland, and has told stories all her life. She discovered Georgette Heyer while at Boarding School and read every one between the covers of her Latin text book. She failed Latin but was not too concerned, having decided to become the Scottish Georgette, and consequently, her first published novel, a regency romance, was written in California while she watched her sons swim. As well as writing articles, children's books, serials, short stories, contemporary novels (none yet published) and Regional Sagas, Eileen is delighted to be able to return to her first love, the Regency Romance. Her first novel, *The Mysterious Marquis* will be an upcoming e-book from Regency Press. You may find out more about Eileen by visiting her website at: **http://www.eileenramsay.co.uk**

When Colonel Cameron delivers military dispatches to Oakwood Manor, he hopes for a steaming bath and a hot meal before he leaves. He gets much more than he bargains for because Lady Sophia has other ideas concerning this very attractive military man.

The Unexpected Guest

Susannah Carleton

Chapter 1

"Well, hell."

Michael Cameron, Colonel in the 10th Hussars and Earl of Dumfries, swore softly as the grey clouds, which had threatened snow since he rode out of London, honored their promise. Squinting through the blur of white created by the whirling flakes, he searched for the lane the innkeeper vowed would cut several miles off his journey. Cold, muddy, and weary to the bone after ten days of hard travel, Michael wished General Armbruster had chosen to spend the holiday in London. But he hadn't, and since the colonel's orders were to place the dispatches in Armbruster's hands, it appeared Michael would celebrate Christmas in Derbyshire, too.

Finally espying the path, he turned his horse. Letting his mind drift, he imagined a blazing fire, a steaming bath, a hot meal, and a warm, loving woman. He would, no doubt, find the first three at Oakwood Manor. The latter was merely a dream, an image that had sustained him through years of battle and lonely nights, but ephemeral as the morning mist.

"Come down, Will, before you fall." The voice roused Michael from his reverie. Glancing about, he spied three men, two standing at the base of an oak tree, the third high up in its branches. The climber's goal appeared to be a bunch of mistletoe, but Michael did not believe the nearby branches would support the man's weight.

A limb snapped loudly, producing a moan from the climber, renewed exhortations from his companions, and a command from the colonel. "Come down before you break your neck!"

The man responded as obediently as a trooper, descending quickly but carefully. When he reached *terra firma,* the older of his companions heaved a sigh of relief, then turned to the officer. "Thank you, sir. Lady Sophie wished for a bit of mistletoe and Will was determined to get it for her."

"Does Lady Sophie always get what she wants?" Michael kept the sneer from his face, but not quite from his voice.

"No, sir, she doesn't. Her wishes are rarely considered."

Michael felt a cad. It was obvious from the man's tone that Lady Sophie, whoever she was, was highly respected. "Well, then. Perhaps I can help."

"But you're bigger'n me, sir," protested Will.

Michael dismounted. "So I am, but I don't intend to climb the tree."

The two younger men goggled. The older asked, "What do you intend, sir?"

"If you can assure me that no one else is nearby, I will shoot the mistletoe from the tree. I won't get it all, but it should be enough to please your lady."

"The others took the greenery back to the house. And aye, Lady Sophie will be very happy with a small bit."

"You are certain no one else is out here?" Michael probed.

"Yes, sir. But if you like, we can search the wood for any stragglers." At his nod, the two younger men left, one walking north, the other east. Michael heard them calling out the names of, he presumed, their departed comrades.

"'Tis very kind of you to help, sir."

"I hope, in return, you will give me directions."

"Gladly, sir. Where are you going?"

"Oakwood Manor."

The man gestured broadly. "This is Oakwood. I...er...I didn't realize other guests were expected."

"I am neither expected nor a guest. I carry dispatches for General Armbruster."

"I am sure—"

Will rejoined them, slightly breathless from running. "No one about that I could see, sir. Well, exceptin' that Jem is out there now."

"When he returns we will proceed."

Two minutes later, they were ready. With the three men standing some fifty feet behind him, Michael narrowed his eyes against the swirling snow, aimed his carbine, then fired. A large clump of mistletoe—and a small oak branch— fell to the ground.

"An excellent shot, sir!" Will, grinning broadly, retrieved the prize. "On behalf of Lady Sophie, I thank you."

Michael bowed slightly. "I am happy to have been of service."

The older man gestured to the west. "The carriage drive is about fifty yards down the lane, sir."

Michael remounted his horse with a grace that belied his fatigue. "Thank you."

"A happy Christmas to you, sir."

"And to you."

As he rode toward the house, Michael contemplated the date. He'd left Lisbon on the fourteenth and reached London on the twenty-first, so today was Christmas Eve. Would Oakwood Manor, like the inn in Bethlehem, be full to the rafters? Perhaps he wouldn't have a blazing fire and a hot meal, but a bed of hay in the stable.

"Good afternoon, sir." The butler studied him from shako to mud-splattered boots before allowing him inside. Michael knew he made a strange sight wearing a greatcoat instead of his cape, but it was too damned cold to do otherwise.

"Good afternoon. I am Colonel Cameron with dispatches for General Armbruster."

"The General is not here—"

"The War Office told me he was spending the holiday at Oakwood Manor!" Michael's heart sank at the prospect of further travel.

"I beg your pardon, sir. I did not express myself clearly. General Armbruster is indeed a guest, but he is away from the house this afternoon. Do you wish to leave the dispatches or to wait?"

"My orders are to give them directly to the General."

"Very well, sir." After taking Michael's whip, gloves, shako, and greatcoat, the butler led him to a small but cozy parlor. With a blazing fire. "Would you like something to eat or drink whilst you wait?"

"Something warm would be most welcome, but I will gladly eat whatever the cook provides." Michael sank into a chair in front of the fire. "And some coffee, please, lest I fall asleep before the General returns."

"Yes, sir."

Sometime later the sound of footsteps roused Michael from a doze. The butler entered with a tray, from which steam and the mouth-watering aroma of good English food wafted. With quiet efficiency, he placed the contents of the tray on a small, round table next to the window, then pulled out a chair. "Is there anything else I can bring you, Colonel Cameron?"

"No, thank you. This will do me very well."

Michael enjoyed every delicious bite. Warm now, and replete, he leaned back and stretched—and was caught, mouth open and arms in the air, by a petite, attractive, not-so-young lady with merry brown eyes and a wealth of dark, curly hair who entered the room.

As he scrambled to his feet, the woman spoke. "Good afternoon, Colonel. I am Lady Sophie Herrington. Foster said that you have messages for my uncle."

"Michael Cameron, my lady." He bowed over her hand. "I carry dispatches for General Armbruster."

"Will you wait upon my uncle's return or shall I take the messages, er, dispatches, so that you can travel home to your family for Christmas?"

"My home is in Scotland, my lady, but I have no family awaiting me there."

She motioned him to a seat. "Then you must spend the holiday with us."

"You are very kind and generous, Lady Sophie, but I do not want to intrude upon your family's celebrations."

"Surely you cannot wish to spend the holiday alone!"

"Not at all, my lady, but neither do I want to impose—"

"Pooh." Her brown eyes sparkled as she added, "You must know, sir, that a handsome man is always a welcome addition. My young cousins will be delighted."

Michael felt the flush rising to his cheeks. "I have been a soldier for many years, my lady. My social skills are sadly out of trim."

"I see no evidence of that, sir." Tilting her head slightly to one side, Sophie studied their unexpected guest. Well over six feet tall, his broad shoulders and narrow hips were delineated by the uniform he wore. His features were, perhaps, more rugged than handsome—lean cheeks, a narrow nose, a strong jaw centered by a cleft chin—but perfectly framed the emerald green eyes. The wings of silver in his mahogany hair, as well as the lines radiating from those remarkable eyes, indicated he was closer to forty than thirty, but he was, without a doubt, the most attractive, distinguished man she'd ever met. And he was exhausted.

Sophie glanced at the ormolu clock on the mantle. "Colonel Cameron, my uncle will not return for several hours. Would you like to rest and refresh yourself? I will have you woken in good time to meet him."

"I would like that very much, my lady, but I don't want to interfere—"

"Nonsense! Truly, Colonel, we would be pleased to have you join our Christmas celebration."

He rose and bowed. "Thank you, Lady Sophie, for your extreme kindness and generosity. I accept your gracious invitation." As they walked to the door, he scooped up his saddlebags and said, "It has been so long since I spent the holiday here, I am not certain I recall all the traditions. Tell me, please, what you have planned."

Sophie's curiosity overruled her manners. "How long has it been since you celebrated Christmas in England—or Scotland?"

"Eighteen years." With a rueful grin, he added, "Nearly half my life."

"My word! We will have to do our possible to make this one memorable for you."

Chapter 2

Three hours later, after a nap and a bath, Michael felt a new man, ready to celebrate the holiday—and life. As he walked downstairs to the drawing room, where the footman who'd attended him said the family and guests gathered be-ore dinner, he thought about his hostess. She and the butler had provided three of the things he'd wished for as he journeyed here. And he'd dreamt of Lady Sophie in the fourth role.

He stood in the doorway and watched as she added ribbons and such to a ball of greenery. She was a tiny little thing—the top of her head did not even reach his shoulder—but she had a heart as big as all of England. She...

"Lady Sophie!"

With a guilty start, she turned, one hand still on the ladder. "Oh, Colonel Cameron. I...ah, you—"

"You were not intending to climb that ladder, were you?" He stalked toward her.

A fiery flush confirmed her guilt. "I only wanted to hang the kissing bough"—she lifted the greenery in her other hand—"before everyone arrives."

"I will climb. You keep your feet firmly on the ground." Belatedly recognizing the commanding tone with which he'd spoken, he winced inwardly, then smiled at her and more gently added, "If you please, and direct me in the proper placement."

With a saucy grin, she saluted. "Yes, sir."

"Old habits die hard, my dear." He took the ball and scaled the ladder, then looped the ribbons over the arms of the chandelier as she instructed.

As he descended, he noticed mistletoe hanging from the bottom of her creation. Finally, his brain made the connection he'd been too tired to make earlier: Will and the others had sought the mistletoe for her! Michael was, suddenly, very glad he'd assisted them. He remembered the holiday tradition associated with mistletoe, and he vowed to try to catch Lady Sophie beneath her kissing bough. That kiss would be his Christmas present to himself.

After collapsing the ladder and placing it in a corner near the door, he stood beside her, admiring her creation—and her. "It is very pretty, but not half so lovely as the lady who made it."

A delicate rose tinted her cheeks. "Thank you. I understand I owe—"

Two men entered the room, escorting two ladies. The men, one of whom was General Armbruster, were in their fifties. The lady on the General's arm was seventeen or eighteen; the other lady was on the far side of seventy. Lady Sophie introduced the colonel to her father, the Marquess of Hartfield, and her grandmother, the dowager marchioness; then to her uncle and her cousin, Miss Barbara Armbruster.

As Miss Armbruster assisted the dowager to a chair, the General said, "A colonel carrying dispatches? Most unusual. Well, we will deal with them after dinner."

Michael murmured his acquiescence, then was jolted from matters military by the marquess's query. "Michael Cameron, the elusive Earl of Dumfries?"

"Yes, sir. Although I would dispute the 'elusive.'"

"You might, but the members of Lords would not."

"I will take up my duties there when I have completed them on the Penin‑
sula."

The marquess's "very well" was overridden by the General's startled ex‑
clamation. "What's this?"

Repressing a sigh, Michael turned to the latter gentleman. "Two years ago
I acceded to the earldom after my brother and his family died in a fire."

"And is the estate in order and the succession secured?"

"No, sir. I haven't been in England for more than four years. I was chosen
to carry the dispatches, and given leave, so that I could see to my estate."

The entrance of half a dozen people saved him from the General's interro‑
gation about the succession. After introductions were completed, the colonel
answered a number of questions about the war, foolish ones from a foppish
stripling as well as far-sighted ones from the marquess. When the butler an‑
nounced that dinner was served, Michael stood without moving for several
moments, watching. Precedent did not appear to determine a gentleman's
choice of partner, so he scanned the room for an unescorted lady.

It wasn't until he felt a gentle hand on his arm that Michael realized that
Lady Sophie had spoken to him. Twice.

With a rueful smile, he offered his arm. "If you wish a response, my lady,
you'd best call me Colonel Cameron. I have held that rank for five years and
am accustomed to being so addressed."

"Surely after two years your new honors are familiar!"

"In truth, I cannot recall that I have ever before been addressed by my ti‑
tle."

Lady Sophie looked askance at him, astonishment writ large on her counte‑
nance, but when she spoke, it was in her normal, dulcet tone. "Should you not,
by right, be Colonel Lord Dumfries?"

He nodded. "That would be the proper title, did I choose to use it. I thought
it would be too confusing for my men, however, and have remained simply
Colonel Cameron."

"There is nothing simple about you, my lord colonel." She smiled over her
shoulder at him as he pushed in her chair, then motioned him to the seat on her
right.

Dinner was a lively affair with conversation on a wide range of topics, in‑
cluding leading questions from the younger members about the presents they
might expect. Michael rued his decision to leave his trunk in London. His sad‑
dlebags contained little more than clean linen, whilst the trunk held a number
of gifts he'd picked up over the years for his family but had never been able to
deliver. He had a bottle of very fine sherry he could give his host, but nothing
for Lady Sophie.

After the ladies departed, Michael drank a glass of port, then retired to the
marquess's study with General Armbruster. The old soldier accepted the dis‑
patches, then said, "It will take me some time to get through this pile. Go join
the ladies in the drawing room. You can answer my questions later."

Michael obeyed with alacrity. Lady Sophie's face was far lovelier to gaze upon than her uncle's.

When he reached the parlor, the other gentlemen had already joined the ladies, so he slipped in and took a seat near the door. 'Twas obvious from the gentle teasing and touching that the members of this family loved one other. His heart was gladdened to see such affection yet mourned the loss of his family. After a few minutes, 'twas also clear that the older man had been right this afternoon when he'd said Lady Sophie's wishes were rarely considered. She wanted to sing Christmas carols, her father preferred to play cards, and her younger cousins opted for charades. It appeared she would be completely overruled, until the marquess called upon Michael to join a table of whist.

He rose and bowed. "I beg you will excuse me, sir. I would prefer to sing carols." Walking toward the pianoforte, he basked in the glow of Lady Sophie's radiant smile. And fell fathoms deep in love when she met him halfway, directly under the kissing bough.

Smiling, Sophie walked toward Colonel Cameron, pleased that he thought, as she did, that Christmas Eve was a time for carols, not cards or charades. Meeting him in the center of the room, she grasped his hand and squeezed it. "Thank you, my lord colonel." Her eyes met his and, for a moment, she felt as if she were floating in a pool of deep green. The laughing exclamations of her family drew her back to the present—and to the realization that they were standing under the kissing bough.

"Oh, dear." She felt the blush coloring her cheeks. "I am sorry, Colonel Cameron. I did not intend--"

He smiled at her. "I am not at all displeased by our location, my lady. Be it intentional or otherwise." Then he bent from his great height and brushed his lips against hers. "Happy Christmas, Lady Sophie."

Somehow, she managed to return the greeting, despite the bevy of butterflies suddenly aflight in her stomach. Sophie had been kissed a few times in her twenty-eight years, mostly in circumstances such as this, but never had she felt so fluttery afterward. He plucked one of the berries from the mistletoe and put it in his pocket, then escorted her to the pianoforte. As he seated her, she wondered if her trembling fingers would be able to play a note.

After a few moments, she felt calmer and reached for the book of carols. She was a bit surprised to see all her cousins grouped around the instrument, until she realized they had but followed the colonel's lead. *What a dear man he was.*

Wanting to honor him as he'd honored her, she asked, "What is your favorite carol, Colonel Cameron?"

He thought for a moment before replying. "*O Come, All Ye Faithful.*"

She found the page, played a short introduction, then began to sing. Barbara's alto, Freddie's wobbly tenor, and Tom's baritone immediately joined her soprano. A few notes later, a deep, gloriously rich bass underscored them all sending chills down her spine. She glanced up and met the colonel's smiling eyes. And fell a little bit in love.

When Foster brought in the tea tray more than an hour later, her cousins darted away. As Sophie put away the music, Colonel Cameron said, "I enjoyed that. Very much. You have a lovely voice, Lady Sophie—"

"I? 'Tis you who have the magnificent voice, Colonel."

"Let us agree that God has gifted us both with extraordinary voices."

With a nod, Sophie rose from the bench. He tucked her hand in his elbow and escorted her across the room. "I suspect those carols were no challenge to your talent. I hope to hear you play again."

"It would be my pleasure, sir." She smiled her thanks, then took her place behind the tea tray and began to pour.

By the time they left for church, it had stopped snowing, but the snow was more than six inches deep on the lawn. Two large sleighs would carry the older people to church, but Sophie and her cousins always walked. Her father called for her to join him, but she demurred, offering the place to Barbara or Mary, both of whom squeezed in. Eyeing the mounds with some misgiving, she set off behind Freddie and Tom, only to be stopped in mid-stride and lifted on a horse. A very tall horse, fitted with a man's saddle.

"Wet hems and cold feet will not benefit your singing, little songbird." Colonel Cameron took the reins and, leading the horse, followed her cousins.

"And what of your feet, sir?"

"These boots and I have survived worse than this."

"Does it snow on the Peninsula?"

He answered that question and a dozen more before they reached the church.

❆ ❆ ❆

From the look on Colonel Cameron's face as he escorted her down the aisle, Sophie thought he'd found the service as uplifting as she had. Ever honest, she admitted that part of her joy had come from the presence of the man beside her, his arm against hers as they'd crowded into the pew, his gloved fingers touching hers on the prayer book. But the rest was the magic—the miracle—of Christmas.

When they stepped outside, he lifted his face to the sky and studied the stars, then exhaled deeply. "Christmas is a magical time, is it not? Tonight I can almost believe there will be peace on earth again."

She squeezed his arm gently. "For your sake, and that of all our soldiers, I hope it comes soon."

They did not converse on the walk home, each lost in their own thoughts, but the silence between them was a comfortable one. Stopping the horse in front of the door, the colonel dropped the reins and grasped her about the waist. "Good night, Lady Sophie. Thank you for sharing your Christmas Eve with me." He kissed her, then lifted her to the ground. And Sophie fell a little further in love.

Chapter 3

Early the next morning, Michael walked downstairs still feeling tired. Given the luxurious comfort of his billet and the depth of his fatigue, he ought to have slept like a babe. Instead, he'd tossed and turned for hours, contemplating such imponderables as: Can one chaste kiss—or even two—cause a man to tumble head over heels in love? Might a lady do so as quickly? How soon after meeting her might a man propose marriage to a lady and not be considered a fool? And the question that nipped at his heels like a hound chasing a fox: How long would it take General Armbruster to compose his replies to the dispatches? When Michael had, finally, fallen asleep, he'd dreamt of Lady Sophie, and whilst some of those dreams had been peaceful and idyllic, others had not. Twice he'd woken tangled in the bedclothes, muscles taut, sweating and aching.

As he reached the dining room, he resolved that, however long or short his stay at Oakwood Manor might be, he would enjoy it—and the company of Lady Sophie—to the fullest. Opening the door, he was surprised to see he was not the first to arise this Christmas morn. Lady Sophie sat at the table in a green wool dress with a lace-trimmed bodice, a cup of tea in her hand and a distant expression in her eyes.

"Good morning, Lady Sophie. Happy Christmas to you."

She started and turned, a delighted smile on her face. "Good morning, Colonel Cameron. A happy Christmas to you, too. I trust you slept well."

"Tolerably." Reaching her side, he took her hand and raised it to his lips, brushing a kiss across her knuckles. A delicate blush tinted her cheeks and she averted her face. Michael's heart sank as he released her hand. "I apologize, my lady, if my attentions have displeased you."

The blush blossomed to a deeper pink. "Oh, no. I am not at all displeased, my lord colonel. Merely...flustered." She waved him to the sideboard, where an array of cold and warm dishes waited to tempt even the most jaded palate.

Michael piled his plate with eggs, bacon, kippers, and porridge. Returning to the table, he placed one hand on the back of the chair next to hers. "May I join you?"

"Please do. It is always more pleasant to have a companion at table. My uncle was here when I came down, but he left shortly before you came in."

It would be very pleasant to share breakfast with her for the next fifty years or so, he mused as he seated himself.

"Coffee, tea, or ale?"

"Coffee, please."

As she passed him a cup, she looked at his plate and chuckled. "A Scotsman to the bone, aren't you?"

He felt one corner of his mouth turning up in a smile. "I am certain there are Englishmen, and women, who like porridge. I am only half Scottish, you know."

"I didn't know. I know nothing about you except what you, yourself, have told me." After a moment's pause, she amended, "That is not quite true. My uncle said you are a very good soldier and an exceptional leader." Another pause, longer this time, then, "Tell me about yourself and your family."

Michael granted her request. She, in turn, told him of her life. Two hours later, when the marquess and Viscount Lorring entered the room, they were still talking. After greeting the newcomers, Sophie took her leave to speak with the cook. Michael made his excuses and followed her out.

"Lady Sophie, are there any youngsters here for the holidays who might enjoy a romp in the snow?"

"Besides Barbara, Mary, Tom, Freddie, and me?" she quizzed, smiling.

"Yes, there are. Shall I take you up to the nursery and introduce you?"

"I don't wish to detain you. May I wait in the morning room whilst you attend to your duties?"

"Of course, Colonel. I shan't keep you waiting long."

She was as good as her word, returning in less than ten minutes. He rose when she entered, returning her smile. "Would you truly enjoy a romp in the snow?"

"Indeed I would." Her smile blossomed into a grin. "And a snowball fight."

"I cannot image Miss Lorring or Tom doing so. Miss Armbruster, possibly. Freddie, most definitely."

"Mary may decline, but the others will not. I will take you up and introduce you to the younger Lorrings, then roust the others out of bed."

The nursery set greeted the plan with enthusiasm. Fifteen minutes later, Michael descended the stairs to find Lady Sophie and Miss Armbruster searching for six-year-old Matthew Lorring's lost mitten. It was quickly found and they trooped outside, where the children and Freddie frolicked like puppies.

Michael didn't know who threw the first snowball, but it caught Lady Sophie in the back, nearly knocking her off her feet. Soon the air was full of icy missiles, with the colonel, Lady Sophie, and Miss Armbruster teamed against the five Lorrings. The General's daughter had a good arm but lamentable aim; her balls hit a target, but rarely, she laughingly exclaimed, was it the one she'd intended. Lady Sophie's aim was truer, but her arm not as strong; she soon resorted to fashioning ammunition for her teammates.

An hour later, cold, wet, and rosy-cheeked, they brushed the snow off one another and returned to the house. As they warmed themselves in front of the morning room fireplace and drank hot chocolate, the children gave a blow-by-blow account of the fight to the marquess, General Armbruster, and Viscount and Lady Lorring. The tale told, Lady Lorring shooed them all upstairs to change into dry clothes.

Following her children to the door, the viscountess paused beside his chair. "Thank you, Lord Dumfries. It was very kind of you to take the children out."

"It was my pleasure, my lady. Your children are delightful."

A smile lit the viscountess's face. "Thank you."

Michael listened as the other men discussed a hunt scheduled for the next day. Suddenly, the viscount said, "Dumfries, you'd best change your clothes before my wife returns or you will earn a scold for your folly, regardless of how many years you have in your dish."

Chagrined, Michael shifted in his chair. "I will deserve it. It wasn't until after we returned indoors that I remembered I have naught but clean linen in my saddlebags."

The image of his tiny sister chastising the tall colonel had the marquess laughing so hard, tears rolled down his cheeks, but all three men invited Michael to make free with their wardrobes. Three-quarters of an hour later, garbed in a coat, vest, and breeches belonging to the viscount, a pair of the marquess's shoes, and his own linen, the colonel again descended the stairs. Both the marquess's valet and the viscount's, who'd assisted him, had pronounced him complete to a shade, but, accustomed as he was to wearing a uniform, Michael felt decidedly unlike himself. He wondered what Lady Sophie would think of his transformation from soldier to man of fashion. Reaching the first floor landing, he heard *"The Holly and the Ivy"* being played on the pianoforte, so he turned toward the drawing room to find out.

❄ ❄ ❄

Foolish, foolish girl! Sophie sat at the pianoforte and buried her face in her hands. She'd been building castles in the air since last night. Just because she had fallen in love with Colonel Cameron, it did not necessarily follow that he had fallen in love with her. She had fancied herself in love before and nothing had come of it. Why should this time be any different? *Because Colonel Cameron is a better man than most.* Sophie wanted to believe the little voice whispering from her heart—Michael Cameron was far superior to most men of her acquaintance—but another voice, this one from her head, destroyed her burgeoning hope with its counterarguments. *You are the same woman you have always been. And you are eight-and-twenty, less of a matrimonial prize than ever.*

Sophie was not, and had never been, a Diamond of the First Water. During the years since her come-out, the fashionable world had acclaimed tall, slender, raven-haired girls and blue-eyed blondes, either voluptuous or willowy, but tiny chits with brown hair and brown eyes had never been in vogue. She wasn't ugly, but neither was she beautiful. She wasn't vivacious and she couldn't flirt, but she was an experienced hostess, accustomed to overseeing several households, and she had a heart full of love to give to a husband and children. She could easily imagine Colonel Cameron in that role, had been dreaming of it since he'd kissed her...

Enough. She was not going to fret herself to flinders over air dreams. She would enjoy Colonel Cameron's company whilst he was here—and renew her prayers for a husband and children to love. Resolved, Sophie lifted her hands to the keys and began to play.

As always, the music calmed her. The carols with their message of joy and hope heartened and cheered her. She had much for which to be thankful.

At the sound of a quiet footstep, Sophie glanced toward the door. "Colonel Cameron!" Her fingers stumbled over the notes at the sight of the tall man standing just inside the portal. "Nay, it is Lord Dumfries, is it not?" she corrected as she rose to greet him.

He bowed over her hand, but did not—to her regret—salute her knuckles as he had earlier. "I am the same man, both colonel and earl, regardless of my clothing, Lady Sophie."

"I know that. You look very elegant, my lord colonel." She smiled inwardly as his lean cheeks flushed. "Not that you didn't look very distinguished in your uniform." The blush deepened.

He choked out a "thank you," sounding half strangled.

She studied him, wondering at the too-large breeches and slightly too-tight coat. "Why the change?"

"I...ah...." His face crimson, he led her to the sofa. Lifting her face to his, she patted the place beside her and waited for his reply. Instead of joining her, he paced away, then stood staring down at the fire in the hearth. "You have made me feel so welcome here that I forgot I am not really a guest. When—"

Sophie stood abruptly. "You *are* a guest, a most welcome one."

He nodded as if acknowledging he'd heard her, rubbed his hand over the back of his neck, then spoke rapidly. "When I suggested the outing in the snow this morning, I forgot that I didn't have a trunkful of clothes to wear, only clean linen in my saddlebags."

"Oh, Colonel." Sophie hardly recognized the soft, breathy voice as her own.

He turned and looked at her, his expression softening, then walked toward her. She met him in the center of the room, taking his hand and squeezing it. "What a wonderful man you are."

"You don't think me foolish?"

Sophie shook her head emphatically as she stared at the buttons on his waistcoat. "No. Kind, generous, wonderful, but not in the least foolish."

"Sweet Sophie." He rubbed the back of his index finger against her cheek.

Her breath caught in her throat at the tender gesture. Grasping his hand, she stepped back, tilting her head back to look at his face—and realized they were, once again, standing under the kissing bough.

Should she mention it? Something, perhaps a change in her expression, must have alerted him. He glanced up, then down at her, a delighted grin curving his mouth and brightening those extraordinary eyes. With a gentle tug on their clasped hands he drew her toward him, lifting first one hand, then the other to his lips. Slowly he lowered his head. His lips found hers, brushing them, then returning to kiss her again.

She bit back a sigh when he stepped back and released her hands. "Happy Christmas, Sophie."

"Happy Christmas, Colonel Cameron."

He plucked a berry from the mistletoe, then scrutinized her face for several moments. Finally, he retreated another pace and motioned toward the pianoforte. "Will you play for me?"

Did he truly expect her fingers to be steady after their kiss? Perhaps it hadn't affected him as it had her. "If you like." She walked to the instrument and seated herself, then took a deep, calming breath. "Is there a particular piece you would like to hear?"

"I will enjoy whatever you choose."

She played "The First Noel," but had just completed the first verse when her great-uncle entered the room. "Sophie, your father requests you join him in the morning room."

"Thank you, Uncle Eversleigh." Rising, she turned to the colonel, who also stood. "I am sorry, sir—"

"No apology is necessary, my lady. I have kept you from your duties long enough."

Lady Sophie offered him a wobbly smile, then departed. Michael was surprised her great-uncle didn't follow, even more startled when the Bishop of Eversleigh joined him on the sofa.

"You seem troubled, young man."

"How so, my lord?"

"If I knew why, I wouldn't need to ask, now would I?" the old man said testily, studying Michael's face. "Troubled in your soul. Or in your heart."

Michael fought the urge to squirm away from that probing gaze. "I feel a...conflict sometimes, between my duties as a soldier and those as earl. That I have postponed taking up most of the latter," he clarified.

"Any good man would. But that isn't what is worrying you now."

Michael looked at the bishop, the concerned expression on the seamed face, the kindness in the faded blue eyes, and made his decision. Taking a deep breath, he blurted, "There is a lady."

The old man slapped his knee. "I knew it," he chortled. After a few moments, mirth controlled, his gaze swept the colonel from head to toe. "You are an exceedingly eligible fellow, so where lies the problem? Is the lady not suitable to be your countess?"

"The lady is quite eligible and perfectly suited to be *my* countess."

"You love her then."

Michael nodded. "I love her and am in love with her. But although I feel I know her very well, and she, to a slightly lesser extent, me, I have not known her very long. And I do not know if she returns my regard."

"You have not told her you love her? Or proposed marriage?"

"No. Neither one."

"Why not?"

Michael slumped back against the sofa cushions. *Why not, indeed?* Before he could repeat that he had known the lady for only a short time, the bishop spoke again. "You said that your acquaintance with the lady is fairly recent, but it has been long enough for you to know that you love her. What makes you think that she hasn't had time to realize her feelings?"

"I...ah—"

"I will give you the benefit of a lesson learnt from bitter experience. If you do not open your heart and ask for the lady's hand in marriage, you will always regret that you did not. You will spend the rest of your life wondering what would have happened if you did.

"There are three possible outcomes if you act upon your feelings: The lady may accept and make you a very happy man, or she might ask for more time to be certain of her heart, or she might refuse you, in which case you can get on with your life."

The bishop placed a hand on Michael's shoulder and levered himself to his feet. "You have nothing to lose by asking. It just takes a bit of courage."

A bit of courage? The colonel's mouth quirked at the understatement. Facing French cannon was less frightening than the thought of baring his heart.

Chapter 4

When it was time to dress for dinner, Michael was pleased to find his uniform dry, brushed, and pressed. If he had the opportunity, he would offer heart and hand to Sophie. The uniform would not make such a difficult task easier, but he was comfortable in it and would, at least, feel like himself.

He was plagued by uncertainties, despite his talk with the bishop. Did Sophie return his regard? Would she accept his proposal or laugh in his face? Was it fair to ask her to wait for him? Could he make her happy? He would have answers to the first two after he spoke with Sophie. And he had decided the choice to wait or not should be hers. As for the last, only time would tell, but he loved her enough to believe that he could.

He checked his appearance in the cheval glass, then reached for his gloves. The bottle of sherry on the dresser, his Christmas present to the marquess, reminded him that he hadn't yet asked Sophie's father for permission to pay his addresses. When did the Herringtons exchange gifts, he wondered, touching his pocket to ascertain he had Sophie's present.

The drawing room was empty when he arrived, except for a pile of gaily wrapped packages near the hearth. Turning on his heel to go upstairs and retrieve the marquess's gift, he nearly bumped into that gentleman. "I beg your pardon, my lord. I just realized I left a present in my room."

Hartfield motioned to a footman outside the door. "Tom will get it for you." After instructing the man where to find the gift, Michael turned back to Sophie's father. "I wonder if I might have a few minutes of your time later, sir." The marquess glanced at the enameled clock on the mantle. "You may have them right now, if you like."

The colonel swallowed hard. He had never asked for a lady's hand and had not yet considered how to present himself to her father. Hartfield poured two glasses of sherry and, with an expectant look, offered him one. Michael accepted it, then took a deep breath. "I would like your permission to pay my addresses to your daughter."

Waving him to a seat, the marquess sipped his sherry, studying Michael over the rim of the glass. "This is rather sudden, is it not? You only met Sophie a few days ago."

"Yesterday. I met her yesterday." Michael didn't believe that admission would aid his cause, but he could not be other than honest. "It is sudden, sir, but I know my heart."

"Ah. You love Sophie, then?"

"Yes, Lord Hartfield, I do. I fell in love with her last night under the kissing bough, but by then I already loved her for her kindness, her generosity, her wit and warmth. I want to share the rest of my life with her, to love and be loved by her. I—"

He broke off as the Lorrings, all eight of them, entered the drawing room. As the children ran to examine the pile of gifts, the marquess stepped close and spoke softly. "I believe I know your character, and I am certain you are able to support a wife. You have my permission to address Sophie, but the decision will be hers alone."

Smiling, Michael accepted the marquess's outstretched hand. "Thank you, my lord."

The arrival of the dowager and the bishop claimed his host's attention. Michael joined the Lorrings whilst he waited for Sophie, whom he hadn't seem since luncheon, to appear. What, he wondered, had his darling been doing all afternoon? Had she been thinking of him?

❊ ❊ ❊

Sophie ran toward the stairs, knowing she was late. She had just completed her last gift, the one for their unexpected guest, and while it was an acceptable present, it was not what she would most like to offer him. A knitted scarf was a poor substitute for her heart, although a more practical, and socially acceptable, gift. Pausing outside the drawing room to catch her breath, she wondered what Colonel Cameron had done this afternoon, if he'd thought of her. And she hoped that she'd be fortunate enough to catch him under the kissing bough this evening. That would be a wonderful Christmas gift.

After a quick glance in the mirror to check that her heavy curls hadn't fallen from their pins in her mad dash, she stepped across the threshold. She apologized to her father and grandmother for her tardiness, then placed her present with the others. Scanning the room, she saw Colonel Cameron, resplendent in his regimentals, standing near the window, Matthew perched on his shoulders and Betsy hopping up and down at his side. She wondered if anyone had told him the children would share dinner with the adults tonight, before they opened their gifts. Freddie joined her just as Foster announced that dinner was served. She looked across at the colonel, wondering if he would escort her again this evening, but Freddie was quicker. As she accepted her cousin's arm, she saw Colonel Cameron bend toward Betsy and the nine-year-old's delighted grin. *What a wonderful man he was.*

❈ ❈ ❈

Michael muffled a groan as he pushed back his chair to assist Betsy from hers. The food had been abundant and delicious, the company delightful but noisy. He was not yet ready for six children, he acknowledged ruefully, at least not six as lively as the Lorrings. One would do to start. As his body reacted to the thought of creating a child with Sophie, he quickly resumed his seat and engaged Freddie in a discussion of Latin declensions.

Knowing the children were eager to open their gifts, the gentlemen drank only one glass of port. As they quitted the dining room, General Armbruster caught his arm. "Are you taking my letters to Wellesley? I thought you said you'd been granted leave."

"That is correct, sir. I will take them to London, where Captain Middleford is waiting to take them to Sir Arthur."

"Middleford ought to have brought them here."

"He wanted to spend Christmas with his family. As I don't have one, I volunteered to bring them to you."

Armbruster nodded. "That was kind of you, Cameron. I will give them to you later. You can leave at first light."

Michael's heart sank. "Yes, sir." *Would he have the opportunity to speak to Sophie tonight?*

Entering the drawing room, the colonel chose a seat near the door. Betsy had explained during dinner that the children would distribute their presents first, then receive their gifts. After the youngsters had gone up to bed, the adults would have their turn. Since he had only two gifts to give—one public, one private—and since he wasn't really a guest, he would just sit quietly and watch.

Michael was more touched than he could say when each of the children presented him with something they had made: a drawing of his horse from young Matthew, a badly embroidered handkerchief from Betsy, and a lump of leather he was assured would be a capital pen-wiper from Peter. Asking Foster for paper and pencil, Michael quickly drew a sketch of each child, trying to capture both features and personality. A collision between Betsy and Peter under the kissing bough, and the argument that followed when the eleven-year-old boy realized he had to kiss his sister, gave Michael time to complete the drawings.

Glancing at the pile of gifts, he wondered if anyone else had taken the time to make him a present. Considering how they'd welcomed him, he was certain some of them had. He requested more paper, then settled to his task, wishing he'd thought to do so earlier.

There were three encounters under the mistletoe whilst gifts were distributed to the children: Tom and Miss Armbruster, Freddie and Sophie, and Michael and Lady Lorring. Fortunately for Freddie's continued good health, he bussed his cousin on the cheek. The children proclaimed themselves delighted with the drawings whilst their parents and the other adults marvelled that he'd portrayed both looks and character. Pleased by the success of his last-minute gifts, Michael hurried back to his corner to finish sketching the adults.

When the children departed, after "thank-yous" and hugs all around, the colonel was still laboring. The arrival of the tea tray was a welcome reprieve, giving him a chance to study his last two subjects: the marquess and the dowager marchioness. He gulped his tea and took up his pencil, finishing just as the marquess stood and indicated it was time for the gentlemen to disburse their gifts.

Michael's gifts were, again, a great success. For the bishop, a caricature of himself in the pulpit, admonishing his congregation; for the General and his daughter, portraits of each other; for Viscount and Lady Lorring, a drawing of themselves surrounded by their children; for Tom, Freddie, and Miss Lorring, an individual likeness; for the dowager, a drawing of her son; for the marquess, one of his daughter (and the bottle of sherry); and for Sophie, a portrait of her father and grandmother.

Returning to his chair, Michael was astonished at the pile of gifts on the seat—and very glad he'd drawn something for each of them. He received handkerchiefs embroidered with his initial from Lady Lorring, Miss Lorring, and Miss Armbruster, a beribboned bookmark from the dowager, a knitted scarf from Sophie, a silver flask, well used but prized, from General Armbruster, a book of sermons on love and marriage from the bishop, a gold cravat pin from Viscount Lorring, and a bottle of very fine champagne from the marquess.

Attempting to swallow the lump in his throat, the colonel stood. "I want to thank Lady Sophie and Lord Hartfield for inviting me to spend Christmas here, and all of you for welcoming a stranger and for your generosity. I have not spent the holiday in this country for eighteen years, but I will never forget your exemplification of the true meaning of Christmas.

"I have one final gift to give. Lady Sophie, would you accompany me to the library, please?"

A slight frown creased Sophie's brow as she stood and took his arm. "You have already given me a present, Colonel Cameron."

"Yes, I know, but I gave your father two gifts, also."

When they reached the library, Michael seated her on the sofa, then sat next to her. "Sophie, I cannot thank you enough for your kindness and generosity to a stranger, for inviting me to spend Christmas here and allowing me to share your celebrations. I have never enjoyed the holiday more, not even as a child, and I will remember this Christmas, and you, as long as I live. I wish that I could stay for all twelve days, but the General informed me after dinner that I must leave at first light."

"So soon?"

"Yes." He reached into his pocket and pulled out his mother's locket, which had been his talisman for many years. Fashioned like a heart, it had lost its shape—and saved his life—when hit by a pistol ball three years ago. Taking her hand, Michael placed the locket in her palm, then curled her fingers around it and enveloped her hand in his. "Although I depart in the morning, I leave my heart herewith you. I love you, sweet Sophie. Will you do me the very great honor of becoming my wife?"

She stared at him for a moment, eyes wide, then slipped her hand from his and opened her fingers.

"It belonged to my mother," he said, then explained the reason for its battered state.

"Oh, Michael." Tears pooled in her eyes, but she blinked them away and grasped his hand. "I love you, too, Michael. I would be very honored, and very happy, to be your wife."

For such an answer Sophie was rewarded with a number of Christmas kisses, all without benefit of mistletoe. Eventually, they returned to the drawing room where Michael toasted his bride-to-be with the champagne her father had given him, then consulted briefly with the marquess and the bishop.

Early the next morning, the colonel departed. On January sixth, the twelfth day of Christmas, he returned and, surrounded by her loving family, with her great-uncle Eversleigh presiding, Sophie married her unexpected but most welcome guest. It was the first, and in some ways the most memorable, Christmas Sophie and Michael shared. But the next forty-seven were even more full of love and joy.

Susannah Carleton is a mechanical and biomedical engineer, working as a consulting engineer after fifteen years as a college professor. At the ripe old age of 33, she discovered Regency romances and promptly fell in love, since life among the ton in Regency England is such a diverting change from her workday world. After reading several thousand Regencies, and with more than a bit of prompting and encouragement from author friends, Susannah took the plunge and began writing them as well. Her short story, *The Viscount's Angel*, is in A REGENCY SAMPLER and she contributed Chapter Four of *To Find a Hero*, the collaborative story featured at The Reticule, an e-zine sponsored by Regency Press. (**http://www.regencyreticule.com**).

Currently working on the second book of a Regency quartet, she lives in Florida with her husband and teenage son.

Romance is the furthest thing from Deidre's mind; however, her young "niece" is determined to give her the best Christmas present ever. Read on to learn about Cupid's curly-haired accomplice!

A Very Special Christmas Present

Susanne Marie Knight

"What you need is a husband!"

At her best friend's provoking words, Deirdre Livingston dropped her needlework and gave her full attention to the vivacious dynamo who was also, at present, her hostess. "Emma Fairmont, whatever are you talking about?"

"Darling, I am worried about you." Emma whirled around her elegant drawing room as a spinning top might, after just being launched. "With your dear brother, Thomas, now gone, there is no one left to take care of you."

Even after five long months, the pain of losing Thomas still stabbed at Deirdre's heart. To regain her composure, she blinked her eyes and stared at the snow-capped fir trees huddled outside the large latticed window.

Emma laid a comforting hand on Deirdre's shoulder. "Dee, you must admit, a woman alone at your advanced age is at the mercy of...dastardly scoundrels—of the worst type!"

Sighing, Deirdre picked up her needle and thread to continue embroidering the handkerchief. To some, the age of six-and-twenty might be advanced, however she did not fear a strand of grey or two marring the darkness of her hair. "Are there any other kind of scoundrels?"

Emma was not amused. The lacy mobcap denoting her married status fairly vibrated with her outrage. "This is exactly what I mean. Here you are, talking gammon! A husband would surely provide a stabilizing influence for you."

Pull the reins in on me, more like, Deirdre thought mulishly. However as she was a guest of Sir Hector and Lady Fairmont—her dearest Emma had married well—Deirdre wisely withheld her reply.

A slight movement near the white alabaster fireplace caught her eye. There, behind the plump, upholstered chair, hid a small child eagerly devouring every adult word! But who had the audacity—?

The redheaded minx placed a tiny finger to her lips, evidently hoping Deirdre would not expose this current display of naughtiness. Withholding a smile, Deirdre lowered her gaze and finished tying off a bright yellow string of thread. Spirited Matilda Fairmont was Emma's eldest. A rare handful indeed.

Not feeling guilty about being in league with a five-year-old, Deirdre commented, "You might be right, Emma, about a husband. Since it is the holiday season, perhaps I shall acquire one for Christmas."

"Dee?" A frown of concentration distorted her friend's lively face as she tried to decipher what Deirdre meant. Husbands, after all, were not purchased in a specialty shop and then trussed up with a velvet bow to amuse family and friends.

Deirdre shook her head sadly. It truly was too bad things had to change. At one time she and Emma were as alike as two peas in a pod, with no room for a third. Now, today, a marriage and three children later, Emma had the respectability so demanded by polite society while Deirdre was still in many ways an incorrigible hoyden—with an iron will of her own.

"Christmas!" Emma brightly latched onto the word. "Yes, precisely. Sir Hector and I are so delighted you decided to forego your grieving for poor Thomas and celebrate the holidays with us. We have invited all Woburn's eligible bachelors for tomorrow's festivities, you know. In fact, you cannot imagine my joy when I heard the news that should the weather hold, the Earl of Bainbridge will deign to attend our little soirée."

Will deign, will he? How kind of him! Threading the needle with brilliant emerald green thread, Deirdre then savagely thrust it into her embroidery. She did not know the Earl of Bainbridge from Adam, but she had a bone to pick with England's nobility class. While most of them stayed home to enjoy the bounty of dissipated pleasures, the brunt of England's horrendous, never-ending war was placed squarely on the shoulders of respectable, but common, working men. Men who had more nobility in their left pinkie toe than those so-called aristocrats. Men like dearest Thomas, whose life had been snuffed out on a battlefield, in a foreign land, with no mourners to shed bitter tears.

Even now in this, the ending days of the year of our Lord 1812, tears threatened to stream from her eyes. Hearing a noise in the entryway, Deirdre jumped at her chance for solitude. "Goodness! It sounds as if more guests have arrived. Do go on, Emma, to greet them. I shall be fine here by myself."

Emma nibbled on her lower lip. "Are you certain, Dee?" As a loud, querulous voice penetrated the depths of the corridors and into the drawing room, she slapped her hands to her cheeks. "Gracious me! Sir Hector's grandmama, Lady Pringle. I, ah, I should go attend…"

Her voice dropping away, Emma left to dance attendance on that matronly tartar, which left Deirdre not truly alone. "You may come out now, Tilly. An explanation is in order, young lady."

Instead of creeping with her tail between her legs, so to speak, Matilda hopped out from behind the chair and giggled her way to Deirdre's side. "Auntie Dee! I knew you wouldn't tell on me!"

Enveloped in a satisfying hug, Deirdre smiled sadly, savoring the innocent scent of childhood combined with rosewater from Matilda's bath. With Thomas gone, the chances of her becoming a true aunt were decidedly slim. "So tell me, Tilly, what mischief are you up to now? And why are you not upstairs in the nursery?"

"Nanny has her hands full," Matilda sing-songed as if repeating the nanny's own words. "Too many cousins upstairs! It's not fair. I have to share my bed with a frightful little monster..." She then dimpled an infectious smile. "Auntie Dee, I just wanted to see you. I'll help you get a husband."

Deirdre coughed; she could not help it. She was not sure whether to laugh or cry. "Tilly, your mama and I were talking nonsense. Truly." She gave the precocious child a kiss on the cheek. "You must go back upstairs right now, before you are missed. Remember, tomorrow is Christmas, and there will be presents. I have a special one for you."

"But I have nothing for you." Matilda frowned. "I could give you one of Mama's pretty gowns. Your clothes are too dark."

Mourning clothes usually were, but a child would not be aware of that. Deirdre smoothed Matilda's corkscrew curls off her high forehead. "I need nothing, you silly goose. Now, off with you before your nanny grows alarmed."

The child sucked in her lower lip, duplicating one of her mother's mannerisms. "Don't worry, Auntie Dee. I'll get you a special present, too. A very special present!"

After a quick kiss, a rustle of petticoats, and a door slamming shut, Deirdre finally was alone in the drawing room. No longer interested in embroidering, she set her needlework aside once again to stare out the window. Winter's icy breath had crystallized the Fairmont landscape, turning it into a garden of frozen delights.

Frigid, heartless beauty.

At this moment, Deirdre feared winter's breath had touched her as well. Cold and empty, her heart shriveled within her breast. Without Thomas, life itself seemed pointless. But, duty demanded the living carry on without the loved ones left behind. Which meant tomorrow she would be expected to set aside her grieving and wear a merry face at the Christmas ball.

Sighing, she closed her eyes tightly. Dear God in heaven. However would she manage?

❈ ❈ ❈

After being announced, Jeremy Stafford, the fifth Earl of Bainbridge, sauntered into the Fairmont ballroom, recognizing his congenial host but no one else. He cast an uninterested eye around the huge room, then flicked a bit of lint off his superfine tailcoat. Sighing, he mentally raked himself over the coals. Why the deuce had he agreed to attend?

Damn it all, the buzz emanating from tipsy revelers could do nothing bu encourage his foul disposition. The overpowering scent of greenery—holly ivy, and in particular, mistletoe—caused him to sink further into the dismals Normally that would not have been the case. However, with a variety of mar riage-minded maidens infesting the ballroom, he would certainly have to watch where he stepped. Mistletoe, the main component of the infamous kissing bough, hung from each of the three chandeliers—low enough to brush the top of his hair should he be foolish enough to find himself under the greenery Some females used any excuse to lay claim to an eligible lord of the realm, es pecially an earl.

Blast. Again he scanned the room. Musicians in place, dancers lined up for a cotillion, the taste of wassail punch in the air; the festivities were well un derway. There could be no avoiding the merriment of the season.

Jeremy ran his hand through his hair. Damn. He *should not* have come. But in a weak moment, he had yielded to Sir Hector's entreaties. And a word once given was one's solemn duty to obey. So there it was.

A flicker of movement caught his attention. A rose petal, pink in color now settled at the end of the hearth rug. Next to the petal stood a dandified fledgling, scarcely old enough to shave. However, the young man had not no ticed the petal's descent, for he continued with his conversation.

About to turn away, Jeremy then spotted another petal, fluttering next to a gentleman at the opposite side of the fireplace. As before, no one observed the soft pink rose petal.

Intrigued, Jeremy looked up. Situated high above the room, a balcony overhang ran along all four walls. Peeping through the column-slats on the bal cony was a tiny girl. A very tiny girl with riotous red curls. At this late hour, it was a certainty she had escaped from the nursery. With a frown as large as her cherub face, she prepared to launch yet one more petal at another man. Then she spotted Jeremy.

Her small mouth formed an excited "O" and she gestured for him to come up to the balcony.

Smiling, for the first time in months, Jeremy exited the ballroom to access the upper story in private.

"Ooh! You've come up! How wonderful." The little dab of a thing cooed Not embarrassed about being seen in her nightclothes by a stranger, she rushed over and dragged him by the hand to her position on the balcony.

"I knew this would work. I just knew it. You're perfect!" Gravely, she then made an admirable curtsy. "I'm Matilda Fairmont, but you may call me Tilly."

Perfect? Perfect for what? He glanced down at the swirl of guests, but no one noticed the *tête-à-tête* above them. "And my name is Jeremy, Tilly. My friends call me Jerry." Sitting down on the floor so he would not loom over her, he said, "I admit to being curious. Tell me, why are you raining roses on Sir Hector's party?"

Her giggle engendered another smile of his own. Truly, she was a most adorable child. "Papa and Mama don't know I'm here," she whispered. "But I had to come. I had to do something! I promised Auntie Dee I would find her a..."

She blushed pinker than the roses by her side. Tugging on his sleeve, she then pointed toward a group assembled in the far corner of the room. "There's Auntie Dee now. See how unhappy she is?"

One young woman among the four did stand out—most likely because she was not simpering in an obsequious fashion. Tall, almost majestic, she wore her sleek, dark hair swept high off her long neck and caught up in a silver net with tendrils escaping at the sides. As she listened to the chatter around her, she languidly fanned her wan face while her heavy-lidded eyes glittered, even at this distance. No animation disturbed the young woman's demeanor. Dressed in a grey bombazine gown that proclaimed to all and sundry she was in half-mourning, the woman looked as stiff and aloof from the proceedings as Jeremy felt.

"Your aunt, you say?" He shook his head. Indeed, he could see no resemblance to the energetic redheaded minx by his side. "What did you promise to find for her?"

Hopping from one foot to the other, Tilly shrugged her shoulders. "It's Christmas. And I wanted to give her a present. D'you think, maybe, you could dance with Auntie Dee?"

Surely, that was an odd request from a child. As he gazed down at the sober young woman in grey, a peculiar longing settled within his chest. But what the deuce it was, he had no idea.

Just as suddenly, Tilly shuddered, then sneezed. Afraid she intended to use the sleeve of her white lawn nightgown in an inappropriate manner, Jeremy pressed his handkerchief into her hand.

"Thank you, Jerry." She blew her nose without constraint as only a child could. "Will you? Dance with Auntie Dee?"

"If I agree to partner your aunt, you must return to your bed this very instant. No delays." He stood, then brushed the wrinkles from his evening breeches. "Do you promise, Tilly?"

She bobbed her head, scattering her tight curls this way and that.

"Then, Miss Fairmont, we have a deal." Taking her hand, he then bent over and kissed her tiny fingers. "Good-night, child. Perhaps I shall see you in the morning."

"Ooh," she squealed, racing the length of the balcony. "I hope you and Auntie Dee..." Standing under an evergreen kissing bough hanging near the door frame, Tilly waited for him to open the door.

After he complied, she blew him a kiss. "Good-night, Jerry!" Bare feet padded down the corridor until she was out of sight.

He smiled once again. Returning to the ballroom, he entered with anticipation instead of dread. A good deed was surely an excellent reason for his presence tonight. Tragically, his comrades-in-arms did not have this opportunity to make merry away from the battlefield. Instead, far too many of them suffered the horrors of war even now on Christmas night.

He shook his gloomy reflections away. How was he supposed to cheer Tilly's Auntie Dee if his own thoughts were deep in a brown study? Glancing at the woman's pale countenance, he furrowed his brow. Why was she so melancholy?

She must not have noticed his approach for she jumped when he touched her on the shoulder. "I beg your pardon," he said in his smoothest tones, "I am aware propriety demands I secure our hostess to perform introductions, however, Lady Fairmont appears quite busy at the moment. Would you do me the honor of granting me this next minuet? I am Jeremy Stafford, the—"

"My apologies, Mr. Stafford." With a slight incline of her head, she flashed luminous blue eyes his way. "I do not dance tonight."

A challenge. He appreciated a challenge. "But you must dance with me, my dear, else I will have broken my promise to an enchanting little madcap."

Ah, success! Giving him her complete attention, she seemed puzzled. "How so, Mr. Stafford?"

It had been months since anyone addressed him as anything other than Lord Bainbridge—so recent was his acquisition of the title. Life had been so much simpler back then. He extended his hand. "I will explain on the floor. Shall we?"

She shook her head, sending tendrils of hair swaying about her fair face. Gazing at her, he caught his breath. Up close she was quite comely. Quite comely indeed.

"I do not dance," she repeated with less conviction in her voice.

Perhaps he should try another tack. "What if dancing with me was your niece's fondest wish?"

"My *niece*?"

Now it was Jeremy's turn to sound unsure. "Yes, of course. Tilly."

"Oh!" As a candle suddenly burst into flame, so did "Auntie Dee" unexpectedly come to life. Her generous smile crinkled the corners of her expressive eyes while her shoulders shook with suppressed amusement. "So Tilly is the enchanting little madcap. I see now."

Blushing, she vigorously fanned her cheeks. "Tilly's mother, Emma, and I have been bosom bows for years." Her heavy-lidded gaze no longer languid, she glanced over at her companions. "Shall we walk about the room, Mr. Stafford?"

He held out his arm. "Delighted, Miss…?"

"Goodness, you do not know my name?" She slipped her arm through his. Her touch was light, and somehow inspired protective feelings within him.

"Auntie Dee, is it not?" Patting her hand through her velvet glove, he then proceeded to lead "Auntie Dee" through the throngs of merrymakers.

"Miss Livingston," she corrected as she nodded to several passersby. "Did Tilly bamboozle you into dancing with me? Such a naughty child! But I do love her dearly."

A slight misstep caused her to bump against his side. Contrary to his first impression of her, she felt soft, warm, and supple.

"Oh, pardon me." Her earnest gaze seared him as intensely as the summer heat in a certain foreign land's bloody battlefields. "I release you from your promise, Mr. Stafford. In truth, I am not inclined to dance."

The string quartet began a lively composition by Austrian composer Joseph Haydn, uplifting the festivities with musical rhythm and grace. But Jeremy had lost his chance for this minuet with Miss Livingston. He had played his trump card and it failed. Yet not entirely, for she was now securely ensconced on his arm, by his side.

"Let us partake of some wassail punch then, Miss Livingston. I shall drink to your good health in the coming year if you will drink to mine."

"Agreed."

Pleased she so readily accepted his alternative offer, he lifted two glasses of the mulled cider and handed one to her. The pungent aroma of spices such as cinnamon, nutmeg, and cloves tickled his nose even before he drank.

He sneezed. "I beg your pardon." Reaching for his handkerchief, he came up empty.

Miss Livingston must have realized his dilemma, for she searched in her reticule and pulled out a delicate, embroidered cloth. "Please, take mine," she offered.

Accepting the handkerchief, he marveled at the satin-stitch design and the feminine name of Deirdre stitched upon it. "My thanks, Miss Livingston. I gave mine to that imp of a child! Is this your fine needlework?"

She looked down at the parquet wood floor. Modesty became her. "Yes. I had the pleasure of giving handkerchiefs as Christmas gifts to all Lady Fairmont's guests." Her gaze everywhere but on him, she added, "Would you like for me to make you one, also?"

His response came straight from the heart. "Indeed, if I may, I wish to keep this one. Your name is quite lovely."

By Jove, but her radiant face flooded crimson! Although the music still played, he heard nothing, he saw nothing, except Miss Deirdre Livingston.

A type of madness seized him, overriding his natural restraints. More than anything in the world he wanted to get to know this young woman. "Miss Livingston, I am not usually forward in my address with ladies, however—"

From a distance, a snappish voice intruded. "Where is he, Emma? You promised me an earl and I shall hold you to your word!"

Jeremy exhaled his frustration. Bearing down on him was a mountainous dragon with his unfortunate hostess in tow.

Seeing the direction of his gaze, Miss Livingston whispered as if they were conspirators. "Lady Pringle, Sir Hector's grandmother. I wonder why she is heading this way."

He patted her hand again, desiring nothing more than to remove the glove and feel her silky skin. That, and to be rid of the hatchet-faced matron now panting in front of him.

Wringing her hands, Lady Fairmont darted a panicked gaze at Miss Livingston. "Please excuse us. Sir Hector's dear grandmama insisted on—"

"Do be quiet, you provoking creature!" The lady in question hauled out a quizzing glass and proceeded to inspect him from head to toe. "Gad, but you're a fine figure of a man, ain't you? Hair like midnight and eyes blacker than coal."

He exchanged amused glances with Miss Livingston, then gave his most polished bow. "Just so, madam."

"La!" Lady Pringle tittered. "An earl. Imagine! Who would have supposed Lord Bainbridge to be so amicable?"

Miss Livingston gasped. Her sweet features, so bathed in shyness just a scant moment ago, now blanched white—as white as the distant moon. True, she had interrupted him before he fully introduced himself, but why would his title cause her discomfort?

"Lord Bainbridge." She coldly nodded in his direction. "If you will excuse me, I have some matters to attend to." After curtsying to the ladies, she walked briskly through the ballroom doors, leaving the party, and dashing his hopes to get better acquainted.

"Well, I declare! Such wretched manners!" Lady Pringle shook her massive head and stormed off toward another group of unsuspecting victims.

His hostess remained behind to place a hand on his sleeve. "My lord, I do apologize for my friend. She has but recently suffered a terrible loss." She gave him a weak smile, then followed in her grandmama-in-law's footsteps.

Indecision stayed his movements. This night he had stumbled upon a jewel so rare, and now she was gone. Should he respect her wishes and stay away?

He fingered the dainty handkerchief. By Jove, no! His purpose intense, he strode from the ballroom with nary a look back. However, once out in the corridor, he stopped. Where the deuce was she? A puzzle, that. Stroking his chin, he glanced around for inspiration. By all that was holy if he did not spot a mop of curly red hair hiding behind a decorative pillar!

Pointing up the stairs, Tilly loudly whispered, "The balcony!"

Tomorrow was soon enough to ring a peal over the child's head for not keeping her end of the bargain by going to bed. But then, on the other hand, he had not actually danced with Miss Livingston—Deirdre—either. Waving his hand in thanks, he ascended the stairs. As silently as he had led his men in battle, Jeremy approached the balcony door and opened it.

Away from the balcony's edge, Deirdre sat on the floor with her legs folded beneath her as a child might, at rest. She leaned against the wall where the kissing bough dangled, and she used yet another handkerchief to wipe at her eyes.

"Oh!" She tried to scramble to her feet, but he placed his arm out to forestall her, then sat on the floor himself.

"This is a bit of tricky business," he said as a greeting. "These tight breeches leave me no maneuvering room. If they rip, I shall blame you, Miss Livingston."

She hurriedly cast her handkerchief out of sight. "My lord, it is not seemly for us to be here...together...like this." A smile threatened to reveal itself to him. "Nor is it proper for you to, um, mention what you just did."

"Ah, are you a pattern card of propriety, Miss Livingston?"

"My lord?" Uncertainty furrowed her brow.

"Do not worry, my dear. My intentions are honorable."

The object of his desire folded her arms across her delightful bosom. "You are an earl." Her voice indicated there could be no worse crime.

"Guilty." He grinned. "The Earl of Bainbridge—surely an infamous rake-hell."

Deirdre pinched her lips together, trying oh-so-hard to be severe.

"I was not born an earl, if that makes any difference, Miss Livingston. In fact, I liked it quite well when you called me 'Mr. Stafford.' Indeed, 'Jeremy' or 'Jerry' would also be greatly appreciated. "

Obviously having none of his nonsense, she primly lifted her nose. "My lord, Emma, Lady Fairmont, told me that you *deigned* to make your appearance tonight. You must think you are better than—"

"Miss Livingston, it has only been five months since I have come into the title." The time for frivolity had passed. He reached for her hand and sandwiched it between his own. "The previous earl was a distant cousin. He died rather unexpectedly, leaving me holding the bag, so to speak. Indeed, I served under Wellington up until the day I was notified."

Once more she gasped, her gaze riveted on him.

"Truth be told, when Sir Hector invited me, I was thinking of my fallen comrades. That I did not have a right to enjoy myself while they had made the ultimate sacrifice."

"I understand." Her eyes reflected sorrow. "I lost my brother, Thomas, just five months ago. He, also, served under Wellington, in far-away Spain."

"But this is passing strange!" Jeremy gripped both her hands. "Where in Spain had he fought?"

She allowed him this privilege. "Close to a city that I confess, I can hardly pronounce the name. Sala—"

"Salamanca. I was there. To date, it is Wellington's most impressive victory." He dropped his voice. "However, thousands died."

The silence between them was somehow comforting. High above the deafening clamor from the ballroom, they sat side by side, hands entwined, content in each other's company.

When she rested her head against his shoulder, his heart soared. "I did not know your brother, Miss Livingston. My sincere condolences on your loss."

"I have done you an injustice, my lord, by accusing you so."

"'Jeremy', please. Or 'Jerry', if you prefer. Tilly calls me that, you know."

Looking up at him, Deirdre smiled so sweetly that an ache developed deep within his breast. For thirty-two years, love eluded him. Never once had he been tempted to give his heart or contemplate marriage. And now, in the space of two short hours, he could think of nothing else, of no one else.

"Do you forgive me...Jeremy?" She fluttered her thick lashes at him. "Perhaps when we become better acquainted, I might call you 'Jerry.'"

When. She also believed they had a future together! Elated, he whispered into her hair. "There is nothing to forgive, my dearest Deirdre, if I may?"

She nodded permission for him to use her name.

Now in the shadow of the kissing bough, Jeremy glanced down at his love. "As this is a perfect, private setting for us, I have another request to ask of you, Deirdre. May I...?" He lifted his gaze to the overhanging evergreen decoration.

"Most certainly." She inched closer to him. "I was wondering when you would notice the mistletoe."

Tentatively feathering a kiss on her rosy lips, he then briefly joined with her, drinking in her honeyed taste. Intense bliss permeated his soul. He now knew the true location of Heaven: lodged on the Fairmont ballroom balcony, in the company of the beautiful Deirdre Livingston.

"Ah, wonderful." He brushed his lips against the tip of her adorable nose. "But, Deirdre darling, I just realized I have not given you a Christmas present."

Her response was swift and enthusiastic. "Oh, but yes, you have, Jeremy. A *very* special Christmas present."

His joy complete, he took advantage of the kissing bough's proximity yet again.

Susanne Marie Knight is a fiction and non-fiction writer currently working for a fitness program shown on public television. Regency romances have been a longtime passion of hers. One of her Regency novels received a five star rating from Affaire de Coeur magazine. *A Very Special Christmas Present* is her first published Regency short story. Susanne also writes in other genres, and used her experiences working for two Federal law enforcement agencies to author *Grave Future*, a paranormal romantic suspense novel now available on the Web at www.dreams-unlimited.com. Originally from New York City, Susanne now lives in the Pacific Northwest, by way of Okinawa, Montana, Alabama, and Florida. Along with her husband, daughter, and feisty Siamese cat, she enjoys the area's beautiful ponderosa pine trees and wide, open spaces—a perfect environment for writing. She is completing courses for her Master of Science degree in Natural Health.

Frankie has lost all hope. Or rather she has too much of it because on Christmas day, she's obligated to marry the boring Lord Hope. But things are not always what they seem in this captivating tale about not giving up Hope!

Page and Monarch, Forth They Went

Bethany Schneider

Frankie was procrastinating, but it was growing so cold that she knew she must go in soon. She didn't want to open the massive door of Kildeer Manor and face the disapproval of all inside, from sour-faced Elsie, the chambermaid, on up to her Mama and Lord Hope. She especially didn't want to see Lord Hope's face. "Andrew's face," she muttered under her breath. Now that she was to be married, she must learn to use her fiancé's first name. "Lord Grope," she said venomously to the enormous dog at her side. "His Boredship, Lord Blandrew Grope." She stamped one frozen foot.

The dog—a long-legged, yellow behemoth—laid its ears back and managed to look as if its feelings were deeply injured.

"Not you, Ajax." Frankie laughed, tangling her hands in his snow-matted fur. "That fortune-hunting side of beef I must marry on Christmas day." She looked into the dog's golden eyes. "And if you were half the dog you claim you are, you would save me from him."

With that, Frankie gave the heavy door a push and took a determined step inside. "Go to the stables, Ajax," she said over her shoulder, but the dog was trying his big, muscley best to push in beside her. "No!" She turned to push him outside. "Go to the stables. I know you're allowed inside when we are home in Somerset, but…" She stopped pushing the dog and scratched his honest face instead. "I'm sorry, Ajax. Kildeer is home now, and Lord Hope says it's the stables for you." She gave him a determined shove. "Stables! Go to the stables!" She caught a last glimpse of his stricken eyes as she closed the door. Immediately he began to howl. "Oh, Ajax." Frankie slumped to the floor and sat with her cheek pressed against the door. "Don't cry." Then, to her great mortification, Frankie herself, the bravest lass in all of Somerset, began to sob.

Ajax howled more loudly, and Frankie gave in to her tears, pressing her cold face against the hard wood of the door. She couldn't even have fun on a snowy Yuletide day, but must stay inside by the fire, sewing and making small talk with the Dowager Lady Hope and Mama while His Boredship hunted grouse. Not that she wanted to hunt grouse particularly, and certainly not in Andrew's company, but she did want to play with her dog in the snow. "And that," said a small, strong voice inside her, "is just what you have done, in spite of them all." Frankie smiled through her tears. Even when, in two days time, she became Lady Hope, even when Andrew could lay his big, sweaty hands on her whenever he wanted, and lecture her about propriety all day and night – even then, she promised herself, she would find a way to play with Ajax in the snow.

Tears can't last forever, especially not when one is the stouthearted daughter of a hero. And not just any hero, Frankie reminded herself. Her father had died at Trafalgar, leaving a vast fortune to his broken-hearted little daughter, who even at the age of seven knew the depth of her loss. Thirty thousand a year could never replace the laughing Papa who held her before him on his horse as he rode the boundaries of his land. The Papa who called her "Frankie" when everyone else called her "Frances," who let her ride her pony astride and who taught her how to shoot. Thirty thousand a year could never compensate for the fact that he left her with a mother who cared only for titles and wealth. Frankie stood up and tried to smooth her sodden pelisse with one cold hand, while attempting to pat her snarled, damp hair into place with the other. The hallway was very dark after the bright outside, the grand staircase sweeping up into gloom. No lamp was lit. Frankie almost felt as if her father were there beside her. "If you were living, you would never make me marry this man," she said.

"No, that I wouldn't," said a soft, rich voice.

Frankie spun around. There, beside an open window that he'd obviously just climbed through, stood a man. She squinted into the dark. It was Andrew, Hessians covered in snow, black hair unusually rumpled.

"Surprised?" He shut the window with one hand and strolled forward with an easy, loose-limbed grace that was entirely out of character for the stuffy, pretentious Lord Hope.

Frankie watched him approach, a light dawning in her pale, heart-shaped face. "Do you really mean it, Andrew?" she asked quietly, not wanting to break the spell. "I don't have to marry you?"

Andrew stopped and surveyed her. She knew that even in the forgiving gloom she looked terrible, covered in great paw prints, dog hair, pine needles, and melted snow. So why did his face take on that strangely intent look as he gazed at her? Why did a smile slowly spread itself across his tanned face…and why did he look tanned? "Yes," he said. "I really mean it." And with one step he covered the space between them, scooped her up in his arms, and put his mouth slowly over hers, kissing her softly and long.

Frankie's eyes closed in delight. Why, she thought in the few moments before she gave herself to his kiss, was she letting this happen? Why were her arms going around his neck? This was Andrew! Who had just said, if she wasn't totally mistaken, that he would allow her to break their engagement! Maybe it was the different smell about him, the earthy, salty scent that was entirely different from the cloying cologne he usually wore. Maybe it was this new grace in him. Before, when he'd tried to kiss her, he had always bungled, moving too quickly or too slowly, like she was a trout to be tickled. And she had never allowed him to get further than a damp squeeze of the hand and a moist peck on the cheek. But this was entirely different. His kiss grew more insistent, and Frankie found conscious thought fleeing away. She was warming in his arms like a crumpet before the fire.

"No more tears," he said, when he drew his face away. He set her on her feet and kissed each eyelid. "You are now free as the briskest little North Wind, which is what you are." He smoothed her hair. "My delicious ice-maiden."

"Not so icy now," she said, shyly, and reached up to straighten the folds of his cravat. "Such a simple cravat, today, Andrew! Have you started dressing to please me, just when you release me from our engagement?"

"Do I please you like this, in all my dirt?"

"I can't quite see the dirt in this dark hallway," Frankie said.

He laughed. "I assure you, it is there."

She stole a look at his tall person. He was a beautiful sight, as always—no one could say Andrew wasn't a handsome man, whatever his character flaws. But this time the affectation was gone, the lazy, cruel look in the eyes was replaced by a glinting humor. Why, his buckskins even had a smudge, and his Hessians, after their obvious tramp through the snow, hardly shone at all. She smiled. "Andrew! There are some marks on you! Your man will faint with horror!"

He dusted his sleeves and stood even taller. "I'll have you know, young lady, that I pride myself on my military neatness! But today...today I'm fresh from battle."

"Military neatness? Battle?" Frankie laughed and stepped back. "What's come over you, Andrew?"

"Shall I tell you?" He stepped forward again, and grasped her to him.

With her chest pressed against his and her face uplifted, Frankie suddenly saw the truth in the lines on his face, the leathered look of years spent outside, the obvious age and experience of him. "Oh!" She clung to him for a moment, searching his face, feeling his warmth. Then she pushed at his chest. "Let me go!"

He gripped her more tightly for a moment, his gray eyes locked on her blue ones. Then he let her go.

"You're not Lord Hope!" she said, backing away.

He didn't attempt to follow but stood at his ease, a slight, sad smile on his face. "Don't go, North Wind," he said.

"Who are you?"

"I am Lord Hope," he said. "But I'm not Andrew."

Frankie looked at the face before her. It was Andrew's exactly, but Andrew's face ten years older. Andrew's face with every feature tinted with humor and kindness rather than bitterness. "You're... you're...." She ran to the wall, where Andrew's portrait hung beside another, a painting of a dark-haired young man astride a big gray hunter, a winter landscape stretching behind him, Kildeer Manor painted in minute detail in the distance. It was Andrew's brother, the late Eliot, who had died in Spain before he ever came to be Lord Hope. Frankie had often gazed at it since arriving at Kildeer last week. It was as if someone had painted grim, sanctimonious, lecherous Andrew as a generous, happy youth full of life and fun. "This is you? But you're dead! You died years ago, on Christmas day!" She stared at him, aghast.

He did nothing but stand there, smiling at her. His kiss still burned on her mouth, the kiss that had seemed to promise her freedom. A freedom that she now felt slipping away. Who did he think he was, to tease her like that? She marched back across the broad hall and slapped his face as hard as she could. "How could you pull such a dirty trick, you nasty old...nasty old ghost!"

To her surprise, Lord Hope threw his head back and laughed. "Oh, little North Wind, what a tempest in a teapot you are!" He took her by the elbow and led her to the stairs. "Please, sit!" He gestured to the second step. "I shall sit beside you," he announced, "and we shall talk."

Frankie sat with as much dignity as she could muster, spreading her ruined skirts with the delicacy of a princess. Eliot sat beside her, legs sprawling like a soldier's. Which, she supposed, he was.

"Now," he said. "Are you angry because I kissed you? I assure you, I have no regrets myself, but if I find that I have offended you I will abject myself most humbly."

"Of course you offended me!" But Frankie could not hide the flush in her cheeks. The kiss had been the most delicious thing she'd ever experienced, and she had a feeling he knew it.

"You don't lie well, my little North Wind."

She pursed her mouth up and tried to look prim, but this only set him laughing again. "If you're not careful, I shall kiss you again!"

"You insult me, my lord."

"Balderdash. But I see you are too gently raised to admit it." Lord Hope settled himself more comfortably on the step, so that he was almost lounging beside her. "Let me tell you something. I came here today to look at my old home and maybe to catch a glimpse of my mother at Yuletide, her favorite time of year." His eyes were staring at a distant, invisible horizon. "In another life before the war, it was my own favorite season as well."

Frankie thought of the unusual portrait; a young man painted in a winter landscape. But it suited him, she thought, stealing a close look at his face now that he was distracted by memory. He was warm, full of life, and in a strange way, winter makes the living feel more alive. She thought of her own joy, wrestling with Ajax in the deep drifts, the way her blood had felt rich and hot in her veins.

With a start, she realized that he was now perusing her face, a slight smile touching the sadness in his eyes. "But then, my little North wind, while I sat on my horse, hidden behind the box-hedges, I saw you playing in the snow with that overgrown creature you probably call a dog."

"His name is Ajax," Frankie said, picking at her pelisse. She wasn't sure she liked the idea of Lord Hope watching her play. It had been a headlong romp through the snow banks, with much heels over head rolling and open-mouthed laughing. Not at all a lady-like way to spend an afternoon.

"And that," Lord Hope said, as if he could read her mind, "is what I found so fascinating about you. Who is this wild child staying at Kildeer? To whom does she belong? I felt I had to know the answer. Which is why, when you went inside, I came to the window to watch you confront the family. I felt sure they would all be waiting just inside to ring a peal over your head. Imagine my surprise when down you toppled by the door, crying like a fountain! This was not the rough and ready girl I'd just watched wrestling with a beast twice her size! Up came the window and in I popped to comfort you. You mistook me for Andrew, which amused me until I learned that Andrew, who is, I'm sure, as dull today as he was five years ago, is to marry you. It all seemed terribly un-fair, and suddenly your wildness and your tears made sense. That kiss," he said, lightly stroking her cheek with one knuckle, "was meant to console you, not trouble you further."

"I'm not troubled," Frankie said bravely, although her insides seemed to be floating up into her throat.

"You're not?" He sat up. "Then I shall do it again!"

Frankie turned her face away. She didn't know what to say, and was angry when she felt, rather than saw, that he was smiling at her confusion. "Don't be cruel," she muttered.

"Truce, little one," he said, and she knew that his smile grew even wider. "I shall leave kisses behind and proceed to the next question. Are you angry because I am Lord Hope? Are you upset because your fiancé, my esteemed brother, is now dispossessed of his title and wealth? Are you angry because you will now be merely Mrs. Trethorn when you marry?"

Frankie leapt to her feet. "If your purpose in coming here was to raise and then dash the hopes of a woman you have never met, a woman young enough to be your daughter, a woman who never gave you a thought until now, you have succeeded! Not with a paltry kiss or by deflating Andrew's consequence.

I don't care one fig if Andrew is King of England or a mere blacksmith, but I am honor bound to say that I also don't care who you are, sir. I don't care if the whole lot of you turn into pigs and run squealing into the night, you, your bantam cock of a brother, and yes, your mother too!"

Eliot got up slowly, with the grace of a big cat. He caught her hands in his. "Softly, my little North Wind. Surely you don't mean to say that of my mother."

Frankie looked into his eyes and saw in them the deep sadness she had often noticed in the Dowager Lady Hope's, the gentleness verging on pain. She knew, looking in his eyes, that the Dowager was a good and patient woman who had seen many sad things in her day. "No, I don't mean it of her." A long silence. "And I don't mean it of you, either."

"But of Andrew?" A light danced in his eyes.

Frankie gripped his hands impulsively. "Lord Hope," she said. "You told me when you came through that window that you wouldn't make me marry Andrew. I was speaking to my dead father, but you answered. On Christmas Day I am to marry Andrew in front of the entire parish!"

"Cry off! It is a woman's right."

"I cannot!" She dropped his hands and sat back down on the steps. "It was my father's dying wish."

"What?" Lord Hope looked incredulous. "These are not the Dark Ages!"

"My father perished at Trafalgar," Frankie said, summoning all her dignity to her aid. "Your father was with him when he died. Together they made a pact, that I should marry Andrew." She held her head high. "My father was the only person in my life whom I respected and admired. I think he was in error, but I cannot go against his dying request."

"You are Captain Janson's daughter?" He raised her to her feet.

"Yes? You knew him?" Frankie searched his face eagerly. "You were friends?"

Eliot tried to swallow a smile, and failed. "No, no. Contrary to appearances, I am not old enough to be your father. Far from it, my little North Wind! I only admired your father from afar. He was the hero of my youth! To think that you are his child! Little you!"

Frankie stretched herself to her full height. "I'm not so little!"

Eliot laughed and drew her to him again. "Just as high as my mouth!" And he kissed the crown of her head. "You shan't marry Andrew. If Captain Janson and my father ever made a pact like that, I'll roast my buckskins and eat them for dinner! I don't believe it for a minute!"

"I've seen the paper with my own eyes! Andrew showed it to me. There's my father's signature on it, and your father's, and even a bloodstain."

"Hogwash!" And with that he stepped away toward the window. "Now then, little one. Not a word about me! Watch!" He raised the window without a sound. "Due to some boyhood sanding and greasing, this window is absolutely silent. Unlike the blasted door." In a moment he was outside, leaning in. "Come here, North Wind."

Frankie went to the window.

"What's your name, Miss Janson?"

"My name?"

"Yes, your Christian name. I want to break all proprieties and call you by your first name."

"Frankie." She whispered it, afraid he would laugh. But she wanted so much to hear that name on someone's lips.

He smiled. "Frankie," he said, and was gone.

Frankie made it upstairs and out of her ruined clothing without anyone noticing. She was rummaging in her wardrobe when a knock came on the door. "It's Elsie, Miss," came the grumpy voice.

"Come!" Frankie flung open the door, not caring that she was in her shift. "Help me dress, Elsie. I must look wonderful tonight."

"Well!" Elsie's sour face puckered even further into a rare smile. "This is a new song you're singing, Miss! Are you finally reconciled to your Christmas wedding? Your bridegroom has been hanging mistletoe all over his rooms, I'll have you know!" Elsie laughed cruelly at Frankie's blushes. "Come, come, don't go all over missish with me! You're a wild termagant and a sailor's daughter, to boot. And you're lucky to have his Lordship, I don't mind telling you to your face." She bustled to the wardrobe and began pulling dresses forth and laying them on the bed. "You're a pretty piece, that's true," Elsie continued. "But why his Lordship must *marry* you..." She let the implication hang in the air like a bad smell.

"I know how you feel about me," Frankie said. "And I know you don't appreciate my father's worth. You think he tricked Lord Hope into marrying me."

"That's saying more than I ever did," Elsie said, satisfaction shining out of her eyes. "And you to marry him on Christmas day, the very day poor Master Eliot met his death in that heathenish Spain..."

"Christmas was not my choice, Elsie. It was Lord Hope's."

"I don't claim to know about that, but I'm sure her Ladyship the Dowager feels the insult most painful-like..."

Frankie held her arms up as Elsie drew the white silk dress down over her head, and stood still as Elsie tied the long, light-blue satin sash that went round Frankie's ribs, just under her breasts. Through an effort of sheer will she relegated Elsie's torments to the background, and tried to remember the warmth of the *real* Lord Hope's arms. It was almost impossible in the bitter cold. *Perhaps Elsie is trying to kill me*, Frankie thought idly, glancing at her goose-pimpled arms. *I know I have warmer garments in there somewhere.*

Thus began a fantasy involving heavy woolen capes and a certain handsome peer. Frankie could see the whole picture. It was Christmas morning two days away. She would be standing at the altar, nobly ready to sacrifice herself.

But then Lord Hope would save her—never mind how—and ride with her into the white distance. She would be warm as warm could be in her woolen clothes and her thick pelisse and big furry mittens...but of course, she would really be wearing her silk wedding gown, thin as air. Admittedly, the white dress against the white snow would be a pretty sight—and she would be warm in his arms! They would stop somewhere after the gallop through the snow, and Lord Hope would gather her into his arms again, and he–he would kiss the open palm of her hand with his burning lips.

"Stop sighing!" Elsie's sour-apple face swam into view.

"Sorry." Frankie closed her eyes and tried to summon the fantasy again, but it gave way to despair. He had told her he only kissed her because she was crying, she reminded herself. He was simply comforting her, as if she were a little girl. He probably didn't even mean to help her break her engagement. She remembered his teasing laugh. He thought she was little more than a school-room miss! He must be, oh, fully twelve or thirteen years older than she, worldly, experienced. Frankie felt the real cold again and heard Elsie's words filtering through her shattered fantasy.

"...And Master Eliot, mind, he would never have allowed the likes of you in this house, an upstart sailor's widow and her skinny daughter..."

Enough was suddenly enough. Frankie turned and spoke softly. "What do you know of Master Eliot?"

"He was the best and kindest lad anyone has ever known," Elsie said with pride in her sunken eyes.

"If that is so, can you honestly say that he would have turned us away, the wife and daughter of his father's oldest friend? At Christmas time?"

Elsie's little eyes shifted around the room, then came to rest on Frankie's face. "Lord love you, girl, you have the right of me. Master Eliot would have taken you in and warmed you by his fire and given you of his best to eat and drink and toasted you with good Christmas punch. He'd welcome you to his Christmas table even if you was conniving to marry him with false documents, and plotting to steal from him, and ruin his poor mother's health and happiness. And for the sake of his dear memory, I won't rail at you no longer, Miss." With that she shut her lips tightly and took up the hairbrush.

Frankie turned and allowed the older woman to brush her curls. "You know I am not here to connive and cheat and steal," she said. "I am bringing money into this household. That's why Andrew wants me."

Elsie brushed vigorously for a moment. "We shall see what we shall see," she said, and would say no more.

If Frankie's cheeks glowed that evening, and if her eyes sparkled, no one knew why but she. Andrew looked at his bride to be with covetous greed, glad she was looking more the thing after the last days of wan misery. She was a beauty, he thought to himself, a rare thing in a chit with thirty thousand pounds. Most heiresses managed to be wall-eyed or knock-kneed or unable to speak or unable to stop speaking. He looked from Frankie to her mother, a well-preserved woman of forty, whose lust for position and whose sense of her own importance marched well with Andrew's own overblown self-esteem. Now there was a woman, Andrew thought. If the little filly would only grow up to be like her dam, and bear him sons instead of daughters! His eyes traveled back to Frankie, who was sipping her wine with a far-away look in her eyes. Andrew frowned. He would break her of these strange starts. Why, just today he had looked out the window to see her romping with that great overgrown rag of a dog, just as if she were a lad and not a grown woman of nineteen winters! The dog would be easy to take care of. A bullet between the eyes would do the trick. But the girl might be harder to bend. Ah well. Just another day—one long Christmas Eve day and a night to go until she was his, to do with as he pleased.

✻ ✻ ✻

Seated beside Frankie at the dinner table, Mrs. Janson looked at her daughter uneasily. There was no understanding the girl! This morning she had been in her usual state of silent and morose despair. Then she flitted off to spend the afternoon Lord knows where, probably kicking up her heels outdoors where anyone could have come across her. And now the child was all smiles, sipping her wine and grinning at the air. Well, it would serve her right if that bloom in her cheeks and the fire in her eyes turned out to be the first signs of consumption. Not that Mrs. Janson wished any ill to her only child. It was just that she was so much like her father, and that wasn't a good thing in a girl destined to be Lady Hope! She was so bold, so reckless, and so friendly, so loving to everyone! Everyone, including the footmen and the scullery maids! Now, in Captain Tom Janson, those qualities had been annoying but not improper. Mrs. Janson thought back on her marriage with a touch of frustration. Her fury the day her father introduced her to Tom—the younger son of a mere baron—saying this was the man he'd chosen for her. She had hoped for an earl, but after three seasons in London, no one had come up to scratch. Tom's charm had won her over, but the easygoing ways and joyful voice ringing through the house had grown more than a trifle threadbare by the time the poor man met his end. One wanted a steadier husband, a husband who sat quietly in the background and provided one with money and a title, which Tom never did. Not the title anyway. Not even the tiniest little title, although she had hourly expected him to be at least knighted for his endeavors. To be sure, he'd made his fortune five times over—it all had to do with capturing ships and winning prizes, and then there was that instance of the treasure found in some godforsaken bay somewhere at the bottom of the world...Mrs. Janson never did understand it all. And little enough he'd cared for the money he had, giving so much of it away to this or that charity, and all anonymously, and what good did that do? Frances was just like him. Didn't care for money. Didn't want this marriage to Lord Hope, didn't care for his title. Lord Hope—and who could hope for a better man? She smiled at her own little joke and attacked the venison. Lord

Hope served a proper meal, the table literally groaning beneath the hearty Christmas fare. It was what one approved of.

The Dowager Lady Hope also had her eyes on the young girl at one side of the table. A pretty girl, but very young, the Dowager thought. Young in her ways. Still playing in the snow, romping about with that wonderful dog. Ajax, his name was. The dog reminded her of her own dear King, dead now these fifty years and more. A beautiful dog, King. He had saved her, oh yes, more than once in her wild days.

Once from drowning and once—she smiled into her wine—from an unwelcome suitor. How Andrew would frown to know the follies of his own mother back in the days of her youth! She remembered the hot kisses of men now in their venerable years, still vigorous some of them, still riding to hounds and sitting in the House of Lords. And others were dead, like her own beloved husband, cut down in his strong old age by a silly accident, a fall that made no sense. He'd taken that fence a thousand times! But she wouldn't let her thoughts dwell on that. No, she would think of something else. Oh, if only it hadn't happened! Not only would she have no broken heart, but also there would be none of this trouble with Andrew, who thought he was Lord Hope. She looked at her son, stuffing his mouth with meat and grimacing at the poor girl he was to marry. Inside that big, handsome body (so like Eliot's!) was a paltry, deluded, self-satisfied popinjay. God knew she loved her younger son, but there it was: he was a boor at best, a scoundrel at worst.

If only her husband, dear Edgar, weren't dead! When Eliot began his secret missions for the Duke of Wellington, there had been no thought that Edgar might die and leave the inheritance in such a mess. If her husband were still alive, there would be no problem with Eliot's return; he could come home a hero. But now, with Andrew prancing around calling himself Lord Hope, the real Lord Hope would have a rough time of it. And when would Eliot return? When would he stop this secret life, or rather, this secret death he was leading? She had three letters from the Duke himself.

The first one, the secret one that she kept at all times on her person, explained that Eliot's work for the army was indispensable, and necessitated a false demise. The second one, the public one, consoled her and Edgar for Eliot's "death" on Christmas Day. How Edgar had laughed, little knowing that he would go to meet his maker in a few short months! And Christmas Day! Why did Wellington have to ruin her favorite holiday? Every Christmas now for years she had had to play the heartbroken mother, when she knew perfectly well that her beautiful, great-hearted, laughing boy was out there saving Europe from Bonaparte. But now that Waterloo was long past, surely he must return? The Duke had written his third letter to assure her Eliot was safe, but gave no clue as to his homecoming.

The Dowager let her sad gray gaze rest on the girl Andrew would marry on Christmas morning. Christmas again! Andrew believed his brother was dead; was his marriage on that day some sort of perverse celebration of Eliot's death?

The Dowager shook her head. She couldn't believe it. But then again, she knew she didn't trust her younger son. She'd never told him about Eliot—and why not? Deep in her heart she knew she didn't tell Andrew because she feared for Eliot—and England. She couldn't be sure that her own son wouldn't turn on his brother, or turn on England, turn traitor! And the proof that her instincts were correct was that pesky document about young Frances's betrothal to Andrew. That document was a forgery. The Dowager knew it; there had been no agreement between Edgar and Tom Janson. They had been two men who understood love. Edgar because he had it, plenty of it, with her! She smiled at the memory. And Tom because he hadn't been able to feel any for his wife; his was an arranged marriage, and a horrible pairing it was, too. No—Captain Tom Janson understood love because he loved his daughter to distraction. He loved her too much to have made a pact like that.

What she didn't know was whether Andrew had forged the document, or whether it was that wily Mrs. Janson. The girl was certainly innocent of the plot that surrounded her pretty person and her money. It was clear she didn't love Andrew, but the Dowager supposed she was marrying him for the title. The poor child thought she was going to be a great lady, living out the dream of every nineteen-year-old girl in England. The Dowager sighed. She'd known no better at that age, either, and really, it was just luck that led her into Edgar's loving arms. *You poor thing,* she thought, watching the way the girl sipped her wine and smiled to herself. *You think you're a clever sausage, landing a big fish like Andrew. Little do you know the depths of duplicity surrounding you!*

Frankie herself paid no attention to the three people watching her so closely. She was waiting for Lord Hope. Would he come tonight? There was so little time until Christmas morning! When would he make his appearance? And what would he say? Or did he plan to let her marry Andrew after all? He was Andrew's brother—perhaps he was no better than Andrew. Perhaps he had simply stolen a kiss and told some lies and then disappeared into his mysterious life again. And what did the kiss mean? Frankie shied away from thinking about it too hard. No matter what Eliot said about his youth, it was clear he was an older man, a man of the world. Just because she'd lost herself in his arms, just because his kiss had warmed her right down to the cockles of her heart, just because his voice had started a tremor in her hands that hadn't yet died away... *Peagoose!* she scolded herself. *Just because he has you chirping like a fuzzy baby chicken doesn't mean he feels the same way.* She took a sip of wine and stared at a rugged, tanned, smiling face that she could see perfectly well, hovering just above the blanc mange.

Christmas Eve morning dawned cold and clear. Frankie ran to the window and looked out. She felt a Christmasy thrill go through her, but then she remembered. Tomorrow the Christmas feast would taste like ashes in her mouth. She would be married to Andrew. "Until death do us part," she whispered, and it sounded like a death sentence, indeed. Yesterday's encounter with the real Lord Hope seemed like a faraway dream.

There's nothing for it but a good, stiff gallop. The last gallop of your maiden days! she told herself. *And this morning you'll ride astride!* Five minutes later she was dressed in her father's buckskins, saved all these years. Fifteen minutes later she was in the stables, saddling Jilly. Ajax whined, longing to be off. And thirty minutes later she and Jilly were picking their way across the South Lawn of Kildeer, Ajax bounding ahead, then bounding back, then bounding ahead again. The snow, she realized, watching Ajax slip and slide, was far too icy for a run. But at least she could feel the strength of the mare under her, and pretend for just an hour before the rest of the household awoke, that she was free to go where she pleased.

The morning was silent and beautiful. She felt as if she had stumbled into a time long past. On impulse, she raised her clear, sweet voice in song. *"Good King Wenceslas looked out, on the feast of Stephen,"* she sang. *"Where the snow lay round about, deep and crisp and even! Brightly shone the moon that night, though the frost was cruel, when a poor man came in sight, gathering winter fuel!"* The last of her silver notes died away, and Jilly gave a soft nicker.

Another horse nickered, and another voice picked up the song – a rich baritone. *"Hither page and stand by me,"* the voice sang, *"If thou knowest telling. Yonder poor man, who is he, where and what his dwelling?"* A tall gray horse stepped from behind the trees, Lord Hope leading him across the snow. He smiled as he strode toward her.

Frankie stared at him. In the quiet, snowy morning, wrapped in his greatcoat, and followed by the beautiful gray stallion, he did look like a king of old. Or at least, she thought with a smile, like a lord. Lord Hope.

"Answer me," he said softly, his breath clouding his handsome face.

Frankie remembered the song. *"Sire, he lives a good league hence,"* she sang, surprised that she could find her voice, *"underneath the mountain, right beside the forest fence, and Saint Agnes fountain!"*

Lord Hope swung himself into the saddle and rode up beside her. *"Bring me food and bring me wine, bring me pine logs hither!"* His voice rang out, full of Christmas joy. *"Thou and I shall see him dine, when we bring them thither!"*

Then, as if they'd practiced, their voices rose in unison, hers harmonizing with his. *"Page and monarch forth they went, forth they went together, through the rude wind's loud lament, and the bitter weather!"*

They were riding among the trees now, and Kildeer was out of sight. "Let's not sing the rest," she said, "about how I get too cold to go on and how you must support me."

"Why not, little North Wind? You know that you may always follow in my footsteps!"

"Yes, but in the song, 'heat was in the very sod that the saint had printed,' and something tells me that you aren't a saint, and that your footsteps may lead me very far from home!" She laughed.

Lord Hope reined in, his face serious. "I think you are home, Frankie. Here at Kildeer."

"No!" Frankie reined in as well. "I won't marry Andrew and stay at Kildeer to live in misery or...or die bearing his children! You said you would help me!" She felt tears rising and hoped desperately that they wouldn't spill over.

Lord Hope watched her, his eyes unfathomable. "I think that Christmas morning may dawn to find that the roles have switched, and that you are the monarch, and I am the poor beggar." He reached out for her gloved hand and broke the serious mood with a smile. "I hope your wedding dress will not be a pair of buckskin breeches held tight with an old leather cord!"

Frankie couldn't smile at this, although she knew she looked like an urchin dressed up in her father's old clothes. In fact, she didn't know how to answer this man beside her, who seemed to say two things at once. Would she marry Andrew tomorrow, or not? Did Lord Hope ever mean to reveal himself to his family, or did he plan to torment her for the rest of her life, appearing and disappearing at will?

"You look troubled, my North Wind," Lord Hope said. He lifted her hand to his lips. "But be not afraid, as the angel said. It's almost Christmas, and if we're lucky, there will be some tidings of great joy. Goodbye." He turned and rode away, the gray stallion blending quickly with the blue-white snow.

Christmas Eve passed slowly, filled with the minutiae of wedding and Christmas preparations. Frankie moved through it all as if underwater, allowing herself to be dressed and undressed and dressed again, her mother buzzing about her like a whole swarm of bees. "You must have orange blossoms in your hair, never mind if they are silk. No, you must hold them in your hand, like this. No, like this! Will you mind me?"

Andrew kept coming upon her, making endless crude jokes. "This time tomorrow, eh, Frances? This time tomorrow!"

And the Dowager Lady Hope, gazing at her silently. Was it reproach Frankie saw in those gray eyes? Pity? *Your eldest son is alive,* she wanted to scream at the old woman. *You may put aside your grief and be merry!*

The servants, who seemed to be carrying endless burdens of evergreen branches, were practicing already. "My Lady," they would say, a smirk across their faces.

When she finally climbed into bed it was well past midnight. *Already Christmas Day,* she thought as she fell asleep. *And I'm too tired to care what becomes of me.*

In the morning it was snowing. Frankie awoke to find her mother bending over her. "Get up, darling," she said in a honeyed voice. "It's your wedding day!"

"Mother, you know I don't wish this," Frankie said, swinging her legs over the side of the bed.

"I know nothing of the kind," Mrs. Janson said. "Mine was an arranged marriage, and I was very happy in it. You will be too." And with that, she personally dressed her daughter in her wedding dress.

"Of course it's white," Frankie thought. "Just like everything else I own. White or pale blue." She shuddered. "At least I'll be able to wear colors when I'm married." But looking in the mirror, she had to admit she seemed elegant rather than girlish. The back panel of the dress lengthened into a short train, trimmed with white fur, and as she walked, Frankie could feel it slipping across the floor behind her. Its weight made her hold her shoulders very straight. The low-cut bodice made her look regal rather than—as her other dresses did— merely cold. It was cut *very* low, Frankie thought, looking down at herself. But she supposed display was part of the whole game.

"You look like a queen of the snow," her mother breathed, standing back. "Even I was not so lovely on my wedding day!"

"Thank you, Mama," Frankie said, feeling genuine dislike for her mother. She glanced once more at the pale, black-haired girl in the glass. Her blue eyes did look like ice—emotionless and cold. "Snow queen indeed," she said to herself. "I feel as if I am dressed for a lifetime of winter. Or for the grave."

Standing at the back of the church and seeing Andrew standing at the altar waiting for her, Frankie felt as if she had already died. The church was decked with evergreen boughs and smelled of winter spices. The parish had turned out in their very best Christmas outfits, and the congregation seemed full of rich crimson and green velvets. She could swear, as she walked up the aisle, that a deathly silence reigned – but she could see that a merry carol was being sung. She was sure she could hear each footstep echo, each beat of her heart reverberate as she marched to the altar. *I did my duty*, she thought, as she took Andrew's arm. *I did my duty.* They were Nelson's last words and, she thought, would be her own last sentiment before she began a life of mechanical action.

When the curate asked if anyone knew any reason why Andrew and Frances should not be joined together in Holy Matrimony, Frankie's heart felt like a stone in her chest. She watched the curate's thin lips as he pronounced the words, "speak now, or forever hold your peace," and she felt that stone crack and crumble into sand.

Then, from the back of the church, came a ringing voice. "I will not hold my peace!"

Frankie turned, as if in a dream—but the man at the back was not Lord Hope. He was of middle years, with a very striking nose. As he walked up the aisle, Frankie felt that he was somehow familiar, but it wasn't until he turned his head to smile at her that she recognized him from the cartoons and portraits that had flooded England in the past decade. This was the Duke of Wellington himself! Come all the way to Kildeer, a full five-hour's ride from London. Longer, perhaps, in this snow! And on Christmas Day! Suddenly, Frankie felt like laughing. How appropriate that England's savior should arrive, on Christmas, to lift her from her bondage! For she was sure Lord Hope had sent him. She glanced at Andrew and saw that his face was a mask of surprise and growing fury, and a tiny giggle actually bubbled to her lips.

The Duke reached the altar. "Hello, Frankie my dear," he said. "You are all that I have heard, and more." He winked, and Frankie felt that here was a charming man indeed. She smiled and, drawing her arm from Andrew's slack grasp, sank into a deep curtsey.

"Your Grace of Wellington!" she said, and a gasp came from the congregation, as they realized who this was in their midst.

The Duke smiled and raised Frankie from her curtsey. "Stand here, my child," he said, and drew her elbow tightly against his side. "I'll give you away in a moment, never fear! Now, Mr. Trethorn."

"Your Grace." Andrew bowed. "Have you come to bless our union?"

"Don't be a fool, boy. You are in the stew. I don't envy you."

"I...I don't know what you mean!"

The Duke smiled thinly at Andrew's confusion. "Attend." He held up a crumpled piece of paper. "This is supposedly a document written by young Frankie's father, as he lay dying on a bloody deck at Trafalgar. It reads, 'I, Captain Thomas Janson, do hereby state as my dying wish that my daughter Frances Anne should marry the heir of Edgar, Lord Hope.' And it is signed," the Duke continued, "by Captain Janson and also by Edgar, Lord Hope, who adds this note: 'It is my wish also.'" The Duke let his cool eye range over the gathered parishioners. "You knew the old Lord Hope," he said. "Would he have put his name to this document?"

The congregation was silent. Frankie looked into their stunned faces and felt the urge to laugh, but the Duke's arm tightened around hers and she contained herself.

"The answer is no," the Duke said. "No for both Lord Hope and Captain Janson. I have here another letter, from my dear friend Captain Westgate, who, although he is a Navy man, is one of the most honorable gentlemen I have ever had the privilege to know. He was there when Janson died. He swears, and I quote, 'Thomas Janson died surrounded by his friends. He signed no paper, although he did speak of his daughter to Lord Hope and the rest of us. He said she was the best girl the world has ever seen, and that he hoped he left her rich enough to live the life she chose, and to be free to marry or not marry as she saw fit. I hope your Grace finds this information useful. If your Grace wishes, I can provide the names of all others still living who were present at Janson's death.' The Duke paused for a long moment, then turned to Andrew. "What say you to that, Mr. Trethorn?"

"Fr...Frances marries me of her own free will!" Andrew said, his gray eyes bulging with rage.

The Duke held Andrew in his gaze for a moment, then spoke in a voice that was both quiet and resonant. "What young girl would not choose, of her own free will, to obey the last wishes of a dying and adored father? A father who died a hero's death?"

"She loves me!" Andrew said, and he reached a hand out to Frances, desperation in his eyes.

"I do not love you, Andrew," Frankie said. "I have never told you so."

Andrew's eyes darkened into fury. "You love me, you little baggage! You sailor's by-blow!"

"You have your answer, Mr. Trethorn," the Duke said, and it was the voice of supreme command: quiet, but final. Andrew's lips tightened, and he said no more.

The Duke released Frankie's arm and strolled to the great, butter-colored candle burning on the altar. "I am destroying the evidence, Mr. Trethorn, for which you may be grateful. But know that I only do it to protect the good name of Miss Janson, who has suffered more than any young girl should on a Christmas morn." He put a corner of the document to the flame, and held it burning before the congregation. When the flame came close to his fingers, he let go, and the last scrap of paper burned in mid air, the ashes floating heavenward. "If I were you, Mr. Trethorn," the Duke said conversationally as he dusted soot from his fingers, "I would offer Miss Janson an apology."

"I will not!" Andrew said. "We are practically married! We will finish this ceremony, and we will go home. Your Grace has meddled where your Grace was not wanted! I am Lord Hope, not Mr. Trethorn! I am the head of an old and noble family. Our title was not created yesterday, to be idly laid aside by upstarts!"

A startled gasp came from the congregation, then shocked silence. The Duke let the silence grow and fill the room before he spoke. "In honor of Miss Janson's wedding day, which my instinct tells me it still is, I will consider that speech unsaid, Mr. Trethorn." He stared at Andrew until the younger man dropped his eyes.

Frankie could barely suppress her laughter, but with an enormous effort, she succeeded in looking severe and sorrowful. Out of the corner of her eye she saw the Duke's mouth twitch. She liked him more and more! He reminded her of her father, and how her father would have laughed to see this moment!

"I do have something to tell you, Mr. Trethorn, about your ancient and most venerable title," the Duke said. "It is my great pleasure to inform you that you are not Lord Hope."

"Impossible!"

"Your elder brother, the real Lord Hope, is alive and well, and about to re-enter his life after a few years spent 'dead' in the service of his country. He was, in fact, executing some of the most dangerous missions undertaken in the late war, all accomplished in strict secrecy. Meanwhile you, Mr. Trethorn, were sitting idly at home, basking in borrowed glory."

The Duke turned to the congregation. "Joyful news!" he said, in a ringing voice. "You may now welcome back to your bosom a son whose travels beyond the grave have helped greatly in our hard-won triumph against Bonaparte. If the secrecy of his mission and the false report of his death have caused pain and misadventure, I take all the blame upon my own head, for it was I who called young Hope to a duty from which he could not, and would not, turn away." The Duke bent his gaze once more on Andrew. "Lord Hope's title sits lightly on his shoulders. He is a man who judges men by their character and actions, not by lineage and rank." The Duke smiled at Frankie and said, so that only she could hear, "As for women...apparently he judges women by their love of large, boisterous dogs. And I warn you, with Lord Hope that kind of love is exactly what you will need!" He raised his voice again. "Hope!"

The door at the back of the church swung open and Lord Hope entered. A shout went up from the congregation, and Frankie's heart turned over and awoke. His lordship was dressed to perfection now, in his glorious red Regimentals. He looked, Frankie thought, as handsome and hopeful and bright as a Christmas morning: as this very Christmas morning! His eyes went immediately to hers, a question in them. She felt rather than heard herself answer, and saw that answer reflected back to her in his dawning smile.

"You see, North Wind?" he said as he reached her side, the congregation still cheering at his back. "You are now Queen Wenceslas, and I the poor beggar."

"Oh, no, my Lord! You are the gallant page, at least!" She slipped her hand in his and smiled into his eyes, which shone with a clear, happy light.

"And I will serve you for many Christmases to come, Frankie!"

"Well I should think so! And Easters as well! And all the days in between!"

"Except Mondays," he said, tracing a finger down the line of her jaw. "Mondays are my days."

Bethany Schneider was born and raised in Western Massachusetts. Aside from getting her hair cut at the "Regency Salon," she lived in ignorance of the Regency period and Regency fiction until a few years ago, when she accidentally read a Georgette Heyer novel. Since then she's been making up for lost time. For the past three years she lived in Oxford, England, where she wrote this, her first stab at a Regency story. Recently, she moved with her partner to northern Ohio, where she is plugging away at a career as a teacher and journalist.

Christmas is the season of miracles. A wounded war veteran learns just how miraculous this time can be.

A Strange Occurence
Near G___

Susan McDuffie

December 28th, 1815

Dear William—

I write to tell you a story I scarce believe myself—yet I swear, on the bones of those men who fought with us and died on that plain in Belgium, and those many others who died for our cause in Spain, that every word of it is true.

The last few months have not been kind to me. Upon returning home, having recovered my health to some degree, I confess I found the amusements of society so superficial, and my disappointments so severe, that I betook myself to my club. Like some wounded badger, I spent the better part of some months there, in my den. I rarely stirred from my room until noon, and then only for another bottle of brandy.

Only you, my fellow officer, can imagine the darkness of spirits that assailed me. Upon returning from our illustrious victory, I found that, although a *victor* in the field of *Mars*, I had been *defeated* in the field of *Eros*, and that Deirdre's affections were no longer mine—as vanished as my missing arm. And the pain has been as great—I still seek to move the limb that is no longer there, just as my heart sought vainly after Deirdre, who became Lady Ardington these eight months since.

I tell you this, dear friend, so that you will understand the total desolation of spirits which oppressed me as I rode, some few days ago, towards G____, finally to visit my parents at their estate for the Yuletide holidays. I confess I had gone to some lengths to avoid making the trip, and it was only my sister's ultimatum which eventually induced me to go. Cecily, now that she is a married woman and a mother, is no less the little termagant you may remember from your visit with us some years ago. She accosted me, *at my club*, roundly denounced me for being both a fool and a coward, and told me that although Mother would quail at the sight of my missing arm, she would undoubtedly die of heartbreak if I did not make the visit. So, under such orders—and had Cecily been on the Peninsula, I can assure you the campaigns would have been concluded there more quickly—what could I do but set out towards G_____, as directed by my little sister.

I took no carriage, only Trafalgar, who leapt at the chance to be on the open road. As it is only a ride of some few hours from London to G_____, I thought to make the journey in one day, but the storm last week slowed my progress. The sun set, snow kept falling, and I remained far from my destination. To make matters worse, I thought to take a shortcut through a boscage I thought I remembered from my youth—and the landscape having been overgrown somewhat in the years since I had been there, I found myself lost, in deep snow and bitter cold, on Christmas Eve.

At such times, one would think that I longed for the warmth and comfort of my childhood home and the completion of my journey, but such was the darkness of my mind that I preferred the bitter isolation of the forest. There were moments when I thought it would be for the better were I to die there, in the forest, and end this life. For what was I? A one-armed man, who would never be whole in body or heart again.

How long I remained in this state I cannot say—hours, for the evening star had risen high in the sky, and the moon was setting—when I came to a small clearing in the forest. The snow had stopped some while back, and the clouds, which had hitherto obscured the glory of the heavens, were now blown away. The moonlight reflected off the snowy boughs of trees, all covered in a frigid and icy beauty.

Here, I thought. *Here, I shall dismount, and make a little hollow in the snow, and sleep. And sleep, and never wake again. Thus, my miserable life will end, here in the snowy countryside, after surviving French bullets and bayonets.* I fancied, as I thought this, the wind went sighing through the trees and the branches moaned a bit, in sympathy. A cloud blew over the clearing, obscuring the starlight, which had shone down a moment earlier.

"Oh God," I prayed, "Help me; forgive me. Let no one find me here, let me make a hole, go to ground in it, and die in it. For I confess I no longer want to live."

I fancied at this time that the wind increased in strength, but after a moment or two I dismounted and found some shelter behind a large tree trunk. I found Trafalgar a place out of the wind as well, and, wrapping my cloak around me, I lay down upon the snow, hoping my last slumber would bring me pleasant dreams of Deirdre before it brought me to Hell—for there I was surely bound.

I dozed a bit, and then awoke to a bright light in the clearing. A star of great magnitude blazed down, turning the snow to a brilliant white, and all seemed mild, despite the snow. I wondered not at this, for I had heard stories of the pleasant warmth one sinks into as one freezes, but I wondered at my alert state. All torpor had vanished. It was as though I had awakened from a dream and, refreshed and alert, was ready to begin another day.

And then I saw the child. A young boy, feet bare, dressed in a ragged smock, came walking across the clearing. I could clearly see the prints his bare feet made in the snow by the starlight. His face was thin, and his features showed a sadness no child should know; and yet, his eyes, more ancient than the hills, looked strangely kind.

"Here," I called, "You will surely freeze. Come here child, and get warm in my cloak."

The boy obeyed, and huddled against me. His flesh did not feel cold, instead, strangely, he seemed to warm me.

"Where are your people, boy?" I asked. "What are you doing out here in the hills, alone?"

"They be at D_____" he said, gesturing in that direction. "They left me, as I was to wait here. That be what they told me. But they haven't come back for me."

He looked at me with that odd trusting look you sometimes see in children. "You came for me. I was waiting for you."

"We will surely freeze if we stay here, boy, " I said, somewhat gruffly, forgetting that freezing to death had been my intention a few moments ago. "Come, now, I have a fine horse over here, out of the wind. He can carry us both, and take us to your people."

And so we found Trafalgar, I mounted and set the boy in front of me, and we set off through the snowy night in the direction the boy indicated. The boy had almost no weight, and Trafalgar barely noticed him, except that he carried us even more gently through the frozen forest.

For some reason, I did not feel the cold. In fact, I had the oddest sensation, as if the warmth of that slight child poured into my body, into my heart, and thawed it, breaking the icy prison that had held it for so long. I found myself breathing deeply, and tears fell from my eyes, while at the same time an odd sense of well-being flowed through me.

I could not say how long we rode through the forest. At some time, the child's even breathing indicated he slept, and Trafalgar's steady pace lulled me to sleep, as peacefully as a baby myself, while the horse continued his steady walk and that bright star above bathed us in its light.

I awoke again, to find Trafalgar still walking, a pink dawn creeping over the white hills, and the drive to G_____ just ahead. But the child had disappeared from my arms, taking my burdens with him.

We followed Trafalgar's trail back through the woods, to that clearing. We found the hollow where I had slept, Trafalgar's hoof prints, and my own prints. But the small barefoot prints of a child were nowhere to be seen.

I confess I did not expect to find them. But I will tell you that I kept Christmas with a glad heart this year.

Yours,
Stephen

Susan McDuffie was raised in the northeast US but has since relocated to New Mexico. She discovered Regency fiction a few years ago and found it a wonderful antidote to her day job in the public school system.

She has since completed two novels and several short stories set in that time period. Her historical mystery story, *An Unusual Correspondence*, was published in *A REGENCY SAMPLER* last year by Regency Press. Lately, she has been accused of "channeling the Regency" in her writing.

True love knows no boundaries: not distance, time, nor even death. Duncan is about to discover this truth on his annual Christmas walk.

The Christmas Walk

Steven Abaroa

Duncan MacAlister looked out his third-story window at the new Christmas Day that had just begun to dawn. There was a light powdering of snow around the city of Edinburgh. *It will be cold this morning*, he thought as he pulled on his overcoat, being very careful not to crush the precious gifts in the inner pockets. Slowly, he made his way out of his flat and down the long flight of stairs to the ground floor. There was a time when he would run down as fast as he could, anxious to begin his annual walk to the love of his life, to his Maggie Rose.

As he reached the bottom of the stairs, Mrs. Potter, his housekeeper for the past forty-some years, met him with cup of tea in hand.

"Morning, Mr. Duncan. Warm yourself up before you go out this morning,"she said as she handed him the cup. "Now mind you, you're to have dinner with the Dean and his wife at three o'clock sharp, so do not be late."

"My dear Mrs. Potter, where would I be without you?" Duncan said as he took the cup from her. Mrs. Potter came to be employed by Duncan when he first moved into his house. That was forty-five years ago in 1766. Duncan, born and raised in Edinburgh, had left when he was eighteen to attend the University of Cambridge in England. When he returned in 1766 it was to teach history at the University of Edinburgh. His father had set him up in his house with Mrs. Potter to help. His house was quite a walk to the University, but Duncan enjoyed his time "to think," as he would put it.

He would use this, his Christmas walk of 1811 to think...to think of Maggie Rose. He left his house and turned toward Holyrood Castle. He would take the road past the castle to High Street or, as many called it, the Royal Mile. As he turned toward High Street, he stopped to gaze at Queen Mary's Bathhouse. He would always laugh when he told his students how Queen Mary would buck the traditions of the Tudors and bathe once a month, whether she needed it or not. Not with water, but with White Wine. Today, however he would look at the bathhouse and not remember Queen Mary, but the day he stole a kiss from his Maggie right there on the steps of the bathhouse when he told her the story of Queen Mary.

He felt a cold wind hit him as he turned to go up High Street. It was a long walk uphill from the Castle to St. Giles's, which would be Duncan's first stop before he would go see his Maggie Rose. There were many shops and pubs on both sides of the road. Most of them would be deserted on this Christmas morning. Only the Bakeries would have signs of life, movement around the shop and, a wonderful smell as they worked to fill Christmas dinner orders.

Normally when Duncan walked High Street he would be followed by his students. He knew everything about each building, and enjoyed telling his students about each one. Most of the students enjoyed this walk until they returned to his class and found that he wanted them to write a paper on the history of High Street. It seemed to Duncan that the only thing anyone could remember was the public house where Queen Mary hid after her escape from Edinburgh Castle.

At last Duncan arrived at St. Giles's. This Gothic edifice was the high church in the Scottish Presbyterian faith. It was here, as Duncan would tell his students, that the very Protestant John Knox had preached to the very Catholic Queen Mary. There would be no preaching today. Duncan came into the church and sat in the very pew where he first met his Maggie Rose. It was on a Christmas day much like today. On his Christmas walk, Duncan had stopped at St. Giles's to warm up a bit. The only people in the church were a few workers who were getting the chapel ready for Christmas Mass. Maggie was one of those workers. Her father was one of the ministers. Duncan was shy around this beautiful, young girl, but she was not shy around him. Before he knew it, he was helping her with the work around the church.

After that Christmas, Duncan would call at the Rev. Edmund Lumsden's house to sit and talk with Maggie. By Easter, there was a wedding at St. Giles's. That was thirty-five years ago. Tears began to fill Duncan's eyes as he watched a young couple work on setting up candles near the High Altar.

I must be going, Duncan thought to himself as he quickly left the church. He crossed the street to the City Building. From here he took a back alley that led him down a long flight of stairs. Edinburgh was built on several hills, and this alley took him down and away from the old part of the city. As he came out of the Old City, he came to a bridge that crossed the river, and led to the New City. In the Old City, buildings huddled close together and streets were narrow. In the New City the streets were wider and buildings sat around parks that allowed people more room to walk about. Mrs. Potter wanted Duncan to move to the New City. "You'll be closer to your Maggie Rose," she would say. But Duncan would not have it. He loved his walks, no matter how far they were.

As Duncan crossed the bridge he came to Princess Street. He turned left and followed the Royal Park that ran between the street and the bottom of the Old City. On his left loomed the dark foreboding Edinburgh Castle. On the right, the light, welcoming buildings of the New City. At the end of the park was St. John's Church.

Arriving at the church, he turned down a small path that led to a ravine. This ravine was part of St. John's Cemetery. Because of the steep cliff, the sun had not yet touched this area. Just past a leafless tree, Duncan stopped at a headstone.

"Merry Christmas, Maggie." Duncan carefully lifted a large Christmas Rose from his breast pocket. "Just as I promised," he said as he laid it on her grave, "a Christmas Rose for my Maggie Rose."

Reaching again into his pocket, Duncan produced a small wooden rocking horse. He had worked on it all year. "And this is for Daniel," he said as he placed it beside the rose. He stood and stared at the tombstone for a while. It read, "Rest in Peace, Margaret Rose Lumsden MacAlister, April 23, 1757-December 25, 1777, Loving Wife and Mother. Rest in Peace, Daniel Edmund Mac-Alister, December 25, 1777, Loving Son."

Daniel was to be their Christmas present to each other, but something happened. Maggie passed away shortly after he was born, and Daniel died in his father's arms an hour later. For thirty-four years Duncan had come on his Christmas walk to place a rose and a toy on the grave of his Maggie Rose and his Danny.

Bells began to call the people of Edinburgh to the churches for Christmas services around the city. Duncan wept as he turned and left the cemetery. He retraced his steps back to the bridge that led away from the New City to the Old. He was feeling a bit tired as he reached a park bench near the bridge. *I'll sit a moment*, he said to himself as he brushed off some snow and sat down. He had just closed his eyes when he heard a familiar voice.

"Well, Duncan, there ye be," the voice said. "Don't you think it is time you came home?"

Duncan opened his eyes. In front of him stood his Maggie Rose.

"Come Duncan," she said, reaching her hand to him. "Daniel will be awake soon and he'll want to see his Father."

Duncan touched Maggie's hand and stood and brought her into him. Together, arm in arm, they walked in the mists of the Royal Park.

Many buggies, filled with families on their way to Christmas Services would pass that old man sleeping on the park bench. It would be late in the afternoon by the time they discovered that he was not asleep, but had gone home to his Maggie Rose.

Steven Ramon Abaroa was born and raised in San Diego, California. He attended Brigham Young University where he met and married DeeAnn Lewis. They are the parents of four boys; Tyson, Jordan, Cameron, and Austin.

Steve now lives in Gilbert, Arizona where he teaches World and British Literature, Shakespeare and Journalism. Currently, he is also the Speech Coach, and directs the One Act Competition Play at Highland High School.

He has been a featured writer in the Arizona Republic. Once a year, Steve takes a group of Highland School seniors to England and Scotland. This is his second story to be published by Regency Press.

"Be careful what you wish for" is the theme in this comedic tale of switched identities. But then, "All's well that ends well" as Lionel and Geoffrey also decide to try each other's fiancées!

The New Year's Wish Tangle

Jennifer Ashley

"Good morning, my lord."

Lionel Moreland cracked open his eyes on New Year's day, 1817, and knew all was wrong with the world.

First, the grey-haired, correct personage who poured steaming water into shaving basin was not his valet. Lionel's valet was a former footman called Martin, who stood six feet tall, and performed his duties with bumbling good humor.

Second, Lionel lay in a decadent palace of a room he didn't recognize. Gold frescoes climbed to a vaulted ceiling painted with classical figures, most of them unclothed. Lionel's own bed chamber in Picadilly was dark, comfortable, and simple.

Third, his headache. A head-splitter like this only came along after a night imbibing port with his old school chums. But he'd drunk little more than lemonade the evening before at the ball hosted by his fiancée's father.

The valet draped the towel over his arm. "I have laid out the silver and blue for you, my lord. Is that to your wishes?"

And why the devil did he keep calling Lionel "my lord?"

"Yes, of course." Lionel threw off the covers.

And nearly screamed.

The legs attached to his body weren't his. The beefy, muscular appendage belonged to a huge brute of a man, while Lionel was only moderately sized, fact that Millicent constantly twitted him about.

Lionel scrambled out of the bed and stood up. And up and up. He looked down at his huge feet far below, his head spinning.

"What's happened to me, man?"

The valet glanced up. "You were a trifle inebriated last evening, my lord."

A trifle?

"If you will sit, my lord."

Lionel moved his huge frame to the chair the valet indicated, seated him-self, and looked into the mirror.

And bit back another cry. The man looking back at him was not pleasant-faced, brown-eyed Lionel Moreland. Instead a powerful giant with blue eyes, blond hair, and handsome, chiseled features peered out at him.

What's more, Lionel recognized him. Geoffrey Seton, Viscount Ashbury.

Lionel clenched his big hands as memories of the previous night rushed over him. *My own fault,* he thought. *My own bacon-brained fault.*

Lionel had spent the evening at the New Year's ball hosted by Millicent Deveaux's father. Millicent had hung on his arm most of the night, chattering about the upcoming Parliamentary sessions and what a mark Lionel would make in them. She'd outlined her plans to court those who could boost Lionel's career, and reminded Lionel many times what a wonderful wife she would make him when they married later that year.

When she'd finally let him alone, Millicent's father had pinned him down, to reiterate at length how he expected Millicent to be the most sought-after hostess in Town.

Lionel had escaped to an empty anteroom shortly before midnight. He'd opened the window wide, letting the cold December air pour over him. He'd leaned against the sill, gazing out over the frosty cobbles of Portman Square, and saw his future stretching before him, bleak and featureless.

A year ago, Lionel had easily won a seat in Commons, and he'd gotten en-gaged to Millicent, a pretty and charming girl with a wealthy and influential family, perfect for a gentleman with political ambitions.

But then Lionel's father had died, and he'd barely recovered from the blow when Millicent and Mr. Deveaux had latched firmly onto him and made it no secret that they intended to guide his every move.

Lionel had believed he could live that sort of life for ambition and fortune, but no longer. His heart needed something more.

A group of gentlemen had stumbled into the frosty square below him— gentlemen of wealth, Corinthians out on the town. They walked arm-in-arm, laughing drunkenly. A carriage trailed slowly behind them.

"Come back in, Ash. We're cold." A buxom lady put her head and torso out of the carriage window. Feminine giggling followed.

Lord Ashbury, a tall, blond, fiercely handsome gentleman had turned 'round. "Stubble it, m'dear. Don't interfere with a man's wager."

"But you'll ruin your boots!"

Lionel peered at the fine Hessians on Ashbury's feet and agreed. Probably his lordship had never walked out of doors in them before.

"I'll sacrifice 'em. Got a monkey with Warburton that says I can't walk around the square without falling over. Devil take him, I can't."

Ashbury, supporting himself on his equally fuddled friends, passed beneath Lionel's window.

He looked up. The two men's eyes met.

Lionel thought suddenly, Wish I could be that chap. Bet he does only what he wishes, and nothing else.

As the thought took shape, church bells around the city began the muffled toll of midnight, the end of the last hour of the old year. Laughter and music rose in the ballroom behind him. A mist shimmered before Lionel's eyes, a faint fog on the frigid air.

The mist cleared. Lord Ashbury turned away, bellowing a bawdy ditty...

The valet tilted Lionel's head back and the mirror was lost to view.

Lionel let out his breath. Well, he'd wished himself into Lord Ashbury's pristine Hessians all right. Did that mean that Lord Ashbury was enjoying New Year's breakfast in Lionel Moreland's rooms in Lionel Moreland's body?

The devil. There was nothing for it. Lionel would have to charge round to his own digs and see if he'd meet himself—or rather, Lord Ashbury—as soon as this valet finished with him.

❄ ❄ ❄

It took two hours for the valet to finish with him. After shaving Lionel carefully, the valet dressed him in the finest lawn shirt, biscuit pantaloons, and white-on-white waistcoat.

Next, he carried forth a pile of snowy linen neckcloths and laid them reverently on the dressing table. He turned Lionel's collar up and draped an immaculate white cravat around his neck.

"Shall you tie it yourself, my lord?"

Lionel hesitated. He had the idea that his usual plain knot wouldn't suit noble Lord Ashbury. "Why don't you do it?" He pinched his eyes closed, pretending the headache had flared.

The valet turned him around, and Lionel lifted his chin. After an excruciating interval, the valet asked, "Is that to your liking, my lord?"

Lionel glanced in the mirror. The cravat was tied in a perfect "Ashbury," the knot made famous by the man who normally occupied this body.

"Yes, quite," Lionel nodded. "Just the thing."

He heard a silence. He looked down and found the valet staring at him, open-mouthed. "Are you—certain, my lord?"

"Of course."

The valet swallowed. His assistant darted forward, eyes wide, to take up the unused neckcloths. "Only one?" he whispered.

"Mind your manners, lad," the valet hissed back.

Next, the valet produced a frock coat cut so perfectly that valet and assistant took ten minutes to maneuver it over Lionel's athletic shoulders. Hessians went on Lionel's feet; if they were the same boots from the night before, Lionel couldn't tell, but they shone with polish.

Lionel surveyed his fashionable self for a moment, trying to stem his rising panic.

"I'm going out," he said off-handedly. "Send my rig 'round, will you?"

The valet raised his brows. "Surely Lord Alexander will arrive momentarily, my lord. It is three o'clock."

"Lord Alexander?"

"Lord and Lady Alexander, and Lady Lucinda. They were to call at three."

Lionel racked his brains. He knew of Lord Alexander, but wasn't acquainted with him, or with Lady Lucinda, his daughter. He was surprised to hear they were in Town at all. He was surprised Lord Ashbury was, as well. Surely Ashbury should be shooting things at his country estate this time of year.

The valet's tone turned sardonic. "Your fiancée, my lord, and her family. Surely your lordship remembers? Though your lordship has been rather inebriated since the announcement."

Lionel hid his start. Ashbury's fiancée and her family. Good lord. He didn't much like dining with his *own* fiancée and family.

But there was no avoiding it. He'd have to get rid of them quickly, then go 'round to his rooms and have a talk with himself.

His headache wasn't getting any better.

※ ❈ ※

"Bring me some real clothes, man! I'll look a damned quiz in this!"

Martin, Lionel Moreland's valet cum footman, dashed out of his master's bedroom, followed by a well-aimed waistcoat.

Geoffrey Seton, fourth Viscount Ashbury, was in a foul temper. He'd woken with a headache in a strange bed in dull digs, and he didn't know where he was or *who* he was for that matter. The personage in the mirror had brown hair, brown eyes, and a dashed drab demeanor—definitely not the handsome, much-sought-after Lord Ashbury.

He still must be cup-shot. The last thing he remembered was wagering five hundred pounds that he could tramp around Portman Square in the middle of the night. He'd lost the bet, devil take it, tumbling over before he'd reached the third side. He didn't even have the blunt to cover the debt.

And he'd awakened *here*, with a headache and this cursed incompetent valet. What the devil was the matter with everyone?

"Mr. Moreland!" a man exclaimed from the doorway. "You surprise me, sir."

Ashbury swung around. A thin man with a beaked nose stood on the threshold, staring at Ashbury in disapproval.

"And who the devil are you?" If he weren't in this spindle-shanked body, Ashbury thought, he'd dash over and throw the nuisance out himself.

"Mr. Moreland, you forget yourself."

"No. *You* forget yourself. How dare you insinuate yourself into my private rooms?"

The gentleman looked affronted. Ashbury didn't care. He must be a creditor, come to gather in his notes, and Ashbury knew he couldn't cover them. It would be Fleet Prison in no time, viscount or not. He needed to marry Lady Lucinda and her fortune quickly before everything caught up to him.

"How dare *I*?" The gentleman puffed up. "I will be handing over Millicent, my only daughter, to you in a few months. It is *my* position and *my* money that will boost you up the ladder, my son, don't you forget it."

What was the dratted man blathering about? Ashbury picked up a boot; ill-made, he noted in irritation. "Get out, blast you, or I'll have my servants throw you out."

"Mr. Moreland, I am appalled."

Ashbury hurled the boot. The gentleman turned and fled.

Dashed creditors. Pretending to be a fellow's father-in-law-to-be to get past the servants.

Ashbury stopped short, ideas at last penetrating his thick, Corinthian skull. Perhaps the reflection in the mirror wasn't the product of being fuddled. Perhaps others too, saw him as this brown-haired chap. Perhaps the gentleman really had thought his daughter would marry him.

That meant that the bookmaker and his bully who would call on Lord Ashbury today would not find him. And Ashbury was supposed to have spent a cursed boring afternoon with his fiancée and family—but if he were here, looking like this, then he wouldn't be expected to court her today. Well, well.

Humor restored, Lord Ashbury threw himself onto the divan and called for the valet to bring him a newspaper and brandy.

❊ ❊ ❊

Lionel made his way nervously down the huge staircase, following the butler to the blue drawing room and the waiting Lord Alexander and family. In his pocket lay an unmarked box his valet had pressed on him, declaring it was the New Year's gift to Lady Lucinda that he'd fetched from Bond Street.

Lionel anticipated the upcoming interview with a shudder. Lady Lucinda was probably a simpering miss without a thought in her head, the kind of young woman Lord Ashbury would be certain to attract.

He strode across the black-and-white marble hall and waited for the butler to open the door. Three people in the Wedgewood-blue room rose as he entered. The large man with white hair was no doubt Lord Alexander, and the tiny lady in the lace cap, his wife.

"Good afternoon," Lionel said, trying to sound cheerful.

Behind them, Lady Lucinda, their daughter, stepped forward. Lionel gazed upon her, and fell head over ears in love.

Lady Lucinda had fair hair that shone in the candlelight, oval cheeks tinged with pink, and a womanly figure that dazzled him. Lionel bowed over her hand, his heart racing, murmuring something he hoped sounded polite.

When he looked up at her, his breath deserted him. Her eyes were an un-usual shade of grey—silver almost. He became lost in their shimmering depths and held her hand for much longer than was proper.

"My lord." Her tone was resigned, her expression, tired. Lionel understood in a flash that Lady Lucinda married Lord Ashbury out of duty, not personal desire. A shame. This fair creature deserved better than the drunken lout who stumbled about Portman Square with Corinthians and demi-reps.

Reluctantly, he released her then invited his guests to sit.

Fortunately for Lionel, Lord Alexander liked to talk. He dominated the conversation, and all Lionel had to do was make responses. But Lionel found himself liking Lord Alexander, despite his garrulousness. The man had intelli-gent opinions and a bluff good-heartedness. Lionel listened politely, and let his gaze stray to Lucinda as often as he could.

He should be ashamed of himself, losing his heart to another man's fiancée. *But, who knows? I may have to marry her in the guise of Lord Ashbury after all.* And, he thought, catching her eye again, that might be no bad thing.

When he focused on the world at large once more, he found the conversa-tion had turned to New Year's customs. Folklore, Lord Alexander confessed, was one of his hobbies. Lionel's interest seemed to gratify him. They specu-lated on some of the more interesting superstitions, such as it being bad luck to receive a woman on New Year's Day. Lionel glanced at Lucinda and remarked that in his case the luck was all to the good.

"Some stories have it," Lord Alexander warmed to the subject, "that any wish made at the stroke of midnight on the last day of the old year has incredi-ble power."

Lionel looked up, attention caught. "Does it, indeed?"

"Apparently, the wish may be *un*-wished any time during the first day of the New Year, but after that, it is binding."

"Interesting." Lionel tried to sound casual. So all he had to do was wish himself to be—himself again? But perhaps the real Lord Ashbury had to wish it too. He glanced at Lucinda. *Binding.* He could marry her. Temptation plucked at him.

"Lucinda found that particular story," Lord Alexander said fondly.

Lucinda smiled, but looked uncomfortable.

The honorable thing to do, Lionel thought, was to wish himself back to himself and let Ashbury marry her. Maybe Ashbury was head over ears him-self. He didn't really believe that, but Lionel had honor. He sighed inwardly and told himself to enjoy what little time he could with her.

As his visitors rose to depart, Lionel pulled the box from his pocket. "Lady Lucinda," he said. "I have a gift for you." Good lord, he was stammering like a schoolboy.

"Have you, my lord?"

Lord Alexander suddenly became taken with a painting on the opposite end of the room, and insisted that he point it out to his wife.

Lionel blessed him for his tact. Left alone with Lucinda, he opened the box.

They both gasped. On black velvet lay a string of diamonds, which caught the light and glittered like silent stars.

Lionel's lovestruck heart recognized in them a perfect compliment to her beauty. "They match your eyes."

The eyes in question widened. "My lord, this is a princely gift."

"It is nothing to what I want to give you, Lucinda."

Suspicion edged her tone. "And what is that, my lord?"

"All that I have and all that I am."

She flushed. "Your words are pretty, but I must say they surprise me. I was led to believe our alliance was purely for convenience."

"Perhaps it began that way." Lionel drew out the diamonds and laid them around her neck. "But I was a fool if I did not love you sooner."

"Love?" She started.

"Love, esteem, adore." Lionel fastened the catch, his pulse quickening as he brushed the softness of her neck. "You warm my heart, my lady."

"Flummery, my lord."

"No." He took her hands. "Will you do me the honor of allowing me to salute you in the tender way I long to?"

Lucinda stared at him in amazement.

What kind of bacon-brained barbarian had Ashbury been with her? he wondered, if Lionel's admiration struck her with such astonishment?

"Very well." She braced herself, but lifted her face.

Lionel, his heart soaring with joy, leaned down and softly kissed her lips.

❊ ❊ ❊

"Mr. Moreland," came a petulant, female voice.

Ashbury looked up from his sporting paper. A trim young woman with auburn curls wearing a pale, long-sleeved gown stood in the doorway. She carried a basket on her arm, and her brown eyes held worry.

"My, my," Ashbury tossed the paper aside. "What a pretty gel you are."

The young lady regarded him severely. "Mr. Moreland, you *dismissed* papa. No one dismisses Papa. He is most distressed."

Ashbury recalled the annoying gentleman he'd tossed out a few hours before. "He was a troublesome lout. Why shouldn't I dismiss him?"

"It was quite foolish of you. His good favor could land you a cabinet post, you must remember." She stepped into the room. "Are you feeling at all well, Mr. Moreland?"

"I am now that I have you to look at." He remembered the name the man had spat at him. "Millicent."

A pretty blush bloomed on her cheek. "You've never before called me by my Christian name, Mr. Moreland."

Ashbury grinned at her. "What are you doing here, you fast baggage? Visiting a man in his rooms is most improper."

"I feared you were unwell. I brought some of my remedies for you. And we *are* going to be married—"

"So you slipped away before Papa could notice." Ashbury chuckled. What a spirited little thing. Quite unlike that milk-and-water miss he would marry. "Remedies, eh? I'm feeling quite poorly, as a matter of fact. What have you brought me, m'dear?"

Millicent peered into her basket as she crossed to him. "Chamomile for your headache; tansy to soothe your humors. Shall I ring for hot water?"

"Not yet." He laughed, caught her 'round the waist, and pulled her down into his lap.

"Mr. Moreland!" she squeaked.

Ashbury studied her flushed face and sparkling brown eyes, and admitted himself smitten. He slid his arms around her, and pulled her down to him.

"*Lionel*," she whispered happily, then their lips met.

❄ ❄ ❄

Lord Alexander and his family departed to prepare for the round of New Year's balls. Lord Alexander expressed the wish that they might encounter Lord Ashbury later that evening. Lionel nodded and made noncommittal noises, then the family took their leave.

The idiot Ashbury hadn't offered to escort his fiancée and her family that night, Lionel reflected as he turned back to the stairs. He would have to have a little chat with Ashbury.

"My lord?"

Lionel turned to Ashbury's butler, who regarded him with a faintly worried expression. "There's a gentleman to see you, my lord. I told him you weren't home, but he said he'd wait. He and his servant were—rather insistent."

Lionel lifted his brows. He couldn't imagine anyone bullying Ashbury's stately specimen of a butler. The man's air could freeze water at ten paces. "Very well. I'll see them."

"Yes, my lord."

The butler led Lionel to a reception room at the front of the house. Lionel entered and found himself facing two mismatched gentlemen.

No, he corrected himself, *gentlemen* was not an accurate appellation. The smaller one looked a seedier sort of man of the City, and the other, a huge ape of a man, had "criminal" stamped all over him.

The butler left them. Lionel remained standing. "How may I assist you, sir?"

The small man bowed. "You can give me two thousand pounds, my lord." His voice was soft, controlled. "It is the first of the month. I extended you three months out of mercy, but now I want my money."

Lionel kept his look bland. "I'm certain I can write you a draft." He picked up a handbell from the writing table and rang it.

The small gentleman stepped forward. "No, my lord." His eyes went flat. "No bank drafts, no vowels. I want cash from you, my lord, and I want it now."

Lionel let his brows drift upward. "I don't know if I have such a sum in my house, but I will enquire."

As they waited for a servant to respond to the bell, Lionel wondered. These gentlemen were not the usual sort of moneylenders. They had an air of East End toughs who'd risen in the world, probably by collecting money from nobs like Lord Ashbury.

The butler returned. "My lord?"

Lionel drew the man aside. "These gentlemen want two thousand pounds. Can you fetch it for me?"

The butler's eyes widened. "I—don't think so, my lord."

"Oh, come now, I must have some loose cash about the house."

The butler resumed his air of hauteur. "I'm sure your lordship's secretary would know more about that."

"Ah, very good. Just send him in, will you?"

"He is not here, my lord. He took a holiday to see his family in Surrey."

Drat the man. "Of course. But you can bring me his books, can't you? There's a good chap."

The butler narrowed his eyes at being called a "good chap," but he bowed and glided away.

"Won't be a moment." Lionel smiled at his guests. The small man returned a sullen look.

Lionel wondered if Lord Ashbury was the sort of man too top-lofty to pay his creditors. Many in the Polite World were, and Ashbury had a title to protect him from much trouble.

Or so Lionel supposed, until the butler and a footman gravely set the account ledgers on the writing table. Lionel leafed through the uppermost ledger, and his blood chilled.

Ashbury was deep in dun territory indeed. Not only did he owe the usual bills to tailor and boot-maker, but he had vast sums due to moneylenders and pencillers and still less reputable people.

Lionel realized in an instant that Lord Ashbury's carefree life was a sham. The man was two steps shy of having to flee to the Continent in the wake of Brummell and other indigent compatriots. No wonder he'd holed up in this house over the winter. He probably couldn't stand the expense of opening his country estate.

"If you could call back tomorrow, gentlemen," Lionel said carefully. "Perhaps I can have the money for you. I may not have the spare change in the house, and it is New Year's, as you know."

The large gentleman folded his arms across his chest and gave Lionel an evil look. The small gentleman smiled. "We'll wait."

Lionel sucked in his cheeks. Well, if they wanted to sit idly, perhaps he could untangle this mess of accounts and find some of the ready *somewhere.*

Within an hour he realized that Lord Ashbury's secretary was embezzling him something fierce. He'd been clever, the secretary had. He'd salted away money while keeping the books so confused that it looked as though Ashbury were horribly in debt, when in fact, he had plenty of blunt.

But Lionel was clever, too, and he knew he could unravel the secretary's web.

He looked up at the waiting gentlemen and beamed. "Well, sir, I may be able to help you after all."

❄ ❉ ❄

Lionel had to extract from the butler the fact that the secretary lived in, and that the butler, indeed, had a key to the man's rooms. A short search by Lionel turned up a nice casket full of money—gold coins, and bank notes, all pilfered from Ashbury's accounts.

Lionel counted out two thousand pounds in bank notes and coins, and returned with them to the waiting bookmakers below. The small man seemed surprised, but readily snatched up the money. He gave Lionel Ashbury's note, and departed.

Lionel opened the account books again. He could do this one favor for Ashbury at least, to compensate for falling in love with the man's fiancée. He found pen and ink in the writing table, seated himself, and began the interesting task of straightening out Ashbury's accounts.

By eight o'clock, he'd done it. He rose, stretched, then took himself back upstairs to the bed chamber.

He ordered the valet to dress him in Ashbury's most comfortable clothes: loose breeches, top boots, greatcoat, and a neckcloth looped once and tied comfortably.

The valet collapsed to a chair and fanned himself. Lionel ignored him and called for Ashbury's carriage to take him to Picadilly.

❄ ❉ ❄

Fifteen minutes later, Lionel hammered on the door of his own digs, and his valet, Martin answered it.

"Mr. Moreland is not feeling well, today, sir," Martin ventured.

"Then he's here? Good. I'll run up and see him." Lionel pushed past his young valet, who was no match for the beefy Ashbury.

"But sir—"

"Don't worry," Lionel called out. "I know the way."

He ran up the familiar staircase, and down the dark-panelled hall, which was a cool relief after the ostentation of Ashbury's mansion.

Lionel opened the door to his chamber, and stopped.

His own body lounged on a divan in his favorite dressing gown, with Millicent Deveaux sprawled across him. Her disheveled hair tangled on his chest, and both lady and gentleman were fast asleep.

"Good lord!" Lionel cried.

Millicent jumped awake. She stared at Lionel in the doorway for one dazed moment, then scrambled to her feet. "Oh, sir." She put her hand to her loosened hair. "What you must think! But this gentleman, he is my betrothed—"

A roar issuing from the throat of the now awakened Ashbury drowned out her words. Lionel saw with shock his own blandly handsome face twisted into a snarl of rage as Ashbury launched himself at Lionel and grappled for his throat.

Lionel stepped back, his strength easily breaking the other man's hold.

"You!" Ashbury bellowed. "By Jove, I—" He broke off, looking Lionel up and down in horror. "Devil-a-bit, no one *saw* you wearing that, did they?"

"I'm not concerned about fashion at the moment," Lionel answered, tight lipped.

"But, good God! Breeches and boots at this time of night! What were you thinking, man?"

"We haven't got time for that." Lionel closed the door. "Tell me quickly. Last night, did you wish you were me?"

Ashbury lifted his brows. "I did, by Jove. Saw you standing in a window. 'What a dull stick,' I thought. 'Must lead a dashed dull life. Wish I could be him when that penciller and his bully come calling for their money tomorrow.'" Ashbury eyed him narrowly. "You seem to be in one piece."

"I paid him."

"The devil you did? With what?"

"Your money. You have pots of it."

"That's a clanker. Who told you that?"

"No one told me. I looked in your books." Quickly Lionel explained about the embezzling secretary.

Ashbury went chartreuse. "That blunder-headed villain! I gave him the post because I felt sorry for him. Was at Eton with him. Of all the bloody—"

"Listen to me." Lionel cut him off. "We have to wish ourselves back. If we don't, it's binding."

Ashbury stopped. "Binding?" He shuddered. "I certainly don't want to be you for the rest of my life. I mean to say, *look* at these rooms." He gestured at Lionel's comfortable bedchamber. His sweeping hand took in Millicent, and he grinned. "But it might have its compensations."

"I have yet to ask what you were doing with my fiancée."

"*My* fiancée tonight, my friend." Ashbury waggled his brows. "I'm thinking, though, of marrying her. Such a gel deserves better than a dull stick like you."

Millicent gazed back and forth between them, her expression puzzled. "But I am already going to marry you, Lionel."

"That is what you think, my pet," Ashbury returned.

"What about Lucinda?" Lionel demanded.

"What about her?"

"Who is Lucinda?" Millicent asked.

Lionel ignored her. "You would simply walk away from her?"

"Why not? If I have pots of money, as you say, I don't need to marry her."

"That's hardly fair to her."

Ashbury shrugged. "She's a pretty gel. She'll have other coves hovering round."

"Lionel!"

Both men turned at the same time. "What?"

Millicent flushed. "*Who* is Lucinda?"

Ashbury jerked a thumb at Lionel. "His fiancée."

Lionel met his eye. "And I'd like her to remain so. Do you understand me?"

"I understand you perfectly." Ashbury stuck his hands in his pockets. "Though I don't know what you see in the chit." He pursed his lips. "I suppose you have a way worked out where we untangle all this in the morning?"

Lionel nodded. "If you gather Lady Lucinda and her family to your house tomorrow at noon, I will bring my party. And then we will sort it out."

"Very well then. Time's getting on. Shall we wish?"

Lionel squared his shoulders and looked into his own dark eyes. "Yes. Let us wish."

"Lionel," Millicent said, "I am very confused."

❇ ❇ ❇

In the sharp cold of the second morning of 1817, Lionel Moreland, himself once more, stepped down from a hackney and mounted the steps of Lord Ashbury's Berkeley Square mansion.

He was admitted by Ashbury's correct butler, who led Lionel to the reception room where Lionel had received the moneylenders the day before.

All were assembled there. As Lionel entered, heads swiveled to him. Lord and Lady Alexander sat in a pool of winter sunshine on the Egyptian-style settee near the window. Lucinda stood behind them, her deceptively bland countenance belying the hurt in her eyes. Lionel bristled, wondering what the devil Ashbury had told her. He longed to go to her, but he couldn't. Not yet.

On the other side of the room reposed the Deveauxs. Millicent's father looked up, then, to Lionel's utter astonishment, gave him a deferential nod. Millicent rose from her seat and gazed at Lionel adoringly.

"So the thing is," Lord Ashbury said, "I want to withdraw my suit for Lucinda and marry this lady here." He pointed a thick finger at Millicent.

The room erupted in noise.

"What?" Millicent screeched. "How *dare* you! You burst into Lionel's rooms last night and now you—"

"Sir, there is such a thing as breach of contract." Lord Alexander quivered on his feet, throwing Ashbury a look of fury.

"No need to bother about that," Ashbury said. "Lucinda can marry my friend, Moreland, here. He's got a brilliant career ahead of him."

"*What*?" Millicent's father shouted.

"Gentlemen! Ladies!" Lionel stepped forward, raising his hands in a subduing gesture. "Let us sit and be civilized. No doubt Lord Ashbury has astonished you, but we may unravel this."

For a moment, everyone froze. Then Millicent's father subsided. "We should do as Mr. Moreland says."

Lionel blinked. To hear such a respectful tone from his fiancée's father was beyond belief.

"I have no wish to offend the ladies," he said. "But I am certain we can come to some sort of understanding. And I would be honored," he continued, giving Lucinda a bow, "if I could be allowed to call on Lord Alexander's daughter."

It was a sticky moment. If Ashbury hadn't been so devilishly high-handed, Lionel might have found a gentler means of rearranging all their lives. Now, he could only hope that Lady Lucinda and her family didn't simply walk out in high dudgeon.

Lord Alexander shook his head. "I was not certain I wanted my daughter to become Ashbury's wife anyway. I had grave doubts about his character. Yesterday, I'd hoped that I was wrong, but I see now that I wasn't." He looked Lionel up and down. "You, sir, may be no better than he."

"Oh, he's heaps better than I am," Ashbury broke in. "He's got brains and can unravel a bad financial situation quick as a knife. And he's so much more respectful than I."

Lionel shot Ashbury an irritated glance, then faced the doubtful Lord Alexander. "May we at least speak on it, my lord?"

"But Lionel!" Millicent started for him. "What about me? Last night you said—you dared make me think—"

"Be silent, gel!" Ashbury caught Millicent's arm. "If you marry me, you get to be Lady Ashbury. That's much better than being plain Mrs. Moreland and praying one day he gets a baronetcy, now isn't it?"

Millicent looked up at him, her interest caught. "Well—"

"That's settled then." Ashbury slid his arm around her waist. "You're a beautiful chit and I'm a handsome gentleman. We'll make a decent portrait. Better than you would with a chap like Moreland."

Lionel knew then that Ashbury had won her. Her father, too, looked suddenly cheered at the prospect of having a peer for a son-in-law.

Lionel turned back to Lord Alexander. "My lord, may I speak to your daughter for a brief moment?"

Lord Alexander hesitated, understandably, Lionel thought. But Lady Lucinda raised her head.

"I'd like to, father. I want to hear what he has to say."

Lord Alexander looked from Lionel to his daughter, then nodded. Lucinda met Lionel's gaze proudly, and Lionel's heart tumbled end over end.

He led Lucinda into the little reception room that opened off the large one. Leaving the door ajar, he turned her to face him.

Her grey eyes glittered with both hurt and fury. Lionel ached to take her in his arms and soothe away her anger.

"Lucinda." He caught her hands. "You are the one most injured in this mess. Lord Ashbury and I have used you cruelly."

She met his gaze, hers unwavering. "I should say you have. But I am curious, Mr. Moreland, as to your part in this. I don't even know you."

"But I know you. My lady, the words of love Ashbury spoke to you last evening—they were my words."

A pucker appeared between her brows. "Your words? What can you mean, sir?"

"I saw you, Lady Lucinda, and, forgive my impertinence, I fell in love with you at once. I was appalled at how Ashbury treated you, and I admonished him for it. What I instructed him to say was what I would have said, had I been in his place."

There. It was almost the truth—or at least as close as he could come without sounding a complete madman.

"You fancy yourself in love with me?"

"I do." Lionel squeezed her hands. "And every moment I spend with you, I become more and more certain."

"You speak prettily, sir." Lucinda searched his face, and then her hard countenance softened a little. "There's something about your eyes, though. Something—"

"Something?"

She shook her head. "I'm not certain. But, very well, Mr. Moreland, if you wish to call on me, I will speak to you. How I will answer I cannot tell."

"Thank you." Hope leapt in his heart. "My lady, you will never regret the loss of Ashbury—or rather, his loss of you." Boldly, he lifted her hand to his lips. "I do love you, Lady Lucinda. When I made my New Year's wish, I never dreamed it would result in such happiness as finding you."

Lucinda flushed in sudden confusion. "You made a New Year's wish? But I too made one, Mr. Moreland."

Lionel lifted his brows. "Did you? What was it?"

"You will think it silly."

"No indeed. Please, tell me."

Lucinda gazed up at him, her diamond-grey eyes full of longing. "I made the wish that the man I married would love me with great intensity."

Lionel stopped, thunderstruck. Was it possible? Had the whole tangled mess woven itself so that Lionel could find and fall in love with Lucinda—to make her wish come true?

And did it matter? Whatever wish, or fate, or magic had brought them together, it was welcome.

"And so I will love you." Lionel kissed her fingers again, unmindful of who might be watching. "If you'll let me."

Lucinda breathed a sigh. "I might, Mr. Moreland. I just might."

"Long life and happiness, my lady? Shall we wish for it?"

She smiled. "I would rather like to see us take it as it comes. I believe I've done with wishes."

"So have I, Lucinda." He leaned down. "Because my greatest wish has come true."

Her lips parted, her silver-grey eyes shining. Daringly, Lionel pressed a kiss to her mouth, happiness flooding him.

Someone at the doorway snorted.

"Sentimental twaddle," Ashbury scoffed as they sprang apart. "Come out here, Moreland, and help me celebrate our good fortune. I have champagne, the best of the Frenchie stuff, and there's more where it came from. Now that you've found me my money, I'm going to *spend* it."

Jennifer Ashley has lived all over the U.S. as well as in Germany and Japan. She married a wanderer like herself, and insisted her honeymoon be spent in London, where she lodged near White's and strolled St. James's, Hyde Park, and Mayfair. She has published short stories in three genres: romance, fantasy, and mystery, and is working on several romance novels and a mystery series, all set in Regency England. Her short story, *The Gentleman's Walking Stick* appeared at The Reticule, an e-zine sponsored by Regency Press. (**http://www.regencyreticule.com**). She and her wandering husband have settled, with cat, in warm and beautiful Arizona.

*miline discovers how much fun it is to live next to a determined, incorrigible
ake. Follow her progress... and the rake's in this charming Regency short
tory.*

The Rake's Progress

Paola Addamiano-Carts

Excerpts from the Private Diary of
Miss Emiline Sommerset

December 29, 1813

I am keeping this diary because Edgar, dearest and most vexing of brothers,
as broken his leg. That is to say, he was to have accompanied me to London
nd Aunt Imogene's town house for her annual Twelfth Night festivities. In-
tead, however, he is confined to the sickroom to recuperate from a fall. Why
he nodcock was climbing up a vine at the side of the house not two days be-
ore Christmas, in the middle of the night, wearing his best suit and reeking of
he most obscene mixture of drink and perfume is beyond me. My maid,
Hedgepodge, who knows about these things, winked at me and informed me, in
meaningful voice, "Mrs. Jenkins, Miss," referring to a young and comely
widow who lives in the village.

As Mother is continually charging me with being indiscreet and blurting
ut things that ought not to be said, I have decided to attempt to be more virtu-
us and ladylike and not pry into Edgar's affairs. The Reverend Tyndale says
hat the Christmas season is full of rebirth and hope. I believe he is right, al-
hough I cannot help wishing he could be a bit more lively and brief in his
peech, and have sent up a small prayer on my behalf, so I daresay even I
might be able to hold my tongue on this one occasion.

So it is that poor, sick Edgar has asked that I relieve his tedium by reading
his journal to him upon my return. He asks, as well, that I make the retelling of
events more interesting by including several adventures. I certainly plan to
have some adventures, but I have no intention of reading this diary to him un-
ensored. It seems to me he finds enough mischief to get into without being
privy to the innermost thoughts of his sister. And, I ask, of what use is keeping

a diary if one cannot put down one's deepest and truest feelings? Even Edgar, possible friend of country widows, would be shocked at all the things that pass through the mind of his "little angel Em" as he sometimes calls me.

Of course, I suppose that I could develop a secret code of some sort. For instance, ∾ could represent each occasion when a gentleman looks at me with speaking eyes. My former dance master called them *occhi parlanti* and, despite all of Edgar's dreadful teasing that Signor Ferrari was using his *occhi parlant* on me, I find this much more romantic than the English equivalent.

Now, let's see, what else might I need a code for? Being that this is the season of hope, I could designate ⌘⌘⌘ for the times a gentleman, overcome by my scintillating conversation and beauty, forgets himself and whisks me away to a secluded corner of the garden where I, equally overcome by his good humor, fine looks and impeccable—up to this point—manners, permit him to embrace me in the manner I once observed Edgar and Miss L. G. doing.

Well, I daresay that the pages will be dotted with ∾'s and hopefully at least one ⌘. For though I may be outspoken and "unnaturally lively," as Mother would say, I am given to understand, without being vain, that I am not uneasy to look upon. I recently received a poem from one of my beaux at home in Kent. He says "thy young blue eyes, they smile." Perhaps I should not be insulted that he has plagiarized the notorious Lord Byron, for, after all, that bard does have a pretty turn of phrase. I rather fancy my blue eyes, besides. Certainly, they are my best feature. I think the way my hair is done up now, in little curls all over my head, is rather flattering, too. I fancy I look like a sprite. Monsieur Blanchard, Aunt Imogene's hairdresser, oohed and aahed over it after he had finished cutting it yesterday. But then, he would hardly say "*zut*" if he had cut it badly, would he?

Aunt Imogene is a dear. She is Papa's youngest sister and a widow. Her husband, the earl, left her very well situated, and Aunt Imogene has a life of independence. I think she is eccentric. She has none of the ladylike accomplishments that have been so firmly ensconced in me—despite my unnatural liveliness. She cannot ply a needle or play the pianoforte or sing or draw. She does dance, though, and has a fine hand and seems to delight in writing letters and keeping accounts and ledgers. Papa says this is because his mama died when Aunt Imogene was little and she was indulged by their papa. He certainly must have indulged her wanton expenditures on fine clothes, for it is her favorite excess.

Yesterday, the day after my arrival in town, Aunt Imogene whisked me off to the modiste's and ordered several stylish new gowns for me, as well as several for herself. I am to have the most darling celestial blue carriage dress, a fur-lined cloak with matching muff and hat—quite dashing!—and the most wonderful gown of sea green that shimmers in the light on account of tiny silver threads shot through the fabric. This last gown is for Aunt Imogene's Twelfth Night party.

Despite the fact that I loved the fabrics and designs dearly, I remembered my vow to be virtuous, and protested that the dresses were too dear. Aunt Imogene only laughed and said that it was Christmastime and I was to have pretty things. She reminded me of the parsimony for which Papa is famous and said I was to enjoy myself at her expense. Then we set about procuring stockings, slippers, gloves, and so forth until my head was reeling. Finally, when we were done gallivanting around town, it was time for Monsieur Blanchard to work his miracles.

After he was gone, Aunt Imogene and I retired to her parlor and propped our feet up on cushions. A maid brought us tea and we devoured the dainty cakes in a matter of minutes. As I sipped a cup of steaming bohea, marveling at the wonderful decadence of the day, Aunt Imogene informed me that this Christmastime we are to have a special treat: her next-door neighbor is in residence. I have not yet laid eyes on him, but I am told that he is handsome beyond all reason and has a rakish reputation to match. He is Lord Barracat, a marquis, but we naughtily call him "The Rake". His house sits back from the road, and we expect to have a fine view of his comings and goings. Aunt Imogene has surprised even me by moving her opera glasses to her escritoire in case they are needed on short notice! Thus prepared, we lay in wait by the window, Aunt Imogene with her ledgers and I with my embroidery, in hopes of viewing "The Rake's Progress."

December 31

I have seen The Rake. Today, Aunt Imogene and I had taken up our favorite pursuits in the parlor when we heard a commotion next door. I say a commotion, but it was truly the most awful cackling and screeching, rather like the time father's hunting dogs chased a fox into the hen house. As discreetly as possible, we both inched closer to the window, shielding ourselves from view by draping the curtains across our shoulders and faces like women from Araby. What we saw was astonishing.

There, before my very eyes, was Adonis, albeit a dark-haired version of the god, with a female over his shoulder. She was kicking and screaming and all her petticoats could be seen, and her stockings and garters, besides. The Rake finally set her down. He has the most wicked smile. I believe I should like for a gentleman to smile at me in just such a way. The female sported a fur cap, not so fetching as mine, but sweet, brilliant red curls and flaming red cheeks, whether from artifice or nature, I could not determine. If she comes again, I will remember to use Aunt Imogene's opera glasses. Undoubtedly she said something impudent, for The Rake laughed. He gave her a playful push toward the street, and she went to the waiting carriage, brazenly blowing him a kiss before she departed. He waved and turned to go into the house.

Aunt Imogene sat back then, but I was too astounded to move. A curious thing happened...or perhaps I only imagined it. I was rather dazed, but I thought I saw The Rake stop at his front door, turn, and bow in our direction. I snapped out of my trance, and stepped back. It was then I noticed a greasy smudge on the window pane. I will not even contemplate the possibility that I forgot myself so much as to press my nose to the glass.

Aunt Imogene and I spent the rest of the afternoon speculating on what could be the meaning of such goings on. We reached no conclusions, but lamented that rakes hold such fascination for the gentler sex, while stable, reliable men go unnoticed.

January 1, 1814

The new year begins and I have had an adventure worthy of Edgar. This morning I went for a walk in the square. A monster of a dog flattened me to the ground whereupon it proceeded to lick my face with a tongue the size of a dish towel. I lay there like a rag doll, frightened to death because I have never liked dogs, and giggling hysterically because his tongue tickled. I was able, at some length, to get a sufficient grip on myself to scream wildly in between fits of laughter. I can only imagine what the passersby must have thought—two caterwauling females in the square in as many days. In any event, it is of no consequence. Eventually the owner of the dog came over at an insultingly lazy pace. When I looked up, who should it be but The Rake! At this point, I am sure I had a delayed reaction to the accident, for the wind was suddenly knocked out of me. I became breathless and could not utter a sound. My giggling and screaming ceased.

The Rake seemed to find this amusing. He gave me a cunning look, cocking one eyebrow impertinently. "And all this time I thought that Madame Catalani was practicing in the square."

Comparing me to that screeching opera singer was bad enough, but there was not one inquiry as to the state of my health, nor one offer of assistance. I sniffed in anger. "Is this beast yours?"

"Ah, Brutus. Yes," he replied smugly. "Are you done playing with him?"

"Playing with him!" I sputtered.

The insult gave me renewed strength and I managed to throw the dog off me. Finally The Rake offered a hand to help me up, but it was too late. I gave him what I hoped was a spiteful look and rose unassisted, shaking the dust from my skirts once I was finally upright.

When I looked at The Rake again, his shoulders were unsteady and his eyes were watering. The insulting man was laughing! At me! It became obvious that something about my appearance was askew. I reached my hand up. My bonnet was dangling by its strings and my hair was full of straw. There had been a death in one of the families that resided around the square some few days earlier and the straw used to hush the traffic noise had scattered everywhere. I could only imagine what I looked like, a scruffy scarecrow with a mulish expression on my face. I found The Rake's humor to be contagious and burst out laughing. The Rake gave full vent to his mirth as well. He has a very nice laugh.

When we had recovered our wits, The Rake managed to speak. "Allow me to introduce myself. I am Lord Barracat. Brutus and I live across the square. There," he pointed.

"I know," I admitted, giving what I hope was an ingenuous look. "I am a guest of Lady Harpersfield. She is my aunt."

He cocked his eyebrow in what I was beginning to understand was his quizzing expression, "And do you delight in peering out the window, as well?"

My face grew heated in embarrassment. He knew I was guilty.

He spoke *sotto voce*. "Never tell Lady Harpersfield that I am on to her. Do you know that I once believed I had a calling for the stage? I have found an outlet for my thespian talents by enacting a few little dramas right below your aunt's nose. It delights me to give her something to fuel her salons with."

At this point, I'm sure my jaw dropped open and I was standing there like a gapeseed. It dawned on me that the little scenario Auntie Imogene and I had witnessed was all a hoax. I managed to pull myself together sufficiently to ask, "But, why spread stories about yourself that are not true?" It would have been better to stop there, but I could not help asking, "And who was that redhead?"

The merry twinkle in his brown eyes spoke volumes. "Tut, tut. So many questions? And you think the stories are untrue? I am wounded. But can you not guess? Surely a young woman as delightful as yourself must be plagued with dozens of suitors. You will understand what a nuisance it can be. I prefer to keep match-making mommas and their simpering daughters at bay."

"And the redhead?" I persisted.

"Tenacious little thing, aren't you," he observed with some amusement. "Let us just say that Miss Delacourt from the King's Theatre owed me a small favor. Now," he said, adroitly changing the subject, "Let's see what we can do about setting you to rights." So saying, he removed his gloves and began plucking bits of straw out of my hair. When he was done, he gave my hair a final fluff and looked at me with his fine brown eyes. Apparently I was still not recovered from Brutus's attack, for of a sudden I felt weak in the knees.

Lord Barracat offered his arm and we returned to our corner of the square in thoughtful silence. Brutus followed behind, scrunching his haunches so that he looked dainty and petite, no taller than my knees, but he didn't fool me.

January 2

Lord Barracat has sent round the most charming little nosegay of violets and a note asking me to go on a ride in the park tomorrow. I am dizzy with excitement, not all of it attributable to Brutus and my fall, and know it shall take a long time to go to sleep tonight. I think I shall dream of wicked smiles and 〰.

January 3

Edgar will be green with envy, for I have been in a high-perch phaeton. A flood of Edgar's cant expressions come to mind: all the crack, tiptop, bang up to the mark, etcetera, etcetera. I was "togged out to the Nines," too, in my new blue dress, fur-lined cloak, and the darling little fur cap. Lord Barracat expressed warm approval of my fine feathers as he helped me up to the seat and I felt my cheeks turn red in delight. At the last Brutus bounded up onto the bench. I daresay Lord Barracat was afraid of what would happen should he try to foist the beast off, for he let him stay. I did not protest as the three of us wedged together on the bench meant extra warmth. Of course, Brutus was most likely the warmest of us three, as he was in the middle. I felt sure Auntie, peering through her opera glasses from the parlor window, approved of the mutt playing gooseberry.

We drove to Green Park. It is not so fashionable as Hyde Park and this time of year is nearly deserted. We could move about at some speed and I was actually glad to have Brutus to cling to, for the combination of height and speed left me a bit light-headed. Lord Barracat explained that he preferred to let his horses get some exercise as they turned into slugs when confined to drudging around town. Apparently both he and the horses prefer the country. He has an estate not too distant from Papa's in Kent.

After he had put his horses through their paces, Lord Barracat stopped the phaeton and helped me down. Brutus descended on his own. Two or three boys came running over and Lord B. paid them all to watch his team. We took a short walk, letting Brutus guide us as he zig-zagged here and there, chasing birds and, one presumes, marking his territory. Lord B. and I talked of inconsequential things, laughed a great deal, and felt quite contented to be in each other's company.

On the ride home, Brutus bounded up once again, but this time Lord B. put him on one side of the bench and I sat in the middle. I was fearful that Brutus, who had taken to slobbering at this point, might soil my new cloak, so I scooted perhaps closer than what was proper to Lord B., but he did not seem to mind. It was a most pleasant excursion and I was sorry to see it end.

January 4

Lord B. has sent around a note to Aunt Imogene explaining that he has had to go to Kent on urgent business, begs pardon for not being able to provide her with more fodder for gossip, but assures her that he will return in time for her Twelfth Night fête whereupon he will try to create a sensation worthy of being printed in the newspaper. "Incorrigible lad," Aunt Imogene commented good-naturedly. She tapped the note to her chin and added in a thoughtful voice, "I wonder if he will be able to bring us news of Edgar." That Aunt Imogene would think Lord B. would enquire about Edgar merely because he is in Kent is surely a sign of the state of her mind. She is much distracted with preparations for her fête, particularly the loss of the little baby Jesus figure that Cook is to bake in the cake, so I shall spend these next few days doing what I can to lighten her burden. (N.B. The little baby Jesus was a present from her mother-in-law, who was French.)

January 5

Brutus has come sulking over to Aunt Imogene's house. I found him in the kitchen as I was helping Cook find a suitable replacement for the lost baby Jesus. We have decided to bake a dried pea and a ring into two Twelfth Night cakes. One cake will be served to the men and whoever finds the pea shall be crowned king. In the same manner, whichever lady finds the ring shall be crowned queen. As Brutus was eyeing the cake batter in a particularly avaricious manner, I decided to avert disaster by giving him a bone and bringing him to my chamber. At bedtime tonight, he thrust his paws and chin onto my covers and I had no choice but to let him sleep at the foot of my bed. I am afraid I have a soft heart for scoundrels.

January 6

Noon–I have dashed to my room to make this entry. Lord B. has returned! Brutus and I have seen his carriage pull up next door. Lord B. descended, wearing a stylish great coat with several shoulder capes and his hat tipped at a jaunty angle. He danced a little jig, undoubtedly for the benefit of his next-door neighbors, so we conclude that his business has been conducted successfully. I shall enquire tonight.

January 7

I have made a discovery: It is impossible to sleep when one has lived through an absolutely perfect evening. I am dancing on air, reliving every glorious second of Aunt Imogene's fête and wishing it had never had to end.

I, or perhaps I should say Hedgepodge, began my toilette early in the afternoon and the results were everything that could be hoped for. The sea-green dress was splendid and I think I have never looked finer. Aunt Imogene lent me a dainty necklace of pearls and emeralds which added a certain dash and elegance to my appearance.

Aunt Imogene was done up in a lovely plum-colored silk gown with a turban of shimmery gold fabric perched on her head. There were three ostrich plumes adorning her turban and they quaked magnificently when she moved. She seemed quite pleased with the effect. Around her neck resided a splendid ruby necklace, a gift from the earl on their fifth anniversary, she said. Curiously, she also wore a gold chain from which hung a quizzing glass. When I asked her about it, she said, "Emiline, my dear, you can't have forgotten that Lord Barracat has promised us a newsworthy item tonight! I plan to be ready. I thought of wearing my opera glasses, but that would be a bit much, do you not think? The quizzing glass is much more subtle." So saying, she raised it up to her eye, where I was able to count every eyelash on her inquisitive grey eye.

I came downstairs after the first of the guests had arrived. I cannot begin to say who they were, for all rational thoughts fled my mind when I set eyes upon Lord B. He was splendid! Certainly, his formal black evening dress and snowy neckcloth showed him to advantage, for he has a very fine figure, but he seemed particularly pleased about something, and he glowed with happiness and good-humor. His eyes, well, they shone with something more intent. I will abbreviate: ∿.

Dinner was a success, if you can overlook all the flushing and choking on wine that occurred at my place during the meal. It was all Lord B.'s fault, for he kept sending the most unsettling glances my way (∿, ∿). When finally the cake was served, we all nibbled with caution lest we break a tooth on the prizes. As luck would have it, I found the ring. Lord B., the slyboots, managed to switch slices of cake with a rather fat and florid friend of Aunt Imogene and get himself the pea. Amid much hoopla from the crowd, we had to don capes and paper crowns and lead the first dance.

The last dance was the Sir Roger de Coverley, and I stood up with Lord B. At some point in the progression, I managed to enquire about his recent trip. "Your trip was a success?"

"Quite," he said with infuriating brevity.

I prompted, "Aunt Imogene says you bring news of Edgar."

"Yes. Your dear brother is recuperating rapidly. A nurse has been brought in from town. A Mrs. Jenkins, I believe."

My eyes must have opened like an owl's at this news. Papa would never allow for such an arrangement as I envisioned.

"It seems she was widowed on the battlefield. She had followed the drum, don't you know, and learned a good deal of nursing in the process."

"Goodness! Edgar may linger in recovery for months."

"Yes, the clever fellow. You know, my dear, you and Edgar bear a striking family resemblance. I can't see where you get it from. Your parents seem so sensible. By the way, they send their greetings and felicitations."

"Felicitations?" I voiced hazily, some shape finally taking form in the muddled thoughts in my brain. "But....but how is it that you came to run into them?"

He knew something I did not, that had been obvious all evening, but he teased me mercilessly. "You mean you still haven't figured out what I was doing these past few days?"

"Oh!" I uttered, my eyes popping open wide again.

"Slow top!" he teased. "But lest there be any doubt, I intend to make things perfectly clear." And so saying, he pulled me off the dance floor, totally oblivious of the chaos we were leaving behind. I took one futile look around. Amidst the disarrayed couples looking after us, I spotted Aunt Imogene, quizzing glass already in place. She smiled delightedly and wiggled the fingers of her free hand in a cheery little wave. Then Lord B. pulled me out onto the terrace.

⌘⌘⌘ !!!

Paola Addamiano-Carts was born in Cleveland, Ohio. Her love of things British started even before this landmark event, however: her Italian father and Nebraskan mother met at Oxford University. After a career in the aerospace industry during which Paola stunned the technical world by proving that some engineers can write, she began the infinitely more challenging job of raising children. She and her family, along with their chickens, rabbits and cats, live in Accokeek, Maryland. When not home schooling her three children, Paola enjoys gardening, bicycling, camping, and reading and attempting to write Regency and inspirational literature. Her latest hobby, begun when a neighbor gave her a fleece from one of his sheep, is felting.

A Regency Sampler

Edited by Kelly Ferjutz, August 1999 ISBN 1-929085-001
= = = = = = = = = = = = = =
Fifteen prize-winning stories by new and previously-published Regency authors. The bestselling *A Regency Sampler* has garnered rave reviews from a wide variety of sources, including *Library Journal*, which described it as "a charming, uncommon collection." Still available! $5.95

The Marplot Marriage

Beth Andrews, October 1999
ISBN 1-929085-01-X paper $4.95 / Cloth 1-929085-02-8 $19.95
= = = = = = = = = = = = =
This clever romp has one of the best opening lines in Regency fiction! Stuffy Charles Hargood and mischievous Phoebe Bridgerton, caught in a compromising situation by Charles's fiancée and future mother-in-law, must make the best of it and get married, though they loathe each other. A witty and satisfying comedy of manners.
Also available in electronic versions!

The Reluctant Guardian

Jo Manning, December 1999
ISBN 1-929085-06-0 paper / $4.95 Cloth 1-929085-07-9 $19.95
= = = = = = = = = = = = = =
When ex-soldier and man-about-town Sir Isaac Rebow assumes the guardianship of the Martin sisters, both his lifestyle and relationship with his beautiful mistress, Lady Sophia are threatened. Unexpected twists and turns lead to Mary Martin's life being endangered and Isaac must come to the rescue.

Peerless Theodosia

Rebecca Baldwin, February, 2000
ISBN 1-929085-12-5 - Cloth $19.95
= = = = = = = = = = = = =
When American siblings, Theodosia and Thomas Jefferson Clement are removed from a ship taking them home from the Continent, they become the unsuspecting guests of the Earl of Claremont. Surprises abound on all sides!

Also available in electronic versions!

Lady Lessons
Sarah Starr, April 2000
ISBN 1-929085-17-6   Cloth $19.95
= = = = = = = = = = = = =
Ginger Traynor's godmother, grandmother to the very proper Earl of Ashley, sends for her and her brother in a last-minute attempt to sabotage Ashley's marriage to a wealthy but cold-hearted Cit. Ginger, brought up by an irresponsible father and a doting governess, lacks all the social graces prized by the ton. Even as her spirit and natural charm intrigue Ashley, he's repulsed by her lack of good manners. Only a complete makeover will do—but can an edge-softened Ginger win the earl's heart?

The Franklin Affair
Ty Drago   March, 2001
ISBN 1-929085-75-3 - Cloth $22.95
= = = = = = = = = = = = =
Sixteen-year-old Henri Gruel thinks he's serving the King of France when he agrees to act as spy against the visiting American, Dr. Benjamin Franklin. As his friendship with the elder stateman grows, Henri finds his loyalty tested and his conscience pained. Before long, Henri is swept into a world of politics and intrigue beyond anything he has experienced. When a murderer strikes and Dr. Franklin is implicated, Henri must somehow navigate the lies and double-dealing all around him and decide, finally, whose side he is on.

Our first mystery novel!
Also available in electronic versions!

The Wrong Miss Richmond
Sandra Heath, August, 2000
= = = = = = = = = = = = =
Bestselling Regency author Sandra Heath is at her most skillful in this tale of two half-sisters; Jane, impetuous and lively, Christina, bookish and steady. No sisters could be less alike! Robert, engaged to redheaded Jane, seems to be drawn to capable Christina, who becomes his ally in rescuing Jane from a series of mad escapades (including a soaring flight of fancy in a balloon over the rooftops of the staid city of Bath!) Which is the right Miss Richmond for him? A treat for fans of the ever-popular Sandra Heath and for Regency lovers everywhere! (*A Reprise Book*)

Available in electronic versions!

All Regency Press titles may be purchased directly from us, or are available to libraries through Brodart Co; Amazon.com., and Ingram Books. Call/fax us at (216) 932-5319 or 1-877-343-6299, and ask about our library discounts and standing orders!